# The
# South
# Florida
# Book
# of the
# Dead

# The South Florida Book of the Dead

## ROBERT MERKIN

William Morrow and Company, Inc.
New York    1982

**Library of Congress Cataloging in Publication Data**

Merkin, Robert.
  The south Florida book of the dead.

  I. Title.
PS3563.E7413S6        813'.54        81–22598
ISBN 0–688–00988–3        AACR2
ISBN 0–688 00984–0(pbk)

Printed in the United States of America


2 3 4 5 6 7 8 9 10

BOOK DESIGN BY PATTY LOWY

For Cyndy

"So stand and sing the Hymn of the Poorest of the Poor, whose difficult lives you've portrayed today. For in real life, their final fate is especially bad. The king's messengers come riding to the rescue very seldom, and those who get kicked kick back. So one shouldn't prosecute too much wrongdoing."

—BERTOLT BRECHT, *The Threepenny Opera*


"Of all the pains that afflict mankind, the most bitter is that we should know so much, but control nothing."

—HERODOTUS, *The Histories*

# The
# South
# Florida
# Book
# of the
# Dead

# Part One

## ROCK FEVER

# BECKER

That second day on the road, boy, I'd remembered what that shit was. It was *cold,* Jack, that's what it was. Try to buzz through it on a motorcycle and you had *real* cold, nipple-tightening, scrotum-constricting cold, cold that makes you want to flat-out get out of the cold, no lie. I'd say it was a novelty for about one hour and then it wore off fast, but there I was committed to another one of my Excelsior Ozone trips and there was no way I was going to turn around and go back to Key West for another sweater or permission to ditch the cycle and borrow the truck. That just wasn't the way for a bona fide member of the Royal Order of Flaming Assholes. I'd left Key West in the middle of an epic blow-out between me and Annie, loud and public, feeling pissed off and pissed on. I was packing the bike in the back yard when she came out and sealed my fate. She warned me I was going to freeze my ass off up north at the beginning of what they euphemistically call spring. She was right on the money with the advice, but I wasn't in much of a listening mood. Now I was pushing my act through the bracing highway air with half-frozen snot all over my moustache and tears sloshing around in my goggles, and forty-five minutes or an hour at a stretch was the most I could stand—although the bike, that sweet English thing, just zipped along like a little air-cooled purring kitten.

Annie should have known better. What the hell good is advice in the middle of a fight? Nobody can listen to it. But she'd pointed it out so goddam matter-of-fact and I'd been so raw that it had sounded to me as if she were rubbing it in, and I'd kicked the machine over and roared out. I was so unprepared for this jaunt that unless things loosened up on the weather report fast, I was ready to find a cheap, sleazo motel on the side of some bypassed highway —at this point, Tony Perkins and the Bates Motel would do fine— and check in for a couple of weeks. Turn in, drop out and warm up, as Dr. Tim never quite said. But the fight had left me with a big hair up my ass and I was steaming north on pure outrage; even though half of it was now aimed at myself, it was still enough to keep me moving for the time being.

The fight—I won't say I don't remember what it was about because I sure as hell do and if it would make anybody happy or nudge the thermometer up a couple of points, I'd be more than willing to confess to the dufus-assed play that started it all. But like many another dufus play between friends, it wasn't meant to piss her off. It was meant for a very different reason entirely, and she should have seen that and given me a little credit for it, even if she hadn't liked it. But she didn't see it or didn't want to see it when she got back from her whore-hopping Cook's tour of the islands on that lame shmuck's sloop—well, off it by that time. She told me she'd given him a peck on the cheek and jumped ship a couple of days before she'd flown back to Key West. I'd felt the tension when I'd picked her up at the airport, thick and silent. I kept my mouth closed (no simple feat for me, Jack) on the way home and dumped her off and then made myself scarce down at Mallory Square because it was just about sunset. It was on occasions like that that I frequented the sunset ritual at Mallory because after the first fifty times or so I'd begun to get weary of being panhandled and hit up for drugs or medical advice for the crabs from the scuzzy burned-out flower power crowd that assembled there for no other reason than that Mallory pier was as far south as a soul can get in America, and these lameos were the flotsam of the whole country that ended up in Key West and Mallory in particular whenever the rest of the country shook them up a little. Mallory in effect was the gravity hole all the little steel balls fall into that can't score any more points in the pinball game called American Life and Laughs. But I checked sunset at Mallory out about once a month because there were always some hardcore permanent types there that I knew with the latest blues and dues and news about who had scored a free game fish from some great white hunter who'd had his picture taken with it and then didn't know what the fuck to do with it besides truck it back to Miami in the trunk of his Hertz rent-a-car. That would mean a free feast somewhere for the crowd that wasn't too choosy about those little silvery mercury balls that rolled out of the flesh, provided it was a fish that was edible in the first place, the great white hunters not being enormously picky about that point. Or there'd be some word floating around about a party I hadn't sniffed out earlier, or a bulletin about the latest Key West and Monroe County police atrocity that had crashed down on some random acquaintance's life. It paid to stay in touch at Mallory, especially if the deep purple vibrations had chased you out of the house.

I scored what I was looking for, anyway. My buddy Luck was there zipping around on his skateboard and looking for some respectable tourists to play his hobby on, his year-round version of broad-daylight Halloween trick-or-treat, flashing the crowd with what he didn't have rather than with what he did. He'd been a jarhead playing point man in a mine field—a perfectly sensible way to employ manpower in the Marine philosophy—when the inevitable happened and an antipersonnel had gone off under him. Back on the other side of the world in Walter Wonderful (which was what the inmates called Walter Reed because when they woke up they weren't in Vietnam anymore but in Washington, D.C. and only a spit away from tit bars, abundant reefer, a real city with more than two movie theaters and a whole pharmacopoeia cornucopia of every weed, spirit and pill humankind had ever offered for sale, all in fantastic abundance) his ward mates had started calling him Luck because the way they figured it he either had the worst luck in the world for setting off the mine or the best luck in the world for still being alive and having the use of most everything north of his navel. As usual he was singing his raspy blues and bad-mouthing the crowd as he wheeled himself around the pier on the fancy skateboard. Between verses he said there was going to be a party on

Stock Island that night. I knew the dude throwing it and it seemed at the time it might make an acceptable place to hide out for the night, if nothing more. I told Luck I'd meet him there later and wandered off down the pier to get away from the central concentration of transient creeps. I wanted a cigarette, but if I'd lit one in that crowd from a fresh pack, it would have been like dangling a bleeding toe in a canal filled with big barracuda. I drifted down to the end, still close enough to hear the musicians who knew enough to give the crowd something in exchange for their handouts.

The girl had the accordion. She was good at it, too. I guess she'd paid her dues playing "Sunrise, Sunset" at bar mitzvahs and weddings until it was sloshing around in her shoes, but she was doing something a little better now, and she had a good voice she had no trouble keeping on key. I hadn't seen them around town before so they couldn't have been in Key West long. I wondered if they knew how far ahead of the game they were just because they knew the words to at least one song and their instruments hadn't been ripped off or lunched on Route 1 on the way down. Just that little bit tended to make them aristocrats among the six or seven dozen losers and turkeys who wound up in town every week.

I wasn't the only one at my end of the pier listening to them. As I lit up against the breeze, I looked around at one of the Coast Guard cutters tied up a few yards farther down. The flag party had already done its *Semper Paratus* trip and headed off for the crew's nightly ration of broken-bottle mayhem in the Duval Street establishments, but one young squid was still roaming around the deserted fantail watching the real people's sunrise and listening to the music. I took him to be no more than eighteen. He looked like shitkicker Texas or redneck Baltimore, friendly, just a little sociopathic enough to barely hack it through high school, and then only on his solemn promise that in exchange for the graduation ticket he'd slide straight down to his local recruiter and become a credit to the community rather than the debit he'd been for the last few years. No big deal: one hot-wired Mercury Cougar taken for a midnight spin through each consecutive green and fairway of the private golf course and the girl down the block who'd had to spend half a year with her aunt up in Long Distance Elsewhere, but it had been enough for a panel of friends and neighbors to point the jerk down the path of righteousness, patriotism and civic absence. He didn't seem to see me on the pier; he just looked out and over me toward the crowd. His face had all the expression of an apprentice hit man or a pin spotter in a bowling alley. His eyes were big and vacant and fixed the way squids' eyes get from pulling too many night watches and trying to see things on calm horizons that either are there or aren't. Because he didn't see me I looked at the lad carefully and tried to imagine what was going on behind those cow eyes and that face with this space for rent. I made a mental note to buy a better deadbolt for the front door.

It was getting dark. The tourists and parasites were drifting away and the music proper had stopped, although the girl was still squeezing a few asthmatic notes out of the accordion as she put it away in its case. The squid was wondering what he'd done to have to watch the ship all night while his buddies got to tear up the town and listen to Tammy Wynette tunes on the jukebox. I strolled away, into the cobblestoned streets behind Duval, and started making my way home by the lengthiest route I could think of. Bicycles built for two passed me with weekenders down from Miami and I could hear the gay folks' cacophony start to spill out onto the sidewalk as I walked past the disco that had become their roost. It was early enough to catch them unawares if I was lucky, and I was—no one met me by the gate to cruise me or ask me if I was up for a thrill.

The route took me across Duval and near the Pier House where I recognized some of the waitresses' bicycles in their rack, then by the perfume factory and into the neighborhoods where real people, Conchs and their families, lived in the houses instead of tourist traps. Mothers were screaming for their kids to give it up and come inside for dinner and some of the downstairs windows were already glazed with the harsh blue glow of the big screen inside. Warring smells mugged me on the sidewalks—hot food floating out open kitchen windows, trash bags the dog packs had ripped open the night before and the thick tropical blossoms dripping a perfume that always seemed to be too early or far too ripe, never just on the mark.

The route wasn't long enough and the pace hadn't been slow enough. Annie was in the living room when I walked in and we started to duke it out almost as soon as I sat down. We didn't get down to the nitty-gritty right away; that took a couple of minutes. But the tension was thicker now and it was all set to start tumbling down over everything. I don't remember just what started it. Maybe I'd taken down a phone message wrong or used up all her Cuban coffee. Whatever; it was just all ready to go and we started yelling and having at one another, so that in a couple of minutes we were down to the main item on the agenda.

It was the message, the little note I'd stuffed into her bag the morning she'd left to go island-hopping. The little note plus all the hassles we'd had about her going in the first place, and who she was going with, and the fact that it was none of my fucking business whether she went or who she went with. She was dead right there. It wasn't any of my fucking business. So naturally I'd just gone ahead and jumped right into her business because of the dude she was going with, mainly. After she ran into him at the marina, she brought him over to the house a couple of times and that's when things started falling apart for me. He was just such a fucking titanic creep. He didn't know jack-shit about shit. He had money coming out of his ears and if anybody couldn't see it, he made sure to make a point of it every five minutes or so. He'd talk and it would grate me, like a sudden and horrible reaction to some food or an insect sting. The moment I met him I wanted this refugee from *Gentleman's Quarterly* out of my living room, out of my house, out of my sight and more. I wanted him out of Annie's life, and that's where the trouble started, but there was nothing I could do to stop feeling that way. It just kept leaking out of my mouth like drool when you're taking a nap. I started calling him Slick, *Hey Slick; what's happening Slick?* I think it went over his head, but it didn't miss Annie; she started shooting darts at me and letting me know I was pissing her off no end.

I felt sorry for the shmuck. He wanted to be loved badly and was willing to lay hard cash down on the line for it if necessary. Lawrence-Larry-for-short had apparently just wandered off some hot campus where he'd been or bought the title of Big Man On, and now his daddy had bought him a year cruising on the sloop to check out selected and approved slices of unsupervised reality, in the course of which he'd bumped into Annie down at the marina where his sloop was tied up. He just thought Annie and I were the cat's pajamas and ginchy beyond belief and none of the surly things I was shooting him under my breath could change his mind. I never flat-out told him to get fucked or lost. I don't know why. I guess it wasn't my style. No matter how badly he was grossing me out, he was Annie's guest and it was as much Annie's house as it was mine. But I really felt I was being chased out of my house by this geek and I was grinding out a lot less than my best behavior.

It was no deep mystery to figure out what her act was. She was willing to spread for this creep in return for a few weeks on the bounding main. For this she wasn't likely to get the Nobel for original thinking. Thousands of honeys before her had shaken it a little for a boat ride out of Key West. God bless 'em all and *bon voyage.* Hell, more than a couple of them had shaken it in my face and been rewarded with a cruise on the *Kelpie,* yours truly at the helm—the arrangement itself probably went back to Neolithic days and dugout canoes. But this time the act was being played out in my living room with a turkey I couldn't abide, and that involved me just enough to bring out my bad side. It was there ready to be brought out. When Annie lassoed this prince, I was pretty much in the throes of a double dose of the Rock Fever that had me irritable as shit. Maybe if I hadn't been that way I would have been able to barely tolerate the creep or ignore him in a more constructive way. But the Rock Fever—Jesus, you hang out on this little island week after week and year after year dancing around with the same stale folks, seeking some kind of action at the same goddam bars—the redneck bar, the gay bar, the itinerant drugged-up freak bar—and paradise (even for those who started out convinced that it was paradise) starts slip-sliding into hell behind your back. For a hot time, as they scrawl on phone booths, you can shoot up to Miami and hang out in the Grove—which is a little like getting tired of Irkutsk and going for a laugh-filled week or two to Vladivostok. When your head is convinced that Key West has become lame beyond all belief, Coconut Grove isn't much of an improvement, and you can hang it up hoping to find anything better in the rest of Miami or in Broward.

It was a double dose because I'd been losing almost everyone I cared about in Key West. I don't think I'd ever thought of the place as paradise. At best, the island had an act I could live with pretty comfortably, as long as I was surrounded by my little hard-core circle of bad companions. Annie was one of them, just about the last one, and I guess that was part of the reason Larry irritated the shit out of me—he was spiriting one of my tried-and-true buddies out of town. My Coconut Grove cadre had split. Michael was in Mexico for his personal version of forever. Lee was—oh, fuck, there was death and desertion all around me. And Richard had left, a year ago now, on his deep-thinking scholar trip up north, freezing his butt for who the fuck knew what; he sure as hell hadn't been able to explain it to me. But whatever he was doing, he was gone, off the island, just like everyone else but Annie.

Desertion, death and desertion. Maybe it was nothing more than good old change, tropical growth, death, rot and decay, faster down here than in most places. But there was betrayal in it some-how. None of us had ever cut fingers and touched blood to blood. No one had ever demanded oaths and declarations. Just the same, there'd been slow and subtle infections and invasions of the heart, hundreds of little knowledges and understandings. God knows I had no right to make the live ones stay and no power to make the dead ones live, but each one who left ripped things, fibrous things out of me, and it was all the worse because none of them had meant to.

A lot had happened to try to shake me off the island, too, and if I'd gone, it would have been a toss-up about which way I would have left, standing up like Richard and Michael, or horizontal like Lee. Each time I'd dived for cover or held on to some tree trunk for dear life and I'd refused to be shaken off. The others—well, maybe they'd been as strong, but they'd dived for the wrong cover or grabbed a rotting tree. I'd dived best and hung on best; they hadn't, nothing more subversive than that. Now I was alone, pissed off that I'd won and half the time wishing I hadn't. Without them I was a prime candidate for the Rock Fever, and steeped in the Rock Fever I was ripe for a knockdown dragout with Annie as she packed her bags and headed for the island with her dufus-assed Slick. Fuck, I was out of control. I knew it, but that didn't help.

She hadn't even listened to me or looked at me straight the night before she'd left and I didn't blame her. We were so raw and pissed off at each other that if I'd tried to kiss her goodbye it would have turned into a fist fight. We just retreated to our separate corners of the house and tried to avoid each other. She was up in her room with her blue-blazer boy child and I was hunkered down in the dark living room with a hunk of hashish and twenty pounds of doom and gloom hovering over my head. Her canvas bag was on the couch ready to be grabbed for the great wordless escape in the morning, half-zipped for a last dunk of toothpaste and suntan lotion. I wish to fuck it hadn't been there and I wish to fuck I hadn't seen it and had the Bright Idea, but it was there and I saw it, and three-quarters blitzed as I was off the chunk of hash, it seemed to make sense. Fuck, even straight it made sense. I'd been worrying about it ever since she'd told me about the trip on the sloop. If I hadn't been such a pain in the ass about Larry I could have talked to her about it. But I had been and now it seemed the only way I could tell her what was on my mind was to scrawl the note and stuff it in her bag where she'd see it, but not until she was away and on the boat. I knew what she'd make of it. It would just be one more piece of fucking meddling in her act after I'd already been bugging the shit out of her for three days straight, and when she came back there'd be hell to pay. I knew all that. Blame it on the hash; blame it on my youth; blame it on the doom and gloom. But the note didn't come from the hash or flaming youth. It came from that idiot-child nobody knows what to do with, from love. I loved her. She was my buddy. I cared. I was worried.

I scrawled the note on a scrap of paper and stuffed it into her bag and then I stalked out of the house to find some place to hang out until the sloop sailed the next morning. I ended up with Luck again up in his room off Duval Street, and together we demolished the rest of the hash. I passed out on the floor around three in the morning. When I woke up the next afternoon I strolled by the marina and looked for the sloop, but it was gone.

The note had said

*Coriolis watch your ass.*

# BECKER

**W**ell, the important thing was that she got the message and she had to think about it while she was out there bobbing up and down on the waves in Geekland. She obviously had thought about it. She'd thought about it and come home and thrown it in my teeth as if it were some kind of mortal sin to worry about her a little. The sin hadn't been worrying about her. The sin was meddling. Too goddam late now, but I really was going to have to teach myself to worry without the meddling.

So I'd stomped out of the house with my camping crap, strapped it onto the tank and the tail of the machine with bunji cords as well as I could, kicked the damned thing over and headed north out of town. In some grudging fashion I told her I'd be back, probably, and said I was heading up to see Richard. Then I started to put some miles between me and the island.

Moisture in the carburetor was making the engine miss, so when I hit the long, lonely stretch north of the Navy station I pulled on the throttle with the clutch handle in to burn the crud out and then tried a little speed. The thing stopped missing and proceeded to move out. It was full dark by then, somewhere around nine o'clock, with a quarter moon low over the Gulf, the last Gulf moon I was going to see for a while.

I stopped for a hamburger in Islamorada and then took the Card Sound alternate, the longer and lonelier way to get to the mainland. Near a microwave relay tower I stopped to repack my load and do a little toot to gear up for the long cruise up the peninsula and the Miami traffic. From the sandy clearing around the tower a dirt road went down toward the Sound to the left. I tried to make out the types of car or truck tracks in the road, but there were no heavy pairs of ruts. Dirt bikes and neckers' cars, mostly.

I knew the spot pretty well. The first time I'd come here, I hadn't known where the fuck I was. Everything had been disoriented. I'd wondered if I was on the Gulf side or the Atlantic side. It was supposed to be that way then. Richard had called me at the house and told me to pack a few things in a knapsack and be ready. He'd come home in a rental van and picked me and Annie up after dark and headed out of Key West. No one talked for the whole trip; we were just going. I'd been in Key West for about a month and a half then. That was about two, three years ago.

On the drive north Richard was always looking at his watch, listening to the AM radio for weather reports and hints and rumors of this and that, anything that might strike him as out of the ordinary. I was in the jump seat and Annie was trying to make herself comfortable on a pile of old canvas sacks some previous renter had left behind. The windshield was dirty; oncoming headlights we passed highlighted the dirt streaks and made it impossible to see shit.

We'd stopped in Islamorada then, too. Richard pulled a duffel bag from behind his seat while Annie jumped out of the side doors to get some food from the drive-in. He rummaged around in the duffel bag: flashlight, walkie-talkie, cheap work gloves. Then he got out of the van and went to the pay phone near the drive-in window and made a call. As he talked he looked at his watch again.

That had been the night of the *Coriolis,* of *Coriolis watch your ass,* a night of considerable Mickey Mouse, of Chinese fire drills, of Richard at his nervous and pessimistic worst, of rendezvous and half-watt communications squawking almost imperceptibly above the frog songs, of deep truck tire ruts and mosquito plagues, of clothes drenched in the black salt mud. It had been a night of dark faces, some that I knew, some that I didn't at the time.

Now the motorcycle was parked at the entrance to the road we'd used that night. Of course I'd known then where we were going and what this midnight picnic was all about. Only the details, like the faces, were obscure. I could reconstruct a lot of them now. Lee had been there. He'd been waiting with the big truck in Florida City a few miles north, just on the peninsula, for the phone call. Michael and R.J. had come in on the boat later. Michael had jumped down off the bow and splashed his huge bulk into the water next to me as I took the line and tried to ease the bow parallel to the shore. I expected just another dark and anonymous temporary stevedore with nothing to say to me. Then I realized his hand was on my ass. I turned around; maybe the grizzly bear was just looking for a better handhold to balance himself in the waist-deep warm water. He was grinning at me.

"Hi," he said.

"Oh, fuck."

"You're cute. You a buddy of Richard's?"

"Please. Get your hand off my ass. We got some work to do."

Well, Michael was like that. A little nocturnal felonious activity wasn't going to keep him from cruising. He was like that on that first *Coriolis* night and I imagine that wherever he is now, he's much the same, not much sadder, not much wiser. We're alike in that way, anyway.

And there was R.J., scurrying back and forth on the deck, whispering commands, looking around with his weasel eyes, down on all fours on the bow in a dark blue sweatshirt with the sleeves cut off, his ears pricked up for noises the way Richard's were, cursing and impatient when things weren't going fast. And looking at me. That night I'd just assumed it meant he didn't like seeing surprises, people he hadn't known were coming even if he knew them, which was understandable. But that wasn't it, or was only part of it. He looked at everyone that way, lovers, friends or what passed for them, door-to-door salesmen, the Avon Lady, police, housing inspectors. One basic look of indifference, of *Who the fuck might you be,* with little components tacked on to suit the moment, a little component of hate, of annoyance, of pleasure. That last one was rare, but I'd seen it. Maybe I had, anyway. I still don't know if it was pleasure. Maybe the best R.J. could come up with was satiation.

Down that road where I paused on the bike, the events that first night had seemed to last for hours. They hadn't, of course. For all the cursing at delays and fuckups, the halts to listen for imaginary engines or helicopters, we'd been in and out in less than an hour. R.J. stayed on the boat and Richard joined him. I drove the van north to Miami with Annie. Lee and Michael took the big truck.

Richard was back the next night. He came into the house with something that approached a smile. Annie and I were eating our dinner in the living room, listening to a Miami station do its FM drifting in and out. He squatted down next to us and pulled his wallet out of his back pants pocket and paid us for our services, in fifties. I was glad to get it. I'd been running out of money. Not that anyone had said anything about it since I'd motored south to hang out with Richard and see what his Key West act was. Nobody had hit me up for the rent. Nobody seemed terribly concerned. If Richard said anything at all back in those days, it was that all good things come to him who waits. So I'd waited for the *Coriolis,* for my ship to come in, and it had.

Of course I didn't know it was the *Coriolis* then. It had been dark, for one thing. For another, the name had been painted over on the stern.

# Part Two

## THE

## CORIOLIS

# RICHARD

**B**ecker didn't know what he was doing. He was just shooting off his mouth as usual in his bullshit nonsensical scattergun approach. A scattergun, though, is designed to hit mostly nothing most of the time and to scare the shit out of everybody because every once in a while it hits a little bit of something. I knew what Becker knew and I knew what he didn't know, and I knew he didn't know anything about the *Coriolis.*

But Michael didn't know that and I couldn't give him any kind of reassuring high sign right there; sticking my foot into it right there and then would have made things worse. It would have indicated to Becker that he'd bumped into something that made Michael and everyone else practically shit in their drawers, everyone who knew about it, and that was me and R.J. and Michael in detail, and maybe Lee in a general outline, already a vastly huge group for a weird tale like that, and no one had had to emphasize that three or maybe four, call it three-and-a-half people were more than enough.

Michael was shitting in his drawers. I could see that. He was down on the floor with Becker playing every south Florida neophyte degenerate's favorite game, backgammon, and between moves Becker was expounding on the nature of space and time and reality, acquainting a small audience that was trying to ignore him with the warp and woof of the fabric of the cosmos. I never minded this floating, perpetual lecture particularly; it was a little like rooming with a reference library (Becker was dynamite with acrostics and crossword puzzles). Also, like the public television station, you could shut him off if you wanted to, just by saying, *Down, Becker, enough already.* He'd get a little ruffled and put on his pearls-before-swine expression and clam up, but no harm would be done and within twelve or twenty-four hours he would crank up again for lecture seven in his open-ended series, perhaps *Alternate Extraterrestrial Chemistries* or *Incest Taboos around the World* or *Digital Techniques in Contemporary HO Model Railroading* or *The Balkans in Transition.* Sit him down and stick some reefer in his face and who knew what would come out or where his mind had been recently. Sometimes in that tiny ramshackle two-story house it seemed as if not mosquitoes or flies were buzzing around in your face but ideas, phrases, topics, and you felt yourself walking down the narrow hallways swatting noxious things like one-to-one correspondences and ion-propulsion engines and fast-breeder reactors and the Kennedy Round of monetary agreements, little useless loathsome things that buzzed around in your ears whenever Becker was in residence.

So of course something like this had to happen sooner or later, pretty much the way it did happen. If I'd been alone with Becker when he'd started to propound on the Coriolis force (which, I had to admit, I'd never heard of) I could have done a pretty good job of pretending that it didn't faze me, that it meant no more or less to me than microwave or fiber optic laser communications or eating squid in Mexico. But that wouldn't have put an end to it. I couldn't have told him not to bring up the subject again without telling him too much of why. So he would have brought it up again pretty much the way he did that afternoon over the backgammon board with Michael. Becker's back was turned to me and I could see Michael's face above the beard turn a little pasty; in return I shot him arched eyebrows and shrugged my shoulders, which was supposed to mean *No big deal; it don't mean shit; mox nix; let it slide.* Although Michael seemed to understand and tried to control himself and pay attention to the game and stop paying attention to Becker, his concentration was pretty much shattered. On the next move he made a stupid mistake and Becker proceeded to clobber him, and after that Michael didn't want to play anymore. That was enough to tip Becker off. He looked at Michael a little narrowly to see what he could read off his face. Michael almost got ticked off but caught himself and went outside to take a walk.

Becker didn't know about the *Coriolis,* the boat he'd helped unload with a cargo of Colombian reefer a couple of weeks after he'd first tooled into Key West. Becker knew only about digital HO trains and fiber optics and the Balkans and bimetallism in currency and the Coriolis force, and he'd chosen that inopportune time to comment briefly on the latter. It had something to do, he said, with the reason that sink water whirls down the drain clockwise in the southern hemisphere and counterclockwise north of the equator. It was a hypothetical force that keyed off the rotation of the earth, he said, named after some Italian gentleman who'd decided that the world was in a sorry state without a hypothetical force like that to explain important matters like water draining out of sinks and toilet bowls in two entirely opposite directions. Hurricanes also decided which way to spin around because of the Coriolis force, he said. And then he started to get really wound up and get himself in deeper and deeper (with Michael's face getting pastier and his eyes bulging out as if his thyroid had ruptured) and tell how he'd always wanted to get a big boat with a big sink and sail it down to Colombia for a big load of reefer (I guess that was about the time Michael started to feel his bowels loosen up) and take a special detour to watch what the water in the sink did as he let it down the drain just at the moment the boat sailed across the equator. I suppose if the phone had rung at that precise moment Michael and I would have smashed ourselves senseless trying to leap for it first, but the phone failed to ring and the door failed to buzz and I tried to let Michael know with hand jive and facial English that despite Becker's unfortunate topic everything was still largely or entirely copacetic. It didn't do very much good, and Becker slaughtered him at the backgammon game.

Much later that night:

"You mean all that stuff was just so much hot air?"

Michael and I were driving north to get some pizza from a place I liked a couple of keys up the pike.

"You know him by now," I said. "He just talks and talks and talks about all kinds of bullshit. This wasn't any different."

"He scared the shit out of me. You sure he doesn't know anything? I mean, he was there when we off-loaded."

"Nope. Just you and me and R.J. How about Lee?"

"Well, he knows things got a little heavy, but that's all he knows. That's all he wants to know."

"Well, if Becker knew anything at all, that's all he'd want to know, and if he knew anything at all, you could trust him the way you could trust me. That's assuming you think you can trust me," I said.

"It doesn't matter. I have to, you know. But for a minute there I thought he knew, too, and I didn't dig it at all."

"Think about it as if you had something besides shit for brains, Michael. If he knew, would he start shooting his mouth off about it in front of you?"

He was surly; it made too much sense to agree to right away. "I don't know. I don't know him that well. I don't know what he'd do."

"Well, he has this much brains. If he went and dicked your twelve-year-old sister, he wouldn't run right up to you and tell you all about it."

"I don't have a twelve-year-old sister."

"That's not the point. He doesn't know and he can't know, but if he did know, he'd keep his goddam mouth shut, certainly in front of you. That makes it obvious to me that he doesn't know anything."

"Look, don't get me wrong," Michael said. "I like your little buddy. I've even cruised him a couple of times, and it's a tragic waste of talent that he doesn't swing my way. But I just don't know him that well, and he makes me nervous."

"No. What happened makes you nervous, and you're just going to have to live with that. It's not just Becker and his physics lectures, man. There are going to be more times than this that something's going to happen to make you think the word's out. Your stomach's going to churn over weirder bullshit than Becker.

You just have to expect it, and if you can't get used to it, you're still going to have to put up with it somehow."

"Okay. But you're sure about him?"

"Becker? Well, I'll put it this way. If it hadn't been for Becker, this problem wouldn't have come up at all, because I'd probably be doing forty years at hard labor in the army. If Becker wanted to fuck with me, he could have put me on ice a long time ago without lifting a finger. Literally. To think that he's fucking with us now over this bullshit is just a little too Byzantine for my imagination."

"Okay. If that's the way it looks to you, okay."

"No. That's not the way it looks. That's the way it is. Do you want me to slip him some kind of word?"

"Jesus, no. Just leave things the way they are. I mean, you're right about other things coming up. It's not just him. I'm willing to let things slide."

And things slid. Michael pulled himself together and Becker didn't seem compelled to give that particular physics lecture again, not that I ever heard. I guess the only thing I really worried about wasn't Michael, but R.J. I really didn't want Becker doing anything or saying anything in front of R.J. that might give the old geek the idea that Becker knew anything about the boat, because then things would be entirely out of my control.

R.J. might think logically about it and come to the independent conclusion that Becker didn't know anything but was just farting off. Or he might come to the independent conclusion that Becker knew. Or he might take a middle course that it was better, safer to assume that Becker knew, whether he did or not. In any case, things might get heavy again, because whatever R.J. would come up with, he'd do it without talking to me or asking my advice. And I couldn't even imagine what R.J. might choose to come up with in that strange little porno theater behind his no-giveaway eyes. Even though he knew Becker a lot better than Michael did and might believe that Becker didn't know anything, R.J. wouldn't trust Becker. R.J. didn't trust anyone. People could fuck R.J. over or rip him off, but never solely because he had trusted them, because he had never trusted anyone.

R.J. tolerated people, allowed them to see things and know

things because I think it tickled him to let people in on little glimpses of his dark, convoluted act, to let them think they had learned something about him the way they thought they knew things about themselves or other people. But they didn't really, not with R.J. His life and his act were compartmentalized like a stage magician's routine. If you got a glimpse of something appalling or intriguing and went back to R.J.'s to look for it again the next day, it was routinely and systematically gone, vanished so completely that you wondered whether you had really ever seen it to begin with. If you asked him about it, sometimes he might smile and verify it and other times he'd look at you quizzically and wonder what you were talking about or ask you whether you were out of your mind. His life was filled that way with trap doors and flies and pulleys and mirrors and platforms that glided away silently on casters. Only R.J. remained on stage as a permanent and central figure like some Mogul emperor surrounded by palace intrigue whose wives and ministers disappear and are replaced by new ones from day to day or hour to hour without notice or explanation.

Of course Lisa was a permanent fixture at R.J.'s, or had been since about the time he moved down to Key West. I suppose that made her the magician's lovely assistant, though is it ever really clear whether the magician's lovely assistant really knows how all the tricks work? Or is that an illusion, too, the grandest illusion of them all, an illusion intended just for her, a perpetual illusion of trust and confidence that rests on nothing more solid than the illusions the audience sees during the show? It was strange, but when I was at R.J.'s, I watched Lisa much more than I watched the wizard—and maybe that's what the lovely assistant is for, basically, to distract the eyes and the concentration; maybe that was the whole idea. But I watched her more than I watched R.J. because I no longer expected any surprises from R.J.

R.J.'s version of the man-woman bond was also constructed along the style of grand illusion. He was very much the open-house stay-at-home potentate providing Turkish-style decadence for any and all of his acquaintances who wished to participate at nearly any hour, and yet so long as Lisa was in residence he only watched the dancing girls—real ones, from the topless bars that catered to the Navy base crowd—and never moved himself from his chair (a huge overstuffed ottoman, appropriately, that he had trucked down to

Key West from his earlier court in the Atlanta house he kept as a refuge when we were at Fort Benning). What everyone except Lisa knew or acknowledged was that R.J. could get out of the chair and become an active participant the moment Lisa was out of town or accounted for somewhere else on the island for the evening; he could and he did. Yet he never felt any pressure when she failed to get out of his hair for weeks or even months at a time; the parties went on continuously, with R.J. content just to be a spectator and master of ceremonies, and as far as the world (that cared) could tell, he and Lisa might have been Ozzie and Harriet or geese that mate for life.

Then Lisa would go off somewhere and the moment she went off, R.J. set the party on automatic and had his pick of the more attractive visitors. He cleaned up the evidence just in time for Lisa's return, not out of fear, but just in keeping with good magician stagecraft—no sloppy handkerchief corners sticking out. In return for the good housekeeping, Lisa didn't pry, or didn't even assume there might be anything to pry into. Her reward was the featured spot, second billing on a very lucrative long-running show with all the benefits and amenities.

Dozens of confrontations might have occurred if R.J. had been just a little sloppier and Lisa had been just a little nosier, but they had long ago wordlessly worked out the limits of sloppiness about R.J.'s in-house and on-the-road activities (there were always extended road trips R.J. had to go on solo while Lisa tended the house) and the limits of Lisa's nosiness. There were no confrontations. The topless bar girls kept dancing, the pipe was always being refilled and passed around, lines were always being chopped and laid out, people kept walking in and out through the beaded curtain that separated the foyer from the living room.

R.J. had tried Annie first in the Lisa role at the Atlanta retreat. She was as much a fugitive from Benning a hundred miles or so to the south as R.J., Becker and I were, and R.J. had plucked her from a waitress gig at the Omni, her first job after leaving her folks at the fort. (God knows you don't leave your military family at Benning and drift across the line to Columbus; you have to put some miles on you and invariably it's always Atlanta.) Her dad was an infantry bird colonel deeply into the sauce who knew he was never going to see a general's star and her mother was pretty much standard GI issue for that kind of an act, too. It was a bad setup just to live and be sixteen or seventeen in, but Annie had started adding ladies to it. I suppose mom and the colonel were prepared for the usual hit-the-roof scene when boys started dragging her molested body home at three or four A.M., but when other ladies started providing the night-owl escort service, there was some real down-home nonsymbolic mayhem in officers' housing and the little white house with the colonel's name and rank on it had an increasingly hard time containing the steam and the drunken freakouts.

By that time R.J. had established his little house off Peachtree Street and installed Annie in it. I never asked and Annie never told me if she and R.J. ever got into anything that might be called body contact, but by the time Becker and I started drifting up there for weekends, Annie was content to play hostess and keep the house together during the weekdays while we all did our bit in fatigues at Benning, waiting for our time to run out there and to be shipped off across the pond. R.J. was just waiting for his time to run out, period, and when it did—it was a complete surprise to Annie, she told me—he cleaned out the house and announced that he was moving Dope Central to bigger and better headquarters in Key West and that Annie was invited to come along.

I was the first to drop down and check out his new act a year later, after a vast amount of trouble that involved stockades and courts-martial and pissed-off Army lawyers and a seedier class of discharge than I might have hoped for. Drifting down to Key West and shacking up with R.J. and Annie—she and I had become good buddies in Atlanta—just seemed to make sense at the time in comparison to everything else, which made no sense at all. And then Becker got back from his stint in the Nam and I started getting these little screwy postcards from him and writing back and he decided to cruise down. By that time R.J. had taught me the family business and Annie was into it as well, muling through international airports with cash and toot concealed here and there about her person, and Lisa had popped up in R.J.'s life and moved in. Annie and I scraped the cash together first to rent and then to start buying the house across town, and Becker eventually made three.

Lisa was, as Becker said when he was casting about for a polite word for dumb cunt, a bubblehead. She talked nonsense when she spoke at all. She talked about astrology and at least two or three even more arcane systems of paraknowledge with conviction but not with education; she wasn't even a knowledgeable astrologer, which irked Becker no end. I'd watched him listen spellbound once for an hour while an astrologer explained the fundamentals as he saw them to Becker and Becker listened with respect and asked questions with respect. But Lisa had nothing to offer but drivel.

She was the most abject drifter I'd ever known, but because R.J. had stopped her from drifting geographically by putting her in his house, she drifted now only in her mind. Annie and I had taken her to the hospital more than once, not so much for attempting suicide as for just failing to give much of a fuck about staying alive, for failing to practice the rudimentaries of good sense that will guarantee your waking up in the morning. The more R.J. left her alone the more prone she was to these things—not because she was angry that he left her alone and not because he wasn't there to supervise her or watch over her like a child. It was just that without him there to distract her, to make her put on some coffee or cook him a meal, she fell into her permanent fixation of sensuality with drugs and liquor, her fixation with astral projection by brute chemical force. Sometimes she'd show up at our house in an incoherent blither the likes of which always astonished me—beyond drunkenness, beyond tripping. And yet even when things would get out of hand and she'd have to go to the hospital and subsequently be dried out, she emerged not burned out; in those rare moments when her bloodstream contained just blood, she looked good, spoke well, even laughed convincingly.

But those times couldn't last. At the best of them, she was itching to drift again. And because she no longer drifted up and down highways the way the rest of the drifters do, she drifted in pill bottles and vials and bags—in syringes, too, when R.J. was gone out of town. R.J. got furious when his house started to display spikes and Lisa started to show tracks. He beat up on her, and out of conviction, in cold blood. He told her in sobriety that he'd smash the shit out of her if he came home and found her spiking up, and when he came home and found her spiking up, he neglected to get angry, but he never went back on his word; he beat the shit out of her. Annie had taken her to the emergency room on those occasions, too. Beaten up and bleeding or spaced out and OD'd, Lisa would be helped into the emergency room and the night shift would help her to a chair and call her by her first name immediately, "Here, Lisa, drink this. . . . The doctor will be here in a couple of minutes, Lisa. . . . Hold this on your arm, Lisa." Whatever it was, R.J. never stinted about the hospital bill. He paid the bills as he paid his bills at the hardware store and as he paid his long distance phone bills—never out of sorrow or anguish or regret or alarm, but just because they were the logical and necessary expenses of his lifestyle, his choice to have Lisa live in his house or his choice to beat her up when he came home and found bloody spikes on the windowsill.

R.J. could have shared everything in his life, every secret with her indiscriminately and never worried. She had no memory, no ability to differentiate or evaluate things one from the other, no reason to hold on to any particular piece of information. But did she know about the *Coriolis?* Would he have told her that? That was the big question for guys like Michael and me, and lacking anything solid, we could mull it over either way. R.J. could easily have told Lisa out of caprice, for kicks. It would have made sense to R.J. to go out of his way to deprive Becker, whom he knew he *could* trust but just refused to trust, of any knowledge about the *Coriolis,* but at the same time to spill all the details about that strange voyage to Lisa, to the biggest fucking bubblehead on the island for absolutely no reason except that it would strike him as amusing to place three or four lives entirely at the mercy of someone like that, of someone who could disappear at any moment and end up living with any man on earth six hours later. That kind of thing would strike R.J. as very funny. If he told her, it probably also struck him as funny that I was one of the people whose asses were on the line.

I guess it hit me about then that we had the seeds of something unstable going on in our little community in Key West and the Grove, and the seeds had been carried in the hold of the *Coriolis.* The boat was scuttled now, but we'd all taken some of those seeds to shore with us, and we were germinating them carefully and slowly and lovingly. I wondered when they'd mature and what they'd look like when they did. I wondered how quick I'd be at recognizing them. I wondered who would harvest them first and who would eat them. I wondered what would happen to us after that.

# BECKER

**H**ow I found out that I was prospering and making my mark upon the land was through the uninvited comments of a kid from Minnesota, but not a farm boy. At least he said he was from Minnesota, and later it turned out that he was telling the truth, not that it did him or me a hell of a lot of good. And not that I wanted *him* to tell me I was prospering and making my mark upon the land in the first place. That was the last fucking thing I wanted.

But he did anyway. I was sitting at the quarter-a-throw slightly private motel beach bar next to Dog Beach one afternoon, minding my own fucking business in the classic American manner, putting a soft legal buzz on with rum and Coca-Cola, not so much because I liked the drink, but because I liked the buzz and I liked the rhythm of the song about the stuff. It just seemed like the Caribbean sort of thing to do, like backgammon.

He came toward my table from the direction of the bar and was about to pretend he was going to sit at another table when he saw me sitting alone and made a gesture of inquiry. I made a gesture back and he sat down across from me, in the shade of the umbrella that grew out of the little hole in the middle of the table. He was definitely from out of town. His hair was styled and he had a midwestern freckled grin that I wouldn't have wanted to be the last thing I saw on this earth because it expressed absolutely nothing except somebody's Junior Chamber of Commerce greeting. He followed the grin up with an outstretched hand and I took it very limply; it turned into a hippie thumb grab that didn't make me think much better of the whole deal.

"Bob," he explained to me.

"Carl," I explained to him. I don't know why I picked Carl. I guess it was just lying there in front of me waiting to be picked up if ever I wanted somebody else's name. That made me wonder if he'd just picked Bob from the same plate.

"I'll bet you live down here. You sort of have that look," he said.

"Yeah," I said. "Not bad."

"Well, I cheated a little. I saw you wave to people, nod at them. I notice things."

"Far out. Where you from?"

"Minneapolis. Damn glad to be down here this month. It must be great to have this kind of weather all year around."

"Actually it's a royal pain in the ass," I said. "But everybody else seems to be queer for it, so I don't squawk too much."

"You like the snow?"

"In moderate, natural quantities, yes. I'm pretty fond of the shit."

"Huh. I've had enough of it. Hell, I've been trying to work it out so I could move down here. I mean, this place is really paradise."

"Well, we all have our different ideas of paradise. Mine's a little more austere. You probably tend to the Islamic version, gardens and fountains and pools and peeled grapes and that sort of shit. Concubines and little boys—well, nothing personal. It just goes with that vision."

"What are you into?"

"I don't really know, to tell you the truth."

"You look pretty comfortable to me," he said.

"Well, I learned to get comfortable just about anywhere in the army. It's easier to be uncomfortable anywhere, but you learn that with a little effort, you can make do in just about any old shithole. I will admit, I do like Cuban food. That helps a lot."

"It probably helps a lot if there's a lot of coke around."

"I don't know. There's a lot of Coke everywhere. I'm a Dr. Pepper man myself, but they don't stock it at this bar."

"No," he said. "I meant the stuff you put up your nose."

"Do tell," I said. "How stupid of me."

"Not really. Just cautious. I would have expected that. But on the other hand, I was sort of hoping that sooner or later while I was down here I could pick some of that up to take back."

"I wouldn't know where to tell you to start," I said.

"That's not what I hear."

I stopped myself and took some time out to think about my next couple of lines. Or maybe I just ought to bid the man good day and stroll. Yes, that was the best thing to do. I should have done that. I didn't.

I looked across the table at him. I looked him right smack dab in the middle of his Jaycees smile and his freckles, just north of his alligator shirt.

"I don't care what you heard. *Nada pasa,* and you're rapidly pissing me off. I don't care what you heard and I don't care whom you heard it from. I don't care if you know my name and the circumference of my tumescent dick in millimeters. *Nada pasa* at this table, buddy, and I think it's time you shoved off, because I was here first."

"Hey, hey, take it easy, man. I'm sorry if I came on too strong. But I had to break the ice somehow. You see, your name isn't really Carl, but that's all right with me. I can dig it. But my name really happens to be Bob. Bob Liggett. Junior, as a matter of fact." He reached into the pocket with the alligator and took out, of all things, a business card. Just a calling card, really. There was no business listed on it, just a Minneapolis address and phone number. "You see, all I wanted to do, even if I did start off on the wrong foot, was to give you this and all the time in the world to do whatever checking out you might want to do about me. Because I know you're a very careful guy."

"Why would I possibly want to check out a dickhead like you?"

"For any reason you might want to come up with. And I'm not really all that much of a dickhead. Or if I am, I'm a dickhead with a lot of these." He reached into his pocket again and took out a C-note, very new, very crisp. It wanted to stand up on the table and sing the Star-Spangled Banner. He pushed it into the center of the table, sort of neutral territory.

"Am I supposed to be interested in that?"

"Not particularly. But maybe you'd be interested in a hundred more of those. Or more. In exchange for something for me to take back to Minneapolis. Look, man. I know this seems just really lame to you, but look at it from my point of view. I don't know any people down here who might want to do a little business. I know you. I know that's probably a rude surprise to you, but I know you anyway. What am I supposed to do, not even try to get your attention? Just gaze at you from afar for a week or two and then fly back to Minneapolis with nothing to show for it?"

"You're fucking-A right. This is a rude surprise, and what you're supposed to do is fly back to Minneapolis with nothing, at least nothing from me. You can keep the bucks. That's free advice. It's worth a hundred smackers, though."

"Then keep it."

"No thanks."

"Keep it and think about it. If I don't hear from you by the time I go back, keep it and spend it on anything you want. Flush it down the toilet. Send it to the Communist party. Have a ball. Free money."

"Still no thanks. By the way, who the fuck told you to ring my chimes?"

"Let's just say a mutual friend. I know it's a terrible cliché, but it's a mutual friend. You trust him, I trust him, he trusts you, he trusts me. He said he didn't want me to use his name, but that with a little luck you and me might do business."

"We're fresh out of luck, but if there's all this fucking trust flying around between us three pals, why the fuck couldn't you use his name? Or why couldn't this gentleman make the introductions?"

"Just didn't work out that way. Time and circumstances."

"Well, from what I've heard—and mind you, it's just rumor

and hearsay—that's the way things like this are arranged. You're asking for love at first sight, and most people prefer some kind of marriage broker. No dice."

"Still, keep the money."

"Fuck off."

"Okay." He put the note back in his pocket but kept the card out on the table.

"No," I said. "Give me the fucking money."

He looked a little surprised, but he took the bill back out again and handed it to me. I grabbed it and stuffed it in my pocket.

"Now listen to this, because it just cost you a hundred bucks, and a dickhead like you probably only thinks things are worth something if he has to pay big for them. First, don't ever, under any fucking circumstances, talk to me again or I'll beat the shit out of you. That is a hard and fast forecast. Enjoy Key West for as long as you like, but keep the fuck away from me. Next, don't try to do business like this with anybody else down here. You're fucking luckier than you'll ever know, pal, because I happen to be all sweetness and light, but the rest of the population would already have slit your fucking weasand from ear to ear for about half of what you put on the table for free. If they find out you're offering a few hundred of those, they'll start taking numbers outside your motel room door for the privilege.

"I guess what I'm trying to tell you is that by all rights, you should be dead by now—and you will be dead in very short order if you try that bullshit on anyone else in Florida. And all that advice, which I tried to give you for free a few minutes ago, is certainly worth the hundred bucks I intend to keep for my trouble now. But I was still at this table first, and I want you to get up now and disappear from my view, immediately."

"Okay," he said. "I'm sorry we couldn't do business. That's what the man said about you, that you were a nice guy and out front."

"He was certainly right about that, but I have every intention of beating the living shit out of him if I ever find out who he is. I can still see you."

"Okay. Sorry again. Take it easy. But you've got my card if you change your mind. I'm at the Sea Breeze."

"Don't hold your fucking breath, and don't pass out a lot of those cards."

And then he left. He stood up, picked up his drink, turned around and breezed back past the bar and back into the motel. He did his best to skate out of my life forever, I'll give him that. It wasn't his fault that he dropped back into it; it was more mine than his, but it was pretty much of an accident either way. Still, I never had to talk to him again, and that was all I gave a flying fuck about.

I finished up my drink and strolled back into the streets, heading for home and hoping nothing else berserko stood between me and it. The simplest of intentions that morning, nothing more complicated than a buzz-on and some tits and ass to look at on the beach, had turned into something remarkably and uncomfortably complicated. Strangers wanting to do dope deals with me. Strangers putting hundred dollar bills on the table in front of me. Strangers who said they knew who I was and that we had mutual friends and that I was a nice Joe or Carl or David. Strangers who wanted me to call other strangers in Minnesota. Strangers who had a pretty good angle on what I was doing to pay the rent these days.

I'd handled it pretty well, whatever the motherfucker's act really was. I'd handled it well if he was a cop and I'd handled it well if he were a disciple of the the Rev. Sun Myung Moon. I wasn't terribly worried that he was a cop; no cop would have been that lame. What worried me was that he had a substantial handle on my act, whoever the fuck he was. That had to mean that someone else also had the same handle, maybe with my intentions, but maybe not. And even if this third party knew about me because I'd wanted him to know about me, I sure as hell didn't want him passing what he knew on to shmucks like Freckleface.

I got home and found the place deserted, which was just how I wanted it to be under the circumstances. I sat down on the couch by the window air conditioner and rolled myself an ample doobie that I intended to consume all by my lonesome, with no freeloaders. I fired it up and began to think about this very complicated day and how to bring it down to Mr. Thoreau's simplification program again.

It boiled down to this. I'd done a pretty good job of handling the dude under the circumstances. Score one for me. I was pretty sure he'd gotten the message that I didn't want to run into him again. Score two. Hope springs eternal in the subhuman breast, so there was the possibility that he was going to hang around the Sea Breeze waiting for me to call and invite him over for some Florida lobsters, but that was his problem; it was still two to nothing on my side. And if things should get weirder somehow, I was pretty sure I had an accurate handle on who he really was. The guy was just lame enough to have told me the straight skinny about that. I had to count that as another point for me.

After that, everything stopped being quantifiable and just slushed into a mess of pure paranoia, in which case he didn't score any points, but I was going to forfeit some. I could start tearing my hair out and losing a lot of sleep over this crap. I could start looking over my shoulder to see if I was being followed. I could start carrying a bazooka and a roll of dimes. I could lie low and suspend operations for an indefinite period. I could turn myself into the authorities and get it all over with.

For what? You don't spend a couple of years in Heavy Dope Central, cruising around in an atomic bomb of a boat, with no visible means of support, without some kind of loose talk getting around. I'd probably been pretty fucking lucky so far, and Big Bob from the Land of a Thousand Lakes was just the first inevitable security leak of many I was going to have to put up with. Okay, so each time it happened I was going to have to churn a little—but just a little, goddam it. Chalk it up to dues, but dues is dues, not the end of the world, not the Big Knock.

Finally, there was the great wheel of karma, and here I had to be ahead, at least for this little exchange. I'd sold the man some exceptionally superb advice that just could save his dufus ass if he chose to take it to heart. The young fellow had come down south courting some 99 and 44/100 percent pure disaster, and I'd tipped him off on how to steer a considerably safer course. Who could fault me there? It certainly was about as close as coke dealers could ever come to walking old ladies across busy intersections or donating a kidney.

There was just one more trick to pull. I'd convinced myself that the asshole and I were square, that he and I had passed in the night without a major catastrophic collision. But I wanted something just a little better from the exchange, and I was loosened up enough to pull it off. I took the C-note out of my pocket and examined it in its pristine purity. I checked it for little tick marks or ink spots and didn't find any. Then I walked it upstairs and put it under Annie's sunlamp (funny . . . I never asked her what the fuck she was doing with a sunlamp in Key West) to see if the ultraviolet did anything exciting to it. It didn't. The goddam thing was a bona fide, spendable one hundred dollar bill, good for all debts public and private. I savored all the hot times and cha-cha tickets I could buy with it.

Then I torched the sucker. It didn't burn fast and it didn't burn slow. It burned responsibly and seriously, the way a product of your government and mine ought to. I manipulated the bill in my thumb and first finger until the flame had turned about fifteen-sixteenths of it into black ash, and then put the remains gingerly in a big ceramic ashtray from Pennekamp, an awful monstrosity that showed the underwater Jesus statue. The last sixteenth of it—the last six bucks and a quarter, I guess—turned black and unrecognizable, and the whole mass shrunk into a little charred scroll there in the ashtray.

Felt great. I'd never done that before and I got a great charge out of it. If I couldn't keep that turkey off my back, I was going to charge him ten times as much next time and torch that, too.

## BECKER

**S**ometimes when the fits were on us we'd drive up to the Grove in Miami, usually unannounced, and descend on Michael and Lee in Lee's little shack buried behind a jungle of shrubbery and Australian pines down one of the dozens of winding out-of-the-way residential roads south of the center of the Grove on the canal system that linked up with Biscayne Bay and eventually the Atlantic. We'd also wind up at Lee's when it was time to fly some toot up north or prepare for a deal by moving some cash around at Lee's bank.

Sometimes if we felt sportin' we'd take in the odd pastimes Miami had to offer big spenders, a pigout on stone crabs at one of the specialty restaurants and then a night at the dog track or jai alai or the horses. I went for the dogs for the simple reason that no matter how hard you try, you can't bribe a dog to throw a race. I wouldn't go with Lee to jai alai because I knew those suckers were all on the take and I resented it. Of course there was always somebody around who'd say that although you couldn't bribe a dog, you could always drug him, but I didn't mind that. That was a chemical problem, not an ethical one; even if the pooch was staggering out of the starting box and seeing triple rabbits, he was still honest.

Lee was my age and I guess he came from something pretty

close to my own background, but he was a real Jew's Jew and he ate it up with a spoon. He loved to flash that roll at the track and sport a honey or two on his arm. He loved to grab for the restaurant tab at Wolfie's or Rascal House and it didn't start to get interesting for him until it was up around fifty or sixty bucks for a few lousy bagels. He loved to dress like an explosion in a neon sign factory when he went out on the town, and the town he liked to go out on most was Miami or the Beach. Although he lived in the Grove and he lived pretty quietly, the worst, the most lurid and rancid stretches of the strip on Miami Beach were his favorite playgrounds. He cruised them in his Mercedes, even though a Mercedes in Miami Beach is about as distinctive as a cockroach in Harlem. Sometimes the insane gaps between his sense of taste and his lunge for the absolutely tasteless made me dizzy. It used to drive me crazy trying to figure out why I got such a charge out of the motherfucker. Half the time he was actively and aggressively everything I hated in the loud, ill-dressed and flaming kike and he knew it. He knew how I felt about vomiting Jewish all over everyone's shoes and when he saw me start to squirm, he just increased the juice in my direction and made me squirm some more. His accent would get more New York, more Brooklyn (although I don't think he ever spent more than a month at a time in the Apple in his life) and he'd begin to spout his kike aesthetic—that the world was a dichotomy of the *hamishe,* the Jewish and worthy, versus the *goyishe* and worthless. Only *goyishe* ass had value, great value; *goyishe* food had no taste, *goyishe* cars and clothes had no class, *goyishe* attitudes and mannerisms made no impact on the cosmos. He constantly turned on me and accused me of deserting my roots, that my true feelings were for white bread instead of pumpernickel and rye, and that I went down for Dinty Moore beef stew instead of chicken soup with a couple of gigantic matzoh balls floating around in it, and that I rode my motorcycle to emulate limeys and greasers. "C'mon, Davie," he'd scream in the middle of a restaurant, "you're ashamed to be a Jew. C'mon, admit it."

"No," I'd hiss quietly, "I'm ashamed to be a loud kike like you."

"You're a closet kike. You think we should all shuffle and

scrape so nobody'll know we're Jews. Well, I'm proud to be a goddam Jew, and I don't care who knows it."

"Everybody knows it now."

"That's the way it should be. What are you afraid of, Davie, a pogrom? Well, if the cossacks ride in here, *boychick,* I'm not getting speared alone. I'm pointing you out. You can put on all the *sheg* airs you want, Mr. Taste, but I'm fingering you. You're going to the gas chambers with the rest of the sheenies."

He was crazy, of course. I don't know what held him together. He was as close as I ever want to come to one of those dime novel schizos with the twelve different personalities all of whom are out to bugger all the others.

When I had to make the cash deals, I'd walk in on him at his daddy's bank, where he was an exec. His clothes were Florida somber and his attitude was handshake and pat-on-the-back friendly businessman Jaycee *avec* the ever-ready business card. He would sit me down in the stuffed chair in front of his mahogany desk with its oversized telephone with the six incoming lines and the hands-free speaker and chat while he called his secretary Laura, the ultimate classy *shikseh* girl Friday and mistress with the whispy voice and wraithlike countenance, to stroll in and fetch the stacks from the vault. She smelled of the slightest hint of extremely expensive perfume that probably was squeezed from Himalayan wildflowers or essence of Baptist virgin, but the real nasal blast I got from her the very first time she and I eyeballed one another was of hot nuclear trouble that probably felt so good you didn't notice you were starting to glow in the dark.

She fetched tidy little sums like eighty, a hundred thousand in scrambled and unrecorded cash with a nonchalant expertise and efficiency that chilled me about twenty degrees cooler than the bank's air conditioner. And she eyed me that first time, sharp and deep. She eyed all Lee's nefarious pals, either on the job at the bank or at Lee's house in the evenings where she presided as hostess. She eyed me and I had the feeling she was thinking *What will drip out if I squeeze this fellow like a wringer mop and how can I do it?* God knows she was taking Lee to the cleaners emotionally—financially he didn't care; there was always more where the first lost pile had come from—but emotionally he didn't have a great deal to spare, certainly not the volumes a honey like that could leach out of a high-strung lovable flake like Lee. This was a true finishing school honey, and she was well on the way to finishing Lee.

I really did love the guy and I always wanted to tell him that our loving God in heaven just hadn't constructed him to sustain the kind of psychic whammies a honey like that could whip out six times a day and ten times a night, but he fancied himself a sort of Jewish Valentino whose mere gaze could reduce any woman to rubble; it would have taken the Israeli Air Force six weeks of sustained precision bombing to reduce that honey to rubble, and plenty of bombers wouldn't have made it back to base in the process. She let him go on believing that for as long as it suited her, for as long as it paid the rent in a killer of an apartment on Biscayne Bay, and for as long as it kept her loaded with all the coke she could snort, and that last item worked out to something close to her weight, ninety-eight pounds give or take a couple, each week. And it never showed on her. At the bank, even the couple of times I showed up at nine on the dot, she still looked as if the most damaging thing she'd done the night before was to swim eight laps and read a good book and go to bed at ten, alone.

I never exactly found out how Richard tumbled into her. It was probably on one of those midnight visits to fetch an attaché case, but while I always saw to it that I kept my visits short and businesslike, he stayed on until well past sunup. And he started coming back for more of that stuff. That in itself didn't fuck things up between him and Lee. For all Lee's pretense at being Laura's main man and primary hot-time sugar daddy, Lee knew that stuff didn't belong exclusively to him. I think Richard's visits bummed him out at first, but he had to lump it or lose his visiting privileges altogether, so he lumped it. And when Richard was good and hooked, he had to lump her time with Lee and whoever the fuck else was in line the same way.

That made things easier on me in one way. I didn't want to be around her any more than I had to, and there were plenty of times now when Richard was stag because Lee was squiring her around or when Lee was in the same boat because Richard had the privilege. Then there were times when they were both in the Grove and she'd shut them both out, so all three of us would cruise around and

I'd ask them, if they didn't mind, to keep their mutual misery society down to a dull roar; I didn't want to listen to either of them moan about Laura.

So one night it was like that—Laura elsewhere, her jilted swains and me doing the town up and ending up in the Taurus. A very hefty deal had just gone down as smoothly as Ex-Lax and we were all considerably better off for it. So were our reputations: it had been primo stuff, and for quite a few months after that, a shitload of the beautiful people from Miami to Key West thought of us when they thought of parties and fifteen-year-old cheerleaders, spare no expense.

So we started buying rounds for each other and toasting financial independence and all that Three Musketeers crap, and the clock that wasn't on the Taurus wall let a lot of time lapse without any of us giving a flying fuck.

I should have been too drunk to notice—I *was* very drunk—but I never seem to be able to get too drunk to notice footnotes and apocryphal details that have connections, however gossamer, with my own dearly beloved ass. Far away on the other end of the crowded, sweaty, shoulder-to-shoulder singles bar crowd was Minnesota Bob. He was talking to a dude I didn't know, buying him drinks. I didn't know if he'd seen me. Maybe he had and was taking part of my C-note advice about steering clear of me. That was good, because I had every intention, liquored up as I was, of decking him in the middle of the Taurus, or trying to, if he even bothered to smile at me.

But he didn't seem to be taking the rest of that expensive advice. The dude he was talking to had a nice tan, an open collar with a coke spoon dangling off a gold chain, and all the charm of a dose of the clap. I watched them talk and drink and exchange philosophies and pleasantries, until Minnesota Bob reached into the pocket of his sports jacket and took out another one of his famous calling cards. Fucking-A. The dude took it, looked it over, and put it in his very tight chinos.

# BECKER

**S**ix days later I was back on the island and I picked up a copy of The Herald to read over my lunch at the Fourth of July. The waitress had brought me some black bean soup and I'd started to slurp it down when I turned to the metro page and read all about Minnesota Bob.

They'd found him the night before in a car with Minnesota tags in the underground garage of one of the slick hotels in the Grove across Bayshore Drive from Dinner Key Marina. The back of his head had been blown off, and the Dade County coroner guessed a .45 had done the job. Minnesota Bob had been in his Minnesota car for several days by the time they found him, probably by the sense of smell. He was slumped to the side of the front seat, and if the cops found any of those crisp C-notes he liked to travel with in lieu of an American Express card, they weren't talking. I took a wild guess that he was fresh out of them by the time they pulled him out of the car.

I didn't need this. It seemed I didn't need any of the crap that was always going on in Miami. In Key West things seemed to make sense, it seemed I could always just barely keep them under control, but Miami was always out of control, a big surprise every trip, and surprises in my trade were always by definition lousy. I knew my little island crowd, but the crowd in the Grove, even the ones I had to work with regularly, was always cooking up some kind of shake-up, always pitching the screwball curve. Especially sweet Laura.

One night Lee's money magic scheme had worked out to send me alone to Laura's little pad on the nineteenth floor to pick up an attaché case full of bucks she'd brought home from Lee's bank for a Colombian buy I was making the next day. The place was immaculate and surprisingly Spartan. She sat me down and waited on me in that long-gone southern charm way—coffee, how did I like it, a plate of cheeses, some hash (a very rare item in Florida, glutted with straight reefer as it was) in a Moroccan pipe with its tiny clay bowl, soft quasi-jazz playing on the stereo. She showed me the view from the balcony of the causeway to the Beach and the peons shrimping along the sides of the bridges, of the sailboats tacking on the Bay for her viewing pleasure at any hour.

The salt air was heavy and touched several appetites at the same time. I nodded my driest and most perfunctory approval. We talked politely. She tried to do all the listening the way they train the young ladies in southern finishing schools, but for a change I didn't have diarrhea of the mouth. She was in her after-work at-home comfy clothes, faded jeans and an oriental blouse with wide elbow-length sleeves. Her elegant feet were in *huaraches* soled with old car tire treads. I imagined Lee sitting where I was and her gently asking him to make a swan dive off the balcony and I could see him flinging himself out into space with a smile on his face.

She was slick and together; no flies on that honey. She played everything real close to those appealingly tiny and rouge-tinted breasts that liked to peek out of her comfy blouse every once in a while just to stiffen everyone up who had the equipment to get stiff. A couple of ladies used to drip around her as well; she wasn't the type to discard half the human race if she could find a use for it just because it might scandalize Ann Landers. Her apartment hadn't the slightest suggestion that anyone had ever been there before me, even though I knew Lee spent two or three nights a week there. Five seconds after I left, I knew she'd erase any trace that I'd ever been there; the ashtrays would be emptied and perhaps my finger-prints wiped off the arms of the chair. There were no extra tooth-brushes in the bathroom and no towel that said His. You were welcome there, you were made comfortable beyond your Geisha fantasies, and then you were solid gone, vanished without a trace. Back in high school she'd probably found a method for making hickeys vanish between the time her date let her out of the car and the time she walked through the front door. It was unnerving to sense so much passion and potential on the other side of the coffee table and to know that the moment you walked out the front door, she could put it away in a bottom bureau drawer until she needed it again.

I had an overwhelming urge to get the fuck out of there and made my excuses. She went into the bedroom and came out with the suitcase. I counted it, snapped the locks and faded out into the corridor. I remember one trip to Colombia where an undercover cop stuck a magnum against my head and pulled back the hammer (just to see if I had anything to confess; I didn't, but my bladder did), but that short stay in Laura's apartment was the hairiest part of any trip I'd ever made.

And now Minnesota Bob. I had to hand it to him—he'd certainly picked up the Miami style in no time, that knack of darting into the far periphery of my life and making every hair on the back of my neck stand on end even as he croaked. His name really did turn out to be Liggett and Junior, and he hailed from Minneapolis just as he said he did. The paper didn't say anything about him being an undercover cop or a CIA spook or a scout for the Minnesota Twins. He was one of those rare folks in south Florida who turn out to be just what they say they are, a free-lance asshole trying to get himself killed during his summer vacation.

He was from a good family with a touch of heavy real estate money, and several of them were winging their way down to Miami now to clean up the mess and carry it home. The Minnesota cops said he didn't have any arrest record. He'd turned twenty-three the week before he'd checked out. He'd thoughtfully left his fiancée back up north while he took his last trip. She was now free to find another partner.

The cops weren't having a terribly tough time figuring out a motive, but they were fresh out of suspects. That was fine with me because it just might mean that when they'd gone through his pockets and his luggage, they hadn't found my name, address, phone number and waist size written in gold leaf. Still, the whole thing wasn't doing much for my luncheon appetite. I toyed with the idea of going up to Miami, asking to see the body and punching him in the face right there on the slab, the fucking turkey.

Now the stupid stiff was bugging me seriously from out there in the safety zone. Just because I hadn't yet had to answer the Big Knock from the cops who'd sniffed him out in the garage didn't mean they wouldn't get around to me. A shmuck as lame as Minnesota Bob could easily have left my vital statistics for them without even meaning to have done it, and the cops might be decoding them or dancing at the policeman's ball with every intention of cruising around first thing Monday morning.

*Get out of town.* Nope. Not for Minnesota Bob. No way. It was tempting, because I couldn't really imagine anything less attractive than an interview with a couple of Miami detectives about this putrescent stiff they'd found in Coconut Grove who had my phone number on him. Of course if it came to that, I could simply say I didn't know jackshit about it, officer, which was close enough for rock 'n' roll as far as I was concerned. After all, I'd gone out of my way to sever whatever relationship I'd had with Bob almost before it had begun. But I doubted if that would have the ring of truth about it. For one thing, if they did drop in on me unexpectedly, no matter how convincingly I played my Boy Scout good citizen act, our goddam house smelled very heavily of dope dealer. The direct questions about Bob weren't the problem; it was the ancillary questions like *How do you make your living, Mr. Becker?* or *Would you be willing to tell us a little about your personal finances?* At that point, it was Fifth Amendment City via the Good Criminal Lawyer Interchange. They still couldn't turn any of that into a murder indictment. After all, praise the Lord, the central fact was that I hadn't made the boy dead and even if I puked my guts out, I couldn't put the gendarmerie much closer to the fellow who had.

Well, that wasn't entirely correct, was it? Maybe I hadn't seen the iceman with Bob in the Taurus, but the fellow I'd seen with him made me a lot better informed than the cops probably were at the moment. I'd scoped him out pretty well, well enough to help the cops play Etch-a-Sketch, well enough to snag him out of the mug books, even well enough to nail him in a lineup. None of which

I had any intention of doing, of course, but it was going to be an unpleasant trip to have to rap for a few days with the SS, all the time knowing that I knew just the jolly thing they wanted to know, or something pretty damn close to it. And it didn't seem too much of a fantasy to guess that the less help I gave those suckers, the more they'd try to suggest that I was their hottest prospect so far.

The irony of the whole thing was that the geek who'd iced Minnesota Bob probably wasn't squirming nearly as much as I was. As far as he knew, nobody had the slightest inkling that he'd been keeping company with the handsome stranger from the north, and looking both ways up and down the dark garage before he'd pulled the trigger had convinced him that the whole thing would forever be a matter between him and his conscience. The phantom psychopath probably didn't have a care in the world this week as he gingerly laundered and spent Bob's C-notes, which Bob had already gone to the trouble of carefully cleaning.

So my nuts were hanging by one hope, that Bob hadn't left anything the cops could link up with me. Although they could probably trace him to his stay in Key West, it was unlikely that anyone would remember us talking on the beach for five minutes. Unlikely, but not impossible; I was known around town. The whole thing was going to be pretty unsettling for about a week or two. It was really a pity he was dead, and so painlessly, too. While he'd gotten what he'd been asking for, he'd really deserved a lot worse, something much more painful and lingering, something that might have had a chance of bestowing a little illumination on the boy just before he took the train out. It wasn't a tragedy that he was dead; the tragedy was that he'd died as stupid as he'd lived.

And who was the asshole who'd sicced Minnesota Bob on my tail? The mutual friend, as Bob had put it. Grinding my gears to check out a few dozen likely suspects wouldn't have produced anything certain, just a lot of misdirected and dissipated suspicion and anxiety that would have left me staring at everyone I knew wondering if he or she was the mystery dork, and with Minnesota Bob making it big in the Miami papers, it wasn't likely a lot of people would want to claim the middle-man honors. So I resolved to do the best I could to put that competition out of my head and not to lose sleep about it. I was going to lose enough of that anyway.

What a hell of a way to think about the dead. Somewhere buried deep beneath how pissed off I was at Bob, I also felt sorry for him. He hadn't been that different from me, except in smarts and luck. He'd wanted a piece of the South Florida action just like me, and he'd been willing to take some risks and pay cash out front, just like me. He just hadn't had the connections I had, or lacking that, the patience I had. So he took shortcuts and as a result he'd met up with Mr. Death in the garage. It was pretty pathetic. Even if I was smarter and luckier, how long would my ass stay in one piece through sheer brainpower if my luck started to take a steep plunge? These things happened, even to honest folks who did their nine-to-fives and locked their doors at night. The Random Number was out there waiting for quite a few of us, and only the Random Number knew who and when and how.

All in all, it wasn't much of a surprise that I bought the Miami papers religiously the next week or two. It was a relief and it was sad at the same time to see Bob's story shrink a little more each day—*No Clues in Garage Slaying . . . Still No Clues in Grove Death . . . Slay Victim's Family Flies Home.* Each day his story shrank a little and retreated farther away from the front page. It was as if Minnesota Bob, dead and buried, was still trying to hang on, to make his pitiful little impression, but fewer and fewer people were listening. He'd pulled his last act in Miami, and two days didn't go by before three or four better, fresher murders took his place—more mysterious, more fruitful of solution, more gruesome, of more famous people or of local residents rather than dope-dealing transients. He didn't stand a chance. After giving the papers two or three days to revive him after his story stopped appearing, nothing new came up, so I stopped buying the papers. He was solid gone. He'd done it the hard way, but he'd finally taken my advice and gotten out of my life. I wasn't terribly worried anymore. Even Miami cops weren't that slow; if they'd had anything, they would have been down on my case by now. They didn't have anything.

But I had something. I had the face of that coke spoon geek Minnesota Bob had handed his card to in the Taurus that night. I had his face in profile and full-front. It moved slowly in my day-dreams, sometimes almost looking my way across the room. Sometimes it did look at me, eyeing me with the same chilly indifference

I'd used on him. If he wasn't Mr. Death, he was probably the guy who could get you an intro. I didn't like that face floating around in my head. Yet I didn't want to get rid of it, either. It was a good face to remember, not so that I could help the cops draw it, but so that I'd know to think twice and think fast if I ever saw it again in my neighborhood.

I trained myself to remember that face and to listen for the hammer click of a .45 if I ever saw it again. Although Minnesota Bob didn't die for my sins, maybe he died to save me, even if that wasn't what he'd had in mind. Minnesota Bob only thought he had my number. He probably knew I was a Jew, and he probably assumed I didn't believe in a savior. He was wrong. I was loose. I couldn't believe in Jesus, but I could consider believing in Minnesota Bob.

## BECKER

**T**hat weekend I decided to cook up a cure for the Minnesota Bob blues. I hadn't told Richard or anyone else about Minnesota Bob or the number he was doing on my head—nobody's business but my own is the way that particular blues tune goes—but the therapy I was leaning toward seemed to be a cure-all for a lot of accumulated ills, and not just my ills alone.

Lee, Laura and Michael were coming down to the island to party for the weekend, so the cast of characters would be right provided I could peel Laura away from Richard and Lee for a little while. Richard seemed to be ripe for a special three-star Becker presentation, Lee could be bludgeoned into it if he wasn't ripe, and Michael—well, that boy was always up for a thrill, no problems there. All I'd have to do would be to party it up with them and hit each one of them up when I got him alone and the mood seemed right. Weird old R.J. wasn't going to be a problem, either. His partying was strictly a stay-at-home affair and from what I heard, the go-go dancers he'd hired on for the weekend were going to keep him occupied and out of my hair.

Lee and Laura had reservations at the Pier House and when they hit town early Friday night, they dumped Michael off at our house where we were putting him up on the guest bed. After dinner, Richard, Michael and I strolled into town, had a couple of drinks at the Bull, and then Michael said he was going around the corner to the Monster disco to cruise. That suited me; Richard wasn't a whore like me, and with Laura out of the picture for the night, I could have plenty of time to get down to business with him. He and I strolled leisurely through the back streets vaguely in the direction of home.

We were taking a shortcut through a vacant lot when I tossed the pitch. "Listen, pal," I said, "I need some action."

"Go back and fling yourself through the door of the Bull," Richard said. "There's got to be something with tits that'll go home with you if you make yourself obnoxious enough."

"No. Not that kind of action."

"Oh. *That* kind of action. *La vida loca.* Yeah, things has been pretty dull."

"We got to pull the *Kelpie* out of the water and rip the fucking engines apart again anyway, so this would be a good time."

"What kind of a deal did you have in mind?"

"How about a mama ship trip? A quick dash out beyond the limit, rendezvous with *La Cucaracha* by the light of the moon. Bring the shit into the canals and off-load it at Lee's place. Something like that."

"You going to fly down to Bogotá to set it up?"

"I suppose. I'm the only asshole around here who can order a fucking taco without looking it up in the phrase book. Maybe Annie'll want to come with me. You can set the buyers up on this end."

"I don't know."

"You don't know what?" I asked.

"I don't know if it feels right. Are you strapped for cash?"

"No. I mean, it's all relative. But the *Kelpie*'s going to need the overhaul one way or the other eventually. Why doesn't it feel right?"

He was silent for a minute. "It just doesn't. Or I don't feel right. Maybe I'm on the rag. Maybe it's Laura. Maybe I really don't want to get it on with Lee with a business deal right now. Maybe we've been pushing our luck lately."

"I'll buy all that. Or at least I'll go with the flow, if that's the way you feel. I don't want to push you in where you don't want to go."

Richard looked at me and he sighed deep and melancholy.

"What's got you by the ass, man?" I asked.

"I don't know. Lack of nooky. That has a lot to do with it. I can't get no satisfaction."

"Well, you've been focusing on some very weird and generally unavailable nooky the last couple of months. Maybe you should get less particular, like the rest of the world."

"Yeah, I can dig it, but it's just words. That's what I want, and I can't get very worked up over anything else. I feel pretty stupid about it, but that's the way it is."

"Okay, but what's that got to do with business? A little more success and a few more stacks of tens and twenties certainly never hurt anything with that gash."

"Please," he said. "You're describing the bitch I love."

"Oh, no. It's not on that level, is it?"

"Certainly not for her. I didn't mean to suggest that. With her it's strictly metaphysical, or vegetable, or something. Beats the shit out of me what it is with her. An itch. Yeast infection. But I'm pretty strung out on my end, and I just don't know if my head's right for this kind of trip. Maybe I'm not running a good efficiency rating this month. You could consider that."

We'd found a deserted gas station and were sitting down on the rails of a drive-up lube rack, smoking squares in case the heat decided to roll by and check us out. Although you could make advance arrangements with the city police to import reefer, you still weren't supposed to smoke it in public.

"Think about it this way," I said. "Maybe you need a little whacko action to clean your cobwebs out. You know, we've been sitting around on our butts for a hell of a long time now. Maybe that's your problem. A little jaunt on the high seas, a little midnight cargo handling, some of those intriguing pay phone conversations with the boys from the frozen north and you'll feel like a new man. Then you can come back and flex some muscle and kick sand in Lee's face, and Laura will want to bear your love child."

"You think so?"

"Sure. I got to level with you, man. Sitting around on this

fucking island waiting for the radio stations to play something besides disco is getting to be a real drag. I don't mind telling you that I want some action just to get the fuck out of this burg for a while and have something to show for it."

"Becker, have you ever considered the possibility that you're insane? I mean, just as a conversation piece, to pass the time?"

"Yeah. So what else is new?"

"No, really. You're a great partner. You're dependable some of the time, and you're smart, you speak Spanish. . . . I really dig all that about you. But you're insane. I mean, you got to be sitting on at least eighty thousand clams in various safe deposit boxes, tax free, in cash, and you want to go out and get our asses shot at by entire divisions of law-enforcement officials just because you're bored with the local radio stations."

"I admit it."

"It's almost not funny, Becker. We're talking about my ass, the one that still only has one hole and one crack in it so far. I just don't know if I want to put it out on the line for target practice again just because you're feeling a little jaded."

"It's your choice."

"That's what they always used to say in those fucking high school movies about the clap and drunk driving. *The decision is yours—a life of blindness and insanity locked away in a state institution for advanced syphilitics, or a happy, stable American family with the clean, wholesome girl of your dreams in holy matrimony.*"

"I know. I always used to choose syphilis. It just used to piss those health teachers off no end."

Richard sighed again. "How big a deal?"

"Let's go for the American Dream. I'd like to fly down there with a million, maybe a million and a quarter. You think Lee's up for that?"

"Oh, fuck."

"No, seriously. He could scare it up. His old man promoted him last month, didn't you know? He's in charge of big institutional trust accounts now. Convents and Moose lodges and a union pension fund. He could get his hands on that kind of cash."

"You've got to be kidding me. What are you so fucking greedy for?" he asked.

"It's not that. We've been doing these trips for a couple of years now on a small scale. That was like practice. And we did good. We didn't fuck up, we didn't get killed, we're ahead with the rent and the phone bill. But now that we've got our chops down, there's just no fucking sense sticking our asses out for the same minimum wages. If we're going to do this shit at all, we may as well do it for some serious returns."

"I don't know, man. That kind of money draws a lot of bad flies."

"No. *Any* kind of dope money draws flies. We could have gotten ourselves snuffed for those ten-thousand-buck deals just as easily. Fuck, up in Lauderdale, there's guys'll snuff you for six bits and give you change. That's not the problem. There is no problem. We've proved we know how to get all this shit together, and it's just a fucking waste not to use what we know for real money."

"You're very persuasive for a psychopath, Becker. But just what fleet of trucks do you plan to use for that much reefer?"

"Fuck reefer. I'm thinking of straight *cocaína*. That's what people want. That's what they pay the big bucks for. And the weight and volume per unit price tradeoff is so much fucking better it's insane. That's how we retire, with coke, not with fifty tons of fucking reefer."

"Okay," Richard said, "I'm obviously not down here for my health. I'll start talking to Lee about it. Maybe we ought to get together with R.J., too."

"What for?"

"That's a good question. Still, a deal this big—he's going to find out about it. For one thing, we're using his money man, Lee. He's not going to be too happy that we didn't offer him a slice."

"I don't give a flying fuck. Do you think he beats the bushes for us on every deal he throws together? The only fucking time he uses us is when it suits him, when it's convenient. For all the reefer we've helped him bring in, he's brought in ten times as much we didn't know anything about. He doesn't tell us shit. I'm for staying friendly with the man, but quite frankly, I'm getting less and less overjoyed doing business with him. You and Annie I'm comfortable with. Him I'm not."

"I can dig it. We all got to leave mom and dad sometime. I suppose it's always a wrenching experience."

"I'm a little less than heartbroken," I said.

"You think Lee will go along without R.J.?"

"Yeah, I think so. He sort of worships R.J., but that can work two ways. He thinks he's loyal to R.J., but on the other hand, he wouldn't mind a big independent deal that would show he's as good at that bullshit all by himself. I think that would appeal to him."

Richard took a pull off his cigarette and leaned back against the lube rack as a car drove past.

"You know, he's a pretty weak son of a bitch," he said.

"Who, Lee?"

"Yeah. We need him to generate that kind of capital, and I trust him. He's a straight dude as far as he goes. He's also got Michael to watch over him most of the time. But Lee himself—he's always pretty much on the edge, and a deal like this is going to put a lot of pressure on him. It's not an easy trick to go to work every morning knowing there's a little over a million missing and you're the shmuck who borrowed it."

"Look, if you can find somebody with a better mental health picture who'll be willing to get us a couple of suitcases full of cash, be my guest. Sooner or later, you just have to settle for what's available, and Lee's it."

"Yeah," he said. "Lee's it. I just think he's the weak link in this little scheme. I think he could fold."

"He hasn't folded yet. Maybe the sums haven't been quite as heavy, but he's still been risking twenty years every time he did it. Like I said, sometimes you just got to go with what you got."

"He couldn't handle National Guard boot camp. Did you know that?"

"No."

"He got his daddy to buy him a slot, and he freaked out in the second week of summer camp at Dix. They mentaled him out. He asked me one time how we made it through."

"It wasn't very hard," I said. "I just knew if I didn't, they'd send me to Leavenworth."

"You could have mentaled out. Regular boot was rougher than fucking National Guard bullshit."

"I do well in shitholes. That's no argument for anything one way or the other. A guy like Lee, he'd never been around. Nobody'd ever yelled at him before. Nobody'd ever threatened him with having to carry a wall locker around a field all night. He didn't have time to adjust. I managed to adjust, that's all. This isn't basic training. We're asking him to do something he's already done eight or ten times before. He's had time to adjust. And Michael will be in on it, and like you said, he can keep an eye on him and feed him Valium if he has to."

"Okay."

"Look, if your heart ain't in this, Richard, we can drop back ten and punt. We can just forget it or go back to the nickel-and-dime crap. But I don't want to. Sooner or later, we're going to risk our asses on this kind of bullshit again, and I just want it to start to pay a lot more. And I know damn well we can put it together. Even Lee. You know, he needs it, too. Look at him. He's got almost as much socked away in the vault as we do, and he's still fucking pulling a nine-to-fiver for his old man. Let's get him the money to get free. He's dying in that place."

"I didn't know this was a charity case. I'm touched."

"This isn't a charity case," I said. "Or if it is, we're the beneficiaries. You and me and Michael and Lee. Only I'm tired of the slow pace of the research. I want to find a fucking breakthrough cure this summer. I mean, I feel that we are very close to it, Richard. We've paid our dues down here. We've learned the tricks and we've taken the risks, sometimes just for a couple of hundred bucks profit. Now I want it to pay off. Goddam it, Richard, we are smart people. You and I are two of the motherfucking smartest people I know in this or any other world, but what is the fucking use of it all if we can't turn a fucking profit with it? The only guy I know rolling in bucks at this business is R.J., and he's not smart. He's just sly and sneaky. We should be able to top that."

"Rah, rah."

"I fucking mean it, and if it sounds like some kind of a lame pep talk to you, that's tough fucking bananas. I'm ready for the big Kahuna, and I want to know if you are, too."

"Oh, I am, dad. I'm ready."

"All right, then. Let's do it."

"Becker, you really are psycho. I want you to know that. You really are a dangerous person."

"Thank you, Richard. That's very sweet."

"No, it's not sweet. It's scary. Do things scare you, pal?"

"Yeah. Things scare me. Some things scare me shitless. Old age without bucks, for example. Middle age working for goddam IBM scares me. Handing control of my ass over to a benevolent and wise government scares me. I did that once."

"What about getting your fucking head blown away? Do things like that scare you?"

I thought for a few seconds.

"I really don't know," I said. "I suppose things like that scare me. But so far, everybody's missed. And I don't really feel scared until afterwards.

"When it's actually happening," I said, "the only thing I feel is that I've got things to do. I get scared later."

# RICHARD

**I'**d put up my expected and largely ceremonial objections when Becker presented the plan in the gas station. I'd pointed out that smuggling dope was against the spiritual and temporal laws and that armed people had publicly gone on record as opposing activities like that. I'd pointed out that both of us had money in the bank and no crushing debts that I knew of. It was naughty and it was risky and we didn't need the money all that fucking badly. I'd brought up all those points. So if the shit hit the fan, pal, my ass was covered. I could say I told you so. I'd done my bit.

And he'd waved it all merrily away as just so much pink cotton candy. As I seem to remember the conversation, his overriding and compelling reason was that he was bored and I was, too, or that if I wasn't, I should be. And I guess that must have been good enough for me, because the next morning we were working out the details.

Although he was just dragging himself in from skippering the *Kelpie* out for the sunrise and back, he didn't want to crash out and didn't want me to crash out, either. There were things to do, he said, check lists to make, personnel to contact, figures to toss around. Christ, he was nuts. The man wanted us both to swan-dive off the roof of a skyscraper naked, but first we had to sit down and make plans without even a decent night's sleep. And I had to help him find a pencil with a decent point on it.

So it got roughed out this way. He'd talked to Annie the night before out on the *Kelpie* and it looked as though she was going to be out of the deal, at least at the beginning. She was off on a jaunt to California and she'd apparently been cooking up the plans for some time, enough time and enough plans so that she didn't want to chuck them or postpone them now. She might have if she'd known how big a deal Becker was churning out, but when Becker had brought the subject up, she'd assumed it was another deal of about the size of the others, and he'd let her assume that for the time being. She'd probably also assumed R.J. would be calling the shots, and Becker hadn't said otherwise. "For one thing," he told me, "she says she'll be back from California in a couple of weeks, the better part of a month at most, and that'll be plenty of time for her to get back on board. Until then we can do without her. If I tried to talk her out of it, we might end up with her body here and her mind in California, and that's not going to do any good for any of us."

"I think you could of talked her out of it, and I think she would have been glad to stay," I said.

"Yeah, maybe. But to do that, I would have had to tell her how big the deal was and that R.J. was out of it. And then she still might have said she had to go to the Coast, so we wouldn't have had her with us, but we'd have told her everything about what was going on. I wouldn't have liked starting things out that way. Right now she just thinks R.J.'s cooking up the usual shit, which he probably is anyway, and that we can all do things without her. She'd even prefer it that way. You know, she don't like to work with R.J. anymore unless the wolf's howling at her door. She muled for him from Colombia a lot of times, and she never got a good feeling off him, especially the last time. She had a really bad time bringing the toot back through customs, and when she got through it, he wasn't even at the airport to pick her up. She hit the roof about that."

"But R.J.'s not in this one. You might have told her that."

"And she might have gone off to California anyway. And R.J. might have picked up some vibes about what we were cooking up. No, it's better this way, and she'll link up with us for her share of the weird and heavy stuff when she gets back. Some of this you just have to play by feel, Richard, and that's the way it felt."

"Okay, I guess," I said.

Then Lee was going to have to cook up the cash by hitting up his institutional trust accounts, juggling the books and brewing them into the kind of cash we needed. We'd have to tap him about it right away and lean on him with visions of greed and eternal financial independence, and get a hard and fast reply from him on how soon he could make the bucks materialize. Becker mentioned the amount again and I wished he hadn't because it practically gave me a nosebleed.

"Don't let big figures throw you," he said. "Just remember that a man with seven million is as happy as one with eight. Keep everything in perspective."

And of course logically he was right. Poor slobs were getting knifed in the back every day over eighty-eight cents, and as Becker pointed out, in such a world it made more sense to get knifed in the back over a couple of million. The road to hell was always paved with Beckertalk, with Beckerlogic, and after he got you there and the gates closed forever behind you, you looked back through them at the trail of Beckerlogic and you *still* couldn't see the flaw in it. "It's flawless," he still insisted. Your feet were starting to char on the coals and the demons were thrusting rusty icepicks in your calves and Becker stood beside you and said, "It's flawless."

Once we knew when we could lay our hands on the attaché cases, Becker was going to shuffle off to Bogotá solo, impersonating a sane and lawful person, to make contact with some wild-eyed berserk blood-lusting Colombian nightmare who didn't take his morning piss without revolvers and automatics strapped to his hairy torso. And over a cup of Juan Valdez's best java, Becker and the *Sudamericano* lunatic would conduct business. That was all Becker's part, and he was welcome to it.

My part north of the border was hairy enough. I'd be darting in and out of airports and motels for a week or ten days arranging wholesale deals with people who were certainly not friends yet not quite perfect strangers. In my opinion all of them were never more than a centimeter from the edge and were always ready to go over it with a healthy sneeze from behind. All of that assumed that none of them was the Surprise Policeman or that none of them had fallen on hard enough times to be now secretly in the employ of the Surprise Policeman.

But what Becker was doing from the moment he stepped aboard the Braniff and waved bye-bye in Miami was completely beyond the pale. He'd done it before. The first couple of times, as R.J.'s interpreter and factotum and gopher, he'd made the contacts and learned the ropes. Later R.J. had stopped bothering to go himself and had just sent Becker as his representative. Once again, it was not entirely trust, but much less. For one thing, the fewer people who actually went through that Colombian experience, the fewer people who could possibly get killed in that highly likely killing ground. I'd seen R.J. do a few acts of physical bravery, and each of them had the common denominator of being absolutely necessary and completely involuntary. Consequently, once he had taught Becker the name and address of the proper Colombian kill-crazy wild man, why bother to go himself? Becker being drilled full of holes would be an even more agreeable end to the business than Becker and R.J. being filled full of holes. Besides which, R.J. didn't speak one goddam word of the lingo, so why bother, right?

And if R.J. wasn't sending Becker down there simply out of trust, Becker wasn't going out of gratitude and pure loyalty. The prices for those trips jumped something heavy, you betcha, and Becker took it out front before leaving. Beyond that, Becker knew that someday it wasn't going to hurt to know who to see down there all by himself, and that someday had now obviously arrived.

But the main reason he had gone and kept going was the very reason that I'd always done whatever I could to avoid going: the white-knuckle express. He loved it. He loved or craved days on end when anything goes or might go, himself included. He loved or craved putting himself on the line, putting himself *out there,* out in the Zone. He'd come back looking ashen sometimes and trickles of dried blood would have formed little lines at the tops of the remnants of his fingernails—probably his toenails, too—since these trips necessitated long hours of waiting in the least cheery of Colombian hotel rooms waiting for (pick one): (a) the phone to ring, (b) the door to knock, or (c) the end of the world, click, bang, splat.

Meanwhile, what was left of Lee would sweat out whether he would ever see his money again to get it back to the accounts before the auditors came. Michael and I would attend to the other details and get the *Kelpie* ready for the rendezvous out in the Atlantic, or the Gulf if it was a momma ship heading for New Orleans.

Michael was in it because Lee was in it and no one wanted to keep him out. It was always Michael's responsibility during deals like this to keep Lee from losing it entirely at some odd moment, like in front of a traffic cop or a school crossing guard. Michael kept watch over Lee and kept him plied with downers while Lee pulled his hair out and muttered Yiddish curses at himself and at the rest of us for leading him so far astray to his obvious inevitable ruin. Michael understood that part of his job if he understood no other and he did it ace every time. Ultimately, since he lived in Lee's Coconut Grove villa, he could just heave his substantial bulk in front of the door and bar Lee from running outside to turn himself in to the authorities when his nervous system couldn't take it anymore. And then when Lee couldn't get out the door and would fall to his knees weeping and cursing and sobbing, Michael was brawny enough to pick him up like a kitten and carry him to the bedroom and give him a couple of pills and talk softly to him. He'd tell Lee about the better days soon to come when all the cash got returned to the right place in daddy's bank with nobody the wiser, and the big cut Lee was going to make out of the deal and how it would make Lee so happy, all that money that didn't have to be returned to anybody because it all belonged to Lee and he could spend it on Laura until it was coming out of her ears and she didn't want any more money—fat chance, but a soothing vision for the feverish Jewboy bank official who had to get some sleep so he could go to his office on Brickell Avenue the next morning and make it through the glass doors all the while certain he would find strangers in cheap three-pieces poring over the accounts.

Laura must have done a number on Lee all night. Wherever she was by now, I doubted that it showed on her, but as Becker and I schemed and dreamed, Lee was crashed out in the living room exhausted: heavy week, heavy suicide sports car drive down from Miami with the Friday night traffic, heavy date. We kept watch over him informally because the first thing he'd want to know when he woke up was where Laura was, and the answer to that was that she was solid gone.

She'd had a merry little lunch with me, and then when I'd started talking about what we might do together for the rest of the day (I was in the batter's box now that Lee had conveniently passed out and Becker and I were through with our first briefing), she'd announced simply that she thought she'd catch the bus back to Miami. In her tone there just wasn't any room for wondering, *Well, what about me? How about asking what your red-hot Key West lover man might be interested in today?* No room for that at all. No need for an argument about it, either; the lady had announced her plans and whatever they were precisely, they weren't with me. And they weren't with Lee, either. The bus was what she craved to boogie herself back up to her little high-rise apartment and catch up on her reading while she undid the damage to her face and nails that a drive to Key West will do to a girl, heaven knows. I offered to drive her back to Miami, no strings attached, or as few attached as I could manage: Thank you no thank you, she said, a bus trip back was really, sincerely and honestly what she craved, just a walk to the bus stop would do fine and company on the bench until the bus left. That was what she got. We waited and talked about precisely everything except the things I wanted that involved her that day, that week, that year. Of course I had learned those topics were vinegar cocktails to the lady. I couldn't even inquire when I would see her again because the answer to that would be that I would see her again when I would see her again.

So I watched the Greyhound sail off through town and I drifted slowly back to the house, where I found Lee still dead to the world and Becker alarmingly alive and awake and ready for more strategy sessions. Becker getting organized, Becker putting the world together the way it had to be for the next couple of weeks, Becker way ahead of any of my thickheaded little suggestions, waving them all away with a tight little shake of his head like some kind of Prussian hippie, a kind of Erich von Stroheim in blue jean cutoffs and the sleeveless remnants of a sweatshirt that smelled like salt spray and bleached sweat as he sat next to me and outlined the future in detail, certain that it would respond the way he expected it to.

So by the time Lee woke up and asked where Laura had gone, we were ready for him, ready to take him by the hand, take full advantage of his semi-confused state, buy him a good meal at a Florida lobster place on the wharf, and initiate him into the cabal whether it was what he had in mind or not. We had the answers to everything, and every answer was a straight and fast conduit to big bucks and easy bucks, and this time with a considerably better split than he would have received if R.J. were calling the shots.

"Still," he said over his lobster, "I've always done these deals with R.J. Granted he's a crude motherfucker who'd probably stick it to me for a quarter—well, he got me into this bullshit in the first place, and I guess I owe him something. Don't know what, but it seems to be the appropriate sentiment, you know what I mean? I just don't like cutting him out of this deal cold. And I don't know if we could if we wanted to."

Becker was unexpectedly serious. He leaned back in his chair a little. "No," he said. "This one's not for him. It's for us. It's time we all grew up about this crap, him and us both. It's time for us to grow up and do our own deals, and it's time for R.J. to grow up and understand that this isn't the Mafia and he's not Vito Corleone. He'll find out about this deal. I plan to let him find out about it, by sticking a great big wad of primo coke up his nose and partying him out, but that's after the deal goes down. But while it's happening, it's our deal. No advice from him, no split with him. This is our deal."

"Well, maybe we should tell him beforehand we got a deal going . . ."

"No," Becker said. "For a lot of reasons. There's absolutely no percentage in it."

"Look, he wouldn't mind. He's got deals going on his own all the time. I just think he might get ticked off if he finds out some other way but from us."

"That's the point, Lee. I got nothing against R.J. Maybe I owe him a lot like you do. But I don't owe him that kind of puppydog bullshit, and neither do you. He'll find out when he finds out, and he'll take it the way he takes it, but this is our deal, and we're doing it without him."

"Well, what if I don't want to do it without him, or without him knowing? What if that doesn't feel right to me?"

"Then we do it without you, too," Becker said. "I think if we look real hard, we might find some other guy from here to Fort Lauderdale who wants to make a quarter million without taxes. Who works in a bank just like you."

That was the clincher. When you stripped and shrunk him, Lee was essentially a four-year-old in the driveway who freaks out when mom's car leaves for the store without him. The only thing he wouldn't be able to stand about our deal was to be left out in the cold, to hear Becker tell him stories about it later, stories that didn't include him.

"Okay," he said. "When do you need it?"

"Something else first," Becker said. "Laura's also out. You move this cash without her helping and without her knowing."

I was looking at him, too, a little less shocked than Lee was. Lee needed her and Michael and everyone else he could find or rent for moral support during these pathetic deals. He needed R.J. and me and Becker and people he met in elevators. He needed. And now Becker wanted to take his key crying shoulders away. As for me, I'd always worked as beachmaster and truck fetcher in the deals. I'd never depended on Laura or worked closely with her in the business; that was all on Lee's end. Doing a deal without her hit me as no big deal, mox nix, and if I was supposed to resent it, I was having trouble working up a sweat. I'd let Lee do my squawking for me.

Michael wasn't going to have any trouble with the decision if it stuck, though. He could always do without Laura. Lee and Michael never tumbled, but they were pretty thick, and when Laura strolled in, Michael (six feet two, built like a truck) might not even have been there. She also brought out what pathetic little amounts of machismo Lee could muster, and he tended to take it out on Michael for being a fag the way he took it out on Becker for being a Jew. Although his imitation of John Wayne was unfortunate at best, Laura let him know without words that she liked to see him flex and get heavy and hetero as an approvable and rewardable image. She often came on the scene to toss a few petite friction bombs between old friends, but she did it in such a subtle and unspoken manner that if real trouble came of it, she could beam like an angel and disclaim any blame. She was comfortable in the middle of discord if it couldn't be laid on her; she liked to see a handful of people on the verge of fist fights so she could feign a little shock and soak up the accompanying fear.

"Why?" Lee asked Becker, working up to a pout.

"Because," Becker said.

"Don't give me that. Okay about R.J. I can dig that, minimally. But I always use Laura to help me move the cash. We've worked out a great system."

"Not this time, dammit. We got us three and Michael and that's all we need at this stage. Every other person is another mouth and another set of mistakes. Maybe the mouth won't talk and maybe there won't be any mistakes, but we keep this deal as small as we can or we don't do it at all. I'm starting it without Annie, too, and you know how I like to have her around."

"Goddam it, Becker, you're sure setting up a lot of do-it-my-way-or-else conditions on this thing. Who made you the Jolly Green Giant, huh?"

Before Becker and Lee started to duke it out over the cold lobster shells, I cut in between them. "Becker's got a good plan and he's trying to keep it as safe as he possibly can for all of us. I like it. For that matter, I don't mind having him lay it out this time. It sounds clean and quick and simple. Let's just do it and skip the ego struggles. I mean that."

Lee looked at me. Double-teamed and set up and hyped and bounced around, he still wanted in very hard. Being in was like being loved to him; anyway, it was probably the closest thing to being loved he had going for him. His family thought he was shit and Laura didn't make a habit of treating him considerably better.

"All right," he sighed at me. "Personally, I don't know why you put so much faith in this kike, who has to be one of the stupidest shleps I know. Can you imagine, a kike who couldn't duck the draft? And we're supposed to follow a shmuck like that down the cocaine trail? It's all very strange to me, White Person."

"It doesn't seem strange to me. I was drafted, too," I said.

"Yeah, but you're a *goy*. For you, that was the idea. It was proper for you."

"It didn't seem that way to me at the time," I said. "I don't really want to talk about it, if you don't mind. You and Becker can have another round about it if you want, but after I've gone. Are you in?"

"Yeah. I'm in."

So we worked out the rough details on the way back to the house as the sun started fading out. The major problem was the Federal Reserve regulations, the new ones about cash movement, to identify cash movement. That was really why we needed Lee, not so much as the source of the cash itself, but as a source in a bank who could move the stuff around the Fed regulations. We could do deals without him, but without someone like him, a dealer had to stuff his capital and his profits in a mattress or bury it in Mason jars. Just depositing five C-notes in a straight bank (assuming there was one and you were stupid enough to try it) was enough to get reported and scrutinized, and we were going to be spending and receiving a shitload more than five hundred bucks. Someone in Lee's position was really the only indispensable figure, the only guy you couldn't do without. Big drug concerns bought their own banks just to make sure they had someone like Lee in their employ. The way I figured it, telling Lee we could do without him had been Becker's only real bluff. Without Lee, I don't know who else Becker could have turned up who could make that kind of cash materialize with no paperwork behind it. R.J. probably had three or four other fools just like Lee ready to jump through hoops, but Becker didn't. Yet he'd looked at Lee and told him to stuff it if he didn't like things Becker's way, and Lee, being too stupid to realize he had Becker over a barrel, hadn't seen the bluff and so hadn't called it.

With Becker, a bluff like that wasn't all bluff. Becker could be very big on cutting off his nose to spite his face at the least provocation, and at best he suffered bullshit from fools like Lee poorly or not at all. Neither of them was simple and their backgrounds gave them a lot in common, but to Becker, Lee was neurotic, unstructured, unrestrained, unpredictable, unbalanced. Even though Lee was that to me, too, with Becker it was something that carried a deep and secretive contempt about it. Somehow, if he had to, he would have done without Lee; it hadn't been all bluff.

So then Lee hemmed and hawed and finally told us (and himself—that was the part he was postponing for as long as he could) that it would take him about five working days to get the cash in hand; he could have done it quicker, he whined, with Laura to help him.

"I don't need it that quick," Becker said bluntly, to put a period to that subject again. And then he went through the details that Lee didn't really need, the kind of bills, old and nonconsecutive, and the denominations, twenties, fifties and hundreds in a particular proportion or as close to it as Lee could come up with.

The Pier House, where Lee had left his Mercedes, wasn't far, and we walked him to it and waited outside while he checked out. He came out with his leather traveling suitcase, a fancy brown job with straps and buckles coming out the ass. He walked slowly across the gravel lot, scuffing his shoes on the stones, trying to express as much misery as he could without opening his mouth and triggering Becker to leap down his throat. He opened the trunk of his car and threw the bag in disgustedly and then moved around to the driver's door. To get in and start the car and drive away would have been too simple for Lee. He still had issues to bring up and bitching to do—*kvetching* was the word Becker used for it. Becker was always deeply apologetic for Jews like Lee as if he were somehow responsible for them.

Lee first looked at me and seeing no sympathy or help in my direction, looked at Becker, but not directly.

"I'm nervous," he said to Becker.

"Back out," Becker commanded simply. "Do it now and let's get it over with. Do it now so I'll know to start getting someone else, because I don't intend to fart around with you if you're not with us." That was also the wrong direction, even more wrong than mine. Becker's voice was completely devoid of sympathy.

"No."

And then Becker reached over to him and took both of Lee's hands in his own, right in right and left in left. He held them and squeezed them and forced Lee to look up at his face, to look right into it.

"People are counting on you," Becker said gently, with friendship and comfort and solace. "People are counting on you. Be a *mensh*.

Lee was looking back and he seemed to be straightening up, mustering up what confidence he could.

"Okay," he said. "I'll be a *meshugeneh mensh,* just like you boys."

And he got in his car, started the powerful little engine and roared off for Miami and Brickell Avenue to pervert his dad's bank and emulsify his stringy constitution for a couple of weeks. It was strange. I didn't know how Becker could get that out of someone like Lee, but I'd seen it and he had. Lee wouldn't go back on his commitment. I sensed it and I knew it. He would go back to Miami and throw himself against the worst that luck and fate had to throw back against him, and he'd keep throwing himself at it until somebody counted him out for good or until Becker released him.

*Be a mensh* . . . the wizard's magic words, and the monster sat up from the slab and came alive.

## RICHARD

**M**ichael wasn't any problem. He never was. As long as we were cutting him in, we could cut anyone out we wanted. We finally got around to him and told him the amounts of coke and money we were figuring, and that was okay with him, too, with a large smile.

"I like your spirit," I told him as we shook hands. "It's faggots like you who made this country great."

"You bet your tight little ass it is," Michael agreed.

Sometimes I wondered where or even if he ever drew the line. Of course the particular wrinkles on this deal just happened to be ones he could live with real easily. He liked Becker and he liked me and he lived with Lee. He couldn't stand Laura, and he never went very much out of his way to have dealings with R.J., social or even business; he'd even let a few of R.J.'s deals with Lee slide by during the last year rather than have to get into a trip with R.J. Becker had asked him about it; the money had been good and the deals had been pretty straightforward and Sears & Roebuck style. "Lack of inspiration" had been about all that Michael had grunted back.

That troubled Becker more than it did me; I had the edge on knowing a few things about Michael and R.J. that Becker couldn't have known, or I was pretty sure he couldn't have known, nosy raccoon that he was and always getting into everybody's private business as he was. What I knew I guess more than explained Michael's lack of inspiration and it had a lot to do with my own lack of inspiration about R.J. It didn't explain Becker's, which I put down to a sort of infectious spread; you can't live with someone who's always doing the shallow bad-vibe on someone else without picking up those same attitudes sooner or later. Although I still liked to keep up diplomatic relations with R.J., Becker could sense that our friendship had waned over the last year or so. R.J.'s house didn't supply much that I couldn't whip together at my own place in a pinch. Becker still liked to go over there for R.J.'s freak show potential and, it was beginning to seem now, for purposes of what you might call industrial espionage—he didn't mind hanging out at R.J.'s or doing deals with R.J. if it helped him pick up the elements of R.J.'s financial trip. He was willing to suffer through long hours of drug dissipation and exhibitions of topless chorines and an occasional dog show involving some adolescent runaway if he could pick up new skills along the way. I suppose I wasn't as curious by nature even for the lucrative details R.J. still tried to keep up his sleeves or close to his chest. I wasn't as curious and I was less and less inclined to put up with the zoo at R.J.'s just to pick up a few details.

I was also becoming convinced that the law of diminishing returns was at work—I doubted R.J. had many significant secrets that could do me much good or that I couldn't figure out for myself. As far as I was concerned, what secrets he still had were secrets I didn't want to know. And what he had beyond that was just a fat potentate's aura, a very convincing traveling medicine show that entertained, awed, amused but didn't really cure much of anything for anyone; you could skip the show and get the same remedy for a third of the price at the drugstore or at the package store. For me he was now a stage magician whose coat had run out of pigeons and rabbits and vases with flowers, even though he was still waving his arms and saying magic words to play for time until the musicians remembered to play his closing fanfare. R.J. wouldn't miss us in his audience. It was a good act, an effective act, and he could always fill up the seats with yokels and rubes who hadn't seen it before.

The few trips I made to R.J.'s now were just for Lisa, charity trips I made when Annie would wail around our house that R.J.'d deserted Lisa again for a long jaunt somewhere. I knew those were the dangerous times for Lisa and that except for Annie there was no one on the island, no one in the whole world who was going to bother to check up on her or speak a kind word to her. Why that started something in me I don't really know, but sometimes in the afternoon when I knew she'd just be waking up, I'd drive over there and ask her if she wanted to come out on the boat. So we'd cruise out on the *Kelpie* in silence, anchor and take our obligatory swims. She'd strip and I'd practice not looking at her carefully, not staring. Yes, I saw her then, all of her, but I busied myself with other things, with the engine gauges and the lines, at the other end of the boat. And for her part, she didn't flaunt herself. She wasn't a flirt or a cock-teaser. Sometimes I was convinced she didn't even know what kind of a body or what kind of looks she had, that she had more than enough of both to have walked out on R.J. in the morning and found herself set up in a better sugar-daddy arrangement with a perfect stranger by early afternoon. Maybe she did know but it just didn't matter. The arrangement with R.J. was only awful because Lisa, not he, made it that way, and she could have made it equally terrible with anyone else anywhere else.

So we told Michael what we needed from him to start with, which was to babysit Lee during the stressful times ahead, and that was all old hat to him; we barely had to spell out the details. We also needed him to run a commo base for us while Becker was in Colombia and I was up north setting up sales. We worked out some simple word codes with him, largely just to be able to keep in touch with one another and to know that things were still green with Lee and Becker and me.

The codes weren't terribly sophisticated—well, maybe they were. They didn't sound like dope or money talk, so that made them close enough for rock 'n' roll. Becker had a bug against getting too complicated or too slick about the telephone. First, naturally, you had to have a system you could keep straight in your head, a system that didn't make you constantly need to consult reference books or Captain Midnight secret decoder rings. "If your phone's already tapped," he said, "you're fucked anyway. You can use all the goddam codes and scramblers you want. You can get Navajos to do your talking for you like they did in the war. Mox nix—if they're listening to you, that means they already know your trip and they're just tying up loose ends and being voyeurs while they wait for you to show up to bust you. Make it simple just so somebody who overhears your call by accident, some little old lady in Hialeah, doesn't get the whole picture immediately. Nothing fancier than that."

So it went something like this: talk about cameras (it was all quasi-vacation talk) was the reassuring sign that everything was copacetic on that end. Talk about finding scorpions in your bed, about scorpions, meant that something was seriously fucked up on your end and you wanted everybody else to freeze and stop what they were doing and for Lee to get the bulk of the money that was still in the Grove back into the bank. Talk about missing a ferry boat meant that nothing serious was wrong, but there was a delay— everybody else should continue to march. Talk about scuba diving meant you needed help in person and fast; like scorpion talk, it also meant a scrub for everybody else, the end of the deal immediately.

Everyone (except Lee, although he didn't know it) had the authority to call for a scrub at any time and for any reason, from cops smashing down the door to pure intuition. Although we told Lee he could scrub it, too, things were actually set up so that if he wanted to scrub it, Michael had to go along and agree to it. Michael agreed to park his ass by the phone in the Grove from eight at night until four in the morning to allow for phoning hassles from Colombia, but he had to hear from Becker at least once each night. If Becker missed a call, everybody froze. If Becker missed two calls, the bulk of the money went back to the bank right away and the deal was scrubbed. If Becker missed three calls, I hopped a plane with Michael to bring the pieces back home.

As a backup at the message center when Michael and Lee were both out, we had an answering machine. If one of us called and the message said everybody's out, that meant a scrub. If it said that Michael and Lee would be back soon, things were still ace in the Grove, but Becker or I could leave our raps on the tape and halt everything by remote control that way. Our codes certainly didn't cover every eventuality; you couldn't really fine-tune anything from long distance without breaking into fairly explicit words, but Becker was queer on the go-no-go theory, that all you really needed to get across was green light or red light, and that everything else was just unnecessary and confusing.

Becker and I impressed on Michael how important it was that he keep Lee pretty much away from Laura—not entirely away, which would have been impossible, but out of reach of her hypnotic charms. Michael was going to have to steer him pretty tight to make him stick to keeping her out of the deal. It wasn't going to be easy; she was going to be with him at work every day and probably going to have lunch with him every day. After a couple of days she would see that he was strung out and would try to pump him. The best we could hope for was either that she might by accident be on one of her Greta Garbo solitude jags, or that Michael could use the pretext of needing help to man the message center to keep Lee home in the Grove at night. If he could sell that to Lee so that he wouldn't escape to Laura's apartment, Michael could keep a better eye on them even if she did drop over in the evenings. In the long run, though, it was going to be up to Lee and his Boy Scout pledge to keep himself straight.

The three of us spent most of Monday working on the boat down at the marina, Michael grudgingly scraping the hull while Becker and I worked on the engines and Becker calibrated the Loran set he'd picked up secondhand from a lobsterman who'd gone out of business. The electronics on the *Kelpie* were his mysterious passion. He was constantly buying new gimmicks for communications and navigation. The Loran, he said, had an accuracy that could fix his position to a quarter mile of the true position, eyeball distance. All someone had to do was bad-mouth his boxes on the *Kelpie* to incur the Becker wrath and the permanent Becker write-off. "It's fucking dangerous out there," he'd hiss. "There's hurricanes and waterspouts and tsunamis, and sometimes there's stupid people at the wheel, and that'll sink you in perfect weather. If I can save my fucking ass with a couple of hundred bucks' worth of transistors and switches, I fucking-A intend to save my ass, but you can go fucking drown yourself or sail around in circles for the rest of your sorry life for all I care. And if and when they find your bloated sea-change corpse, I'll be glad to write your epitaph: *Died of Ignorance and Primitive Equipment.*"

It was a little more complicated than that, however. In private, he confided to me that he could never outgun the Coast Guard or even evade them in a fair-weather run indefinitely. Besides that, the Drug Enforcement Administration used plane spotters. In other words, the tonnage, firepower and raw money were with the enemy. "But there's got to be an edge somewhere that I can afford and that I can jam onto this fucking boat, and if there is, I intend to have it. If there's some way I can see a little farther in the fog or pick up a little information that can give me just a billionth of a degree of an edge, I'm going to do it. State of the art—that's the way to go. State of the art in commo and state of the art in navigation. This boat is fast, but speed alone isn't going to cut it. This boat has got to be smart, too."

It was all pretty much meat to me. Out on the *Kelpie* at night, he'd shown me all the bizarre and *outré* equipment that glowed red and green in custom cabinets beyond the wheel on the enclosed bridge. He ran through them and demonstrated them and what they could do and made a believer, albeit a pretty ignorant one, out of me. I can't say I got off on the equipment as much as I got off on the daze and trance it seemed to put its high priest into. The actual power of the *Kelpie* he left up to me, the engines and the power train and so forth, because I was an old motorhead and he confessed to being a complete washout as far as the internal combustion engine was concerned. When I needed two men on the engines, he volunteered as purely brute force, to lift or hold or pull or push. But when it came to the electronics, he became inspired. "Another thing," he brooded to me on one of those experimental nights out in the Gulf while he bit his nails and the skin around and under them to make them more sensitive to the fine-tuning of the vernier dials. "This boat is already getting a reputation around the island about speed. People who know boats can look at it and pretty much know what it has and what it can do. You can't hide that. But nobody knows what the fuck it's got here"—he pointed to the equipment—"and even if they did, most of them wouldn't know what the fuck it means. *I* know what it means, and one of these days, you'll know what it means." He was machine-queer and he was always the first to admit it. "Machines treat you better than people do," he said. "If they take a dislike to you, there's a reason, and you can fix it. People'll fuck you for no reason at all and they'll keep fucking you no matter what you do short of pounding 'em. These things are predictable, and they sing for people who understand the songs."

"You're very odd," I said over his shoulder as he fixed his eyeball on a nixie tube readout.

"And I used to feel bad about it, too. That's when I was unhappy. Now I know I'm odd and I like it. I've come out of the closet. I have a lot in common with Michael on that score—just a different perversion."

"I hope your machines make you very happy," I said.

"They do," he said as he clicked a selector switch through its detents. "Consistently. People aren't shit compared to them."

This wouldn't be the *Kelpie*'s first dope run, but it was going to be the first time we put her through her paces without R.J. as supercargo and shot-caller. It was going to be the first time she was going out just for her owners, and we found ourselves far more demanding of her as we looked her over around sunset with all our muscles stretched and screaming and Michael's forearms bleeding from encounters with barnacles. We piled into the truck and drove home; we were too tired to think about eating, but when we got home we found we were too tired to think about sleeping right away, either. Annie was in the kitchen. She yelled hello to us but didn't trundle out to the living room as we fell back on couch and cushion and floor to cool down and decompress. Michael pulled out the dope tray and started rolling a couple of fat numbers and I put a Mahavishnu tape on the box low. We all smelled funky and looked worse and didn't care very much.

"I ought to call Lee and see how he's doing," Michael murmured after the jay had gone around a couple of times.

"Fuck it," Becker said. "You'll see him tomorrow. Even if he's fucking up left and right, there ain't shit you can do about it from here. Relax."

So we rolled down on the oblivion express for an hour or so, spaced out on hard work behind us and strange, bladder-voiding thrills to come, not frowning or smiling, just steady-as-she-goes, trying to look mindless, but not being able to think mindless enough. They didn't make dope like that. The kitchen noises were distracting me; I was closest to the kitchen door and gently shut it. The tape went on and ran out; Michael crawled over and flipped it. It ran out again on the other side, and Becker put on some old Ry Cooder.

*Tomorrow we'll drive up to Miami,* Becker said at last, *and drop Michael off in the Grove and see how Lee's doing, if he's getting anywhere with the money.* I nodded. *And then you and I have business.*

I asked him what kind.

*A side trip,* he said. *A fast dash up north to some old places. Some old faces, maybe. We lack. We need.*

I asked him what we lacked, what we needed.

*Don't ask,* he said, looking up at the ceiling and sighing. *You can ask tomorrow. You don't need to know tonight. I don't need to deal with it tonight.*

# 10

## RICHARD

**W**e got to Lee's house in the Grove at around three. It had been a hot and grubby trip up Route 1 with the Jewfish Creek Bridge being jammed in the up position as usual, completely isolating us and the lower two-thirds of the Keys from the mainland while those in positions of irresponsibility did their Chinese fire drill of calling the fix-it man so he could come south from the mainland through the very traffic jam he was supposed to unsnarl and kick the gears until they decided to mesh again. As soon as we got inside the house, we stripped and fell into the swimming pool and played grabass for a while while we cooled off. Then Michael crawled out and made a bunch of whiskey sours and we sat around the living room drinking them and watching television, waiting for Lee to get home.

He parked his Mercedes in the gravel driveway around four-thirty and plopped himself down in his immaculate hip-but-not-too-hip white suit with white vest and Italian shoes, the tie loosened now and the jacket slung over the back of the sunken sofa. Then the shoes kicked off—he looked real loose, real free, about as free as anyone would look who just got home from his father's bank where he'd spent the day shitting in his drawers about whether dad would find out about his trip to Key West. Or a few other items,

**89**

past and future. Some reefer came out on the coffee table and then Michael headed for the kitchen to crank out some dinner for all of us.

But Lee looked together, anyway, and that was a good sign. Becker didn't bring up the subject of the cash and I followed his lead and didn't either. About halfway into dinner, Lee looked up from a mouthful of food and brought the subject up himself, matter-of-factly. He said he'd started cranking out the first batch of checks on his institutional accounts that morning. The checks, in amounts that looked like loans and investment purchases, were made out to about a half-dozen accounts; most of these, at other banks in his daddy's chain, looked like outside accounts but were really Lee's dummy accounts for this kind of Mickey Mouse. He closed them periodically and opened new ones so that if any of them turned up in random checks and inspired any questions, none of them would have very lengthy transaction histories and none of them led to any of the others, dead or current.

The trick, he explained, was in returning the funds to the original institutional accounts after the deals with larger amounts, larger by about what kosher investments and loans would have earned over the time the funds were out, and to make all of these dividends fairly sweet, better than the average investment track record. "You'd be surprised how little curiosity these people show when you earn them twenty, twenty-one percent," he smiled. "Damn, some of them even insist I keep investing just where I've been investing. I got lawyers for nuns calling me up telling me to do more dope deals, only they just don't know it's dope deals they want to invest in." He was good at this; it was one of the only things he was authentically good at and not just talking a good screw.

Enthusiastic now that he was cranking his bank act up again, Lee was pleasant to listen to. He liked carrying around in his head the account numbers and balances of six or seven fictitious real estate or development concerns and shifting around and laying off huge amounts among them. His trick for turning them into cash was to construct imaginary payrolls for imaginary construction sites and pick them up in cash in the middle of heavy industrial paydays at several different banks, some of them in his father's chain, others outside it. Sometimes he'd make Michael or me or Becker or Laura an officer of the construction company so he didn't have to be on the receiving end himself. This time he was going to have to do some of the pickups himself at banks where the people knew him, but he had that rigged so it wasn't unusual, either with a drinking buddy he greased or with a story about temporarily helping the company to get its payroll systems started. But he was happy, and I found that very interesting for a change.

I generally knew Lee manic or morose. Now, as he juggled books so deviously that sometimes it seemed it was boggling his own mind, he was simply happy. He was a craftsman with a new shipment of his medium and a new commission for his work. His medium was money and institutions that were staffed by people who weren't terribly bright or dedicated, who were compelled to dress a lot sharper than they thought, and who were systematically dulled out by the daily grind—a perfect audience for a sleight-of-hand, song-and-dance man like Lee who kept a stock of crude office jokes in his head to cover up the missteps and the few moments when what he was really doing had to be made visible.

Around us, he was always talking about just a few more big scores so he could leave the bank one last time and drop his drawers outside the big picture window and moon everyone he was leaving behind forever, but that kind of talk—I didn't believe it, really. Oh, sure, he wanted those few more big scores, and he wanted to pull them off without doing five in the federal farm for butt-fucking the Federal Reserve rules about reporting cash transactions, rules that were affectionately dedicated to dope dealers just like us. He wanted those deals. The part about leaving the First Dad National Savings and Trust was the hollow part for me because that was where Lee was really at if he had to choose, that was where he was comfortable no matter how he protested. He liked the executive lunches and the reserved parking spaces. He liked the smell and the feel of the furniture and how it got more expensive as he legged it up in the bank each year. He liked the ritualized way he and the other suited types talked to one another and did business, each knowing which chair to take and how much small talk to exchange over the phone before getting down to the meat, like foreplay.

We were important to Lee, too, me and Becker and Michael and R.J., but not in the fundamental way he paid lip-service to. We were really just another way he could keep one up on everyone else. When he thought about the business types screwing with him or his old man giving him grief, he could think of us as his escape and revenge and his secret identity, people who wore dirty blue jeans and didn't always shave. But if any of us—I guess particularly Becker, who saw through his bullshit and was always just a millimeter away from open contempt—gave him grief, he could fall back in his head on his banking Noh play, where he had his *real* role, where everyone instantly acknowledged his rank and position, where he was a big force in the downtown Jaycees and the United Way drive and the Temple brotherhood. It was pathetic, one of those noble minds o'erthrown—not that it had ever been much of a noble mind to begin with, just another fucked-up schizo wreck of a fairly decent Jewish kid who was always going to be out of his depth whatever he was in. I just never believed he'd ever leave the bank, certainly not for the dope-running beachcomber life where a loudmouth like him couldn't survive for very long. So much of him was always going to need signs, painted names and titles on office doors, plastic lapel badges or metal nameplates on desks, to tell the world precisely who he was without guesswork. And so much of him was always going to need the illusion of knowing who was above him, who was beneath him and who was his near equal; none of that was he ever going to be able to work out for himself without external signs.

We swam around in the pool after dinner and talked about nothing in particular, and then Becker and I hit the road. Dixie Highway turned into Interstate 95 north and Dade turned into Broward County, and technically I was supposed to be in the dark, with only Becker knowing where we were going and what we were going there for. Becker seemed to be getting uneasy about that, or uneasy about my cooperation, why I wasn't demanding to know where we were headed. I wasn't really trying to make him stew in his juices. I knew what we were doing, and I knew why he was having such a hard time telling me. Old pacifists die hard. It bothered me about as much as it bothered him—not really bother, but embarrassment, like two reputable members of the community finding themselves at the same hardcore porno movie matinee when they should have been at home or at work.

"We need guns," he said finally, somewhere around Pompano.

"Yeah. I know. I'm not a complete moron."

"There are implications to this, you know," he mumbled sourly.

"Give me a break. Give us both a break. Of course we need guns. Where are we going to get them?"

"I figure Benning. I mean, let's go to the source. That's where they keep the best selection, and that's where we know the ropes."

"Might not be the same, Becker. It's the all-new volunteer Army now."

"You mean the people there are even stupider than they were when we were there? I figure that works our way somehow."

"I'll go along with you there. How are we going to swing this deal, or are you open to suggestions?"

"Very straightforward," he said. "I brought ten grand in cash with me. If we can't come up with some friendly smackhead in a Phenix City bar in a couple of days, I figure maybe we just ought to retire. I want two or three M-16s and a couple of sidearms and ammo. Nothing fancy, just crash and dash. Whatever's available."

"Well, stop waiting for me to nix the idea. I was beginning to wonder when you'd attend to this detail. I personally was feeling a little weird about the size of this deal and not even a Boy Scout knife to watch over it."

"You're just full of surprises," Becker said. "I threw a set of your fatigues in the back in case we need to go to a costume ball. The ones with the Infantry Center patch. I got some, too."

"I hate to say this, but we could use haircuts if we're going to go that route."

"Between here and Columbus there is nothing but unoccupied barber chairs and eager shitkicker barbers. We get lopped wherever we stop for breakfast."

"Far out."

## BECKER

**H**ey—something worked out right for a change. Smilin'
Michael was waiting outside the bombed-out wreck
that passed for the Miami train station instead of Inspector Erskine
and the other clean-cut lads from the F.B. & I. I'd half been expecting when I lugged my monster duffel bag out into the street.

"Watcha got in the bag, bitch?" he asked sweetly as I heaved
it into the back seat.

"Fartless beans," I hissed. "Let's get out of here, if you don't
mind." It was an ancient Ford Fairlane that smelled like a Salvation
Army soup kitchen and sounded like a pack of dogs chasing a cat
through the canned goods aisle of a grocery store. "How's things
going with Lee?"

"Amazingly well. He comes home every night, takes a couple
of Valium, slides into the shallow end of the pool, and maybe by
nine o'clock he can speak English. Anyway, he says you can have
your first load of bucks tomorrow afternoon. That okay?"

"That's not only okay, it's unbelievable, sport. Has he been
coming home every night like a good boy?"

"Yeah, not dawdling at all. Laura slid over last night but she
didn't stay long, and all three of us pretended like we could stand

**95**

each other and just bullshitted in the living room. God, we watched television. The whole thing was so middle-class it was appalling."

We cut off Dixie Highway and into the Grove south of the downtown section and pulled up in front of Lee's house. I carted the bag into Michael's bedroom and gave him the high-sign to come in with me. I started pulling the dismantled weapons out of the bag and putting them on the bed.

"Christ!" he whispered.

"We been busy. You don't mind if we store these in your place for a couple of weeks, do you?"

He did a little stagger dance backwards and leaned back against his desk. "Knock yourself out," he gasped. "Life in prison never bothered me. Where did you get that shit?"

"Well, it's bad enough you know we got it. Just for fun, how about I don't fill you in on that detail?"

"Suit yourself. God, those things make you look so virile, it just makes me want to grab you around your thighs."

"Later," I said. "Listen, do you know anything about these things? Any of your sisters gun nuts or anything?"

"Well, I know you put bullets in them and pull the trigger and hot lead flies out the other end. That's about it."

"At least you have the essentials. I want to check you out on these things. It could save our asses."

"Those things scare me, Becker. I'm serious—I mean, it doesn't have anything to do with me being a flamer. Those things just scare me. I was polite when R.J. showed me his little collection, but they really make me nervous."

I sat down on the bed and looked across at him, a little disgusted. "Damn you," I said. "Don't you think they make *me* nervous? I mean, let's cut the American cowboy bullshit—these things scare the living piss out of me, if that makes you feel any better. Unfortunately, we have to transcend that for the next couple of weeks. We have to pretend that we know what we're doing with these things, that we'll use them if we have to, and that if we use them, we might even hit someone. That way, the other folks out there who are also scared shitless of these things will think twice about using them and probably decide against it. Lame, but true."

"It's different with you, Becker. You were in the army. You're comfortable with these things."

"Oh, give me a break. I staggered out of a tin hootch twice a day and lofted a balloon on a mountaintop. I'm sorry if I'm shattering your illusions. Besides, look at it as a valuable skill. When Anita Bryant finally organizes her Kill the Faggots mob and rolls into the Grove one night, you can be the big cheese who teaches your butt-fuck buddies how to blow a few of the Baptists away. You could end up being the gay George Patton, you know?"

"It doesn't sit well with me at all," he grumbled. "What do I have to know?"

"For now, not a hell of a lot. I want you to know how to deal with one of these." I picked up a .45, dropped the magazine out of it and cleared the breech to make sure it was empty. "For all I care, you can walk around with it empty. But I want you to know enough about it so that people think you can use it without being knocked off your feet and on your ass."

"That's an automatic, isn't it? What's the difference between an automatic and anything else?"

"We're really starting with the basics, aren't we?" I said. "Okay. There's automatics like this and revolvers, like the cowboys and the cops use. A revolver has six or so rounds in a revolving chamber. They're more reliable, they don't jam as much, but they don't hold as many bullets as an automatic." I held up the magazine. "This is the magazine. It has a spring in the bottom that pushes the bullets up into the gun one at a time. The magazine holds seven rounds, and if you're insane, you can pack an eighth round in the chamber. I don't recommend the practice." I handed him the .45, still empty. He waved it around a little, distastefully.

"Jesus, it's heavy," he said.

"Two rules," I said, "and you may stand a chance of living through this experience with your scrotum still intact. First, learn how to tell if a weapon's loaded and check it every time someone hands you a weapon. Never trust me or your mom or anybody about whether a weapon's loaded or empty. Always assume it's loaded and ready to kill you. The second rule is the biggie. Never point one of these at someone unless it is your intention to kill him immediately. Then do your best to kill him immediately."

"You're serious, aren't you?"

"You betchum. You see, with Becker's two rules, you won't shoot yourself in the foot, and you probably won't ever have to display one of these things or use it. That's what I'm aiming for. We need these things to do what we want to do —unfortunate, but true. But I intend to do my best to see that my troops don't get themselves shot and don't leave a bunch of shot-up meat behind them. I intend to do my very best on that score."

"Well, you've made a believer out of me, Sarge. Show me how to tell if it's loaded."

I showed him. I showed him how to load a magazine, how to breech a round, and how to clear a weapon. I also showed him about the safety, but told him not to rely on it. Then I taught him the two-hands-feet-spread stance for shooting. "Everything else is cowboys and Indians," I said. "This is a tremendously powerful machine and it can't be aimed worth a fuck. This is the only way to give yourself half a chance of hitting someone in the torso. If you do, he's out of the game and you don't have to worry about him anymore that night."

"What about those machine guns?"

"Forget them for now. I just want you to know the pistol. I'll check you out on those when you need to know."

"My mother would never believe this."

"You think mine would? Jewish people aren't supposed to walk around armed, unless they're in Israel. We're supposed to wear glasses and study for the medical boards."

"Where did you go wrong?"

"Beats me. I cut Sunday school and hung around with pinko faggots like you."

"Hey, were you bar mitzvahed?"

"Of course I was bar mitzvahed," I grunted. "Why on earth do you want to know that?"

"I don't know. I went to somebody's bar mitzvah when I was a kid. It looked neat. Did you sing?"

"No. We were Reform. We didn't sing."

"Did you have to learn all that Yiddish?"

"Not Yiddish. Hebrew. Yes, I had to learn it. *Shalom. Baruch ataw.* Impressed?"

"And how. I was a Catholic. Would you believe I was an altar boy? No shit, I really was."

"You suckers stopped using Latin. I was very disappointed with that decision. I studied that crap for years, and the only people that were still using it stopped. Who do I see to file a complaint?"

"Too late. The subject's closed, I think."

"What's it like being a Catholic fag?" I asked.

"Well, it depends. If you're a flamer like me with no secrets, you can hang it up. I went to an underground gay mass in New York once. It was really depressing. I had the feeling everybody was about to beg for forgiveness at any moment. I forgot to go back next Sunday. I am not exactly in a state of grace."

"Well, the door's always open here, my son. We're very loose on moral issues, as long as you don't grab my ornament."

"Thanks, dad."

"You got a file around this place? I don't know what good it's going to do us, because just having these things is enough to fry us, but I think it's traditional to file the serial numbers off."

"Yeah, there's something that answers to that description in the pool shed."

"Hurry up. I want to hide these fuckers before Lee gets home. I doubt he could take it. I don't want him to know we've got these things, okay?"

"Sounds reasonable. I'm sorry *I* know."

It took us about a half-hour to make the serial numbers illegible enough for rock 'n' roll, and then we put everything back in the duffel bag and stuffed it under Michael's bed. The room smelled of gun oil and Cosmoline, so Michael lit some incense and we smoked a couple of numbers in the room. We were pretty blitzed out by the time Lee walked in on us and sniffed around, but the gun smell was gone. Nothing in the world is like that smell.

I'd been telling the truth to Michael. Guns gave me the creeps, pure and simple. My only saving grace was that I knew about guns and they didn't positively terrify me. Oddly enough, I was even a good shot, the terror of NRA-approved paper targets the world over. Dumb-ass things—the distinctive centerpieces of Western civilization.

"Becker! You've come back! Where's Richard?"

"He went up north to scout out the sales force. With what we're going to move, I want some people ready to buy large chunks of it fast, without us having to hang around each burg for a week. How are you coming with the money?"

"Okay, like I said I would. It's weird, but I'm getting it."

"There's a flight to Bogotá tomorrow night at 9:30," I said. "Can you have the first money in my hands by seven tomorrow night at the latest? Here at the house?"

I was pinning him down. He jumped a little, then thought better of it. Not much better. "Listen," he said, "I can't be sure. Why don't you wait till I get you the money and then make your plans?"

"Because I've got to be able to know something ahead of time, and this is one of those things. You say you can have the money tomorrow afternoon. Tomorrow afternoon means that seven o'clock's giving you plenty of time. You should be able to tell me yes or no."

"Maybe it won't be as easy as that," Lee said. "I mean, from here it looks like I can do it, it really does, or I wouldn't have said that. But things have gone wrong, not big wrong, but little things. You got to be realistic."

"You'd be amazed how realistic I can be, including shit like this. I'm being reasonable, but that doesn't mean I'm going to hang everybody and everything up on waiting for you to get your end straight. You've had a week to do that, and you say you've done it. Now I want to be able to plan just a little ahead. I don't want to have to wait until tomorrow night to actually lay my hands on the cash before I think I know I'll have it. Because if you come back tomorrow night and turn Friday night into Saturday morning, or turn Saturday into Monday, I'm going to scrub this whole thing while I'm still ahead of the game. I'm going to call Richard back and regroup, pal, and I'm going to regroup without you as the pivot man in this little circle jerk."

Lee looked down at Michael for some kind of support or reassurance. Michael just stayed flat-looking, not taking Lee's side or my side.

"I'll do the best I can," Lee said. "I told you I would."

"That's only good enough if I know I'll have the cash I'll need in Colombia by tomorrow night at seven."

"All I can tell you now is that from everything I can see, that's the way it'll be. It's as set up as I could make it, and I been busting my balls on it all week, I swear."

"You don't have to swear. You just have to bring me the money."

"It'll be safe down there with you? I mean, nobody's going to rip you off? I've heard it's heavy down there."

"You've heard right," I said.

"Well?"

*Don't whine. Don't whine, motherfucker, or I will jump up and smash you in the face.* . . . I calmed myself down before I opened my mouth again.

"Let's put it this way. To get your money, someone's going to have to make me dead first, dead or pretty close to it, and I can't tell you how carefully I'm going to work to avoid either of those catastrophes. It's sort of the same thing with flying in airplanes, Lee. I trust 'em because I know that anything that happens to me is going to happen to the pilot first."

He thought about that for a second or two. "Okay," he said, not overconvincingly. "I know you don't want anything to happen down there. I guess that's good enough."

"Yes. It's good enough. It's good enough for me and it's good enough for you."

He whistled. "It wouldn't be good enough for my old man if I couldn't get the money back in time."

"Then you have to make it good enough for him, too."

"Nope. It wouldn't work out that way."

"Then we're all going to do our very, very best to see it never comes to that. How's that?"

"Okay," he said.

I had plenty to do Friday to get ready for Colombia. I started things off around eight in the morning with the flight reservation—foolish, considering it was all dependent on Lee, but necessary. I got to the airline's downtown office when it opened and laid down the advance money they wanted to book me tourist class. Then I had to scare up a money vest from a little hole-in-the-wall Cuban tailor I knew on *Calle Ocho,* a dude about seventy who always got the biggest charge making up things like that for R.J. and me. I wasn't terribly worried about him because he didn't speak four words of English. And R.J. already had his outfit, so it wasn't likely he'd be paying the old gentleman a visit in the next week or so. The Cuban took my measurements and my specs and I spent the next hour strolling around *Calle Ocho,* thumbing through the mystery paperbacks in the bookstores and trying to throw back a cup of *guarape,* that lethal sugar cane juice they squeezed out in about a dozen tiny stalls up and down the street. Then I hung around the vest-pocket park and watched the old men play dominoes and chess. *Calle Ocho* was a trip, such a marvelously convenient way to escape from America at a moment's notice, and from the very crummiest America that was Anglo Miami and Hialeah and Miami Beach.

By the time I'd done all my Miami chores and got back to the Grove, it was about five in the afternoon. Michael was splashing around in the pool and the only other noise was the shrieking of the neighborhood peacock somewhere over the fence. Michael was indulging in the private pool owner's prerogative and cavorting around in the hairy buff. I sat down in a deck chair and took my jacket off.

"How'd things go?" he asked.

"They went well. I'm all set."

"What do you think?"

"You mean about Lee? This isn't a fucking dog race, goddam it. I think he's coming with the money. I think he better be coming with the money. How's that for an answer?"

"Satisfactory, chief, satisfactory," he said. "Okay, my money's with you. I think he'll deliver the goods, too."

I kicked my shoes off and pulled my pants legs up and dangled my ankles in the short end while Michael pushed himself off from the edge on his back and imitated a spouting whale. He swam back beside me.

"What do you do if he doesn't? You don't mind if I ask, do you?"

"No use asking. I haven't decided yet. I don't really want to decide," I said. "I can do two things. I can jump in the car and race around town until I find him and kick his ass until he's scared so shitless he'll go back to work and get the money. Or I can just write the whole thing off for now. It's a tossup at the moment with me. It depends on how pissed off I get and how much I lose it if he doesn't show up."

I heard noises behind me at the front door and turned around. Lee was walking across the living room toward me with his attaché case. It was too close, too near the deadline to believe. All that was left was for him to open it and for me to see and touch the bucks. I was afraid to push things, to break the spell. I tried to read his face, but he was playing it impassive. It must have meant he had the bucks. He wouldn't be standing there in front of me with a poker face if he didn't have the bucks. He wouldn't be standing there at all. He'd be running somewhere to hide out and cry.

"Tell me," I said.

"What? That I got the money? You didn't doubt me, did you?"

"Not for a second," I said.

He crouched down on the concrete and laid the case down with the latches toward me. I crouched down and sprung them. The goddam thing was lousy with cash, and I liked the look of it right away. The stuff obviously came from at least three or four different stops and different vintages and styles. The little bit of new, crisp stuff was in a comfortable minority. I went through some of the older bundles. Nothing looked like siblings or cousins. The Federal Reserve marks were different and random, Philly, New York, Cleveland mixed around, Richmond and even some West Coast marks.

"Nice going," I whistled.

"Thanks," he said contentedly.

"Feels good, doesn't it?"

He looked across the attaché case at me. "Yeah," he said. "I guess it does. I was really shitting in my pants, I got to tell you."

"I know. No big deal, if you get through it and make it to the end."

"Please bring it back," he said. "I figure I can string it out for maybe eight, ten working days. Please, no more, even if you got to rob another bank."

"Okay. Understood. I trusted you and you came through. Now you got to do the same with me. It'll be hard, but you'll do it like I did it."

"Yeah," he said, grabbing for as much conviction as he could, and wrapping it in a nervous little smile.

I wanted Michael to stay and man the phone in case Richard called, so Lee and I threw some food down and I got dressed and packed and transferred the money to the vest, and he drove me to the airport in his Mercedes.

I told him not to park—just to drive me up the departure ramp. I was clean-shaven for the trip and still coming off that deranged Valdosta redneck haircut. Just to complete the picture without too much overkill, I had my 35mm camera slung over my neck—with real color film in it, just for grins. But most of all, I had my angelic, nine-to-five two-weeks-vacation, wild-blue-yonder smile on, with reflections of plaza cathedrals and the Galapagos Islands practically visible in my twinkling, nonbloodshot eyes (Visine, what else?). The trick wasn't to look perfect going through Customs; just the opposite, really. It was to look a little bent, to look like you were up for a little whoremongering and black-marketing and smuggling back a few things without paying duty. The trick was to look like a vacationer, but a naughty one. That put you in the boring median as far as the Customs people and narcs were concerned, making everyone else you were traveling with look either more bent than you or much straighter, suspect in either case. I'd seen plenty of people pulled out of the crowd in my Caribbean travels and I'd tried to learn what it was about them that got them yanked, assuming it wasn't a straight tip-off. There wasn't much about those glimpses you could write down or analyze, but you could bolster your intuition with them if your intuition was good to begin with. A little bit of wickedness got you through faster than a nun's habit, as far as I could check, and that was the way I played it.

Ultimately, you had to do the best you could and trust that the day you were traveling, somebody on your same errand was stupider than you, sweated more than you did, darted his eyes around more than you did, or if it was a honey working as a mule, scratched her snatch unconsciously. If the anvil had to fall on someone to make somebody's quota, you just had to do the best you could and hope someone else would run under the anvil ahead of you. It still had all the certainty of a horse race, but that didn't mean you couldn't hedge your bets, lean on the favorite with a proven track record, and put the best jockey on his back; results were what made the horse the favorite and the jockey the best jockey.

I pulled my suitcase out of the trunk of the Mercedes and leaned back into the car to say goodbye. It was dark now, with an early evening lull in the swing of the airport car and foot traffic. I didn't mind that. Maybe getting lost in a big crowd was the best way, but there was also something to be said for letting whoever was checking you out have a long, satisfying look at you so he could feel all that much better about writing you off his shit list; otherwise you could end up continuing down the travel conduit with a question mark penned next to your name.

"God," Lee said with a strange sort of sigh, "I wouldn't be going where you're going for anything in the world."

"You ought to try it sometime," I said. "It's fantastic down there. They eat better than we do, those of them that can afford to eat at all."

"There's no lox down there," he said. "No bagels and cream cheese. Just corn things. Forget it."

"One of these days I'll take you along with me. It would do something for you. You're really pretty fucking parochial, you know. You could use some travel."

"I been to Europe," he said. "I spent my junior year in Europe."

"No you didn't. You only think you did. You ain't really been anywhere. Everywhere you been, you just turn around and there's another fucked-up rich American tourist to speak English with. I'll take you somewhere with me one of these days. It's my mission."

"Spare me," he said. "Well, maybe. I don't know. I don't know if I could take it. I can't see how you can. Anyway, good luck, man. I mean it. Not just for me. For you. For all of us."

"Thanks," I said. "I try to make my own, but that don't mean I don't appreciate any spare luck my buddies have to give me. I do."

"You'll let us know how things are going?"

"Michael knows the routine. You'll know."

"Hurry back," he said.

"Fast as I can," I said. I banged the Mercedes on the roof and he drove away, slipping into a hole in the light traffic. A skycap made a move for my bag, but I fended him off. When you need somebody else to shlep your shit, you've got too much of it.

# RICHARD

I t should have occurred to me that if Becker made it back to Miami International at all, everything was copacetic and there wasn't anything to worry about. But it didn't occur to me.

I was sitting in one of the leatherette chairs with a good vantage point of Customs, far away from it and acting disinterested as all get-out, when I spotted him in the line flopping his suitcase up on the counter. Every few seconds I'd look in his direction to see how things were coming, and then suddenly—oh, God—there was Becker surrounded by two uniformed Customs jerks and all three of them were having an animated argument. I felt like someone was tilting a dump truck full of my lunch down in my bowels. What the fuck was going on? He couldn't possibly be coming back from Colombia with reefer or toot; that was supposed to be somebody else's act, one of the nuns or tourists in the line. He'd have dumped the money in Colombia, the big bucks, the down payment. What the hell was going on? Were they going to take him into the little room and make him stare at the 150-watt bulb for a few hours? How could he do this to me?

I peeked again, and by gum, he was zipping up his bag and stalking out of the Customs area and into Freedomland, heading vaguely in my direction. I gave a short whistle that stopped him in his tracks and he turned, saw me and sat down next to me. He was looking grim.

"What *happened* over there?" I asked.

"Oh. I just had to fucking pay duty on my own goddam camera. I forgot to declare it before I flew down."

"Thanks for making a stink about it," I said. "I almost left a puddle under this chair."

"Well, what did you want me to do, pay them twenty bucks without bitching a little? I'm supposed to be a tourist, not King Farouk. Anyway, they say if I can dig up the receipt for the camera and bring it down to the Customs office, I can get a refund."

"Are you going to?"

"You're fucking-A right I will. I bought that fucking camera in the good old U.S. of A. and they're not going to screw me like that if there's a way around it."

"God bless you, my boy. Well, let's get out of here."

So I gave my report to Becker as we zipped along the East-West and down 95 to Dixie Highway in the truck. All told, it looked as if we'd have all the buyers we'd need, spread out fairly evenly so we wouldn't have to concentrate any vast amount of weirdness in one city. Everybody understood the rules we wanted to deal by and understood it was going to be a quick crash-and-dash, and that if they fucked up or missed the mark we'd be gone, no apologies. They'd bring their own scales and testing equipment, and we'd bring a few weights with us to calibrate things. They'd make their decisions at point of sale and would have the cash with them or within five minutes of a call. We'd steer them to the place of the buy, and once they were there, no one else would find out about it until the deal had gone down and we'd cleared out. No guns allowed on their side; we had pat-down privileges. But primarily things would go down fast and our way or not at all. Apart from two, maybe three asshole buddies with whom we were willing to dispense with the cloak and dagger, everyone else I'd prepared for the worst and we planned to give them the worst. Any objections and they were invited to shop elsewhere.

Now all we needed was the toot, and Becker told me the date

on that little item. "The rest of the money. How's Lee coming along with that?" he asked.

"Fine. He brings it back home every day or two and insists on rubbing it under my nose and making me count it. I move it to a safe box the next morning. I'm using four around town."

"What's the feel for things?" he asked.

"Good. Good. Nothing strange, no funny clicks on the phone, no funny cars parked across the street."

"Well, I guess we lay back and screw off for a couple of days. I'd like to go down to Key West and check the mail, maybe tomorrow. You want to come?"

"It depends. If Lee's bringing money home tonight, I'll want to get it to the bank right away, but if you can wait until the bank opens, I'll truck on down with you."

"Okay. There are still a couple of things I want to do with the boat. You can go to the bank and I'll hit the marine stores in the Grove, see if they got what I want. We can be on the road by ten or eleven."

"I think it's working, Becker."

"Looks that way. It gets you coming and going. I'm nervous as shit about it fucking up, and now I'm nervous as shit because it's working. Damn. First thing I'm going to do when I get to Lee's is jump in the fucking pool."

# 13

## BECKER

**T**he dangerous part, the bad part was now, after we'd greased and oiled and overhauled everything and taken care of everything we could possibly take care of, even piddleshit that didn't really matter but was just something we thought up to keep ourselves occupied. Now even that was taken care of and we had time on our hands waiting for Eduardo's mother ship to make it up here. Without anything to keep us in focus, I didn't know how the time was going to wear on each of us, and we weren't all in the same place. Richard and I were lounging around at home on the island, and Lee and Michael were holding the fort in the Grove. We could phone each other all we wanted to, but you can't get the same feel for what's going on in somebody's head over the phone. It was just a bad time. It gnawed at you.

Me, I spent it fantasizing about the future, airbrushing an old dream that had only required a metric shitload of cash. I'd transcended mules and mother ships and was now the squadron commander of some ancient C-130s revving up in a secret field in central Florida. I was holding a predawn pilots' briefing in a quonset hut just before the big mission—to bomb the East Coast into psychic submission with two hundred thousand tons of primo tops, which would make me High Dope Lord and mythic archetype.

Back on earth the phone rang. It was Michael through the squawk and hiss of the usual crummy connection from the Grove to Key West.

"What's shaking?" I asked him.

"Listen," he said, "nothing heavy, but R.J. just breezed in this afternoon and set up camp for the night. He's out cruising the Grove right now with Lee. There wasn't much I could do about it. I don't think anything's up, and I think Lee's pretty together about the whole thing. I'm going to meet 'em later at the Taurus."

I grumbled to myself for a second or two. "Well, he's solid and he takes up space. He had to be somewhere tonight. Did he mumble anything about what he's up to? Does it look like he's doing business or pleasure?"

"Hard to say, boss, but it seemed like pleasure. I think he wants to get away from Lisa for a couple of weeks. I think he's taking a northern cruise from here, maybe tomorrow morning if he doesn't run into some neat little fucklette on his rounds tonight."

"You really think Lee's together? Let's say R.J. thinks he's sniffed out something out of the ordinary and puts a couple of questions to Lee—"

"I think Lee's up to it. That's all I can say. I think he's part together and the other part's scared shitless that R.J.'ll find out now that Lee's decided to do this one with us on the sly. I don't think he's going to give anything to R.J. except a good time."

"Okay. Here's what I want you to do. Get ready to leave and to come down here. Don't wait until tomorrow. Drop by the Taurus and check things out. If Lee still seems to have it together, if you don't think you have to nursemaid him anymore, tell them you feel like checking out Key West and you're driving down tonight. Then do it."

"Is it time?"

"Yeah, just about. If you don't slide in overnight, I'll assume Lee started to go green around the gills, okay?"

"Okay, boss. But that means I got to leave Lee with the old fart for the next I-don't-know-how-long."

"No. You'll be coming out with me and Richard'll be handling things in the Grove. He'll check in on Lee by tomorrow afternoon. I think it'll work out better that way."

"Yeah, I can dig it," he said. "I'll see you some time in the morning."

"Okay."

Richard had caught most of my end of the conversation.

"Tomorrow?" he asked me.

"Yeah. It's one day ahead of schedule. I want to chance a dry run with Michael. There's also the possibility the freighter had a good sailing. If it's on the loop, we can do it then. I don't want to keep them waiting, even if they're early. They might keep trucking on without us."

"That means I have to bring the equipment to Lee's house, and R.J. might still be there."

"No. When you get to Miami, check into a motel in North Miami, the one we shacked up in that time we were too fucked up to drive anymore, you remember?"

"Yeah, what is that, 163rd Street?"

"Right. Leave the boxes there and then check in at Lee's. Check things out and if they need your attention, stay there and just go to the motel at the necessary times. But I don't want you to take Lee with you. I don't want him to know you're staying in a motel or which one."

"Lee doesn't know when the pickup is?"

"He has to, give or take a day or two," I said. "But if he screws things up and tells R.J. what's going on, I just don't want him to know where it's going to happen. From the time you meet us for the drop, Lee won't be with you and he won't know where the rest of it's all happening. We'll be free-floating from then on."

"What if he's already told R.J.?"

"Play it by ear. Deny everything, and if R.J. doesn't like it, tell him to stuff it. Walk out and keep the deal rolling."

"Things are getting hairy," Richard said.

"No, they're just getting real and there's no helping that. We didn't expect R.J. to disappear through all of this. Maybe it's better this way. We know where he is, and if we're not total assholes, he just thinks we're all diddybopping around as usual, fun-loving and bent for a good time."

"I hope that's how it's going down."

"That's how it's going down," I said. "You hungry?"

"I suppose so. I suppose I could watch you eat, anyway. What you got in mind?"

"Well, let's get a good meal in us. It may be the last decent one we'll have time for the next couple of days. How about the Fourth of July?"

We cruised over there on my bike and after dinner circumnavigated the island just to catch the breeze. There was no chance of getting any sleep after we got home, so I cranked up the Hallicrafters and listened to the marine traffic and the weather bands while we played an endless rubber of backgammon. The weather seemed ace for the next couple of days, and I told Richard I just might take the dry run and then stay out on point for another day doing some sport fishing; that way, with any luck, we'd all be beyond R.J.'s reach if the shit hit because weak-link Lee wouldn't know about the motel and he wouldn't know any of the hard arrangements of the pickup and drop, just that they were probably about to happen soon. The next time R.J.'d even have the opportunity to stick his hand in our act would probably be after we'd done our sales trip up north. *Fait accompli.* I'd buy R.J. a steak dinner if he felt hurt and out of sorts about our independent venture.

Michael rolled in around three-thirty in the morning, looking a little ragged from the suicide drive down 1, but bearing good news and ripe for some action. R.J. had behaved like R.J.—getting something out of that was like pulling elephants' tusks—and Lee had behaved pretty soundly for Lee. Nothing seemed weird, nothing fishy. Michael had said his goodbyes and gone his merry way.

We toked up on the off-chance it might mellow us out a little and give us a few hours of anesthetized sleep, and as the bong went around the living room, I dragged the duffel bag out from the utility shed and issued the weapons, a .45 and three magazines for Richard, an M-16 for me and for Michael, three regular magazines each, one tracer-interspersed magazine each, and a .45 for Michael and me. After we'd checked the weapons, Michael and I put ours back into the duffel bag to go along on the boat. The grease gun was still in the bag, along with some surplus canvas bandoliers that would handle the M-16s' NATO ammunition. The whole scene, of course, conjured up a fearsome firefight, but I played it straight and businesslike and nobody else said anything about nasty implications. Fair enough.

Around five we went to our separate corners and sacked out. I set an alarm for ten—Michael and I would have plenty of time to catch up on our sleep on station in the boat, and Richard could snore away in the motel in North Miami. When I rolled out and started breakfast going in the kitchen without bothering to wake anyone up, I made enough clatter so that within about fifteen minutes I heard bathroom noises upstairs and then downstairs. Cuban coffee was just made when Richard walked into the kitchen and Michael strolled in a minute after that.

We ate quietly and quickly. Everyone seemed itching to move. Although it annoyed me to have to do the dishes, if you don't in the tropics, you come back two hours later and the whole kitchen wall's been taken over by a green mold that's harder to kill than the Blob and stinks worse. By the time I was done, Richard and Michael were loading various goodies into the truck.

The final thing I did before I closed up the house was to get the bulk of the cash from its hiding place in a tackle box behind a board in the upstairs linen closet. It looked all there. It looked marvelous. It was amazing how it was going to grow within a couple of weeks and how much we'd have if we lived to spend it.

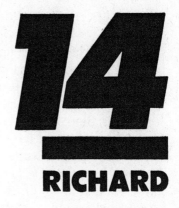

# 14

## RICHARD

There wasn't much to say at the marina after everything had been loaded on in a fair imitation of a couple of young, bent Conchs out for a few days of marlin fishing. Becker and I went over the commo signals for the fiftieth time and they were remarkably the same, which seemed to surprise the wizard. After that, there wasn't much to say, so we didn't say it. We shook hands hippie-style, the thumb grab, this being no time to shake like straight people, I suppose, and Becker said *Buena suerte, Dickhead,* and then climbed into the *Kelpie,* turned her over from the flying bridge while Michael and I took care of the bow and stern lines, and the crime of the century, give or take a few hundred others that season exactly like it, headed for the open seas.

I watched the bully boys fade into the distance at a leisurely clip until they reached the first bridge and went under and out of sight, and then I climbed into the truck and headed it north. I passed the usual stream of refugee hitchhikers heading north to make way for the ones I'd meet a few hours later on the other side of Dixie Highway heading south. I passed them all up—no extraneous thrills this trip, thank'ee. It was going to be hard enough just making it to the mainland at this hour, and while I wasn't in much of a hurry, I wasn't in any mood to set a slow record, either. No riders.

I broke the trip at a hot dog stand on Tavernier a little up the highway from the marina where Michael and I had checked out the first boat, the *Coriolis*. It struck me that since then, this was probably the first high seas deal Michael had been on—yeah, it almost surely was. Since then it had either worked out in R.J.'s deals that Michael had worked the dry land end of the few deals he'd been on, or else Michael had seen to it that it worked out that way on purpose. I suppose Becker's taking charge this time had liberated him from that taboo if it was a taboo, but I wondered how cheery he was about it nonetheless. As the *Kelpie* had pushed off a couple of hours earlier, I'd seen Michael resting his back against the midships bulkhead underneath the flying bridge, not happy, not sad, not waving—a little wistful, maybe?—or maybe I was just reading invisible ink in a short and sweet notice that meant to say nothing of the kind. Anyway, he hadn't waved goodbye.

I made Florida City and the mainland by half past three in the afternoon and twenty minutes later started passing through the horror of the southern 'burbs of Miami—monster shopping malls, out-of-control highway intersections, innocent cars lost for hours trying to make a simple left turn across Dixie. It was all of goddam five o'clock when I pulled into Becker's motel in North Miami and the only thing nice I could think of about the battle with the Friday evening rush hour was that it had very likely been the most terrifying thing I might have to face in the next couple of weeks. Beyond that, I was half crashed-out from lack of sleep and surliness, and I had neither toot with me to get farther up nor reefer to slow things down. Personal choice: no way I was going to get popped at this stage for a personal stash when I was sitting on the receiving end of a veritable footlocker of flake. Better to go out with a nuclear fireball and get hauled in for the mother lode.

I didn't try any funny games with my name or the truck license plate at the motel office, there being too many cops from too many jurisdictions with too little to do in this neck of the woods. Two, maybe three nights, thanks. Pay in advance? Sure. Yes, I've got some luggage, but if you'll just show me where to park near my room, I can get it myself. On my way out of the lobby I read the announcement board. If things got dull in the room, I was just in time for a monthly science fiction convention that ran through the weekend. I picked up the mimeographed program from the registration desk no one was manning yet. For four bucks each session, I could wile away my spare time watching *Forbidden Planet*, three or four episodes of *Star Trek* and the *Star Trek Bloopers*, *Invasion from Mars* and *2001*. There were also going to be talks by two sci-fi authors I'd never heard of and another by a NASA representative. Comic book swaps. Souvenirs. The time of my life. Maybe I was lucky to get a room.

Lucky to get it or not, once I'd carted everything from the truck into it, I locked and chained myself in, started running a very hot bath, stripped and started looking over the gear. Becker and I had packed it well and it seemed to have survived the trip. The last thing I looked over was the .45—Jesus, I'd forgotten how big those suckers really were and how heavy. There was no magazine in it and nothing flew out of the chamber when I pulled the action out. What to do about this sucker for the duration . . . under the pillow? I tried that and decided it sucked the hairy wazoo. Likewise the night table between the twin beds, although there was a certain charm pairing it with the Gideon Bible. Fuck this . . . back in the kit bag. No, back out again. Magazine in, snap, still nothing in the chamber, *now* back in the kit bag. Hot potato. Ready for grizzly. Surprise, surprise, hot lead in your eyes . . .

I took a shower, put on some fresh clothes and strolled out of the motel for a couple of blocks looking for a pay phone. I didn't want to chance making a call to the Grove from the motel room in case the funny clicks from the motel switchboard suggested anything to R.J. if he picked up. He didn't. It was Lee.

"Hey, motherfucker, how's things?" I asked.

"Okay," he said. "Where are you?"

"I'm in town, just getting something to eat. You guys at home tonight?"

"Yeah. R.J. took off this afternoon, a couple of hours ago. Guess where he's going?"

"I'll bite," I said.

"He wants to cruise up to Tallahassee or something, where the magic mushrooms grow, and get his ass shot off by some farmer while he hunts through the cow pies. He asked me to come with him."

"Chance of a lifetime."

"No way. Besides, I guess things are happening around here this weekend, right?"

"Could be, could be. Okay, I guess I'll cruise on up and bother you guys for the evening if that's okay by you. Anybody else there?"

"No. Just me. I'll scare you up some nooky if you want."

"Sounds grand, but I'll pass. I'll see you in about an hour."

Back at the motel room, I repacked the indispensable gear into one bag, the stuff I'd be terribly bummed out about if the room got ripped off while I was gone, including the monster gat. It all stowed away nicely in the tool chest bolted to the truck flatbed. It was dark by the time I pulled out of the parking lot.

Lee had left the front gate and door unlocked and I found him watching television in the porch room off the swimming pool patio. He looked up and gave me the high sign but didn't make any moves to lower the volume or to turn the thing off. I wished I hadn't come. The house was too quiet. The darkness was becoming oppressive. Finally a brassiere commercial came on and Lee clicked the sound off with his remote control dingus: *sproing!*

He got right to the point.

"Think I'll get the bank's money back?" he asked. He spoke flatly, as if he were only wondering out of the most idle curiosity.

"It's always happened that way before," I said.

"How about this time?"

"Okay. I look through my crystal ball." I picked up a glass off the white wrought-iron porch table. In it was a half inch of leftover whiskey and water and the last memory of an ice cube. I looked into the glass. "By George, here it is. I see the speedy return of the capital and a vast profit besides."

"Fuck the profit. I just want to know if I can get the bank's money back in time."

"Auditors coming?" I asked.

"No. Nothing special. I just got a bad feeling about everything. I can't tell you how bad I'm up shit's creek if I don't get the money back."

"Look. Why don't you sit here and drink yourself shit-faced

and dwell on it for the rest of the night? That ought to do wonders for everything and everybody."

He got sullen and quiet. He got up and left the room. From the bedrooms I heard water running and a toilet flushing. He came back about ten minutes later. The TV sound was still off, but the guy and gal were back. They were in ski togs, exchanging their lines at the top of a slope.

"I'm sorry. You can see why I've got *spilkes,* okay?"

"I think you told me what that meant once, but it plum slipped my mind."

"You're such a *goy.* Anxiety. Hysteria. Whatever."

"Then I have *spilkes,* too," I said. "We all do. Unfortunately, everything's going okay so far, so nobody has anything to blame it on."

"It's not going okay. I almost shit a brick when R.J. showed up last night."

"Did he say anything? Ask anything?"

"No. I don't think so."

"Yes or no? Give me a break," I said.

"No. He didn't say anything or ask anything. It's just that under the circumstances, it bothered the piss out of me, okay?"

We played gin for a couple of hours and he trounced me. I didn't play the game very well to begin with and my head was off in space. Although his head wasn't much better off, obviously idiot card games like that cooled him out and gave him the illusion he was functioning. Finally I'd had enough, and I figured I'd been there long enough to check his oil and verify that R.J. wasn't hovering.

"I'm going to cruise for a couple of hours, pal," I said.

"What for?"

"I just feel like getting the fuck out of here for a while. You got telephone duty—not that anybody's going to call, but you've got it anyway."

"You going up to Laura's?"

That was snide and I fought back an impulse to contribute my half of an argument around it. "Nope. Not even close. I just want to get out. And I sure would appreciate it if you didn't call her to find out if I'm there."

"I wasn't going to," he said.

"I'd also appreciate it if you go light on the drinks for the next couple of hours. If you have to know, I've got business that has to do with getting your famous money back to the bank on time, can you dig it?"

"Yeah. I figured."

No you didn't, you asshole. You thought I was going to skunk your time with Laura while you sat up with a sick telephone. "Okay. It's important. I may not sleep here tonight, but I'll phone you if I don't, and I would really be terribly unhappy if I call and you're not here, okay?"

"Okay." It didn't sound okay, but it was the best I was going to get.

"Is there any chance R.J. might get back from his mushroom hunt tonight?"

"I don't know. I don't think so, but I guess he could. He just comes and goes. Not much I can do about it."

"Okay. If I call and he's there, let me know right off, but stay calm. You think you can do that?"

"Yeah."

"This is serious bullshit, Lee. I ain't fooling. You're the guy who wants that little piece of cash back in the bank, so you'd better keep things together."

"Okay. I can dig it."

I heard him click the sound back on as I walked out to the truck. The goodies in the tool chest hadn't been tampered with and the street looked as if nobody gave a damn who shouldn't. I cranked the engine up and headed out of the Grove, north on US 27 through the split between Coral Gables and Little Havana.

The *Kelpie* should have been on station now since late afternoon. If the freighter was a day early and the pickup was going to be tonight, the *Kelpie* would get its mango or guava or pineapple code message sometime around midnight and get a course, also in code, to start steaming on to make a rendezvous sometime around two or three in the morning. I pulled into a 7–Eleven parking lot, bought a microwave submarine sandwich, and cracked the tool chest in the back of the truck for the CB, the Dixie Kicker and the marine VHF radio. I ate the sandwich in the cab with one hand and with the other installed the equipment into Becker's homemade racks under the dash. Then I put the magnetic antennas on the roof of the cab and drove off, farther north.

One way or the other, go or no-go, Becker would contact me with his CB and Kicker at midnight and follow it up with another transmission at one and at two, just in case the deal was going down but the freighter was late getting its transmissions together. After two in the morning, Becker and Michael would scrub things for the night if they got no word, and I could crawl back to the motel. With the Kickers, illegal power boosters, there wouldn't be any trouble communicating with the *Kelpie* from its location and mine, and around transmission time I was supposed to be somewhere in Broward, preferably as far north as I could make it, certainly well north of Lauderdale and on the coast. Route 27 wasn't the most direct way to get there, but I had a lot of time and I was feeling my way along, doing things the way they felt best, and going into Broward well inland just felt best along the deserted highway that skirted the Seminole reservation off to the west. Cheap cigarettes there, but closed, alas.

I cut east on 84 before 27 took me into the Everglades and made my way on residential secondaries east of Dixie Highway all the way up to Pompano Beach. About ten to midnight, as I made for the coast and the beach bridges, I switched on the CB with the squelch all the way down low. We were truckers, boys and girls, me answering to the discordant tune of the Tennessee Stud for the night and Becker signing himself as the Wheeler-Dealer, CB handles researched long and hard for their innocuous and cornball qualities. I switched through the channels to the one we'd arranged, and it was a good pick; Becker knew his stuff. We didn't have it entirely to ourselves, but it was pretty clear. Two women with Cracker accents were jawing about somebody's husband and how everybody knew but Corrine that he was going through some heavy reproduction moves with someone's underage niece. Well, hell, now that it was on the CB, even Corrine probably knew. Excellent choice—any outsider who could stand to listen to that crap for more than fifteen seconds sure as shit was no menace to our schemes.

Becker came up on the channel at five after midnight, drawl and all. "Skipland, Skipland, how's about you, Skipland?"

"Roger, Skipland. You got this one and only Tennessee Stud here. How you copy?"

"I copy you fine, Tennessee Stud. You got this one Wheeler-Dealer here. What be your twenty?"

"Wheeler, we be doing those double nickels outside that Fort Pierce in that Sunshine State"—which meant that I was where I was supposed to be—"bring it back with your twenty."

"That be a roger, Tennessee Stud," Becker said. "We be coming to you from Greenville, North Carolina, you copy?" I did; he was on station, too. "We be pushing this eighteen wheeler far ahead of schedule and we so happy, we gonna be seein' our mama for breakfast." That was news. The freighter had contacted him and the pickup was tonight.

"Well, that be wonderful news, Wheeler," I droned as if I could care less. "Give her one powerful kiss for me." A question: did he want me to go into the next part of my act, and when?

"I reckon that if she still be up and watching the late night movie, Stud, we be catchin' mama along about an hour and fifteen minutes." *Ad nauseam.* We'd practiced and I guessed I was passing for a redneck trucker, the emerging American fool as hero, but Becker was an absolute terror from his end. It was getting hard to keep visualizing his face. I kept seeing Gene Autry instead. But through all the shitkicker jive, we'd managed to trade all the information we needed.

Just to be on the overkill side, I started driving north for the next hour and fifteen minutes, slowly, no rush to be anywhere. Delray Beach would do, and it did. I cranked up the VHF as Becker'd taught me, and when the time was right, I taped down the microphone and began broadcasting a marine distress signal. It was a pretty pathetic speech, and Becker and I had pulled out all the stops. Assuming anyone picked it up, which was almost a certainty on the marine emergency channel I was using, they'd get about eight minutes of a Sad Sack who didn't know how to use his marine radio or else was too scared to switch over to listen for an acknowledgment. He didn't know where he was too precisely, just somewhere out in the big bad ocean off the coast of Vero Beach, maybe fifteen or twenty miles out. All he really knew for sure was that he was sinking. He was definite about that and a little on the panicky side about it to boot. The name of his boat was the *Martha's Pride,* no port mentioned, and he had four other people aboard. Although he didn't say specifically that they were also fools and that everyone was drunk on beer, it wouldn't take an expert listener to read those details through the crackle and sputter.

Becker had reckoned that if and when the message was received, it stood a damned good chance of drawing the Coast Guard cutters and choppers out of the *Kelpie's* sector for at least half a day, and that the prime effect would come at daybreak, when Beck would be drifting back into the outer fringes of Miami's weekend fishing fleet. Lives to save, no time to check out every goddam sport fishing boat, lives to save. It sucked, but it made good sense.

After my initial broadcast, I was supposed to snap back to receive, to listen for the response, which Becker had said would probably start swamping the emergency channel. It had. The second I let the transmit button on the microphone snap back, I could hear at least five different voices trying to raise me. One of them sounded more authoritarian or experienced than the others and asked everyone else to clear the air. Then he tried to raise the *Martha's Pride* again and again for a solid fifteen minutes, interspersing his questions about a better position (sorry, Bub, that's the best you get from me) with encouraging messages that the Coast Guard had been notified and that if the hapless quintet could hold on for just a little while, help was on the way.

I turned west and made for Interstate 95. When I came to the entrance, I pulled off and put the Kicker and the VHF marine and its antenna back into the tool chest. I was clear for the night, but I kept monitoring the CB in case Becker was trying to raise me. If he was, I wouldn't need the Kicker to hear him—his Kicker would do the trick and mine wouldn't help. The things were illegal, even if nobody gave a rat's ass about them except the FCC, and just like my lack of reefer and toot, I wasn't going to run the risk of flashing anything illegal for any longer than I had to.

It only sunk into me when I swung south onto 95 that Becker and the *Kelpie* were committed and moving in for the score. I wasn't sorry I wasn't with them, that I'd drawn the shore duty this time. I just wasn't sorry, that was all. Not that I thought much would go wrong. Becker had turned out to be a hell of a lot slicker at every detail than R.J., and yet not really too fancy. I was just glad to be ashore and away from it. I felt shitty about that.

## BECKER

A short news update at 1:30 from a Miami AM station was coming in pretty well. It had a tape of a Coast Guard public affairs officer over the phone announcing the report of the sinking and the sending of helicopters and a Miami-based cutter in that direction. I didn't know how novel this cry-wolf story was—we'd never used it in R.J.'s deals—but even if it smelled like yesterday's broccoli, they'd still have to check it out fairly seriously, that being their primary mission and swine like me clearly being their secondary. Even without the tragic sinking of the *Martha's Pride,* those suckers were spread pretty thin anyway. If they could have done it, they'd be doing something nasty just to keep us on our toes, so I figured it was fair play to do it to them first. They started it. I never announced my intentions of interdicting Coast Guard cutters on the high seas or of blowing them out of the water or of throwing those people in the can for twenty years. That stuff was all their idea. I never threatened them with shells across the bow. So if Richard's little VHF marine transmission could keep 'em jumping for a couple of hours past dawn, until the harbormasters started answering their phones and the Coast Guard decided there'd never been a *Martha's Pride* and that nobody's wives were jumping up and down on the docks frantic, that was good enough for me and all fair and square. If I remembered after this was all over, I'd call them up and say April Fool's.

The seas were light and only a sliver of a moon peeked through a good cloud cover, which took away one of my major worries, DEA spotter planes. Half the time the DEA couldn't afford to pay the pilots anyway, but when they could and the weather was right for aerial observation, seagoing entrepreneurs like us could get royally fucked. It was the aerial version of the Georgia cop's little jingle:

*You may outrun my old Chevrolet*
*But you can't outrun my old two-way*

and our side lost more mother ships and transports that way. The mother ships, ancient rusting freighter hulks, went to their final rewards near the Miami Coast Guard docks on the south bank of Government Cut. Paperless and ownerless and almost useless, they were on their last legs when they'd been interdicted anyway and the government couldn't give them away. Every other couple of weeks the Miami TV stations showed another one being towed in and off-loaded by marshals and DEA twerps in jumpsuits and shotguns. After that, no one showed an interest in them even for scrap. The smaller private boats like ours, though, fared better and got recycled. They went up for public auction, and most of them with a little something interesting in the power train or payload capacity were snapped up by other dope runners; I'd heard of one that had been boarded and hauled in three times that way.

All my little green and red electronic toys were humming now. The VHF was tuned to the mother ship's loop frequency for updates and course changes, but we were probably on our last leg now and the rest was a straight shot to an intercept, assuming the skipper could calculate a simple vector; it was his ball game and not mine because he knew where I was, while I had to take his word for it that he knew where he was, and he wasn't saying. Sometime within the next hour, he'd either tell us to halt, to let another boat in ahead of us, or he'd take us first and give us the final go-ahead, where he'd be waiting just over the horizon. Although I wasn't sure, I thought I'd caught an acknowledgment from a boat called mango on a different frequency by accident, and every once in a while I tuned back to it, but I didn't hear it again. I made a note to myself to run a second VHF receiver the next time out even if it made the boat look like the *Pueblo*.

At nightfall I'd had Michael rig up the radar sweep, even though it really wasn't much of a help in this situation. The jury-rigged platform it was mounted on didn't give it much elevation, so it had little range; I rigged it only for the edge it might give me if I needed one. I was using it passively, not sending out a signal for reflected objects, but to pick up the beacons of other ships' radar just beyond the horizon in case any ships, like a cutter or the mother ship, were out there. I kept Michael occupied by teaching him to synchronize the Loran waveforms as we sailed along, so that in an emergency I wouldn't have to start the procedure from scratch to have an updated position. When you used a lot of tricky electronic gear, it helped to bite your fingernails, because the pink skin on the ends of your fingers was left with raw and painful nerves that made the fingers more sensitive when they worked the vernier controls that tiny cunt hair's distance they needed to get something just right. Every quarter hour or so I cut the engines entirely to listen for other engine noise, which would have carried well on a night like this across the ocean surface. I didn't hear any, just the sloshing of the waves against the hull of the *Kelpie*.

"How's it goin', boss?" Michael asked me.

"Copacetic as far as I can tell. Of course I haven't taken submarines into account."

"Listen, if they got subs after us out here, we can just hang it up. How much longer you think we got to steam?"

"Hard to say. The mother ship knows. We don't. But if he's not worried about anything, he'll be closer in, closer to us rather than farther out, and things seem pretty clear tonight. Don't smoke."

"Why not?"

"Cuts down your night vision. I'm not saying it's a big deal, but we may want all we've got. I'm not smoking either."

"You're a saint," Michael said. "Okay." He put his smokes away. I gave him some gum and started a stick myself. Some talk started to sputter from the VHF.

*Okay guava you hold your position where you are we gonna*

*have mango come in first guava hold your position and stand by this frequency acknowledge*

"This is guava," I said into the microphone. "Acknowledged. We're holding our position and standing by this frequency." Which was a lie. I'd been right about picking up a snatch of mango's conversation and I flipped the VHF back to that frequency. There was a lot of chatter on it now and it seemed a bit louder. The voice was an Anglo man I'd never heard before, with maybe a little native Cracker or Conch. Perhaps he was one of the lobstermen who were going broke trying to stay ahead in the lobster game and found how easy it was to stay far ahead by bringing in reefer. I'd heard the lobstermen in Maine had discovered that trick, too, during the last couple of years, although I couldn't picture Maine lobstermen hustling out for bales of reefer—my illusions shattered. When the mother ship gave mango his final course, I scratched it down on a note pad glued to the top of the VHF. Then I hauled out the charts and started making an angle of our last course with the course the mother ship gave to mango, assuming that when the mother ship gave us the go-ahead she'd give us our old course back. Although this still didn't tell me how far off the mother ship was, it showed me where mango was, more or less; it gave me a better idea of where the players were on the chessboard. Despite cutting the engines, I couldn't hear any other engine noise, and I wasn't picking up anyone's radar. I cut the engines back in and kept trolling forward, just to keep the boat from the kind of sway that makes you think of nausea.

I called Michael to the equipment bay. "Listen," I said, "when we get close to the ship, we'll start using our radar beam and we may pick up two blips, the mother ship, a big blip, and the other boat if we're lucky. As soon as you see either blip, you let me know, and don't lose them if they stay on the screen. I want you always to know where both blips are, and if one or both of them go off the screen, I want you to be able to tell me where they went off the screen. Got that?"

"Yep. What for?"

"I don't know. I just like to know these things."

"Fair enough."

Most of the time I stayed on my own frequency, but every

couple of minutes or so I checked on the mango frequency. While they'd steam silently they'd probably start to talk again when they sighted the mother ship. If I assumed they were cruising at eight to ten knots, that would tell me how far ahead the mother ship was, a little better idea of it than I had now. The system was still damned good for keeping everybody guessing about where everybody else, particularly the mother ship was, but with a little educated guess-work you could eliminate some of the mystery. After about twenty minutes the mango sputtered up on the radio to tell the mother ship they had it in sight and were going to come up on its port side, which made sense considering the sucker was steaming north, prob-ably at least as far as Long Island, maybe up to Boston. Then the frequency went silent, so I went back to my own. There wouldn't be any more noise from mango once they had what they wanted.

It took a half hour before anyone came back on our frequency to give us our final course—just a continuation of the old one, as I'd guessed. The long time meant mango had picked up a shitload of reefer, probably all it could carry without foundering. That was good to keep in mind. I acknowledged the course and told the mother ship we were coming in. Michael stood next to me with his eyes on the Loran and radar scopes, and I switched on our own radar beam. The mother ship's blip appeared on the edge of the round radar scope after about another half hour, and then Michael caught the smaller blip of the mango north-northeast of us heading due west on a dash back to the mainland canals, probably in south Dade.

Michael saw the freighter first on the horizon running a bare minimum of safety lights, scarcely an outline, so the boats that were supposed to approach it wouldn't smash right into it by accident; I'd had my running lights switched off for about two hours. Ten minutes later I brought the *Kelpie* alongside the mother ship's rope ladder. I made the maneuver from the flying bridge while Michael stood by on the foredeck with the bow line ready to toss to one of the crewmen who was hanging from the ladder. Richard had rigged up a special cleat for the lines that would break away under the strain of the engines, but hold us fast even in bad seas if we wanted to be held fast, these being tricky situations where one never knew if one might want to leave in a large hurry. When we'd sighted the mother ship, I'd broken out the arms so that each of us had a .45 in his belt and I had my grease gun slung over my shoulder. Michael had his M-16, loaded, but mainly for effect. As we zeroed in on the freighter I motioned him to the walkway by the flying bridge.

"Admiral?"

"As soon as you tie up, go down to the lower bridge and take the wheel," I said. "Keep your weapon on automatic and ready, but mainly keep down there out of sight. Keep the engine running and if anyone tries to board you, get the hell out of rifle range first if you can before you try to shoot anybody."

"Jesus, what kind of boutique *is* this, anyway?" he asked.

"Who the fuck knows? I don't expect any trouble. We want dope and they want money, and it should be a pretty simple exchange. But if anything goes wrong, I want you to get this boat out of range. When you're out of range, try to raise them on the radio, but don't do anything they say unless I'm on the radio telling you. If I call you Jerry or anything but Michael, get the fuck out of there. Call the Coast Guard, I guess."

"Hey, that would sure be a switch."

"No shit. Anyway, whatever happens, keep an eye on that blip, the mango. When we get out of here, I'll want to know where it is right away. And if you're not real busy, play with the Loran and synchronize the waveforms."

"How long you expect you'll be up there?"

"As briefly as possible. If I take longer than fifteen minutes, start to worry. Twenty minutes, start trying to raise me on the radio. If they say I can't come to the radio, get ready to bolt."

"Aye-aye, sir."

Michael went forward just in time to throw the line to the crewman on the ladder. The ladder, a pretty sparse deal, was good for their purposes; you couldn't climb it and shoot very well at the same time, and it was definitely a one-man-at-a-time deal. The reefer bales were loaded off the cargo swing crane. Michael took the wheel down below while I groped for the M-16 and the tracer ammo I'd offered Eduardo. I stuffed the ammo in the knapsack with the money and the waterproof bags I'd brought for the coke. If they wanted to disarm me when I came aboard, I'd just have to live with that, it being accepted etiquette in these showdown circumstances.

This was another one of those abandon-all-hope-and-trust-in-the-Lord businesses that were part of the sport, and if you didn't like them, that was just tough luck, like someone who likes football but doesn't like being bruised or smashed around. You found another sport if you couldn't live with all the rules. It just came to pass in this act that even when everything was going well, every once in a while you had to walk into a room or board someone's ship where you faced eight or nine members of the other team, all of whom had guns, and they wanted to hold yours for the duration—the famous Mexican standoff, sawed-off shotguns across a poker table, take it or leave it. Among the many reasons not to tell people you ran dope for a living, the best one of all was that it rendered you uninsurable, and I'd converted my GI insurance to a Metropolitan policy and intended to keep it, by cracky.

And then I reached for the ladder. Someone called to me from above and I yelled *Hola esta guava!* up to him. That seemed to be close enough for rock 'n' roll because no one shot me; that was the acid test. The crewman ran up ahead of me and when I scrambled up the ladder and got to the side, two guys helped me over. They were armed, one of them with an M-1 on a sling, the other with a .38 revolver that he politely pointed at the deck. Nobody asked me for my weapons; the armed escort was enough. The freighter was a mess, as I'd expected, just this side of a derelict, and if this ended up being its last voyage, its owners, Eduardo chief among them if not the sole owner, wouldn't be out a hell of a lot. The ladder was slung amidships by the cargo hold, where in the darkness I could barely make out the rough repetitive burlap shapes of reefer bales, fresh from Juan Valdez's Colombian south forty.

We passed the commo shack where a t-shirted fellow with a salt-and-pepper beard was on the headset, listening but not squawking to anyone. An old green desk fan at his elbow turned this way and that without any fan guard, threatening at any moment to slice his arm into bologna. He looked up and smiled at me as we passed. One cabin forward was the skipper's shack, and one of the crewmen, who wore no shirt and smelled as if the good ship was missing a shower, knocked a couple of times. A voice inside yelled in Spanish to come in, and when the crewman opened the door for me, I went in. The boys stayed outside but left the door open. A young fellow in British Navy officer's shorts and a khaki shirt was looking over the charts under red light. He wore a pair of crummy blue tennis sneakers and had a buck knife in his belt on one hip and a holster for a .45 on the other, flap unbuttoned. He looked up from the charts and beckoned me over to the chart table.

"I'm Luis," he said, and we shook hands. "You?"

"Guava. Becker."

"Yeah. Eduardo said you'd probably be the one. Roll up your sleeve. That one."

I did.

"Okay, nice tattoo, right where it ought to be. Okay. What Eduardo says you want, it's in that chest. You got the money?"

"Yeah." I slung the knapsack off my shoulder with the M-16 and laid the rifle down on the chart table. "Present for Eduardo," I said.

"He'll like that. He said to slip you a little more if you brought it. We'll make a deal. You got tracer ammo?"

I took that out of the top of the pack and laid it on the chart table next to the weapon. Then I started taking out stacks of money and piling them up on the table while he hauled the locker into the center of the cabin and opened it up. He took a tarp off the top and uncovered bags of white powder that I guessed were kilo size, about the size of a big squash each. The bags were heavy clear vinyl and the seams looked like they were cut and assembled in a back room especially for the purpose.

"Pick a bag," he said.

After putting the last stack of money on the chart table I went to the locker. Although I still had the grease gun slung over my left shoulder, that didn't seem to bother him. I bent down at an angle where I could keep an eye on him and the guys at the door, even though I wouldn't be able to do much about all of them if anyone decided to get weird; if I was lucky, I could chalk up something on my side of the scoreboard, but they were definitely the heavy favorites.

I rummaged low in the trunk and pulled out what seemed to be three representative bags that I took to the ancient seesaw balance at the far corner of the chart table. I pulled my pack of weights out of the knapsack and stacked a kilo of weights on one side and the first bag on the other. It was over slightly; the other two were under slightly, not enough to be picky about if the contents were half decent. Taking my knife out of its scabbard, I sliced a two-inch gash in the first bag. Then I took the melt-point kit out of the pack and lit the alcohol burner as the captain counted the number of cash stacks and then started flipping through representative stacks. I packed about a quarter gram of the toot into the little glass spoon wired to the metal bulb of the chemical thermometer, and while I dangled the apparatus in the top of the alcohol flame and watched the mercury rise, I took some more toot from the gash in the bag and put it up to my nose. The rush was quick and bona fide and I couldn't detect any speed or baby laxative or butterfly vomit or whatever it was fashionable to toss into it these days. The thermometer would tell the tale, but it was quite possible I was getting Inca Pride brand here, pretty much solid shit without too many alien substances tossed in. I hoped so, because it was what I'd asked for, and Eduardo and I had agreed on the price. If I didn't like the melt point, Cristóbal Colón and I were going to have to start haggling about the price all over again. But things were looking up. The texture was good and my nose kept telling me nice things.

The little glass bulb's contents started to slide down into the bottom in a slightly amberish liquid slag and I took the rig out of the flame. The numbers were pretty close to what I'd expected, close enough to feel pretty pleased and to want to get the fuck off that boat and out of there.

"The money's right," Luis said, and every indication in his voice told me he wanted exactly what I wanted with no additional spicy seasonings. He threw me a roll of gaffer's tape and I taped up the gash on the vinyl bag and put the weights and the test kit back in the pack. Together we started counting out bags and putting them into my nylon duffel bag.

We were mostly done when I heard the puny little horn of the *Kelpie* start to bleat like somebody double-parked who needs to pick up his passenger and get the fuck out of there. I bolted up and Luis did, too, just in time for one of the other crewmen to run up to the door and start to spit out a heavy string of Spanish, of which I caught *Guardia Costal,* which was all I needed to catch. "Eight more, Luis, eight more—I'm taking eight more!"

"Take as many as you want, man—they gonna board us in a minute"—and he was out of the cabin and dashing out to the bridge, which meant I had about one minute to get down the side to the *Kelpie* before I was going to lose my chance to get back to her. I stuffed the bags (okay, a few more than eight) into the duffel bag and hauled ass out of the cabin back to the ladder about eighty feet forward, with the bursting duffel bag and the lightened pack stuffed inside it slung over my back.

The *Kelpie* started honking again. Crewmen were running to stations in all directions, a couple of them bumping into me and slowing me down more than the duffel bag and the grease gun were. Ahead of me I saw a crewman starting to haul in the rope ladder but having a hard time of it and cursing in Spanish over the side. God bless Michael—he must have been holding on to the bottom of the ladder and cursing back. I yelled *Momentito!* at the crewman who looked up at me as he started to unsling his rifle from his shoulder—the cocksucker was thinking about shooting over the side to make Michael let go of the ladder, and beyond him another crewman had already thrown the *Kelpie's* bow line over the side. I pulled my automatic with my free right hand and yelled *Momentito!* again at the man with the rifle and the ladder. He looked up at me. I wasn't pointing the automatic at him, just dangling it visibly in my hand at my side. The chamber was empty and it would have taken me about two or three seconds to chamber a round and make monkey business, but he didn't know that. He assumed I was ready for monkey business now, which gave me a definite advantage over him. That seemed to be the way he saw it, anyway, because he stopped fucking with the ladder and let it hang loose over the side. Nevertheless he was still halfway to a shooting grip on his rifle, and I didn't want him to change his mind about things or decide he was unhappy with me after I was over the side and doing the hand jive on that crummy ladder.

I felt the engines on the freighter bang together. The captain had called for flank speed, and in about thirty seconds it was going to be hell trying to get where I wanted to get with what I wanted to take there. Michael started hitting the horn again down below. I raised the automatic not exactly at the crewman, but chest level to emphasize the advantage I had over him, or the one he thought

I had. The crewman behind him didn't seem to want to be part of any play between us and moved out of the line of my fire without making any funny moves. *Rifle! Rifle!* I yelled at the ladder man and gestured over the side with my .45. He was at least frozen into not making a play for his rifle; it would be tricky, but if we played showdown, I'd probably have time to use my left arm, which was already crimped and stiff under the strap of the duffel bag, to chamber a round in time, just in time, maybe not in time. While he hesitated and Michael honked and the freighter started to pick up speed and—oh, fuck—the Coast Guard cutter kicked in its pursuit sirens out there in the not-too-distance, his face seemed to read that he wanted to come out of this alive and without big holes. I'd edged my back to the rail and stole a peek aft over my shoulder; what bodies I could see didn't seem to care a shit about the little drama at the ladder.

*Rifle,* goddam it!

The ladder man nodded and gently slipped the rifle off the shoulder strap, his hands in all the safe places along the stock and the barrel, and then the sweet, dear, pimply, shit-scared Colombian teenager flung the rifle over the side. It clattered and splashed below and if Michael saw it, that must have given him something to ponder. The kid gave me a sickly little grin after he flung the rifle as if to kiss and make up. That was good enough for me. The crewman behind him was gone, and as I rolled myself over the side, I could hear the noise of the crane working—they were going to try to run and jettison, not that they'd have time to jettison much and not that it would matter, but I guess it gave the crew something to do and feel positive about while they were shitting in their pants.

I was down about three rungs when I heard Michael below screaming over his own and all the other engine and machinery noise. He was still on the lower bridge, loyal to my orders but a shitty place to be for the parallel maneuvers he was having to make to pick me up. I looked above me and the Colombian kid was looking down at me, not menacingly, but waiting for me to free up the ladder that someone had told him to haul in. None of the others running on the mother ship seemed to care about me, thank heaven for small favors.

We must have been doing five or six knots by the time I got

to the bottom of the ladder, which was about level with Michael at the wheel. He was yelling at me. The deck was about a foot and a half away, give or take five feet as the freighter's wake pushed him out and he tried to steer close back to it. I waited for a near pass and heaved the duffel bag with all my might for the aft deck of the *Kelpie—O Jesus God let* anything, anything *go wrong but this toss please please*—and the duffel bag moved out on the arc of its pendulum swing and floated sluggishly and sleepily out over the increasing trough of water between me and the boat. It hit the *Kelpie's* rail with the sickest of cushioning thuds and fucking-A started to teeter and take some time to make up its mind whether or not to go in the drink when all of a sudden something made up its mind for it and it was whipped into the boat and slammed onto the deck—Christ, it was Cowboy Mike with one hand on the wheel and his right hand grabbing for the duffel bag strap, and a good grab, the best ever grab it was indeed.

Both boats were picking up speed and the cutter's sirens were getting louder and rising in pitch. I looked up and I could see the sucker aiming its headlights at us and moving ass from the northwest; we'd all be hugging and kissing and exchanging salty sea stories in what I gauged to be about two and a half, three minutes at the most. The heavy metal frame of the grease gun made for an easier toss to the boat. The bolt was forward, which made it only a little less likely that it would go off if it jarred wrong when it hit the boat; if I'd been smart, I would have dropped it into the water. But I wasn't and I heaved it. It smashed into the deck and didn't make a peep.

I started gesturing to Michael with my free hand to steer the boat hard to port, away from me and the freighter, and although he was looking at me and could see my gestures, it wasn't sinking in, it wasn't making sense. I gestured and yelled more wildly, and finally something clicked and I saw him tug the wheel hard so the boat careened off to port and the gap between me and the boat widened almost instantly—all the water in the world, all the black, unforgiving, cold clutching water I could ever want. I let go of the ladder and tried to turn what followed into something like a dive to give me some distance from the ship, and for a second it felt as if my right foot was going to tangle in the ladder rung—nice feeling—but it didn't. Instantly I was down in the water about four feet below the surface being churned around by the freighter's eddies, trying like hell to get my up-down bearings as my clothes soaked up the death weight of the water. The water wasn't as cold as I thought it was going to feel. That meant if I couldn't keep my head above the peaks, I was going to drown in the inviting, blood-warm water instead.

And then I was above the surface, at least most of the time, and I tried to turn myself around to get my bearings like the centerpost of a washing machine. The noise of the freighter was mostly behind me. Ahead I could see the *Kelpie* standing to with Michael in the stern with a line. He and the line weren't going to make it, but nice try. I waited until a wave wasn't splashing in my nose or my teeth and shouted to him: *Go around! Go around!* This time he could hear better and he dropped the line and made a dash for the wheel. The *Kelpie* jerked forward (Jeez, that boy could be cruel to the transmission, but this was no fucking time to be picky) and started its maneuver. It must have taken about thirty seconds, but then the fucking boat was right alongside, just lolling in the waves. As I started to swim for it, Michael tossed the line from starboard, about from the point behind the wheel where he'd grabbed the duffel bag. Remind me to give this man a raise. I got to the end of the line and grabbed it for sweet life and dear rescue and he started hauling me in. Then there was this sloppy, wet, squishy grabbing of hands and clothes and belts and ass, in the course of which one of my sneakers came off and floated away forever, and at the end of it I felt myself roll over the rail like a sandbag and smash down on the deck, making a dripping pool underneath me.

"Southeast. Southeast. Southeast for all you're fucking worth," I wheezed. He turned away from me and scrambled to the wheel. I could hear the cutter's loudspeaker now reading the abbreviated riot act: *You ships heave to! Halto! This is the Coast Guard! Heave to! Halto . . .* and then the transmission kicked in and General Motors started to demonstrate what it had been born to do as the plane of the boat picked up about ten degrees and the acceleration heaved me back toward the stern about a foot, sliding on my wet and slippery ass. That put me next to the grease gun. I picked it up and looked at it. There was a little dent in the barrel—I'd have to take a fool's chance that it was just cosmetic, something to give it character. I waited until Michael wheeled the boat around at high speed and got to his course; standing up during the maneuver would have been useless and probably dangerous. Then I groped up to the wheel. We weren't even far enough away to show the freighter as much of a blip separate from the center of the display, just a blur that took most of the stern quadrant. The cutter was distinct, clear and closing or at least matching our speed. And that was the whole picture on the radar scope at its short range. I flipped it to long range and that was still the whole picture.

"Where'd the mango boat go off the screen?" I yelled. "I'll kill you if you say you don't know."

"It kept on that due west course. I was good. I watched it."

"You sweet man." I banged him on the back.

"God, you're sopping," he said.

"Thanks for picking me up, uncle. Much appreciated. Hold this course and keep hauling ass." I turned and made my way back to the stern. It was impossible to see what the cutter was doing in the dark because its searchlight was trained on us, but then it swung away and illuminated the freighter. It wasn't heading for the freighter. It was making for us.

That was bad. I estimated it could match our speed close enough to keep us in sight with its radar for as long as it wanted, plenty of time to call for a helicopter or cutter intercept. We outran it by five knots at the most, more likely three. I groped back to the wheel and took it over. I drew some quick cartoons in my head of angles and triangles and turned the wheel some to starboard, to-ward the west, just a few degrees. Then I handed the wheel back to Michael and dragged out the charts. We didn't have time to do this right, but if I was lucky, doing it wrong might get us there just the same.

"Are they going to shoot at us?" Michael asked. "Why the fuck don't they go for the mother ship?" I couldn't tell if he sound-ed panicky or just excited. I liked him better excited, so I decided he was just excited.

"The mother ship's a sitting duck. They can hit that any time in the next hour and it'll still have enough reefer on it to bust all those suckers and seize the ship. They probably have another cutter heading for it now. We're faster—fuck, I don't know why they want us, but they do. I don't think they're going to fire on us. We're out of range and they could hit us. They'd rather not do that. They're going to try to radio for an intercept."

"I notice you ain't surrendering."

"That's very astute of you. No, we're not surrendering. We're running. We're running until they start to shoot to kill and do it accurately, or until there's a boat in front of us and a boat in back of us and two other boats, one on each side of us. And a helicopter on top of us. Or we're running until we get away."

"Look, I don't want to bring you down, but getting away doesn't seem awful likely. Am I allowed to say that, or are you going to get macho and blow my faggot brains out?"

"You're a good faggot," I said, "and I owe you one. I will not blow your brains out. You better be holding that course, sucker."

"I am. What's the plan, Cap'n?"

"If I can figure it out right, we're going to meet an old friend before daylight, I hope to God, and we are going to do something awful." The Loran waveforms were still almost in sync and a little touch on one of the vernier dials had them locked for an accurate position. That was my starting point. "Cut the speed. First black mark from the top."

"Slower?" Michael asked.

"Right on. Trust me."

"Okay. Might as well; can't dance." He didn't sound very happy about it. The engines dropped down a little in pitch and the boat gave a couple of lurches as the hull set a new rhythm through the waves.

"Who's the old friend?" Michael asked.

"I hope to Christ it's mango. He's got to be out there somewhere, bringing in his load of Christmas cheer. Looks to me like we might pick him up on radar in about forty minutes and overtake him in twenty more, I hope."

"What good'll that do?"

"I'm not sure yet. Maybe misery just likes company. By the way, just for grins keep your fucking head down."

## BECKER

**W**e were making a very large, very gradual loop-around that was eventually going to bring us 180 degrees from our starting course or so, to a course of west-northwest. What would have screwed us immediately would have been the cutter trying not to follow us but to cut us off from that course, to half-follow us and half-herd us toward the land where they could radio for state or county boats to look for us when we tried for a marina or a canal. But however they'd known or guessed about the mother ship or maybe about us, they couldn't know what my plans were now (considering I'd just made them up on the spur of the moment), so however odd my course seemed to be, they weren't second-guessing it but kept themselves contented following us, however we zigged or zagged.

I won't say that made me feel good exactly, but it left me with a little hope in the bilge, and that was all I was asking for at the moment. What pissed me off was that we were stuck in the *Kelpie* freaking out over a choice between ditching a behemoth duffel bag of very pure cocaine or getting tagged for about twenty years in the pen each, while to the crew of the cutter, the whole thing up to now was probably no more than a good training exercise, a jolly night out at sea for the regulars and perhaps a few reservists who wanted

**143**

to see what chasing dope villains was really like. They had all the options, or thought they did, and we were just fools making a short dash into a long, drawn-out but still inevitable tag. Maybe so. I thought about Lee and I was damned glad he wasn't aboard. He'd either be trying to surrender, be down below bawling or be pulling a gun on me because his bank's money was about to vanish to the bottom of ten or twelve fathoms of ocean. Which reminded me.

"Michael."

"Yeah?"

"Untie the anchor line from the bow and tie it to the duffel bag. Securely. Keep the whole thing in the stern."

"Oh, shit."

"Just in case of the worst. I don't intend to heave that bag over the side if I can help it. That's why we're running now."

He was in the stern bent over the duffel bag when he looked up and called out to my back.

"Jesus, I've risked my ass just for a little reefer. I don't believe I'm tying an anchor to all this toot. This is the worst thing that's happened all night."

"Can you still unzip it?" I asked.

"Yeah. The rope's tied to the handles."

"You'll find one of the bags inside with a big piece of green gaffer's tape. Pull up the tape and help yourself. Just don't OD. I'm going to need you later, I think."

"Christ, you mean it's all for me?"

"For the moment, yeah. You and I may end up the only two suckers who ever get a taste. When you've had yours, chop some up for me and hit me up. I could use a little, I think."

I heard him unzip the bag and shuffle around inside it, and then I heard the adhesive of the tape give. Looking over my shoulder, I saw him scoop some out of the bag and then seal it with the tape again, salt sea air being anathema to crisp, dry cocaine. Then he came back beside me at the wheel and started to chop the pile up on the dash in the red light. He poured piles on the top of his fist and alternated his nose with mine about five or six times each. By the third hit, the odds weren't better and I wasn't any less worried, yet something seemed to have changed for the better. Couldn't say exactly what it was and I didn't really care. I guess I felt better about going down if I had to go down with a taste of the fruits of my labor in my nose and my bloodstream.

"Nice stuff," Michael said. "Sure hope we get to sell some of it."

"That's still the plan," I said. "You ever been in one of these little sink-the-Bismarck operations?"

"No, thank God. Never even seen the heat out on the waves. There aren't any alleys to duck into at all. I can definitely do without this in the future. You dry yet?"

"Yeah. Not exactly, but it's warm tonight. Look, if I get out of this and all that happens to me is a bad cold, that'll be just fine. Especially if I still have this toot to clear my sinuses."

"You really think we got a chance? I sort of always imagined that once a big official cutter like that set his sights on you, you might as well hang it up."

"All it is is a boat with guns and a lot of radios. We have everything they have, just a lot less of it. Except speed. That we got a little more of. It's evened things out so far."

"But he's got a lot of help. Other boats and planes and helicopters and Anita Bryant if he needs her."

"I don't see any of 'em yet. Nothing's going to show up in the air until daybreak, or unless we make a dash for the coast where they'll be watching for us. But we're not doing that yet, and we have a couple of hours until daybreak."

"You going to tell me what you got planned?"

"Nope. It's nothing you have to get prepared for yet. Just keep watching that radar sweep and let me know if anything else pops up on it in any quadrant."

"Man of mystery," he mumbled.

About a half hour after we'd come about to the west-northwest course, with the cutter still dutifully on our tail—every once in a while she would signal to us with the semaphore blinkers, which I didn't even bother to try to decode—Michael yelled that he thought he saw a little blip coming in ahead of us on the edge of the scope a few points to port. I kept our course until we had the full blip on the scope, which was still on long range. I wanted to make sure it was what I thought it was and not another cutter or the aircraft carrier *Enterprise;* neither of them would do at all for what I had in mind. It looked as if I'd done my trig fairly accurately. The blip size was right and its course and speed—a real crawl, apparently, because I clocked it for five minutes—were right. It pretty much had to be mango. It could have been another boat about the size of a sport fishing boat, but a clean citizen's boat would have been heading out to sea at this hour, not heading back to port.

"I'm going to change course to port in a second," I said, "and then bang this mother into high gear. I don't know how much more speed the cutter can muster, but she'll do it when we make our move, and she may even decide to make her move. We could get fired on from the stern. You still game?"

"Do I really have a choice?"

"Yep. You can go over the stern and I'll give you a flotation device and a good waterproof flashlight. That's about it."

"I'll stick with you, chief. What next?"

"As soon as I'm on course and at full tilt, I'm giving you the wheel. You just stay on course and try not to soil your pants if the cutter tries anything."

I banged the levers back up to maximum and turned the wheel a dozen degrees to port. Although we were both holding on to something, it was still a body rush as the boat chose new and confusing planes and smashed into the waves to a different and more violent tempo. When we'd straightened out again, Michael took the wheel from me. I sat down with my back to the bulkhead next to him and checked out the grease gun.

"I'm going to fire a couple of rounds. Don't freak out."

"Knock yourself out," he said. I pulled the bolt back and fired a short burst of about four or five rounds high over the stern. The gun didn't blow up in my face. I pulled out the other two grease gun clips and stuck them in my belt and then readied the other M-16 the same way. The cutter had turned its sirens back on and was trying to reach us with its searchlight. It seemed to be making more speed, though it was hard to tell. This was its version of trying to scare the shit out of us without actually firing on us. They'd probably try that in a couple of minutes if we started to make distance on them.

When I had the weapons ready, I stood up and checked the radar scope again. I flipped it to short range and stopped sending out our own radar beacon. The mango's blip disappeared, but at her speed I figured we'd sight the boat in the flesh in a twelve-minute run.

The cutter's radar man had probably been relying on our radar beacon to make it easy to follow us and save himself eyestrain, so as soon as I'd flipped it off he'd undoubtedly reported it to the skipper, even though they could still spot us from their own reflected beacon. That told the skipper we were making some kind of heavy move, even if our acceleration and change of course hadn't. Now we were pretty much at the mercy of a couple of random things, the most important of them the skipper's arrogance, how much faith he had in his own ship, in his own brains and ability, in his backup ships and aircraft, and in my inexperience, panic and stupidity. If he thought he had all the cards and I had none of them, then my big move wouldn't bother him much and he wouldn't rethink any of his strategy—just keep steaming after me at full tilt and start yelling into his radio a little louder for the other Coast Guard vessels to intercept me. I was counting on that pretty big, for him to chalk all my moves up to sheer panic with no brains behind them, because if he thought there might be brains behind them, he'd order his gun crew to start slinging shells at me while we were still in some kind of range.

After ten minutes' run at our new course with no visual on the mango boat, I flipped the beacon back on. It would have been damned easy to lose something that small out here in the dark, but in a few seconds I got the blip back and adjusted my course for the final run, which was less than two nautical miles off to the north-west.

"Okay," I said. "Here's what you're going to do. Get up on the flying bridge and take the wheel there, but get ready to duck down. We're going to try to take these suckers by surprise and I'm counting on you to do the fancy steering. We may only get one pass and it's got to be right." When I'd finished filling him in, I held the wheel while he climbed to the flying bridge and took over. Then I crouched down in the stern with the weapons ready.

"They're going to shoot at us. You know that," Michael yelled over his shoulder.

"Yeah, but we know we're going to fire on them right now

and they're going to have to think about it for a few seconds. They don't have radar or they're not using it, so they won't know who or what the fuck we are until we're right on top of them. I think they're loaded to the gunnies with reefer and crawling along at less than half our top speed. They can't outrun us and if they try too many tight maneuvers, they might founder. They're going to be panicky and they're going to be sitting ducks."

"They're still going to shoot, Becker."

"Just get me in there like I said."

"This sucks, Becker."

"I'm open for alternative suggestions," I grumbled.

And then it was there, not running any lights as I'd expected, a sport fisherman about three or four feet longer than the *Kelpie,* making hardly any speed at all and heaving from side to side very low in the water. A minute later, in the cabin's red map light, I could make out a couple of silhouettes moving from side to side and into the stern to see what was coming up on them. Michael held the *Kelpie* to a course off to their port side, straight as an arrow and about six hundred yards away, as if we were just an accidental encounter with no interest in them. That possible explanation wouldn't last long; a boat loaded down with a few hundred thousand dollars' worth of marijuana doesn't believe in accidental encounters. They'd probably be taking aim on us even before Michael made his move. I cradled the M-16 in my right hand with the butt in my shoulder, pulled the charging handle and grabbed something on the side to keep myself from flying around when Michael made his turn.

"Now! Hit it!" I yelled.

When he hit the wheel hard to starboard, the boat veered violently and tried to fling me back toward the stern and up in the air, but I was braced for it. Then I heard distant weapons fire—nothing automatic, thank God. Although I heard something splinter and glass shatter up on the flying bridge, Michael didn't change our maneuver or yell anything. I peeked over the side and saw the mango boat's stern no more than seventy yards away and closing; we'd be within thirty yards when we passed best. I started aiming and then fired, short sweeping bursts of six rounds apiece as near as I could control the trigger. Gunfire was coming back, but still nothing automatic. Though it was focused on me, on the M-16's small flash now, I couldn't change position. I started making the bursts longer as we neared the mango's stern and I didn't even remember changing clips. I let the second clip go almost continuously and then dropped the M-16 and grabbed the grease gun as we pulled away from the mango. I stopped firing before its clip was emptied; we were too far away now. Michael kept on for a couple of hundred yards and then cut to port to parallel the mango boat and not present our stern to her.

"Keep up speed, but circle ahead of her!" I yelled up at him. He yelled back something incomprehensible and started the turn. I watched the mango boat. At first I thought she'd just slowed to keep away from us and present a better position for her riflemen, but she wasn't slowing. She was dead still. I was about to yell up to Michael to cut the engines when I saw the flames in the mango's stern and heard the crew yelling to one another and running around for fire extinguishers. She was without power now, dead in the water. I scrambled up the ladder to the flying bridge and took the controls, back on the course we'd been keeping ahead of the cutter.

"You okay?" I asked.

"I got shot in the leg!"

"Let me see. Can you take the wheel back?"

"Yeah, yeah. It just felt wet after a few seconds. I didn't feel anything, just warm and wet and when I looked down, there was blood all over my trousers. Jesus, that's weird. How bad is it?"

"Well, it can't be too bad or you'd be lying on the deck having a death scene." I took the wheel back and pushed him into the swivel chair. "Can you keep on this course from here?" He reached for the wheel and managed to get a grip on it by leaning forward in the chair. He looked a little tense; if he looked anything beyond that, it was exhilaration. I didn't blame him. It's very exhilarating to realize someone's shot you but hasn't even done enough damage to put you out of action yet. I scrambled down below and brought the first aid kit and a bottle of tequila back to the flying bridge. I stopped halfway up the ladder and looked back. The cutter was approaching the burning mango boat and maneuvering around it. I finished the climb and started working on Michael's leg. After I put a tourniquet on with rubber tubing, I laced a sterile pad with alcohol.

"This is the part where you bite the bullet or pass out. You like tequila?"

"Just do it. I know it's going to hurt, but I'll puke if I get any of that stuff in my stomach."

"Okay." I placed the bandage over the torn-up flesh around the puncture in his calf. He didn't say anything, but a second later I heard something above my head and he came rolling out of the chair and clattered on top of me. I held him up by the chest to keep him from hitting his head. I took the wheel with my left hand and kept it steady while groping with my right hand for an ammonia capsule. I crunched it between my fingers and stuck it under his nose. He did that sort of angel flutter skyward that stuff makes you do and his eyes popped open. Then he turned his head and started to barf. He was holding on to the metal base of the chair and seemed to be going to make it, so I stood up and took the wheel back. I checked my watch. It was twenty minutes after four. We still had the better part of an hour before dawn.

I suppose he flashed in and out of his faint a couple of times between puking, but finally I heard him cough and sputter and catch like a motorcycle engine coming out of long storage.

"What happens now?" he asked from below me.

"We keep on this course until we're out of the cutter's radar range. Then we make a radical change for some other part of the coast. They're out of the chase now. They got a whole boat full of reefer that's on fire to take care of. How's your leg?"

"It hurts like piss."

"That's good. I don't think you've got a slug in there. I think it went out. We can check better when it's daylight."

"I don't mind saying I'm a bit worried. I was hoping we might get a doctor to look at this."

"I'll call for a Coast Guard rescue if I think you're going to stiff out on me," I said. "That's a promise. In the meantime, you're being looked after by a guy who was supposed to become a world-famous brain surgeon."

"That's great. We still got the toot down there, right?"

"Yeah, but maybe you ought to lay off it for now. Get some sleep if you can."

"Oh, I don't want any of it," Michael said. "I just wanted to know it was still with us."

"That part of the plan is still going our way."

"Far out," he sighed. He lay back against the side and tried to get comfortable and close his eyes while I steered by the binnacle. I was going to make the new maneuver in about twenty minutes. Then I could wake him up and cart him down below so I could do some final checking on the charts.

# BECKER

**T**he best I can figure is that the Coast Guard and all those badass antidrug superheroes tried squares C-8, D-9 and E-10 while we were on G-6, H-7 and I-9. Or maybe they weren't even playing anymore. Michael was sleeping down below when I sighted land around six in the morning. I'd been at the wheel the whole time and I was so spaced I didn't have the energy to figure out what the coastal landmarks were. We were heading west and I was pretty goddam sure it was North America, and if that part was true, all the little details were just fine with me, whatever they turned out to be. I cut the engines down to a troll and went down below to sit on the edge of the bunk. After a few seconds, Michael sensed I was there and started to come around.

"How goes it, Cap'n?" he asked as he sat up in the bunk.

"I don't know how to break this to you. It looks like we're home free. We're some ways southeast of the Grove, just below Key Biscayne. I want to hold here for now and blend in with the fishing boats that'll start to come out soon. We'll start running lights as soon as we see a few of them. Later, maybe nine or ten, we can make for Dinner Key. I can drop you off there so you can scare us up some transportation. You think you can hobble around on shore?"

"Doubtful, Cap."

"Okay. You can stay with the boat, then. You'll drop me off and make for the bay again—as if I just wanted to take a leak or I got seasick or something. I'll get a car and you can come back in about an hour. I think we can take care of your leg pretty well at your place."

"I sure as hell hope so. I don't mean to complain, but it doesn't seem to be getting much better."

"Well, you did get shot in it, for Christ's sake. That's the whole idea of shooting people."

"You can tell those guys on the mango boat that it worked pretty well," he said.

I went topside and steered the *Kelpie* to a spot that seemed about right for day fishermen and dropped anchor. Because of all the mist, I decided to fuck it and trip the running lights rather than wait for other boats to come around. We were too close to a safe finish to fuck up by getting ourselves rammed and sunk accidentally. Just for appearances I set up some tackle in one of the fishing chairs and dangled a line overboard. Then I went below again to cook up some canned soup and split it with Michael.

He'd started to run a little fever, so there was probably an infection going on, but he was pretty close to getting somebody to look at it who knew what he was doing, unlike me. I was just the skipper. I got a passing grade just for bringing him back alive. Stopping infections wasn't part of my responsibilities. Maybe next time we'd ship out with a medical officer. Maybe a nurse who could do double duty. Maybe I'd get smart and not ship out at all next time—just stay at home with the nurse. I could always go on a crash program to try to get myself something approaching mental health.

Michael hobbled up the companionway after me and settled himself in one of the fishing chairs. I turned on the AM radio to a rock station that had half-hour news reports; the first couple of times they rolled around, they didn't have anything that sounded like a search for us. The mango boat getting caught adrift and on fire with a whole bunch of reefer made it as a brief item, but the Coast Guard wasn't saying anything about the one that got away. Another cutter had interdicted the mother ship and she was under escort, heading for the rusting reefer ship graveyard at Government Cut.

Just because they weren't making news about us, however, didn't mean we weren't still a hot property. Getting the dope and the guns and Michael ashore was going to be very skittish. Since the cutter had a pretty good description of our configuration, by now state boats and harbormasters would be keeping an eye out for us as part of the daily routine. Although I changed some of the configuration with the awnings off the flying bridge and stowed the radar scoop and some of the extra antennas down below, we still had the same length and hull. Of course the *Kelpie* was similar to a hell of a lot of other craft around these waters, and that was what I was counting on. I debated jettisoning the weapons, but decided to hold on to them. If I wasn't going to heave the coke overboard, why ditch the weapons? It was either all going to come down on our heads or we were going to miss it all; there wasn't going to be any middle mix. Once they sentenced us for that much toot, they probably wouldn't even go hard for the weapons violations. Besides, if I was going to hold on to my .45, it made no difference if I kept the rest of the armory, too. I unloaded everything but the pistols, though. The judge might think that was a civilized touch.

I pumped some cans of orange juice into Michael while we waited for the morning sun to come up and burn off the fog. I'd doubled the dose of codeine pills. He didn't seem to be in agony as long as he didn't have to shake his leg much. We didn't have much to say as the hours went by and other boats started puttering out past us. We'd wave at them listlessly if they waved at us. Michael just seemed to be holding on and holding out. It must have been pretty bizarre to him that we were really this close to coming ashore with a duffel bag filled with the Andes' finest, and he was doing a damned good job of biting the bullet to bring us all the way home. He had no more questions to ask and I had no more answers to give. From this point, everything was either already clear or had to be played by ear. There weren't any more grand stratagems to cook up. I was already out of my element and reduced to letting chance take a raw roll at us. I hated that. I figured that if you don't have anything going for you but raw luck, then you don't really have anything going for you at all, but I could do nothing at this point

to freshen the odds. We were just one more pair of assholes hoping
for a natural, no smarter or better prepared than any other pair of
assholes. Dangerous David Becker and Michael the Fearless Faggot
were just Laurel and Hardy now, and whatever was going to happen to us was up to the screenwriter, and maybe his mistress was
on the rag last night.

Around eight I gauged that the activity at Dinner Key Marina
would be about as heavy as it was going to get by the time we
reached it on a straight run from where we were anchored, so I
hauled in the anchor and Michael's bogus fishing line and kicked
over the engines. I knew the waters and the markers pretty well in
the Bay, so we had the slight advantage of not appearing to be
totally lost in the waters. After we rounded the state park on Key
Biscayne, we cut roughly north through the lower bay, adjusting
the course to run parallel to most of the other boat traffic, even
though most of them were headed out to sea. I made for the docks
closest to Miami City Hall because they were farthest away from the
harbormaster's office and were the ones other boats made for just
to put someone ashore before heading out in the Bay again.

I was right about the peak traffic; it was pretty epic by the time
the docks were in sight, and having to yield to a few hundred
sailboats that were trying to Captain Hornblower it out to sea
without their put-puts was pretty nerve-racking. Michael, hobbling
to the wheel as we negotiated toward the dock, said he'd give it the
old Coconut Grove try to steam out again after he dropped me off.
I had it all in the duffel bag, ready to jump with it, Lady Luck's
choice: either the start of a very prosperous and carefree existence
if I got to the street unchallenged or the end of the line if anybody
in authority asked, *Hey son I'd like to take a look in that bag.*

A couple of hours ago, the stars and the chicken entrails had
been right for fighting and wild dashes, bizarre schemes and desperate remedies, but now, as Michael turned the boat around and
headed back for the open Bay and I hefted the duffel bag up on my
shoulder, all the signs pointed to a quick and cooperative surrender
if anyone in a uniform asked for a little inspection. The time was
definitely not ripe for desperate ad-libbing with wildly aimed fusil-
lades and defiant exclamations as innocent bystanders thrust baby
strollers out of the line of fire and dove behind ash cans. Not in the

proverbial broad daylight, with no dependable mode of fast transportation at the end of a few hundred yards of narrow and wobbly
floating barrel pontoon dockage, and not with me hunkered down
under a sack that easily tipped it at sixty pounds.

No, in case of the eventuality, the order of drill was to put the
duffel bag down and get with the program straight up to the one
free phone call, lame as it sounded. Logistically there was no problem. I looked harmless enough, and even if some cop thought the
bag might have contraband, he'd probably go through the initial
stages of the confrontation mellow and unarmed. Plenty of time to
reach for the Army monster in my pants and get off one or two that
would put me way ahead in points. That would leave me staring at
about fifty witnesses, strolling tourists and Grove residents—about
five percent of whom probably knew my name—after the act of
blowing a cop away successfully.

From there, it had to be all downhill and beyond even my
creative capacity for broken-field running. First off, I'd find myself
fresh out of friends who had anything more than blunt advice which
they'd prefer not to have to deliver to me face to face. More than
that, even surrendering after killing a cop becomes a very hairy
business because the late officer's brother policemen feel such an
individual has already more than bagged his quota and take great
pains to make sure he doesn't get a second opportunity, even if he
has a change of heart and wants to turn himself in to his Father
Confessor posthaste. If the cop-snuffer manages to make it home
free to police headquarters in one piece in his lawyer's tow—well,
one never knows precisely how the wheels of justice will spin
during the year or so that follows, what with appeals and retrials
and earthquakes and whatever, but the odds are heavy that those
wheels won't land a cop-killer anywhere pleasant. Free trip to Dis-
ney World for two just isn't on that spinner, nor is a date with Cher
likely to pop up in the cards when it's all said and done. But it was
time to walk down the dock and take my chances. I was one very
nervous lad. I was about ready to let a uniformed Boy Scout with
a water pistol put the cuffs on me and lead me away.

*So pal what you do under these circumstances is you just walk.
You just squint your eyes and try to find the muscles that keep your
sphincter tight and clench your teeth until the roots are sticking out*

*of the jawbone on the underside and you walk straight ahead. Don't you look to the left, don't you look to the right. Try to think of happy thoughts, like a world temporarily bereft of policemen—all taking the day off, all at the annual picnic, all helping with the Toys for Tots drive, just for today, just for right now. You walk. You don't even think about how fucking heavy the duffel bag on your shoulder is. Jesus, you don't even let that cross your mind, even if you have to shlep anvils the length of nine football fields. And as boaters pass you on the dock and look you over wondering what a slimeball from Mars like you is doing strolling down the dock where all the ritzy yachts are moored, and as they wonder what's in the bag on your shoulder—liberated silverware, possibly, or little girl baby parts or perhaps even machine guns and bunches of cocaine—as you get these stares and evaluations and speculations you pay them absolutely and deeply no fucking never-mind whatsoever, like Christ enduring the jeers of the crowd on the way up that mountain, Christ with his cross, you with your comparable load of coke and stolen Army weapons. You keep walking and hope that as curious as the crowd becomes, as big a splash as you seem to be making, you hope that everyone continues to let you by, thank'ee, let the man pass, man's got business on shore, man's got to be in church for noon mass, please let me by, thank you.*

*And by cracky, they do let the man pass. He makes it to the concrete docks. The parking lot comes into view and it seems devoid of anything resembling the Justice Department Strike Force or even Officer Dan Your Safety Patrol Advisor. A quick peek down the dock to the left and Lo! No one's doing anything more alarming down at the harbormaster's shack than kicking the Coca-Cola machine. No officials running your way with a clipboard or a questionnaire. No Hare Krishnas trying to sell you flowers. No Scientologists trying to make you clear.*

*To the left of the parking lot was a harborside green where Grovies were tossing the Frisbee, riding bikes and jogging along the little asphalt path, and in general not giving a flying fuck about me or my duffel bag. Jesus, they weren't even noticing how goddam heavy it was, not that I wanted anybody to give me a hand with the sucker: Thank you, I'll handle it myself, thanks anyway. Mmmmboy would some of those guys and gals like to know what's in the bag and mmmmboy could we arrange a real strange little scene down in the Dinner Key park this jolly morning if one of those goatfuckers decided to make a play for the goods.*

*But no one does. You grunt on.*

*And then you are there, on the sidewalk of South Bayshore, watching a shitload of last-minute morning rush-hour traffic negotiate its way north, ever northward, toward downtown Miami and the punch clock (Punch clock! Smash that fucker!) and coffee and the paper and the funnies and that spunky new secretary who wears the shattering barrier of Sears La Femme heavy-duty cologne to complement a set of glands under a décolletage that could start a scandal on Romper Room. Northward, ever workward. And as I watched it and wondered how many seconds I had left until I started to reel and buckle to the sidewalk, a taxicab swerved into the rightmost lane about eight feet ahead of me and spat out a lovely little lady, possibly a clerk up the street at city hall, and as she leaned through the passenger window and conducted the fare and tip negotiations at length, I felt my eyes start to go moist and my throat start to choke up and I heard Joan of Arc and General George Patton and Jiminy Cricket all whispering in my ear in unison, imbibing me with encouraging words—no, it was Knute Rockne at halftime, taking time out from an important game in the Heavendome to inspire Me and fill my spirit up with ethereal Gatorade for that one extra point attempt that he knew I still had in me.*

"Taxi!" I croaked, and it was an awful sound, entirely unlike what I'd hoped it would sound like. But it did the trick. The cab waited for me as I hoisted the bag one more time and started diddybopping up the sidewalk for the rear door handle.

# Part Three

# LAUGHS WITHOUT END

# BECKER

**T**he cab driver was a young guy from the Dominican Republic who wanted to talk about sailing with me in Spanish or English or whatever mix we could agree on, but I guess that after I'd established that I could whip out a little Spanish, I must have established that I didn't really want to talk about sailing or much else. All I really wanted to do was to fall asleep in the back of the cab. Every minute or so I punched myself in the thigh so it wouldn't happen. He wheedled his way up Bayshore to Biscayne Boulevard and dropped me off at the bus terminal.

I didn't want to go straight to Lee's or to Richard's motel with all the weird shit in the duffel bag until I knew things were copacetic all around. I would have preferred storing the bag at the airport, but they'd taken the pay lockers out of there after a few mad bomber types had used them for ground zero at some airport recently. The bus terminal would do just as well. Besides, I was looking a little on the scruffy side by this time, and where I'd stick out at Miami International, I'd fit in just fine at the bus terminal and probably even be among the better dressed types there. A nice duffel bag box was available at floor level; I stowed the bag inside, plunked in the two quarters and took the key. Don't lose that key.

When I tried to rouse Richard at the motel from a pay phone, the clerk said he was still registered but there was no answer in the room. I left a message that Dave had arrived safely and would try to contact him later in the day. I imagined that Richard was taking one of his rare shots at freaking out about now. Although I could have reassured him at sea because we'd agreed that he'd stand by the CB frequency every couple of hours, things had been so bizarre getting our asses back in one piece that I hadn't wanted to break radio silence.

It boiled down to an item that was really disturbing the piss out of me about now, and that was whether the Coast Guard had stumbled on us and the mother ship by accident or by design. God knows that was their job, to hunt creeps like us on the high seas, and it was quite likely they could have dropped in on us as they had just by chance. But it was also possible they'd been tipped off. A lot of folks were connected with a mother ship run up the East Coast, and as much as I'd tried to pare down our end of the business, that didn't have much effect on all the other customer boats or the mother ship crew. Some poor asshole with five years in the can hanging over his head could have popped up as an informer anywhere in this intimate and greedy little crowd. Or someone on my end could have been picking up the phone and asking information for the number of the DEA or the Coast Guard. If it *was* a tip and not just a surprise encounter. It had happened, that was the piss-poor part. If we'd just sailed out to the mother ship, done our business and dashed back to a safe port uneventfully, I wouldn't have to worry about whether someone had tipped off the feds about us or not. But the feds had been there just at the wrong time and had chased our sorry asses all over the fucking ocean, and I couldn't help spinning my wheels about that kind of provocative incident.

And I wasn't just thinking about some vague kind of revenge. We had a hell of a long way yet to go in this deal, and I had to know whether I stood an even chance of pulling the rest of it out of the bag or whether things were still seriously stacked against us, whether there was daylight ahead or whether we were just pathetic slobs going through the hopeless motions while a squad room full of DEA creeps checked their watches and played pinochle until it was time to pull the plug on us. Of course that was exactly what I wasn't going to be able to find out until it was too fucking late to do anything about it.

But even if someone on our end was tipping off the enemy, we still had a chance because since the big victory at sea, I'd been playing everything by ear and making up my next moves as we went along. Nobody could know where we'd be or go with the coke at any particular time, because now even I didn't know until I absolutely had to make a decision. What plans we'd made when we'd started out had all been flushed down the toilet, shot to shit, and if everything since then was a surprise to me, that meant it was an even bigger surprise to anyone trying to crash our party.

Everyone always complained about me being tight-lipped and secretive. Well, fuck 'em. My way was right and their way was wrong, and the proof of the pudding was in the snorting and the spending. All I had to do was to bring it off. No big deal. One of my people with a hole in his leg, another on the perpetual verge of schizing out, a third wondering where the hell his pals had disappeared to during the last few hours, and the whole business going down in a wicked, wicked world filled with greedy fuckers who'd snuff us for the time of day and a heavily armed battalion of cop types. No big deal. I'd have us all home by Christmas.

I was dialing Lee's house in the Grove when I found myself hanging up the pay phone and making another of those ad-lib decisions to keep everybody guessing. Suddenly I didn't want to call Lee's house. I wanted to go there in person and eyeball things myself; a phone call just wouldn't do. Big purely intuitive move. I bought myself a cold can of soda and went out into the sunlight on Biscayne Boulevard to hunt up another cab.

This time the driver was a New York retiree honky, and neither of us had much to say to one another besides destination and fare details. He let me off a couple of blocks from Lee's house at a convenience store, and after he'd driven away, I started walking through the side streets, exciting a few dogs and tropical birds. I approached the house from a narrow overlook by a bend in the canal below it that gave me a pretty good distant view of the back and the swimming pool area.

Used plates and cups were strewn on the poolside table and a towel was draped over one of the chairs. I didn't see anyone. I dropped down to the squat and waited, but not for long. In a few seconds, Laura broke the surface of the pool from what must have been a long underwater length, and in one motion she grabbed the edge of the pool and swung herself up and into a sitting position. She was wearing cutoffs but no top, and she pushed her black, long hair back out of her face and over her shoulders where the dripping water started making streams on her back. She soaked up the sun in that position for a couple of minutes as if Pandora hadn't yet opened her box to fill the world with its petty annoyances and troubles. She looked good, that was for fucking sure, and I suppose that for a good couple of minutes, especially in my fatigued state, I felt a lot of the things that had Richard and Lee both careening around South Florida like crazy people for the last couple of years.

She looked good, but not there. Sitting on the edge of Lee's pool without a care while I was having a fuck of a time getting some very important business together that involved Lee, among other people, she looked lousy, like the major item in the drawing above *What's wrong with this picture?* She was wrong with this picture, and so was the absence of Lee. She reached for the towel and started rubbing herself down lightly. Then she stood up and put on a t-shirt she found on a chair and walked into the house.

For an instant I felt myself shift from Captain Commando on his recon mission to Victor the Voyeur getting his rocks off from behind the bushes. Same stance, same eyes, same guy, but the subject, as she showed her back to me and walked through the open patio doors, made all the difference. Lee loved to squire her around town and to take her down to Key West on weekends when he thought his island pals hadn't seen anything to arouse their envy and their glands in the last month. He showed her off like a pet pink poodle on a leash or like his Mercedes. It didn't sit that way with me. It looked like the boy actually had a very large and very mean snow leopard on the other end of a very flimsy Hartz Mountain leash, and if it wasn't devouring him then and there it was only because by a slim coincidence the cat had just eaten fifty pounds of red meat and wasn't interested in any more. She was feline in that respect, purring in response to all the good food and good money and good drugs Lee always supplied her with, but always a microsecond away from swiping at his eyes with razor claws. When that happened, whether it took five minutes or five years, he wouldn't have a fucking prayer, but it wasn't any of my goddam business to try to slip the word to him. On that score and several dozen more he was one very thick lad. Cornell, would you believe, but that wouldn't help when the time came; he still wouldn't have a fucking prayer.

I walked over to the street corner down the block from the front gate of the house to see if anyone was coming in or out. I waited there for a long time, a half hour or so, every once in a while going back to the canal overlook, but there was no movement at the gate or back at the pool. Once I thought I heard Lee's phone ringing with no one answering it, but the sound could also have come from the two houses between me and Lee's; I couldn't be sure. Then a car turned the far corner onto Lee's street and parked across the street from his gate, and R.J. rolled out of the driver's door and headed for the gate. It wasn't locked, because he simply pushed it open and went inside.

Lee was very big about locking the gate at all hours, to keep the riffraff out as much as a lousy wooden gate could keep riffraff out. It was a great neighborhood for rip-offs, being only a couple of blocks away from the downtown Grove with all its transient scuzzes, all of whom knew that every house in Lee's neighborhood was dripping with great stereos and only the finest toot and reefer. A couple of more things were wrong with this picture. Of course I was feeling pretty paranoid about everything along about then, but I didn't give a fuck about that. Paranoid was a great way to feel on a day like that and I intended to keep feeling that way until Lee showed up and put on his best act to convince me that the kids had just dropped by for the hell of it and that all was sweetness and light on the home front.

Nobody came out, front or back, for about twenty minutes after R.J. went in. A parrot somewhere was screaming raucous and incomprehensible bird obscenities—Christ, I hated those useless animals, even the ones that could recite Keats—and cars breezed by every once in a while along the wider through streets at either end of Lee's block, visible only for an instant through the breaks in the landscaped jungles that kept the residents private and unseen. I toyed with the idea of walking down to Lee's gate and peering through and trying to listen to what might be coming from the house. That, however, was a pretty good way to get some neighbor to call the cops. Where I was, I was just a pooped-out jogger, a pretty standard item so long as I kept away from any particular house. I also thought of slinking on down to the canal, diving in and swimming up to Lee's backyard to peer over the low brick edge, but I wasn't feeling much like Captain Commando at the moment. It occurred to me, though, that if R.J. came out and drove off, his car was pointed toward my corner, so I checked out a nice bush behind which to step in that eventuality.

That eventuality materialized. The man himself emerged, a beer in his hand and Laura at his side, and crossed to the car. He was most of the way to the driver's side when he stopped, because Laura had stopped. I heard them exchange a few words I couldn't make out, and then R.J. backtracked and, blow me down, opened the passenger door for Laura while she graced herself in. That was something you didn't see much of these days, and I remembered Richard grousing about it one night when he was unusually pissed off at the lady—*She wants people to open the fucking door for her*, was the way I think he'd put it, less from annoyance than from an honest sense of stupefaction, *so I open the door for her. Otherwise we just stand there for an hour and nobody goes anywhere.* Well, now I'd seen it for myself, so I certainly couldn't write the whole day off as a total loss. Then R.J.—who didn't seem ticked off by it at all, only reminded of something like checking the air in the tires—walked back to the driver's door, got in, started the engine and headed straight for me, while I did my disappearing act behind the appointed bush. He took a right at the corner, toward Tigertail and away from me.

When the car was out of sight, I came out from the bushes and walked down toward the front gate. It was still unlocked and I went in, jingling the little brass bell above it. The house was open and seemed deserted. I stood in the foyer, which wasn't catching any sun at all at that hour and was strangely dark, darker somehow than it seemed when I walked through it at night, even without the overhead recessed lights on; they were on now, as if someone had forgotten to turn them off from the night before.

I stood in the foyer to listen for sounds: breathing, a shower, a clock radio cranking out a tinny tune, but the only sounds came from the patio leaves swooshing and swaying against each other if a little breeze came up and the repetitive lapping of the waves in the pool on the other side of the house. I strolled in that direction first for no particular reason, maybe just because it was sunny and warm there and I wanted to be sunny and warm again. I could see palmetto bugs swarming over the plates on the poolside table and then I could see into the pool. The pool wasn't very clear and the sun's angle made it hard to see below the surface anyway. After I adjusted my eyes to the difficulties, I could see the shape of a man at the bottom of the pool, a naked man, his back and buttocks aimed my way, his face turned down. He seemed to be leaning upward to the surface, in no hurry to get there, as if he enjoyed sitting on the bottom. Where his feet were grazing the bottom, I saw a square, gray object and a thin cord or rope connecting his feet with the object. It was a cinder block on its side. I walked around the side of the pool and even though I still couldn't see much of the face under the floating hair, it was Lee. From under his stomach, which hid his hands, I could see a free-floating end of the same kind of cord. There weren't any bubbles coming from his head. He wasn't twitching or turning. He was just suffering that old chlorinated sea change, aiming as best as he could for the sun and the sky. He reminded me a little of that good old statue of Jesus in the underwater scuba-diving park at the top of the Keys, a sweet, friendly, robed Jesus with his arms outstretched for the surface and the sky. Underwater Jesus. Cinder block Lee.

I wanted to sit down by the side of the pool then and think about people who liked to swim in pools like that, but the phone began to ring from inside the house and I started walking in that direction. On the way, I saw the patio extension on its side, its receiver off the hook, and the long cord that connected it to the jack just inside the house was missing. I followed the sound of the ringing into the kitchen and picked up the receiver off the wall. Though I wasn't thinking too well, it flashed to me that R.J., whom I didn't really want to speak to, was probably still on the road, so it had to be somebody else. Maybe I wouldn't want to speak to that person either, but I seemed to want to give it a shot. I grunted into the phone.

"Lee?" It was Richard.

"No. It's me, Becker."

"Jesus! Where the hell have you been? Are you okay?"

"Yeah. Where are you?" I asked.

"I'm at the motel. What's going on?"

I sighed and looked back toward the pool. I couldn't see into it from that angle. That was fine.

"Bad things . . ." I stopped and sighed again. "Bad things are happening. Never mind what now. Clear out of the motel as fast as you can and get up to Lowry's Marina in the North Miami Cut. Do you know where it is?"

He started to blubber a lot of questions. I cut him off. "Just do it. Michael's steering the *Kelpie* up there. He should get there sometime in the next hour. He's hurt. He's going to need help. I tried to get you earlier."

"Did you get the action?"

"Yeah. It's safe. But there's trouble. I can't talk about it now. Get out of the motel and get up to the marina. I'd rather have the boat there than at a public marina. Have Lowry put it up in dry dock and have him fix the panels on the flying bridge. You'll see what needs to be fixed. But just get out of the motel and don't go back. Go to the marina. And watch your ass."

"Where's Lee?"

"Look, do what I told you and I'll meet you—shit, I'll meet you in the Rascal House parking lot at noon. If you can't meet me there, meet me at the Versailles tonight at midnight. Just be very careful, pal, whatever you do."

"Okay. Yeah. See you then."

"Hey. Did Lee know where you were staying?"

"Nope."

"Score one for our side, maybe. Look, I got to tell you. It's R.J. and . . . just watch out for R.J. and stay away from Laura, okay?"

"What happened?"

I couldn't deal with the phone anymore, so I hung up. I forced myself to stand there for a minute thinking what I'd touched or what possible traces of myself I might have left. Just the phone, which I wiped off with a paper towel that I pocketed, and about a half hour's glimpses of me skulking around the street that I'd provided for the neighbors if they were interested. It was stupid as fuck to have wiped down the phone. My fingerprints and probably my name and number and a couple of old pairs of Jockey shorts, maybe even with my summer camp name tag sewn in them, were all over that house, and fuck if I was in the mood to play cleaning lady and go over the joint with a bottle of Lestoil now. I was hot meat for this trip when the electric meter reader finally dropped by and blew the whistle, but the trick now was to keep all our asses safe long enough to worry about that problem. Things were coming apart like the wonderful one-hoss shay, and me chief among them. I needed to get out of there and find myself some sanctuary.

I pulled the .45 out of the back of my trousers and checked the magazine: full and true. Then I primed a round into the chamber, just to feel as weird as my surroundings, weirder if possible. And then I strolled down the walk to the front gate, strolled merrily through it and onto the street, and then strolled out of the neighborhood, heading for Dixie Highway.

I caught a northbound bus that looped back into the Grove again, but well away from Lee's neighborhood, on its way into downtown. I'd taken it once before when I'd been staying with Lee without a car or a bike. It was fairly empty. I sat well in the back for no particular reason that made any sense and concentrated on trying to stay awake. The bus driver was shouting at me, not too unfriendly, when I woke up with the bus parked in front of the Sears on Biscayne Boulevard, the end of the line. I gave him a little Boy Scout salute and shook myself out of the seat and out the rear exit. I didn't want to ask him any questions, so I checked out the other bus stops around there until I found a route that went farther north and crossed over to the Beach on the Venetian Causeway. Because the bus wasn't there yet and I didn't just want to lounge around, I went into the Sears and bought a new pair of jeans—the kind they were selling then that were already broken in and even a little faded—and a new shirt I thought would look nice for my arrest and arraignment. Then I went downstairs and bought a razor and some shave foam and a hairbrush. I took my shopping bags across Biscayne to the new park and found the men's room, where I shaved and put the new clothes on. The old ones I put back in one of the bags, and I threw the shaving kit away. Although I still felt like hell, by the time I finished brushing my hair, I didn't look quite as much like Charlie Manson or Richard Speck, and there was a chance I might be mistaken for a solid citizen for the rest of the day.

I was only a couple of blocks from the bus terminal, but there was no reason to go back there now. What was there would keep, and keep better there than anywhere else in Miami at the moment. I double-checked to make sure I'd transferred the locker key to my new jeans; I had. I walked back across the street and caught the bus to the Beach.

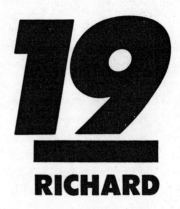

# RICHARD

**M**arching orders under strange circumstances.

What the hell, they were marching orders, and they seemed to have some firecracker burning behind them. Becker speaks and I obey. Besides, he said Michael was hurt, and I was the medic appointed to rescue the lad. I was pissed that Becker wouldn't stay on the phone to give me some details, but even over the phone I could scope out that he was pretty frazzled. Anyway, he said the goods were home and safe, so how bad could everything else be?

Pretty bad. He didn't have to tell me to stay away from R.J. or Laura, not while the deal was going down. Becker must have meant that one or both of them was poking around in our pie somehow, maybe working on Lee. Maybe R.J. had dropped by and sneezed, making Lee fall down on his knees sobbing to confess. Jesus. What pissed me off now was that if Becker said things were bad, they were bad. Why wouldn't he tell me how bad they were? I mean, on a scale from one to a hundred, did we have a 20 situation, which would have been bad enough, or a 50, or a three-alarm 95? No telling, just pack up, get out of the motel, and zip on over to the marina to pick up my fallen comrade.

It was going to take me two trips to load everything into the truck with both hands full each time, which is what made it so easy for the geek who was waiting for me down below in the parking lot. As I started to dump the electronic gear behind the cab seat, I thought he was just somebody at the motel busying himself in the trunk of his own car. A second later I felt a body pressing me up against the truck and a gun in the small of my back. He had a Cracker accent.

"Pick up that shit and let's go back to your room, dipshit," he said. He sounded a little weird. Hard juice, it sounded like. "Give me any crap and I'll blow a fucking hole in your back." Something about his manner and his voice and his phrasing reminded me of boot camp. I tried to remember what he'd looked like before I'd turned my back on him. He hadn't made a hit with me: skinny, red-necky clothes, interest in building a set of muscles that weren't ever going anywhere, just good enough for a few veins to stick out so he wouldn't look like a wimp down at the local pool hall. Crewcut. As he jacked me up against the truck I could smell butch wax mixed with some kind of aftershave that I'd used when I was fifteen because someone had given it to me for Christmas.

I picked up the bags and walked back to the stairs and up to the second deck of rooms. Without turning around, I unlocked the door to my room and went in. I heard him kick the door shut behind us and then felt a foot smash into the back of my thigh just above the knee. I should have expected something like that, but what could I have done about it if I had? I went sprawling toward the can in pain and off balance, slamming my shoulder into the end of one of the beds. Before I could move, he was down on his knees with the gun pressed behind my ear. He did a number all over me with his free hand and pulled the .45 out of my waist and slid it away. Then he pounded me on the side of the head with the barrel of his pistol. I rolled over, pretending it hurt a lot more than it did as an excuse to crawl away from him a little.

Slumped against the end of the bed, I looked up at him for the first time. He had one of those Dirty Harry overkill pistols in his small hand, and he watched me as he rummaged through the first of the bags with his free hand. He dropped each piece of equipment noisily on the floor as he peered at it and dismissed it. Too bad. With a little luck, the dude might have been a crazed radio equipment thief. No such luck, and he wasn't making like a cop, either. Cop gun, cop haircut, cop or lifer manner, but I was pretty sure by this time that I would have heard just a little something from him about an arrest. Not the whole Miranda card or the Declaration of Independence, but cops usually aren't shy about telling you they're cops.

"You got cocaine. A lot of it. Give it to me," he said. He leveled the revolver between my eyes and pulled back the hammer.

"I don't have it," I said.

"Okay, where is it?"

"Somebody else has it. I don't know where he is. I don't know where the toot is."

"Bullshit. I'm just going to blow you away."

"Look—don't, please."

"Listen, dipshit, I'm going to get that coke. If I don't get it or get a line on it fast, I'm going to waste you. That's the deal."

I was staunching the blood from my temple. It was warm and I could feel it gooing up the hair that fell over my forehead.

"Maybe he'll come here," I said.

He got angry and jumped up and danced around with the gun over me. "What the fuck do you mean, maybe he'll come here? Is that the best you can come up with, dipshit?"

"It's the best I can do, man," I said. "I swear. I don't know where he is."

"You were leavin'. Where were you going?"

"I talk to him over those radios. I was going out to try to make contact with him. He's on a boat."

"BullSHIT! BullSHIT! He's back and the goddam drugs are back and you're giving me a bunch of SHIT!"

And then he shot me. The barrel jumped up toward the ceiling and I heard a godawful boom and smelled that shitty firing-range smell instantly up both nostrils, and then I felt something like one of those logs the Vikings used to batter down a castle door smashing into my right side. I toppled over sideways between the beds.

I could still see him. What had happened seemed to shock and startle him and even dismay him more than it had me. He did this frantic little mambo, looking all over the room, and then ran for my automatic on the floor, grabbed it, and bolted out of the motel room door, leaving it swinging open behind him.

Parts of me I couldn't feel at all, as if I didn't have tissue there of my own—just filler like sawdust and some kind of synthetic hide that had no nerve endings but just kept me together. While I stayed awake, I didn't have that much pain. I was sure I could talk and reason and explain things and give descriptions and advise the ambulance crew. The telephone was on the table between the beds, and it occurred to me to make for it while I still had a chance. Something was going on with my legs—no coordination—and then they stopped trying to do anything functional altogether and just balled up into the fetal position. I reached my arm out to the phone, but I was miles away from a grab. Then I remember getting really light-headed, feeling I didn't weigh anything anymore, breathing very fast, and over the dry mouth I'd been tasting since the guy had first stuck the gun in my back, this beautiful Waikiki surfing wave of nausea came over me. My mind filled with dozens of rapid, helpful thoughts: 911 is the emergency number; please have someone pay my motel bill; take me to the VA hospital instead of a private hospital so I won't run up a big bill; if a guy named Dave calls, tell him I couldn't make it to the marina. I never got to tell any of them to anyone.

## BECKER

**F**eeling like death warmed over, I made it to the bus stop across the street from Rascal House with about twenty minutes to spare. I had a sixth sense that things couldn't possibly be going much better on Richard's northern leg of the great adventure than they'd been going for me in the south of town. Chalking it up to epic fatigue, the life of crime I was leading this week, too much real good toot, watching Lee checking out the pool surface from the wrong direction and the fitful kind of sleeping that goes with riding local buses, I still couldn't shake the feeling. Sometimes in Florida you could drive down the highway in a rainstorm and watch the other lanes of traffic zipping along dry as toast in a blazing sunshine just a few feet away from you, but that kind of 180 degree separation didn't usually appear in complicated dope deals; when they started fucking up and coming apart at one end, they started losing it at all ends.

Bad thoughts. Think positive. Richard whizzed to the marina, got the boat into a shed and out of sight, took Michael to a good emergency room where nobody asked any questions and where they patched Michael up and started him on the road to recovery. While all that was going on, the Reverend Moon came out strong for human rights in South Korea and all the Vietnam vets who were still alive were voted a one-night stand with Farrah Fawcett by Congress. All the vets who were dead were voted back to life again. One lousy false start in the Grove this morning didn't mean the rest of the day couldn't turn out to be a real peach, a real red-letter socko boffo day on the calendar. One could always cross one's fingers.

Sitting down on the bus bench, which was courtesy of the suntan lotion with the little girl getting her bathing suit rended by the rabid mongrel, I checked out the restaurant parking lot—completely devoid of either Richard or the truck. It stayed that way for an hour. I needed some fucking sleep, but I couldn't buy it just yet, not under these circumstances. What I could do was to get myself something resembling a headquarters in retreat, a place with four walls, a private can and shower, a bed and a phone and a door that locked. The ghastly Halloween nightmare of a tourist beach motel directly behind my bench fit the bill just fine, and I walked up the driveway, past another hairy eyeball from the bell captain, went up to the desk and made the big contract with cash money up front for a couple of days. It wasn't the most pleasant such exchange that I remember; my intuition said the desk clerk would have felt an improvement in his day if I'd changed my mind and gone to the Elsewhere, just up the strip a couple of blocks. I didn't, and eventually a member of the staff who needed a tip was appointed to guide me through the labyrinthine halls to my room, in case I couldn't follow directions, punch the right button on an elevator or read three digits on the outside of doors. I gave the fucking swine two bucks and smiled, in the hope that if I needed something resembling a personal favor, I wouldn't have to teach him my name and room number all over again.

A great shower bought me at least two more good, functional hours. I bought a couple of extra hours with a couple of lines of toot after I'd dressed, and then plunged back into Sunday or Monday or whatever the fuck the day was. The captain whistled me up a cab that I took up to the marina a couple of miles north. I strolled out to the pier. No *Kelpie*, no Michael, no Richard, no truck in the parking lot. I looked out through the narrow waterway toward the ocean and found the *Kelpie* on the other bank, about a half mile toward the ocean end of the cut, either anchored just offshore of a grassy little island or bumped gently into its mud banks. If Richard hadn't shown here, maybe Michael was waiting for an invitation from me through the binocs. Anyway, it seemed the logical thing to try first. If that didn't work, I'd talk the marina guys into the loan of a little put-put and bring the boat and Michael, if he was aboard, back with the put-put in tow. I waved toward the boat from the pier pretty enthusiastically, and about a second later I heard a blast of the compressed air horn that was really sweet as Dixieland and a couple of seconds after that I heard the *Kelpie'*s engines start to crank up.

I've seen better jobs of channel navigating, but under the circumstances I had to hand it to the wounded pervert. The pier took such a wicked lunge when he rammed the bow into it that it almost knocked me into the water, but I held on to a pile and then leaped onto the boat. Michael was already collapsed below the lower wheel, holding his thigh and sobbing and gasping.

"For God's sake, turn those engines off, please," he wailed.

"Right, troop," I said, and took care of the control panel. "You gonna make it?"

"I don't rightly know. Jesus Christ, where were you?"

"Real busy, no shit. But we're gonna get your problem taken care of right now. Just hold on for a couple more minutes."

I hadn't switched the engines off, just revved them down to a nice match for a quiet neutral. Banging the transmission in again, I steered for the boat shed. A guy I'd done business with before, an old salt who was into Kentucky whiskey and had once personally gone out of his way, while I was buying the drinks, to tell me that he didn't give a flying fuck what anybody did as long as they paid their bill at the boatyard, came ambling amiably out of the office shed and helped with the bow line as I brought the boat up to the channel into the boat shed. I invited him down into the boat.

"Thought that was your boat out there," he said. "Your friend doesn't look too good. Need some help?"

"Whole bunches," I said. "Can I borrow your car?"

"You know, I think hospitals and ambulances pick up these days," he said.

"Yeah, well, how about not this time? We don't want to give the marina a bad name."

"Okay," and he handed me a couple of car keys on a plastic float bob. "What you want done with the boat?"

"There's a little damage on the flying bridge, maybe other places. In fact, you'll probably find a whole bunch of holes all the fuck over the place. I'd like you to do a good job and sort of take your time on it, you know?"

"Job like that'll probably take a week just to get to, if that's okay. We're pretty busy and us Crackers, we're pretty slow that way."

"No complaints," I said. "And if you could, keep her out of the sun."

"Sun's no damn good for this kind of a varnish anyway."

We were already laying a tarp as a stretcher under Michael to haul him out of the boat. My drinking buddy took him under the arms while I tried to do a gentle job with his legs. He was crying and trying to stifle screams that wanted to come out every time we jarred him, which was a lot. We carried him to the car, a bombed-out '69 Continental as well as I could judge, with putty patches and dents all over it, but it had a huge back seat and by the time we could leave Michael alone in it, it seemed he might be able to lie there fairly comfortably.

Despite having some trouble with multiple lanes of traffic and multiple words on the road signs, I managed to negotiate the tank pretty calmly and carefully over the causeway and onto the highways down toward the Jackson Memorial complex. By the time I got to the complex, I'd put together another big scheme to add to my list of snazzy ideas that had fucked up everything so far. I'd been in the Jackson emergency room once before when Lee had cut his hand to shit bashing it through a glass door in the middle of the night for no particular reason that made any sense to us. It was a real big-city emergency-room zoo, and because half the people who came there were certifiable violent loonies, it didn't just have pussy security rent-a-cops but one or two authentic Miami cops all the time. They'd want to know some details about Michael's little mishap and my part in it, and I didn't particularly relish that kind of interview right now. Michael could probably put off answering questions for a couple of days just by acting *in extremis,* and the way he looked in the back seat, he wasn't going to have to put on much of an act.

So instead of heading for the Jackson emergency entrance, I wheeled the monster into a public parking lot by the main entrance. Michael was passed out in the back. I walked through the lobby and took an elevator to a random ward on the second floor cruising for an abandoned wheelchair. I found a nice light manual job and wheeled it back through the hospital, out a side entrance and back to the car, where I shook Michael into something like consciousness and gave him the big pep talk for one last physical effort. He held on to the frame of the car—he had to stop about five times to keep from passing out—until I slid him out and into the wheelchair. Then I wheeled him back into the main lobby and nonchalantly took him for a stroll into the bowels of the interior. I left the chair in a corridor next to a stairway exit and about fifty feet down the hall from what looked like a busy nursing station. He was passed out again, and that was a good way to leave him. He was also dripping blood from underneath the old blanket the marina dude had draped over him when we'd put him in the car, and with any luck, someone connected with the hospital might notice this dying faggot in a wheelchair within the next couple of hours. I ducked down the stairs and was gone.

After laying some nice money down on the marina for the loan of the car and other appreciated services, I caught a bus out front to head back to the Beach and the newly reorganized command post where the Field Marshal could get a little sack time before the next round of the retreat from Moscow. Although I put in a wake-up call for ten-thirty that night with the desk, I didn't trust that worth a shit, so I bought a godawful-looking big brass mechanical alarm clock in the lobby drugstore for about five times what it was worth, and back in my room set it up on the dresser across the room from the beds. Then I fell on one of the beds.

The phone never did ring, or if it did, it rang before the alarm went off and I slept right through it. I didn't sleep through that clock, though. When it went off, I didn't exactly wake right up, even though my dreams indicated that I was in the middle of something resembling the London blitz or the Hiroshima surprise. The big mechanical clanger was the great-grandfather of all air raid

warning systems, so loud that it roused everyone in the neighborhood, but rang only in the event of an impending disaster that no
one's ass was ever going to get out of alive. Somebody in the next
room started pounding on the wall over my headboard and yelling
at me, and that woke me up. He was yelling in French. That was
a nice touch, French cursing. I staggered across the rug to the
bureau and shut the clock off.

I took my clothes off, had another wonderful shower, and then
put the same clothes back on again, same socks, same underwear,
same gun. Sitting on the edge of the bed, I lit a cigarette and clicked
on the television. Apparently you could arrange with the desk for
neat little closed-circuit movies that might help get a couple of
jaded strangers in the mood for a little hide-the-salami, but I pussied
out and opted for the eleven o'clock news instead. The prettiest-
looking, best-dressed sucker I'd ever seen announced all the tri-
umphs and failures of the day and the early evening, and he didn't
mention my name once before he got to the ball scores. He also
didn't mention Lee's name. That was a drag. I was going to have
to blow the whistle on him myself. I clicked the news off and
headed out to the lobby for a pay phone.

After dialing the nonemergency number of the wrong local
police department, the Coral Gables cops, I asked for somebody in
the juvenile office. When a lady picked up and identified herself as
the night clerk, I told her there'd been some trouble at Lee's
address in the Grove. A dead body in the pool, I think I said. She
got real bent out of shape about that and kept telling me I had the
wrong department and she wasn't even a cop. I asked her to read
me back the address, and when she did and I'd corrected the
number and the name of the street so that she read those back to
me pretty much correctly, I hung up. My good deed for the day,
shining like a beacon in a wicked world, you betchum. Different
bell captain, different whistle, different cab.

Since I wasn't Cuban, the cab driver gave me a couple of
pounds of suspicious vibes when I announced my midnight rendezvous in the middle of Little Havana. Neither of us being Cuban
made it twice as suspect, him not wanting to go there and him
thinking I shouldn't want to go there, but I was firm. I was also firm
about making the trip in absolute silence. It was just too goddam

long a trip to sustain a conversation with an already suspicious cabbie and not give him something to remember me by in case anyone asked him about it later, so I preferred to let him remember me as a nasty-ass clam mouth rather than as a gregarious wristwatch salesman from Topeka or some other half-assed ad-lib construct. *Eighth Street, Little Havana, my good man,* and that was about the extent of it. He let me off about three blocks short of the Versailles at a busy little fruit juice stand at about ten after midnight.

I didn't mind being late. Making the second meeting time this late meant that if Richard weren't here and couldn't wait a lousy ten minutes, something was so fucked up beyond all recognition that I could hang it up for any meetings in the immediate future, maybe forever. I approached the restaurant from the sidewalk on the other side of the street. I figured he'd make himself pretty visible for me at a distance, probably at the little juice bar with the window outside by the parking lot. No dice. Just a lot of racy-looking young Cuban gentlemen and ladies out to devastate some discos. I crossed over and went inside the main restaurant. Unless he was at a table all the way in the back, which would have been far too lame-brained for Richard, he wasn't there. I found a seat at the counter and ordered a nine-course dinner sort of centered around roast tongue. When that wasn't enough, I called the waiter back and added a *media noche* mini-sub to that. I stopped ordering more courses when I thought the people sitting near me were about to form a cheering section and notify the Guinness Book to send a representative.

I had eaten slowly and given my main man plenty of time to materialize, but he failed to do so. No telegrams from Western Union either, or mysterious oriental women whispering relayed tidings at me as they wisped past in a cloud of incense. On the other hand, nobody burst through the front door with Thompsons or Stens to spray my section of the counter with hot leaden death, which was a pretty standard twice-a-year act at various night spots on *Calle Ocho.* I was gratified about that. Well, it was well past midnight now, and so technically another day, possibly with an entirely more productive potential than the one I'd just capped. Maybe things were looking up.

I belched loudly as I got up from the counter, apologized to anyone who was interested in the gesture, and waddled over to the cash register to pay up. I bought a copy of the paper and a mint and helped myself to a couple of toothpicks. Then I started strolling down the hot, noisy, neon disco street toward a couple of seedy motels I'd passed. The one with the little swimming pool facing the street and the midget statue of the Blessed Virgin standing lifeguard duty got my trade.

# BECKER

In that motel room over the next couple of days, I started slipping away. I'd started to feel I was getting things together when I'd arrived, with all these wonderful showers and soft motel beds to sleep on and all these little details I was taking care of so well, like getting my three-quarters-dead pal to a hospital, calling the cops to take care of my other entirely dead pal and wondering what the fuck had become of my third pal and in which plane he was residing. But what really happened was that I'd checked into the Dead End Residence for Blown Schemes.

Although the room had no phone, I had nobody in particular to call. All I could do at first was scheme some more and think up nifty solutions to unimportant dangling details. So I started to let things slide. Personal hygiene went first, followed by etiquette. I don't think I noticed common sense slipping down the drain, because by that time I was reasonably convinced I hadn't started out on this venture with any of it in the first place.

The paper I'd bought, a stale edition from the previous morning, had a story on the front page of the local section about the great sea chase and the capture of the mango boat—as I'd guessed, a crew of overachieving Cracker and Conch lobstermen—and the seizure of the mother ship. Pictures showed the hapless Colombian scurvy crew being marched down the ramp at the Coast Guard pier looking ready for a couple of months of seriously crummy times until most of them would be shipped back to Bogotá—the ones who did the best job of impersonating the three squatting monkeys who didn't see, hear or speak zilch. The captain and a few of his senior henchmen would probably sustain your standard federal narco bust and wind up in Atlanta for what would seem like forever. The story made no mention of another boat getting away. Petty of the Coast Guard spokesman not to own up, but I guess when you rule the high seas you can bring home whatever success story you like best. The story read like shredded wheat tastes without sugar, bland, of no particular interest to the writer, the editor, the publisher, the Coast Guard or the public. Everybody had seen lots worse lots of times before. No big deal, just your average encounter between armed-to-the-teeth, crazed, open-ocean druggies and Your Tax Dollars at Work, with the usual outcome. Reading it almost made me want to stifle a yawn. I looked in vain for the telltale *acting on information supplied by confidential informants* or some such bullshit. Had it been there, it would have told me a little something I didn't know or wasn't sure about, a little bit more about where I stood and how many enemies I had and what they were capable of, but I was still on my own, still in the dark.

In the morning I rented a TV from the desk for my room and went out shopping again. There being no crime in impersonating a Cuban, I bought myself some nifty representative threads and another shaving kit, had some breakfast in a little luncheonette, bought the papers and went back to the motel.

Although the Coconut Grove troubles hadn't made the *Herald,* they loomed large on the front page of the *News* street edition, complete with interviews with neighbors who were also doing the three-monkey act. No comment from Lee's father or family, who couldn't be reached, but a couple of nice testimonials from the Miami banking community. Hard worker, honest, good sense of humor, a bit of a playboy, man on the way up. Police were seeking an unnamed man who shared his house for questioning. I'll bet that was the truth. *Hey guys I know where he is . . . .*

That brought me back to the *Herald* and a couple of little items in the local section. Fellow got the shit blasted out of him at a motel on 163rd Street, critical condition but stable, even expected to pull through with a little luck. A police spokesman termed the shooting possibly drug-related. Concerned parties could make inquiries at Jackson Memorial. Well, that wrapped up another loose end. I was beyond feeling crushed at the news or elated at the prognosis. I was in the Zone.

Next page we had—well, shit, I knew all about this one already —a nearly dead gunshot wound victim with no ID whom somebody had dumped in a corridor at Jackson. Also expected to live, just suffering from advanced septicemia, a tad of gangrene, shock, blood loss and athlete's foot.

By the time I tossed the papers in the corner, I was beginning to feel like the pinch hitter for the Grim Reaper. Granted, I'd had help in all this carnage, yet as I flopped down on the old, fat, forgiving mattress, I felt like taking all the credit for everything. I started musing about blowing my fucking brains out, but that was just one of several alternative schemes being considered here at Becker Central. There were others in my crew yet to be slaughtered, innocent bystanders to get blown away, perhaps even the chance of fueling an insurrection in the *barrio*. I couldn't snuff it quite yet, not with so much left to do. And then there were all the arraignments and indictments, grand juries and prosecutors, handcuffs and holding cells peopled with horny swarthy men. And the most intriguing part about it all was that it seemed I didn't even have to stir from my room to keep it all hopping; it seemed to have a great, rich life of its own now. It was merely content to use my name and point to me as its inspiration.

Holed up in the motel, I didn't bother differentiating between waking and sleeping except to catch the six and eleven o'clock news reports. If I couldn't stay asleep as much as I wanted, I filled in the gaps with Merv and Dinah and the *Electric Company*. I ventured out of the room for a meal or two each day and on the way back I'd grab the papers. My good works were fading after the first day, the TV stations and the papers losing interest—God, how hard we try, and for what?—but about three days later things started sizzling again.

The *Herald* had a nice item someone had leaked to them from the Comptroller of the Currency's office, about a staggering sum of money that, by devious and divers means, had been liberated from various lending institutions and institutional accounts, and the trail of paperwork was leading all the bloodhounds to the late Lee. Worse, it was beginning to look as if this wasn't the first time he'd done this sort of thing. No comment from Lee's father and just a little off the top from the bank spokesman, thank you, something to the effect that the bank, as always, was cooperating to the fullest with federal investigators and would sustain all losses. Whispers and innuendoes of links to organized crime and/or drug smugglers. No shit, Sherlock. Nice work.

I felt like puking. I felt like punching out the TV set or setting a fire in the room. I had to get something, anything, however incredibly lame, going. I had to do something pathetic or ineffective, puny or inconsequential, even some kind of fuck-up, because if I didn't, if I couldn't, I figured I had about two more days to go in that motel room before I checked out, but not with the desk clerk. In the army we'd been told during ambush training the big secret of leadership: Just do *something.* When Victor Charles and his pajama pals surprised your convoy in huge numbers with over-whelming firepower, your troops looked at you and this was the message: *We don't really care what the fuck you do, chief, but you better do something and do it pretty fucking fast. . . .* I got up off the bed and prepared to drag my sorry ass back into the fray. Nothing heavy, just a little reconnoitering for a start.

I strolled through Jackson's slippery halls for about three hours before I found Michael. I couldn't take a chance on asking anyone where he was. For one thing, if we were lucky, they didn't know his real name yet, so asking wouldn't have done much good. But if they did know his name, asking someone where he was would raise cop flags, because he was a gunshot victim without a good story to go with the gunshot wound. Probably he had no story whatsoever, or a story so patently unacceptable that the cops were interested in someone else's version, and mine would be just dandy. So I wandered around in my Cuban togs with a large bouquet of flowers in my hand as if I knew where I was going, trying the likely wards and occasionally popping into rooms that gave me vibes that Michael might possibly be inside. I was afraid he might be in the prison ward, in which case I wouldn't be able to get in or even find out if he was there, so I went up there to speck it out from a distance. From down the hall I looked through the sheet of glass behind the cop's desk, hoping to see Michael hobbling around. For the couple of minutes I drank from the fountain and waited for elevators, I didn't see him.

I found him in the lobby of an open mental ward sitting in a leatherette chair reading a Little Lulu comic book. I checked out his wrist wrapper, which had one of the most arcane fictions of a name I'd ever heard. The last name looked Armenian.

"My uncle," Michael said. "They know I'm not really him, I think, but they needed something to call me until something better comes along. They might not let you out of here if you tell them you think that's my name, too."

"Yeah, I'm worried they'll want to talk to me now."

"Naw. They got a lot more to worry about on this ward than me. I figured this was a good place to get transferred to."

"What did you tell them?"

"I told them I was gay and had a compulsion to suck off policemen and Marines and bouncers, and one of them shot me, and that I want to die and that everything's so confused and hazy. Look, all I had to do was tell them I was a fag and that did about eighty percent of the job."

"Can you get out of here? How's your leg?"

"Oh, it's getting better. I hop around. They put it in a cast, see?" He lifted up his pajama leg to show me an odd sort of little contraption around his leg with straps and Velcro and plastic splints. "I got hit in the bone, got a little fracture. I got to tell you, they weren't too fucking impressed with the first aid job, Becker."

"Yeah. Well, I did the best I could under the circumstances."

"No sweat. Listen, what's happening out there?"

"Weirdness. Look, your roommate's dead. Don't make a big scene out of it, but Lee's dead."

"Oh, shit. I knew something was wrong. I was trying to call, I got out to the pay phone a couple of times, and first it was like out of order, and then some wrong person answered the phone. Cop, I guess."

"Probably."

"Oh, shit. Oh, shit. What happened?"

"Well, I think it was R.J. and Laura. Fuck, I know it was R.J. and Laura. They put him down at the bottom of the pool."

"Oh, God. That fool. I knew that twat was no good, and I tried to tell him to stop hanging around with R.J. I just couldn't tell him everything. I should have."

"Everything about what?" I asked.

"You really don't know? I sort of thought you did. I mean, this is no time to be coy, Beck."

"I really don't know. Something about R.J.?"

"Yeah. Oh, damn, now I'll be coy. Let me tell you later, okay? It's not time now. No reason to get into it now. It's just a long, crummy story. We still got the dope?"

"Yeah. Thank heaven for small favors. But it's all fucked down at Lee's bank. They know all about where the money came from. We couldn't stick it back in there if we tried, even if we ever get around to unloading the coke up north."

"So?"

"What do you mean?"

"So who cares about that? Lee's dead. He ain't worried anymore. The bank's insured, and like you said, they wouldn't take the money back from us if we gift-wrapped it. They don't want any of that money. They want us, man. If we can get out of this thing without them finding out who we are, or *where* we are—that'll do for starters, man—then that money's all ours, principal, profit and interest. I'd give it all away to bring Lee back to life, man, but that won't cut it. We are unfortunately some rich people, a lot richer than we expected to be."

"Well. I hadn't thought of it that way. I think I'll experience a severe pang of guilt, and then start thinking that maybe this is a better day than I thought it was going to be."

"Where's Richard?"

"Oh. Yeah. Well, that also turned out a lot worse than it should have. He's here in the hospital somewhere, all shot to shit. He's supposed to pull out of it, though."

"Jesus, what does R.J. want from us? He's snuffing everybody and he still ain't got a dollar or a goddam line of coke. What does he want?"

"I been thinking about that. I'm sure he wants the toot and the bucks, but I don't think that's the most important thing, 'cause you're right—if he just wants the money, he's been going about it real half-assed, and that's not the usual way that cocksucker does things. His moves may look half-assed, but they aren't.''

"So what does he want?'' Michael asked.

"Okay. He wants to take us all out. He wants to do away with the competition. Maybe it's strictly business, or maybe it's personal. Maybe he's pissed that his little helpers went out for a deal on their own. Maybe he's constipated, I don't know. But he wants to take us out as serious competition. It's a very common free-market practice, happens all the time. No rules.''

"Whoa.''

"No. Woe is more like it. We got woe, and I think we're going to get more woe. I mean, the fucker's already set himself up for the gas chamber a couple of times. He's not going to get scruples now, not while we're still shaking a leg.''

"What are we going to do?''

"Well, you got to get out of this place real quick. The cops are looking for you heavy. I think they want to ask you a few questions about Lee being in the pool, and also if you happen to know where all that money is. They're going to put you on ice for a long time, even if they believe you.''

"Yeah, I kind of tend to agree with you. If you bring me some clothes I can meet you in the can down by the cafeteria in the basement after dinner. They let me wander around at night. Around seven,'' he said.

I took the locker key out of my pocket and wedged it gently between the padding of his leg contraption and the plastic splints. "Bus terminal down on Biscayne,'' I said.

"Hey, I don't want this thing,'' he said.

"Look, for the rest of the day you're safer than I am. That man's hunting for me and I don't want that thing on me.''

"Oh, joy. Well, you better watch your ass and show up tonight.''

"Count on it,'' I said. "But if I don't show up, there's guns in the locker, too. Get yourself down there and arm yourself. Then take the dope up north and sell it. Maybe I'll get busted and need some heavy-duty legal fees.''

"You trust me to come back?"

"Oh, fuck, Michael. Yes, I do. No, I don't. What the fuck difference does it make? At least you aren't trying to snuff me, and that puts you real high on my Christmas card list these days. I mean, pal, you and me are very much in the same leaking boat, and this is a piss-poor time to wonder if we trust each other."

"Sorry. Just asking," he said.

There wasn't any reason to try to see Richard. Probably he was in an IC ward with plumbing going in and out of him and not much for conversation, let alone action. And they probably had a set of handcuffs around his ankle to boot, just in case he did come to and decided to leave before satisfying the cops' curiosity about the motel matter. They probably already had him on the army gun business, and if they were really in a bind for something to hold him on, there was always the linear amplifier—a pussy rap, but enough to keep him in custody while they were checking him out and checking the registration of the .45. He was certainly going to need some good legal advice before this was over.

I ditched the flowers in the chapel off the lobby and took a cab to a shopping center out Flagler Street, where I made a stab at Michael's clothes size and picked up a couple of other traveling items for him so he'd be ready to move. Then I found a drugstore lunch counter and killed a couple of hours sipping cherry Cokes and eating egg salad sandwiches on white bread and reading *Popular Mechanics* until the whole experience was coming out of my ears, but it still felt appropriate and comfortable not to be too much out of doors that afternoon, and I didn't want to go back to the motel room. Although I ruminated about checking out the motel parking lot for Richard's truck because I was getting pissed off having to take cabs and buses everywhere, and I was running out of money for that kind of expense account, it finally seemed like a pretty lame idea. The truck had either been towed away to the cop pound as evidence of something or other, or they'd left it in the parking lot just to see who came around and started the engine up. I had to guess the latter was likely, even if it wasn't. That motel was a bad place to go right now. Odds not good, signs point to no.

Michael pulled off his stupendous escape from the bin without a hitch. Although he complained that the clothes I'd bought him didn't fit and were tacky, they covered him up enough for the decency statutes, and nobody questioned us as we found a nice, dull exit out of the hospital and made our way to a taxi stand. We found a Cuban-Chinese restaurant not far from the motel where Michael chowed down and I munched on an egg roll, and then we headed back for the motel room. Nobody seemed to care that I'd decided to entertain a guest. We did up some lines and then sat out by the pool away from the office and the street and passed a jay back and forth. I was almost sorry everything had worked out for a change, because now I was going to have to come up with some more schemes.

We went inside for the eleven o'clock mayhem update and after the first commercial were treated to the ginchiest high school photograph of Michael you ever saw, with a title overlay that said WANTED. They'd finally put the missing roommate of the man in the pool together with the mysterious appearance at Jackson of the man with a hole in his leg, and now the authorities seemed a bit ticked off that they were a day late and a dollar short. It was a nice photograph. Michael was wearing a jacket and a narrow black little knit tie, and his hair looked like a team of experts from the Wild-root factory had been working on it for a week. Even though the photo was blown up, grained out and broadcast on a shitty rented TV, you could still see the photographer's flash shining off it and the comb marks.

"Real slick," I said.

"Man, we missed that trouble by a cunt hair, didn't we?"

"I think this is a bad time for you to try to hobble out of town. They're lookin' for your faggot ass, yes they are."

"They must have found that yearbook in my room. Jesus, if that's the only picture they got of me, I ain't too worried. I've gone through a few changes since then. You might have noticed."

"Still, they got a good description of you from the hospital, and they'll be looking for a gimp. This is a bad time for airports and stuff."

"This isn't a bad place to be," he said.

"For the next twenty minutes, maybe. We got to make the move in the morning, at least get you to another motel. I want you

**193**

to shave and to change your act any way you can. For a couple of days I won't be around to run interference for you."

"Where are you going?"

"Down to Key West. I'm not sure why. Maybe I can catch somebody by surprise or something. Maybe they won't think of looking for me down there. Maybe R.J.'s lying in a hammock soaking up the sun and a bottle of Dr. Pepper. Maybe I can bum out his day a little."

"Sounds like a bad plan to me," Michael said.

"I'm open for alternatives."

"We both get out of town and go north and make some money. How about that?"

"It's coming, but not yet. You can't walk well yet. I don't want to leave town with Richard the way he is. And goddam it, I just want to find something out that might put *us* ahead for a change. I mean, R.J. seems able to do what he wants to when he wants to. He knows where our people are and we don't know where he is. He knows who we are and how many of us there are, and he's taking us out one by one. We don't know who's with him, just that odd bitch, and I got a feeling there's more than just her. If I can get down to Key West and he's not there, I can maybe talk to Lisa. That bubblehead'll tell me everything she knows about R.J., even though she probably doesn't know shit. But she might tell me something that'll give me an edge. Maybe she knows who he's hanging around with or where he's staying up here. In the meantime, you can rest your leg up and do a bunch of drugs and watch the TV."

"Do you want to take him out?" Michael asked.

"I hadn't really thought about it like that. Maybe I just want to try to neutralize him some way. Scare him. Get some kind of armistice going. Just stick my gun up his hard palate and pull the hammer back and try to reason with him."

"Good luck. If you're not going to run, you're going to have to blow him away."

"Why?"

"Oh, please," he moaned. "It's just the way he is. I'm not telling you to kill him. I'd rather get out of town and settle down somewhere else. We're ahead, man. But if you go looking for him, you're going to have to kill him to stop him. I know for sure he means to kill me now."

"What the fuck do you know that you aren't telling me?" I asked.

"Oh, it's just a real rude story, man. Richard knows it. I thought maybe you knew it. Maybe you should have known it before you tried to open up a store down the street from R.J. I guess you should have. It's about that boat you helped unload when you first got down here."

"What about it?"

"Well, I was out with him on that one. That was the last deal I'd do with him. You know it was a stolen boat. You must have figured that."

"Yeah, it did have that disposable flavor to it. I know you took it out and scuttled it."

"Well, there were people on it when we stole it. R.J. and I found it in a marina up the coast and it looked right and easy to grab. It was a bunch of young kids partying on it, sailing it around. They just wanted to screw and do ludes and listen to Rod Stewart. So I got friendly with them and shipped on board as crew for a ride out to the Bahamas."

"How many people?" I asked.

"Six. Couples, boy-girl, boy-girl. Anyway, the night before we sailed, I snuck R.J. aboard and hid him in my cabin. Well, he killed all those people, man. There was big trouble on that boat. I was a mess, man. I was high on money and toot and R.J.'s big plans. I guess it must have occurred to me that once we got the boat he wasn't going to take those people to a French restaurant, but I swear what happened, I wasn't ready for it and I didn't want it to happen. I was just messed up. I messed up."

"What happened?"

He started to groan some and stare at the drawn curtains, and I thought he might shut down or beg off, but after a few seconds he caught himself and started to talk again.

"Well, it didn't exactly go like clockwork. One of the guys found R.J. in my bunk when we weren't too far out. Maybe we were still in sight of land. So another guy came running at me up at the wheel, not really at me. He didn't put R.J. down in my bunk together with sweet little old me yet, but the ship's pistol was up by the wheel. Even though I didn't know how to use it, I held it on him and then started collecting everybody on the boat and herding them down to their cabins. The guy who'd been fighting with R.J. had his throat cut to shreds and was dying down on the floor of my cabin, but he still kept trying to crawl out in the passageway, and the women started freaking out and screaming and crying.

"R.J. locked the women in one cabin and the two guys who weren't hurt in two other cabins, and then we started to get into a big fight. He said I was freaking out on him and that he was just going to do what he had to do, and that I better not give him any shit about it. He had a gun, too. He told me to steer for the big ocean, and I backed off. I guess we were about thirty, forty miles out by nightfall. Then he hauled the dead guy up on deck and cut his stomach open so he'd sink better and threw him over. I started to hassle with him again, but he told me to back off, and he meant it. The women and one of the guys down there were crying and shrieking, and every hour or so he'd go down there and terrorize the shit out of whoever he wanted. I don't really think he was trying to shut them up, though. He said he was, but I don't really think he was. I think he liked to listen to it.

"Anyway, then he offered me one of the guys if I wanted him and I just blew up again and he came down on me worse than ever, waving the gun in my nose and pulling the hammer back and calling me a whole bunch of shit. *You just fuckin steer this boat and leave everything else to me, you asshole pansy, and if you don't like something, you can just shove it or you can just die out here and get buried at sea.* And he went down below and brought up another guy. He pistol-whipped him up the companionway. We'd brought along handcuffs and the guy was stumbling with his hands locked up behind him. R.J. kicked him up the companionway and kept smashing his head against the bulkheads. It was pitiful.

"I couldn't deal with it. I climbed out onto the bow and tried not to listen. That was really pathetic, I mean, trying not to have anything to do with my partner snuffing a bunch of people on a goddam boat at sea. Really pathetic. I heard him shoot the guy and then a couple of minutes later he shoved the guy overboard."

**196**

Michael looked the way I'd felt the last couple of days, as if some-one had reached inside him and removed everything but the last little spark that still lets you be considered alive.

He'd dropped down to a low mumble, but I could still under-stand him.

"I really thought you knew, man. I was sure you did."

"I'm sort of sorry I know now," I said. "What made you think I knew? Who would have told me?"

"Richard. I asked him and he said he didn't, but you guys are pretty tight. That night down in Key West when you started talking about the Coriolis. You scared the living shit out of me."

"The what? Oh, that bullshit. Yeah, what about it?"

"That was the name of the boat. We painted it over, but that was its name, the *Coriolis.* You didn't know?"

"Nope. I'm just one of those guys who can't take a shit without something to read," I said. "You learn a lot that way, names of boats, things that spin hurricanes and water down the toilet bowl, good tips on the greyhounds, how to keep those leftovers fresh in the refrigerator. That's just the way I am."

"Well, you scared the shit out of me," he grumbled.

"Sorry, ace. Didn't mean to. I was innocent as the newborn lamb. Well, anyway, I'm in on it now. What happened then?"

*And he told me what happened then. R.J. told him to steer south for a port he knew where they could work on the boat and change its configuration and color scheme some, just enough to freshen the odds for one round trip to Colombia. The port was two days off and things started to get really out of control during those two days. R.J. finished up with the last guy on board the same way he did with the second, but he kept the women alive and did numbers on them when he chose, and he chose to go down to the cabins a lot. Michael wasn't quite completely terrorized and he confronted R.J. about it down in the passageway; things were pretty tense there for about a half hour. It didn't look like anyone was going to budge. Well, Michael figured that if anyone budged it was going to be himself, but he kept up the staring contest for as long as he could.*

*At one point Michael said he remembered offering to kill the women himself if R.J. would let him do it now and fast, but R.J.*

*just laughed at him, one of those famous R.J. laughs that didn't have the slightest connection with humor or grins or what you might call a good time. You fucking pervert, old R.J. said—I liked that, R.J. calling Michael a pervert—you motherfucking pervert, I fucking hijacked a boat at sea and killed three people. I got three more down there and I'm gonna kill them. You think I ain't gonna get a little nooky off those bitches first? There's plenty to go around for you if you want to swing the other way on this trip, but I sure as fuck am gonna get my fill if you ain't.*

*Part of it was that Michael didn't want to end his days in a pool of blood in the passageway of a stolen boat, even if he could take R.J. with him at the same time. An important part, for sure. But part of it was just the drain of seeing R.J. for the first time entirely free of even the slim constraints he operated under in Key West—that was a big part of why finally Michael just turned around and left R.J. down below. He wasn't getting anywhere with R.J. by threatening to try to make him stop or even slow down. R.J. was building up energy, feeling better and better about things every day, and Michael was just getting depleted of any force or energy or will as he tried not to watch or listen to the screams and the crying down below.*

*But Michael had let R.J. know how he was feeling and even that he might try to use a gun to express his feelings if R.J. didn't cool out. And that crazy loon R.J., knowing all that, knowing he was alone on a boat with a guy who was seriously considering killing him, R.J. didn't even bother to stay awake or sleep in a locked cabin. He'd sleep out on deck in front of Michael during the morning, not pretending to sleep to start something with Michael, really sleeping, and pretty soundly. Once on the way to the head Michael found him asleep in one of the cabins on a bunk and one of the girls who was still tied up had been thrown down off the bunk, jammed up against the wall, and she looked up at him and Michael found himself jumping down the passageway out of sight of her. R.J. had left the door to the cabin wide open, hadn't even given a shit about it. Michael took his piss and just walked back up to the wheel without looking in again; he didn't know that time if R.J. was still asleep or was looking his way and smiling. He couldn't look at the girl again. From then on he took his leaks over the side* and wouldn't go below except just to reach inside the galley for something in a can to eat if he had to. He wouldn't go below anymore, but what was going on below kept leaking up the companionway toward him for the next couple of days no matter how far away Michael tried to get from it. R.J. was beating the shit out of the women and it was all he could do to hold his imagination there. On the second morning R.J. brought the first woman up and got rid of her. Michael was up on the bow again but R.J. shouted at him that she was the one he liked the least, just to get a rise out of him.

R.J. anchored the boat so he could have another night with the last woman who was left, and that was all the detail Michael had for me about that last night, except that he was thinking of that old familiar bagged-out motel-room suicide ending while R.J. was having his time down below and the boat was bobbing up and down at anchor. Michael was playing with a revolver out on the bow and he said that he knew that if he fired that one last shot, R.J. would know what it was and what had happened and wouldn't even stop what he was doing to come out on deck to make sure. He'd just keep at his business until he threw his next weird nut off, got a good catnap and felt like a stroll out on deck for some sea air.

Michael said he thought the last woman was dead when R.J. brought her up on deck just around dawn before they sailed into the little sport fishing village for overhaul. Michael wouldn't help swab the decks and the cabins, but R.J. didn't make a big deal out of that. Well, it just got to be done, he snarled at Michael, so I'll goddam just do it myself. And he did and then they made landfall. R.J.'d been there before and knew his way around, knew just who to talk to and who to pay and who to grease and where to eat. Michael wanted to jump ship but he was afraid to be on his own after what had just happened in South Bumfuckland.

Can you dig that? Michael asked. Can you dig that? After what had been going on I was afraid to leave R.J. I mean, that sounds real rich and ripe. It does now, anyway, but it made sense. I felt real raw and real friendless and dependent. I felt like the only thing worse than going on with a guy who was into mass murder and mass rape and mass buggering was to be alone and on my own that far away from home. I think I felt in a funny way that if we were going *to get popped with all that crime I wanted to be around R.J., maybe just so I'd have the other half of the act there to point at and turn state's evidence and blame it on, but if I got popped in Nadaland all by myself, they'd settle for me alone to draw and quarter in the public square; they wouldn't bother much with the other guy who got away, and me being a fag and all, they'd probably think I was just making the other guy up, they'd figure this is the regular kind of act one of those deranged North American big city queers whips out when he's on vacation. I just didn't want to leave R.J. just then.*

*So I stayed on through the whole dope deal, all the way down to Colombia and back, that night you showed up with Richard and helped unload the boat. And I took my share of the money, more or less what R.J. had told me I was going to net for the trip before we'd started scouting for the right boat. Yeah, I sure as hell took the money. If I had the choice, I sure wasn't going to go through that kind of berserk psycho nightmare for free. If I had to go through it and somebody on the far end was still willing to lay a stack of thousand-dollar bills on me, I sure as hell was going to take it. Take it and get out of there and take the pledge, but take it, for sure.*

"Yeah," I said. "I remember that night. You tweaked me on the ass."

"Look, man, I was feeling high. I mean, the trip was over and I was among friends again. I was home and just about free of that maniac forever, more or less. And I was getting horny. You know, that happens to our lads out at sea from time to time. So I was cruising again. I've always sincerely thought you were cute as a button."

"I'm flattered, don't think I'm not flattered. That's some story."

"Yeah, ain't it, though? A guy could go places telling a story like that."

"Who were they? Do you know?" I asked.

He thought for a minute, as if he were collating or arranging a few threads of a few rumors to come up with something substantial, however small. "I don't really know," he sighed. "I know that a couple of them were rich and had people up in New York, in Westchester and Connecticut. The *Coriolis* was out of Cos Cob, I think. R.J. told me that when he went down below, a couple of them offered him a lot of money to let them go. I guess all they were trying to do was to convert the killings into a nice, harmless kidnapping, a successful one, that they were willing to help him with as much as they could, talking mom and dad into it and into not calling the cops. That's a shame. They should have saved their breath. They were dead—I guess they were dead the minute R.J. and I saw their boat in the marina the first time."

I tried to think of something sage and comforting. *No sense crying over spilt milk* didn't seem to cut it.

"How did Richard find out?"

"I *told* him. I tried to hold it in, but Jesus, only two people on earth knew what had happened on that boat, and one of them was a psychopath who was capable of anything. So one night when Richard was singing R.J.'s praises and counting his share of the bucks and doing up R.J.'s toot, I just blew up and told him what had happened on the boat."

· "What did he think?"

"He didn't say. He was too busy pulling the flies out of his open mouth. Why? Do you have an opinion? I mean, I sure could use an opinion after all this time. It's just what I need, man."

"No. I guess I don't have much of an opinion about it. Bunch of people got snuffed, you happened to be there."

"Yeah. Just one of those things. That's why I don't think you ought to go down to Key West. I think we ought to make a big dash for the drugs and get up north as fast as we can."

"No. I told you, you got to lie up for a couple of days, and I got to do some recon. I'm tired of surprises. I want to surprise some people for a change, or at least know what's coming for me. You got the key. You keep it. Give me a couple of days to come back or to show up in the obit pages and then get the fuck out of town and sell the shit and have a nice life. I'd appreciate it if you'd pay Richard's medical bills and hire him a lawyer."

"I'll take care of that if it comes to that," Michael said, "but you're crazy if you try to tackle that loony. Why don't you go up to the Seminole village and take up alligator wrestling instead? Statistically it's a lot safer, I think."

"No," I repeated. "I'm going down to Key West. I'm tired of surprises." I was, too.

# BECKER

**T**he fellow who'd been talking to Minnesota Bob at the Taurus was sitting in a pretty recent Plymouth with just a little salt corrosion under the doors. He was parked across the street and down a couple of houses from ours. The first couple of times I made a pass near it, walking up to the corner, checking the Plymouth out and walking back before he checked out his rear-view mirror and read me. It was midafternoon and he didn't look like he planned to scoot any time soon. Maybe he was a Bible salesman, waiting for the lady of the house to get home. Maybe he'd sold a Bible to Minnesota Bob. Minnesota Bob could have used one.

I found a pay phone in a gas station a couple of blocks away and called the cops. I was an irate homeowner and I wanted to know what that strange man was doing sitting in his car on my street. Never mind who I was. I wanted something done about it before the kids came home from school. Goodbye.

I strolled back to the intersection by a different route and stopped about a block away. A Key West squad car rolled up the street listlessly and stopped next to the Plymouth. The cop in the passenger seat leaned out and talked to Minnesota Bob's last friend for a couple of seconds and then the squad car rolled on, took a right and moved out of the neighborhood. So did I. The Plymouth stayed.

That was a shame. I wanted to check the mail and shit, shave, shower and shine upstairs and then I wanted to steal my own motorcycle and fly elsewhere. I couldn't do any of those things while he was there. It just didn't seem right. It made me edgy.

Now I needed a southern bivouac and it looked as if it wasn't going to be my shack. I had some touristy threads and an overpriced Instamatic from the drugstore for overkill, so I didn't mind bopping around the streets; it felt a lot safer than crawling through the shrubbery, Key West being one of your more up-tight and suspicious burgs. I steered clear as much as I could of the neighborhoods where I was likely to bump into people I knew, and that worked out pretty well; the worst that happened was exchanging nervous little hesitant waves with a honey I used to run into at parties with neither of us ever being able to remember the other's name.

I had to wait on the wooden stairs on the way up to Luck's apartment for about an hour before I heard him dragging himself up the stairs by his arms on the wooden rails with his skateboard slung over his shoulder clattering against the wall of the house. He didn't even look up until he was just about on top of me.

"Jesus, boy, scare the living crap out of me, why don't you?" he said.

"I was just enjoying the view. Anybody ask you why you don't get an apartment on the ground floor?"

"This one's cheaper," he said. "You could have jimmied the door. Everybody else does, two or three times a month. It would be a nice change to have a buddy do it."

He unlocked an old padlock on a hasp and opened the door and did a monkey crawl inside to a wheelchair in the kitchen. I was sure it was going to topple over in three different directions while he hauled himself up into it and arranged some old, gray pillows underneath and behind him.

"I could use something to drink," I said.

"Don't have no beer."

"Just fruit juice. City water. I'm not proud."

He scooted around the kitchen in the wheelchair, skidding around on the rubber wheels, grabbing drawer handles to stop

himself short or wheel himself in another direction. I closed the
door behind me and stayed out of his way.

"Iced tea. It's all I keep in the box. That do?"

"Great," I said, and put the glass down in one long gulp. He
scooted around and got me another dose, and I put that one down
almost as fast.

"Your name's on the telegraph, boy," he said.

"You don't say. Only good things, I hope."

"I don't know. I could make a hundred quick bucks if I picked
up the phone and told somebody you were in town. More than that
if I told them you were here, I think."

"There's the phone," I said.

"Outta order," he said.

"Thanks," I said. "You been by my house lately?"

"Yeah. I think the man's watching your place. He's a motorcycle troop named Roche. Roach, everybody calls him. Very strange,
motorcycle cop in civvies in his own car outside your house. I was
meaning to ask you about that."

"Parking tickets," I said. "Dare I ask where you'd collect this
bounty on my ass?"

"You know, it's funny—I think R.J. misses you. He's the one
slipped me the word. Personally, I just think it's his way of slipping
a little extra something to a disabled veteran. He's a nice guy that
way."

"A prince. No shit."

"How bad is it?" he asked.

"It's just a little misunderstanding. He's trying to kill all my
friends and me. How much of it did you hear?"

"Well, I know about your pal Michael. Where is he?"

"He's safe."

"You want to stay here?"

"Yeah, just for a short, if you don't need the money that bad.
Is R.J. in town, do you think?"

"Don't know. Looks like he's in his heavy traveling mode, you
know what I mean? Always see him in his short, always heading
north or zipping down for a quick burger and a bop for Lisa and
then out again. Doing deals, big deals. Buying a few months of
uninterrupted hammock time, I suspect."

"Look, I won't shit you. Maybe you don't need me for a house guest right now," I said.

"Nobody tells me what to do." He sounded very recalcitrant.

"I'm serious," I said.

"*I'm* serious. You stay here if you like. I mean, keep out of sight—I'd appreciate that—but you stay here if you need to."

"Well, I sort of need to. That's the truth. Until tonight."

"Okay, then. It ain't fancy like your place. If you sack out, you might get a palmetto bug on your face. Try to sleep with your mouth closed."

Luck cooked us some rice and beans for dinner when the sun went down and it got cool enough to eat. For air conditioning some breezes swept through his apartment and he had a desk fan next to his bed. On the ancient all-in-one box he used for a stereo he played some ancient eight-tracks, usually two or three times around before he got around to putting on another one: Jefferson Airplane, Paul McCartney. He had a pipe and some hash and we did some up. I spent the time cleaning the weapon. He didn't seem to mind.

The man in the Plymouth wasn't out front by eight; the sun must have finally beaten him down. I had the feeling he wasn't on official business, just his own private peep show, in which case he probably didn't have any relief, not even R.J. Especially not R.J. R.J. wouldn't have been fool enough to sit outside my place these days in plain sight.

I got into the back yard and crawled around the house. I didn't hear anything going on inside. I pushed the bike out to the street but didn't try to start it up or turn the lights on until I was down the block a little; I popped it into second and it puttered up and took me a couple of blocks away where I parked it. Since I was going back to the house, I wanted the bike safe and somewhere I could recover it if I had to leave in a hurry.

A lot of mail was stuffed in the mailbox, junk mail, bills and some misspelled and inane dropout postcards from Annie from San Francisco and Phoenix that seemed to say she was heading back to Key West. I really couldn't wait for her to cruise in and ask me what was new. Anything that looked personal had been ripped open, read and then stuffed back into its envelope or not, as the reader chose. This tactful touch from the other side was just to let me know they didn't give a flying fuck whether I knew they were after my ass or not. It pissed me off. It was amazing that R.J. could still come up with something to piss me off all over again, but he could and he had. I guess he didn't think it likely that I was going to file a complaint with the postal inspector that week.

I expected to find the inside a real wreck, but it was pretty much the way I'd left it. A half glass of water on the coffee table in the living room had left a nice ring and butts of Kools were in the ash tray; I didn't yet know anybody who smoked Kools. I didn't turn any lights on. The phone still had a dial tone. Funny how good that made me feel about the house, as if it were still working and functioning and ready to help me in a tight squeeze, not that there was anybody to call who could do much, nobody in particular I could count on. I could call the cops, but they were already here, apparently. My nearest pal traveled around on a skateboard and my other two buddies had holes in them. In a way, all that made things simpler. I didn't have to depend on anyone else and wonder whether they'd fuck up or not or show up on time. If I couldn't do something, it wasn't going to get done, which tended to simplify the problem of resource inventory. I was the only shmuck around with any resources.

I sat in the blind corner of the living room where I couldn't be seen from either the hall entrance or the kitchen entrance. Reading by the street-lamp light that came in through the small window above me while I waited for whatever the fuck the evening had in store, I went through the more interesting pieces of mail. The automatic lay on the table edge next to my elbow with the hammer back and a chambered round. Let the good times roll.

Around two-thirty in the morning, I heard the kitchen door crack and swing open on its rusty spring. That was the best way to come into the living room; not only wouldn't the nighttime caller see me as he came into the room, but by the time he strolled in, his back would be toward me. I could hear my pulse trip-hammering and my mouth was dry as I picked the automatic up and pointed it toward the kitchen.

It was the Roach, Minnesota Bob's pal, and he walked right past me in the near dark and into the living room. He was carrying one of those magnum frame revolvers, either a .44 or a .357, and pointing it into the room as if he didn't really expect anyone to be there, or as if he would have preferred to be carrying a flashlight.

"You are a dead man," I said very softly. It was amazing I could make sounds at all, but I heard them come out and float into the room. Although he did a wild sort of shiver, he didn't try to turn around or swing his gun at me.

"Police officer," he said.

"Then I hope you have a warrant," I said. "Now put the gun down very carefully on the floor and stand up again. Don't turn around."

"You're Becker. Don't do anything stupid, guy. There's a warrant out for you. Let me take you in."

"Do what I told you. I am so fucking serious that you're about an ounce of trigger pull from the end."

He crouched down, laid his pistol on the rug and then straightened up again. "You can't kill a cop," he said. "That's the biggest mistake you'd ever make in your life."

"Maybe. If you're here kosher, like with a warrant. But I don't think there's a warrant out for me, and I don't think you've even got a search warrant to be in here. If I'm right, then I got a free kill right here in my own living room. Because you're not much cop right now and a lot of prowler and burglar."

"I'll show you my warrant," he said.

"You'll show me nothing. That's the last thing I want to look at right now. If you got one, I'd just as soon you keep it where it is, out of sight. That way I can chalk it all up to a tragic mistake when I have to call your buddies to haul your corpse away. Are you getting the general drift that I intend to blow your fucking brains out, pal?"

"I'm on a lawful investigation," he said.

"Get down on the floor, on your stomach," I said. He thought about it for a couple of seconds, and then did it. I stepped over to him and stuck the muzzle of the .45 in the hollow behind his ear. When he started to say something, I told him to shut up and he did. Then we both just stayed where we were, each doing what we'd been posed to do, for an hour. Once during the hour the phone rang. I jumped and he jerked, but the gun didn't go off. I let the phone ring. It rang sixteen times and then it stopped. By the time it stopped, I could smell urine under my nose.

I timed the hour by the kitchen clock. When it was up, with a little extra to spare, I thought it was time to talk some more.

"What do I get if you live?" I asked him. I thought that was to the point.

"You want money? I don't have any money," he said.

"I don't want money," I said.

"What do you want?" he asked.

"Tell me the truth about the warrants."

"I don't have a warrant," he said. "There's no warrant out for you that I know of."

"I still want to know what's in it for me if I let you walk out of here. And it really, really better be good and real tempting."

"I won't fuck with you. Is that what you want?"

"That doesn't sound convincing," I said. "So far you sound better to me dead, you really do."

"What do you want?" he asked again.

"I want you to leave the state of Florida when you walk out of this house. I want you to get in that shit-eating Plymouth of yours and keep driving until you're at least west of the Mississippi. And I don't want you ever to come back."

"I told you I wouldn't fuck with you," he said.

"I'm going to blow your brains away right now," I said.

"Okay, okay. Don't shoot. Please, for Christ's sake, don't shoot. I don't have money to get away."

I pulled his wallet out of his back pocket and looked at it with my free hand. About three hundred bucks in twenties and fifties. I took a couple of them and put them in my shirt pocket, to spend on real foolishness when I got the chance. Then I put the wallet back.

"The instant you lie to me again I will pull this trigger," I said. "You are so fucking close it's pathetic." There was no reason for me to try to sound wired. I could hear myself and I sounded very wired.

"Okay. I'll get out of town," he said. "I swear. Just let me—"

"Don't you ask for shit. I told you the plan. That car, your ass, drive to the Mississippi, right now. Stay on the other side of it forever. That's the plan, and it's the only one you get tonight, or ever. Do you take it?"

"Yeah," he said.

"Turn over," I said.

He rolled over until he was looking up at me. I put the muzzle into the soft cavity under his Adam's apple.

"Where's R.J.?" I asked.

He had a lot of trouble at first making noises, even though I wasn't pressing hard with the gun. Finally he made something come out.

"I don't know. He calls me. Sometimes he's in Miami, sometimes he's in the Keys. He's moving around a lot. I swear."

"When I let you up, you'll be on the honor system for the rest of your life. If you do anything except disappear, if I ever hear you're anywhere near me again, then you better get one clean shot off at me first and kill me. That's your only hope. You better kill me."

"Please. I'm leaving. I don't want to bother you."

I backed up and sat down in the corner again, keeping the gun on his face the whole time. He watched the gun the way he would a snake about to bite. He didn't look at my face, as if the most he could do was try to read the gun and my hand.

"You can go now," I said.

He stood up and stumbled a little as he tried to turn around. I didn't get up to follow him, but listened as he walked down the hallway and out the front door. A few seconds later I heard a car engine start up outside and a car drive off. I could still smell his piss floating around in the stale, hot air of the living room.

I picked up his revolver from the rug and opened up the cylinder. There was a round in each chamber and the couple that I shook out were hollow point, to hit flesh and expand and just take everything out of your middle as it went on through.

Going through the house, I locked all the downstairs doors and windows. Although none of them were very secure, each had enough lock on it so that someone would have to make a racket to get in. Then I went upstairs to my room and lay down on my bed. I put the revolver on the night table and the .45, with the hammer down again, under the pillow in case the Tooth Fairy needed a gat.

What I had in mind was to go to sleep in my house, in my room, in my bed for the rest of the night. I could have gone back to Luck's apartment, but I didn't want to. This was my house, and I wanted to sleep here. Maybe I'd have to do it with two hand cannons a few inches away from either hand, and maybe I'd have to sleep in my clothes with my shoes on. Maybe if I did manage to fall asleep, I'd have very bad dreams. That seemed real likely. And maybe if I did manage to fall asleep, there was a good chance I'd never wake up again.

What the fuck. I was going to try it anyway.

# BECKER

**I** didn't die before I awoke, but I had bad dreams. I remember waking up suddenly twice during the night, confused and disoriented and certain I was under some kind of deadly attack, but before I could reach for a weapon, the attack neglected to materialize. In the dream I remember, I was one of the sons of Njal, the sort of Pa Cartwright of the Icelandic saga. Dad being a seer, for months before it happened we all knew that our enemies would gather in the night outside the cabin and burn the place down with all of us, our wives, our children and our grandparents inside. Although this bothered me a lot during those months and weeks, I never seemed to get around to asking Dad (who looked and talked exactly like my Dad, for some reason) why we all didn't go on down to Reykjavik and sign up for a Caribbean cruise for a couple of months until the troubles blew over. Instead, I just wandered around the cabin doing my chores and talking with various relatives, reminiscing over what a great life it had been and what a shame it was that in a week or two we all had to snuff it, but we all agreed that was just the way the Icelandic ball bounced. The place was musty with predestination, and what little talk there was of installing sprinklers or buying a Captain Kelly smoke detector was pretty much scoffed at as a waste of time.

I think our enemies were parking their ponies in our driveway and soaking their torches in kerosene when I couldn't stand it anymore and made one of those supreme dreaming efforts to wake up. It worked, and as a double bonus, it was around noon and I didn't have to go back to sleep anymore. I'd gone through the recommended nightly allowance and dented the bedclothes enough to say George Washington slept here and get a plaque on the outside, and I didn't have to lie down and have any more of those weird dreams.

I looked out the bedroom window and didn't see the Plymouth anywhere on the street. I was awfully glad about that, but I'd pretty much expected it. That meant I could go downstairs and fry myself up some breakfast instead of going across the street and blowing somebody's brains out all over the front seat of his car in broad daylight. That certainly would have boded ill for the rest of my day.

The *Herald* boy must have been trying to get me to subscribe because he'd left the paper on the doorstep. I made myself comfortable in the living room to read the latest installment of those wild and whacky adventures of me and my pals. I wasn't disappointed. We were getting more outrageous all the time and becoming a regular feature.

Nobody new was dead or tottering on the brink and I couldn't find my own modest name in the goings-on. A large photo showed a fair-sized graveside gathering, with people wearing *yarmulkes* and a couple of young men and one old one trying to comfort a distraught old woman. I had to stare at her for a few seconds before I realized that she was Lee's mother. I'd met her a few times at her house. Sometimes Lee would clean me up and make me dress proper to display in front of the family when he came in for criticism that he was hanging out with too many *shiksehs* and *shegs*. I resented the piss out of it, but except for Lee, I liked the atmosphere in the house, and I liked his old lady. In real life she didn't look anything like the picture. She was bouncy and she liked to toss a lot of Scotch back and get silly and randy and tart and tell stories. She'd been around. She saw through me the first time; I could tell. She told me stories of the Jewish gangsters she used to hang around with when she was a kid in Atlantic City.

**214**

In the story under the picture, the police still didn't have any leads on Lee's killer, but they were more eager than ever to have a long talk with Michael on a number of related topics. He'd been charged with all sorts of wondrous things, conspiracy to embezzle, conspiracy to defraud, conspiracy to violate the Federal Reserve and state banking statutes—in fact, conspiracy to do everything that Lee had done but was now beyond the law's reach to answer for. Lower down in the story was inset a small version of his high school picture again. Good luck finding him with that. *Mazel tov.*

They would have had better luck staking out the funeral. About three rows back in the crowd, as it dwindled from immediate family to cousins and bank employees and business acquaintances, was Michael's face between a couple of heads and shoulders. Dufus-assed move, but I understood it. If I'd been him and been in Miami, it would have been hard for me to fight the impulse, and Michael could be almost as bad as Lee at fighting impulses, even when it meant showing himself at one of the most obvious and logical places even cops might think of. He had the new countenance I'd told him to put on, the shave and haircut. Even in the grainy black-and-white photo he looked sad, real sad and empty, and nervous to boot, but a funeral was a good place for a fugitive to wear a *punim* like that. It fit right in. Looked authentic, too. It probably was. Funerals and fugitive warrants happeneth to us all.

Although I searched the rest of the news columns I couldn't find any mention of Richard. He didn't seem to have died and he didn't seem to have become any hotter as a news item by staying alive. Maybe he'd fallen into the category of Just One of Those Things, private dope deal gone sour at local motel, no big deal, no innocent bystanders plugged, so fuck it. Pretty improbable, but then R.J. and I had been giving the heat and the papers quite a few other things to occupy them. Richard was just some shmuck with a big hole in him who lived—well, how could that stack up against wholesale bank buggering, a wild queer with answers on the loose and a bloated floater in a Coconut Grove swimming pool?

Would Richard be pissed off that I hadn't blown Mr. Roach away when I had the chance? What shape would he be in when I finally got a chance to see him? Maybe he'd contracted The Famous Wound and was out of the gene pool forever, and I'd have to tell him that I'd let the nice law enforcement officer go with nothing heavier than exile on the honor system. That was going to be a bitch. Because of course it had to be Roach who'd waylaid Richard at the motel. Jesus H. Christ, I sure hoped it was Roach, because if it wasn't, R.J. had more than one rent-a-psycho roaming the peninsula and the Keys, and I didn't think I could stand more than one. But dead cops on the floor—yes, there'd been serious pragmatic reasons for not eighty-sixing the man then and there. In lieu of that, though, I hoped the number I'd done on his head had been enough to get my message across. I'd tried to remember the proper formula for getting piss out of a rug and had come up with ammonia, so now the spot where he'd been lying smelled of ammonia rather than piss—a dubious improvement, but at least the guests were unlikely to whisper about lax housekeeping. Not many guests these last couple of days, I thought. Funny how nobody wants to drop by when people are out to kill you. Nobody loves you when you're down and out.

And I was down and out. The motel miasma was creeping back on me. Something about these bizarre and primitive efforts to save what was left of our asses just drained the crap out of me. Every step I took seemed to be a step in lead boots, and a thousand sweet sirens seemed to be harmonizing in my ear: *Give it up. Lie down and rest, sweet David. Lay your burden down. Let George do it. Get out of the drug business and let everyone else take care of himself.* Every day it was an increasingly seductive song that was pressing me to the limit and I knew I was just one straw short of freaking out and heading for California forever—and that was assuming I lived. Heading for the Coast without even bothering to tell Richard or Michael or Annie or the mailman, just the big Shazam, the Judge Crater Express. As a tempting fantasy, it had a lot going for it. I wouldn't have to churn out any more big, complicated plans. I could get far, far away from the most obvious places the cops were going to start looking for me when I became a central character in their investigations. I wouldn't be responsible for anyone anymore, wouldn't have to staunch anybody's leg wounds or haunt the hospital corridors waiting for a peek at one of my troopers with tubes up his ying-yang.

I told myself there was no reason to leave for Miami just yet, either—the trip would go smoother if I waited until two or three in the morning to kick it off and motor out of town. I could get some sleep, clean up my act again, maybe slide by R.J.'s on the way out for a clue to his whereabouts. No big hurry, why fight the feeling, sit back and relax, take it easy on yourself. I crawled up to the bedroom, flopped on the bed and clicked on the TV. That would take my mind off everything. *The Dating Game, Four O'Clock Movie, Bugs Bunny.* The universe was shrieking for some more Becker action, and Becker was up in the sack watching the TV. Well, nobody'd know but me, and I wasn't talking.

TV was about in the same condition I'd left it last time I'd checked on it, no major improvements and just minor deteriorations. You could still do your ironing in front of it without scorching the shirts. It was all pretty pathetic, which matched the way I was feeling pretty neatly. I flipped around the dial looking for the few signals you could pull in over the open water from Miami. Finally, just to pretend I wasn't completely giving in to squash rot, I landed on the educational station.

That was a big mistake. At first it looked just right. Absolutely nothing was happening, even less than usually went down on the public channel. They were having their annual or semiannual or monthly or daily fund-raiser telethon, which was sort of a high-tone terrorist spree in which these strange geeks who looked like real estate salesmen hogged the camera and held *Upstairs, Downstairs* and *The Ascent of Man* hostage until the viewers forked over some arbitrary amount of money by pledging the bucks over the phone. And if you came across with the money, with enough of it, you got a t-shirt with the station logo on it, or an umbrella for a little more, or a director's chair with the station logo on it, or if you were a downtown bag woman haunting South Beach you got a nifty new plastic shopping bag with you-know-what on it. And the geek kept apologizing over and over again that the shows you had tuned in for were running a little late, but they needed a whole bunch more bucks and if you didn't come across with the bread, they weren't going to show you *Monty Python* or let Julia Child show you how to make goat's head soup. He kept whining the pathetic spiel through his nose while behind him a flock of bored honeys from a Catholic snatch college sat at desks wondering if their boyfriends would call and get through to them as long as nobody was calling to pledge money anyway. While just five minutes of this shit got stale, I needed some synthetic voice and smiley face to keep me company while I was conjuring up my epic bummer, so I kept it on.

The light was fading from outside the bedroom windows and the picture on the screen was coming in with a bit more contrast when the telethon started to get hot. A new geek, a lady, had taken over the microphone and was singing the blues about how much it cost the station to acquire one lousy episode of *Crockett's Victory Garden,* when a hand from off screen tapped her on the shoulder and she did a double-take and turned to confront this intrusion into her lecture. The camera panned back a little, and Michael was smiling at her. It was a great smile, a billion-dollar smile, a piano full of teeth flying out of a wild man's face, wild even without his usual grizzly-bear appearance. Apparently he'd just sported for some expensive threads, perhaps careened his way up and down the Miami garment district south of 36th Street, which wasn't very far away from the studios. Though no tags stuck out of his new cream silk shirt and his new blue blazer, it was obvious they hadn't been off for long. He looked so happy. Why not? After all, he had my duffel bag over his shoulder, with half the cocaine on earth in it, a ton of cash and a nifty grab bag of automatic weapons. I would have been happy, too, if I'd been him.

This is about the best I can remember of what happened next.

Lady: *Uh, oh—well, hello!*

Michael: *Hi!*

Lady: *Um, do you have . . . did you . . . .*

Michael: *Oh, listen, I just really enjoy your programs and I saw you were having the telethon and I wanted to help out.*

Lady: *Well, that's very nice of you. Um, can we have your name for the viewing audience?*

Michael: *Sure. Michael Tuckerman.* (It was, too.)

Lady: *And what do you do, Mr. Tuckerman?*

Michael: *Oh, I'm in the importing business. Listen, would it be all right if I just gave you my donation right here?*

Lady: *Well, I suppose so. . . . I don't see why not. John? John? Would that be all right . . . oh, well, our floor director just gave me the nod, so I guess it's fine. How much were you . . . .*

Michael: *How about a thousand dollars?* (He started to reach into his blazer pocket but stopped.) *Nah, how about five thousand? Listen, I'm just going to have to get it out of this bag.* (He limped around a little and put the duffel bag down on the stage and unzipped it halfway while the camera followed him down. Then he started withdrawing some stacks of money and putting them on the floor. Tactfully, without spilling any of the cocaine or the guns. With taste.)

Lady: *Well, while you're, uh, doing that, could you tell us what your favorite PBS programs are, Mr. Tuckerman?*

Michael: *Oh, I like 'em all. I like the rock 'n' roll show that comes out of Chicago and I like Monty Python. Sometimes I watch Sesame Street and the Electric Company. Here you go.*

Lady: *Thank you. This is really very generous. Do you always carry this much—*

Michael: *Well, I had to go out of town on a business trip and I saw you had the telethon going on. You sure you don't mind taking it in cash?*

Lady: *Oh, no, certainly not. Would you like a receipt? We'd like to remind our viewers that all contributions to the telethon are tax-deductible.*

Michael: *No, that's okay. Anyway, I hope this helps you out a little.*

Lady: *Well, it's certainly put us a lot closer to our goal. What part of Dade County do you live in, Mr. Tuckerman? Or do you watch us in Broward?*

Michael: *Oh, I live in the Grove. A lot of people know me down there. But I have a lot of friends down in the Keys, too.*

Lady: *Would you like one of our premiums? I guess you can have any one of them you'd like. The director's chair with our logo on it, that's very nice.*

Michael: *Well, maybe I'll come back for something a little later, but I have to be going now. Good luck with the telethon.*

Lady: *Well, thank you very much from the entire staff here at the station, and I'm sure we all mean that sincerely. This is certainly going to help us put on a lot more of the kind of programming you like.*

Michael: *Right on. You take it easy, you hear?*

Lady: *Uh, okay.*

Then he grinned the grin that spanned oceans right into the camera and straight at me, hoisted the duffel bag strap to his shoulder and hobbled off to the left. The lady and I were stupefied, positively shit-faced. I stared at the screen hoping for an instant replay, but they must have decided against it. Instead, the lady looked right at me and asked me what I thought of that.

## BECKER

**D**rop your cocks and put on your socks . . . .

Yes, boys and girls, like it or not, it was time to roll out of the sack and attend to business again. Michael had lost his mind just a few hours before I'd planned to lose mine, and because he'd beaten me to the punch, it was up to me to drag my ass up to Miami again and clean up his mess, particularly since he was making it with the contents of the magic duffel bag.

Michael could go to hell in a bucket for all I cared. Well, I cared, but when people start losing it like that on such a grand scale on live TeeVee, there isn't really a fuck of a lot that a concerned social worker can do in the face of such determination: the man was heavy into going out in a blaze, and God help anyone, friend or foe, who stood in his way. Yet if I was very, very lucky, I had a wee chance of positioning myself on the sidelines to reach out a hand and liberate the duffel bag as he roared by on the way to the end zone. Not much of a chance, but a chance.

Not that I thought he'd decided to take the toot and the cash for himself and was going to give me a fight over it. That wasn't Michael or even the meteoric trip he was into. The trip came first, and to Michael it was just a slight ancillary matter that he happened to have the equivalent of the gross national product of Luxembourg on his shoulder. First I'd have to find the lad, and that was going to be the heavy part. When I'd left Miami, I'd imagined he was pretty safe in the motel with the Virgin Mary outside and would stay there, give or take a couple of food dashes per day. We didn't have a backup rendezvous to speak of.

So that put me in the position of being one lonely amateur looking for a fellow that a lot of inspired professionals were also chasing all over the landscape, some to jail him, others to interview him and take his picture, and one or two to ice him and relieve him of his luggage. Well, fuck that. If anybody was going to grab that bag, it was going to be me. When I made my play for it, Michael could come along, too, if he wanted, and I'd do whatever I could to cool him out and find him a safe hole to crawl into for the duration, but the bag belonged to some responsible party, specifically Becker, and I was going to get it or go down trying. It didn't belong to the cops—Jesus, they'd just stick it in a safe in a property room somewhere and let anybody who had an ID badge come in and take little bits of it when some cop needed it to plant on somebody in a bust, or when some other cop needed something to trade for a little extra cash. Well, after all, we pay those guys zilch and they can't fucking make a living any other way, so they're entitled to skim a little off the top of whatever happens to be residing in the property room. And the worst fate for all that toot would be if the cops got it and were honest about it. They'd let it sit there until everybody went to trial and then they'd *incinerate* it. No, no, no way. Part of it belonged to Michael, but not if he was going to pull any more of that TeeVee bullshit with it. And it sure as fuck didn't belong to Mr. R.J. No. He'd been too naughty to deserve it. That left me and Richard, but I'd have to act as Richard's proxy while he was having his out-of-body experiences and hovering. That left only me.

I locked up the house around 9:30 that night and kicked the machine over in the backyard. Grass and wet dirt spun out from the rear wheel when I gave it a little too much gas on the way to the street. Cruising through the residential streets, I lazily leaned left and right as I turned corners to get the feel of the bike under me again. I pulled up across the street from R.J.'s, not really knowing what I wanted there. I guess nothing more fantastic than just sitting on the saddle of my bike and gazing across to see what I could see. I could have chambered a round and gone in blasting, but even if R.J. was there and fortune smiled on me, everything would have ended with screams and sirens and a high-speed chase and a crash into some telephone pole. I could have tried my luck by strolling up to the door and having a chat with Lisa if she were there and R.J. wasn't, a chat about the positions of the stars and the amount of Uranus in my trine, with a few innocent questions about where the fuck R.J. was sandwiched in between *Oh by the way, speaking of R.J. might you have any idea where he might be I do so want to have a little talk with him it's been so long,* but that was a pretty iffy plan. Or if R.J. was holding court, I could have walked in and sat down in the chair across from his and laid a little tension down in the room, a little silence, a little displeasure, and then left; he would have been at about the same loss to settle things right then and there as I was, and an unexpected visit with nothing to say might, just might, have unsettled him. Maybe. That depended on whether there was anything in the material plane that had the capacity to unsettle R.J. Probably a flight of nuclear missiles zipping right toward him might annoy him without really unsettling him. So that would make my surprise a pretty wasted visit.

So I just sat on the bike with my feet up on the handlebars gazing across at the white stucco house with the scraggy little excuses for bushes on either side of the front stoop. The house was dark except for the living room, which was spraying out blue light from the TV screen, and it maddened me, just browned me off incredibly that it could have been R.J. inside watching *Dick Van Dyke* or *Columbo,* his feet propped up on the hassock as he took his little entertainment break from the exhausting chores of killing all my buddies and scattering us all over the fucking map and driving us into berserk frenzies. Though it could have been Lisa, it could just as easily have been the Grand Exalted Motherfucker himself, munching on some popcorn while waiting for a troll to phone him to put a black pushpin right where I was on the map of Florida. Even the absence of R.J.'s usual car didn't mean shit, just the way the absence of my motorcycle when Roach had dropped in had been a little on the deceptive side. As I cleared the Naval Air Station up the highway, I tried to convince myself the recon had taught me a lot, that *someone* had been there, that *somebody* was watching the tube, but I let these sparse and unconvincing pickings drift behind me in the airstream. Except for slowing down through Marathon and then Islamorada for the commercial and residential traffic, I hunkered down over the gas tank, my nose and goggle eyes peeking over the gauges to cut the wind resistance.

Gassing up at a big self-serve station in South Miami, parking behind the bank of pumps farthest from the highway, I tried to clear the road out of my head to do a little thinking. One possible rendezvous might occur to Michael now, if he hadn't simply fled or been picked up by the cops. In another forty minutes I had negotiated the causeway to the Beach and the marina. It wasn't a good time to get there. From across the highway I could see through the locked Cyclone fence that one of those half-starved rabid throat-rending Nazi guard dogs inside was getting heavily territorial. No talking to that sucker for sure; the place was his until they took him away in the morning. I wouldn't have minded snuffing him just to put him out of his misery, especially if I could have also had a shot at the jerks who trained things like that, but trying to get into the marina just to see if Michael was holed up in the *Kelpie* was definitely a lame, paranoia-generating idea. After I shot the mad dog, there was always Mad Michael inside, a hell of a lot better armed than I was. The way he'd been acting lately, he might just perforate me all over the docks and then come out and say *whoops*. He'd probably also get beginner's luck.

I killed the wee hours in an all-night bowling alley on 36th Street 'way the hell to the west, getting some chow, playing pool and even bowling a couple of games just to pay the rent. The burgers were greasy and the fountain Cokes had too much fizz water in them. Finally it seemed time to check out the marina again. The Hound of the Baskervilles was just being coaxed away into the security kennel truck when I drove up, and my buddy at the marina was waiting outside for the ritual to be over before venturing in to open the office. As the truck drove away, I pulled the motorcycle into the compound by the office trailer and called to him. He turned around from unlocking the trailer, saw me and walked over.

"Listen, you remember my buddy, the one who was hurt—?"

"The one I'm chargin' room and board to?"

"He's here?"

"Well, I don't know if I know that for sure. I might have seen him around here last night when I closed up. I might have. Of course, he wouldn't have stayed in here after I locked up. That'd be stupid, I guess."

"Yeah. Well, a lot of stupid shit's been going on lately. Think he's in the boat?"

"Best bet. I got it fixed up for you, by the way. He already paid. I think it came to about two hundred bucks. I figured you wanted the panels replaced with the same kind of finished wood."

"Of course. Thanks."

"He said he didn't need nothing, so I left him alone. I got to get the coffee going. Come on over for a cup in a few minutes."

"Sure. Thanks."

Because I was wearing tennis shoes I didn't make much noise clambering up the scaffolding inside the shed where the boat was dry-docked, but when I poked my head over the gunwale, Michael was staring and pointing his M-16 directly at me. The magazine was in and everything looked ready to go. For an instant I wondered whether he still thought I was his pal. That thought hadn't crossed my mind until just then, but there were a lot of things going for it. I'd gotten the man shot, his best buddy drowned, another buddy shot, and decked him out with about five pounds of warrants and federal raps. I'd made the world's most obscure dope-running fag into a South Florida celebrity who had all the cops in the state hunting for him. Now I wanted to talk to him about taking away his duffel bag of machine guns and cocaine—there was just the slightest possibility that he might not be delighted to see me, and now he had the wherewithal to express his displeasure.

"Easy, chief," I said softly.

He smiled and put down the rifle. "Hi. Come on in. Where have you been?"

I climbed over the side and sat down next to him. "Jesus," I sighed, "for a second there I thought you were going to blow my fucking head off."

He looked surprised, even a little hurt. "I wouldn't do that," he said. "What makes you think I'd do that?"

"Times have been rough lately. Caught your act on TV the other day. You really looked slick there."

"Yeah," he said; he was blushing. "I sort of counted on you to watch the educational station. You always were a heavy intellectual type. Anyway, I'm sorry. I sort of lost it there. It was a spur of the moment thing. I won't do it again."

"No, please. Don't apologize. It brightened up my day considerably. You know, you get so used to seeing everything on TV edited and on tape and everything, no surprises, and that gets so boring. It was nice to see a little spontaneity for a change."

"Yeah, I was spontaneous, wasn't I? Jesus, Becker, I don't know what to tell you. I was just going bananas there while you were gone. First I went to the funeral—"

"Yeah. Saw you there in the papers. You've certainly been busy."

"You don't know the half of it," he said. "I tried to hang out in the back row, but Lee's old man recognized me even with the shave and stuff and he sort of lost it there in front of everybody. He started yelling and calling me all kinds of things and then he grabbed me and screamed at some other guys to hold me and call the cops. It was a freak show. I didn't hit him or anything, but I guess I just sort of pushed him away and he landed on his ass and I started to run. It was so weird, man, everyone screaming. I didn't want any of that to happen. I just wanted to pay my respects, man."

"Yeah, I know."

"Anyway, that started doing things to my head. After I ran a few blocks away from the cemetery, I caught a cab back to Eighth Street and got out across from the motel. Guys looking like cops were talking to the manager. Maybe they weren't cops, but I was afraid to get closer to find out. So I cut out and got the bag from the bus station, figuring I'd better be ready to get out of town. I didn't know where you were, man. I was starting to think you must be dead. I was freaking out at every cruiser on the street. And then I started freaking out about R.J. and whoever he might send looking for me. So I dragged the bag up to the garment district to get some ritzy traveling threads, something I could wear to the airport. Anyway, when I stopped for lunch, they had that telethon on the TV. Why did I go there, man? Why did I do that? How'd I look?"

"Grand. Really grand. You don't have to tell me why. I think
I can scope it out."

"Yeah? Well, lay it on me, man, because I'm completely mys-
tified."

"Look—we spend the last week, you and me, peekin' and
a-hidin', ducking bullets and cops, and you can only do so much of
that before you go a little silly and want to just fucking moon all
the people who're after you. You know, you just want to stop all
that hiding under the bed and go in front of the whole world and
whip it out. You did. Congratulations."

"I didn't give away too much money, did I?"

"It's okay with me. It comes out of your profits, anyway," I
said.

"Profits. Man, you sure are an optimist. I'm thinking of getting
out of this with my cock and you're talking about profits."

"We've still got the toot. We *do* still have it, don't we? You
didn't give it to a passing Hare Krishna, did you?"

"Nope." He pushed the duffel bag toward me. "Help yourself. You really think you're going to be able to get that stuff north
and sell it?"

"Oh, goodness gracious, yes. That part of the plan ain't been
shot to shit in the least."

"What about me?" he asked.

"What about you?"

"Well, I sort of feel like a slight liability, with my face and limp
all over the post offices. Have I made the ten-most-wanted list yet?"

"No. They don't put queers on that. Well, what do you want
to do?"

"Christ, man, I think it's time for me to just pull out. I can't
help you guys anymore. Just give me whatever cash you can spare
and we'll call it square, but I got to get out of here and stay away
for a long time."

"No, you're still a partner. After I sell the toot, you still get
a share. But if you want to get out of here, okay. I can dig it. Where
you going?"

"I don't know, man. I'm afraid to crawl out of this boat."

"So don't."

"What do you mean?"

"Well, the *Kelpie*'s as good a way to get the fuck out of here as any other, better than most ways. You don't have to buy a ticket or give anybody a phony name. Once you steer out of here, you don't have to follow anybody's route or schedule, and this sucker'll take you to a lot of places where nobody gives a fuck who you are if you keep reasonably clean."

"Hey, man, I don't know how to drive this stupid boat."

"Sure you do. There's nothing to it. As long as you don't smash into anything or go aground or sink or capsize, no one'll ever suspect you're not Jack London himself."

"You've got to be crazy."

"No. I don't need the boat now. I got the price of four or five more of 'em in the duffel bag if I want another one. And you're right: you do have to get the fuck out of here. They're watching the trains and the buses and the planes and the cars, but I doubt they're watching the oceans and the cuts all that heavily for you. Steer for deep water and practice your seamanship out there. Read Chapman. There's a copy down in the bunks. Head for the Bahamas. The bars there are full of people who island-hop and know something about boats. If you can make it to the Bahamas, you can get yourself a chum, a honey or maybe even a corn-hole buddy who knows how to run this thing and wouldn't mind a free trip to Cozumel."

"Where's that?"

"It's an island off the Yucatán. Tourists and shit. Very in place lately, high-class people, lot of gringos to share a beer with. Hang out there for the duration. Hire out the boat unofficially for sport fishing to keep you going, but don't let the Mexicans catch you."

"Too weird, man. I don't want to take your boat. I'll drown the first night, man, I know it."

"No you won't. Fuck, granted you got to know something about boats, but first of all you do, and second of all this is a fucking emergency. It's the boat or jail, and this boat's your ticket to freedom. And all that goddam equipment, it's the latest shit money can buy and not all that hard to use."

"I ain't got a passport."

"Nobody's going to ask to see one in the Bahamas if you just cruise in for a couple of days, and you don't need one in Mexico, either. Just stay out of trouble and nobody's going to get that formal on you, especially if you got a little bread to hand around. By the time you really need some ID, you can have some cooked up for you, okay? You'll find somebody who can help you out."

"You're sure I can steer this thing?"

"Nope, but I think you're about to find out one way or the other. It's the best plan I can think of."

"Yeah, well, some of your plans have left a lot to be desired the last couple of weeks."

"So get a lawyer. Call a cop. Look, do what you want, but if I were you, I'd take the offer."

"How do I get to the Bahamas?"

I pulled the charts out and spread them over the deck. I showed him how to steer for Bimini and Nassau, after which he'd be pretty much on his own, but with any luck he'd find somebody piloting a boat from there down through the Windward Passage to Jamaica who could be talked into taking the *Kelpie* in a convoy. I showed him how to use the compass for dead reckoning and then how to fine tune his way to landfall with the radio direction finder aimed in on an AM station where he was headed. I told him what he'd need to know about buoys and harbor charts, but basically how to wait for some other boat about his size to go in ahead of him, and then follow it in the first couple of times.

"What about the Bermuda Triangle?" he asked.

"What about it?"

"I mean, is there anything there to worry about?"

"Are you serious?"

"I don't know, man. I mean, this is the first time I ever had to really worry about it."

"That's good. You been shot, R.J. still wants to kill you, all the cops in the world are after you, and you're worrying about the little people from Atlantis. Christ."

"Okay, I'm sorry I asked. I still say this is loony, man."

"Well, I tend to agree with you, but it would solve a lot of problems."

"When can I come back?" he asked.

"How do I know?"

"I mean, how will I know when it's safe?"

"When you get somewhere where you can park your ass for a while, get in touch with me, postcard or a phone call, whatever. If I'm still alive and if the sales go through, I'll hire a lawyer to make inquiries on the sly. But it's going to be up to you, man. All I'll be able to do is tell you what things look like up here. If they don't forget about you, if they still want to lay charges on you, you're going to have to decide for yourself how long to stay away or when to chance coming back."

"Shit." He was looking up at the ceiling, a little glazed in the eye.

"Look, everything cools down, man, sooner or later. Apparently they don't think you killed Lee. Maybe a lawyer can sort of whittle away at all the other bullshit until there's not much of a heavy hit left for you, and then if you agree to come back, maybe he can make a deal so you do maybe six months on that wildlife reservation at Eglin or something."

"It doesn't sound good."

"Well, you should have gone into the real estate business instead of dope. What can I say? I'll do what I can for you. Right now we're both ahead of the game because we're both still walking around in the material plane."

"Yeah. Well, I suppose you could look at it that way. Okay, man. I'll try not to sink your boat."

"Well, it's sort of yours now, skipper. I'll send you the papers to make it official when you get an address and a new name, but it's pretty functionally yours now. You can marry people and hang mutineers and do whatever the fuck you want out there on the high seas. Fuck, you can even use it to run dope for all I care."

"That sounds like an inspired idea, but I think I'll pass for the time being."

"Don't be bitter. *Haec olim meminisse iuvabit.*"

"You got foreigners coming out of your mouth," he said. "I wish you wouldn't do that. What does it mean?"

" 'There will come a time when you will rejoice to remember these things.' "

"No," he said after a few seconds. "I don't think so."

# RICHARD

The doctor who would come and see me each day to check out my condition and update my chart was a Vietnamese intern. I suppose that the first day I was conscious and coming out of a dope cloud I didn't look particularly happy. When I came to, the first thing I saw was an intravenous coming out of my arm and leading to a drip bottle, and it was all downhill from there for everything I saw, smelled, felt or tasted and most of what I heard.

Strange, I suppose, that as soon as I came around I didn't instantly perceive that I was still alive after a point-blank shooting and jump up and do a polka around the room to celebrate. But I felt terrible, nasty, lousy, uncomfortable and in downright pain and I felt nothing coming from the soul to suggest that I make any effort to feel otherwise. And that was when the Vietnamese intern picked me up on his rounds. I imagine he saw a large skin-and-scar-tissue-enwrapped mass of trauma and outraged complaint and not much more except perhaps an experiment in hypothetical physiology and biochemistry that could go either way at that point. So after he sat down on the little imitation wood chair next to my bed and talked to me for a few moments, he picked up my hand, the one not attached to the IV, and held it in his for a few minutes.

He explained that things were looking rosy and constantly improving. The pain and discomfort were only temporary, and eventually even the scar tissue with which my stomach was encrusted could be lessened by plastic surgery so as not to be unsightly. This sentiment I especially appreciated because I hadn't known I had a mass of scar tissue all over my stomach which was unsightly; it was all under acres of gauze and tape, and I had been encouraged not to watch closely when it was changed. His voice as he so alarmed me and held my hand was soft and cooing, the voice of a lover and a gentle healer, and it would have soothed and comforted me if the words it was wrapping were not scaring the fucking daylights out of me.

I didn't have the energy to dispute and I suppose it occurred to me then that whatever the hell had happened to me, these people now had my life by the balls and it would profit me little to do anything to alienate them. So I listened to him as he held my hand tenderly, gazed into my eyes and told me that my holocausted frame would eventually heal and that medical science could definitely find me excellent substitutes for all the things I didn't have anymore.

Of course he was just being a friend the only way he knew how. You could always filter out the real rednecks and assholes among the Americans in Vietnam because they snickered the first time they saw a couple of Vietnamese guys, civilians or soldiers, walking down the street holding hands. Among that filtrate some remained convinced, even a year later in-country, that the entire male population consisted of effeminate fags, so jarring was that initial image of guys holding hands in public. Some just never got over it, and it tended to color their whole style and attitude toward the war. I felt I was doing my intern a disservice by letting him hold my hand and not objecting. His next patient caught unawares might be a Marine or a gym teacher. Well, if the man wanted to be an Amurican, he'd just have to find these things out for himself, even if it did require a little new bridgework. I let him hold my hand.

A little railroad siding type of valve on my IV could administer liquid intravenous medicines without interrupting the glucose and salt and camphor and Chanel No. 5 and wino spit solution they were pumping into me all day and all night, and for the first couple of days about twice a day some nurse would come in with a sort of syringe thing, stick it in the railroad siding, and that was all she wrote—she'd hit that plunger and that was the last thing I'd remember for the next block of time. I never even got a chance to ask What *is* that shit? Maybe once I got as far as What, but when I woke up, whoever that nurse had been was off shift and the earth was hundreds of thousands of miles farther along its circuit around the sun, and in my hospital alone babies had been born and old people had died and some people had come in to complain about the bill and somebody had slipped on the floor outside the flower shop and been taken to emergency. Whatever it was gave me powerful dreams—vivid colors and fantastically lurid landscapes with me decked out in a loincloth and a scimitar leading colorful brigands to overthrow arrogant despots. Every time I woke up from those episodes my head would feel as if someone had swung an anvil into it. The agony would go on for maybe three, four hours, depending on how backed up they were down to the nursing station, after which some new nurse would zip in and slip me the spike. The Vietnamese intern would hold my hand during those waking launch windows, and all the other things that had to be done to me to keep body and soul alive were done without regard to whether I was awake or asleep or busy leading the Mongol horde across the verdant plain. The light in the ward was dim and I hated that, but I barely noticed the coughs or squeals of agony from the other three or four stiffs that were in the ward with me. I was very preoccupied with my own.

One day a cop walked in and sat down in the chair next to the bed. To prove he was a cop he showed me his badge in its little leatherette case with his identification that said Dade County Public Safety Department on it. Then he took off his jacket to reveal the large gruesome automatic under his left armpit, the large gruesome Dirty Harry revolver under his right armpit, and the itsy-bitsy little snub-nose revolver in a belt holster. That was good enough for me. He wanted to know a little about me and what had happened to me in that there motel and who had done this thing to me so they could go out and find the villain. He was very palsy-walsy. He told me it didn't matter at all that I might possibly have been slightly involved with any illegal activities, because whatever they were, they didn't condone attempted murder, no sir. The authorities tended to overlook whatever the victim was up to when murderous scoundrels started shooting up motel rooms.

I told him I wanted to be as cooperative as I possibly could but I didn't know anything about any illegal activities and I didn't have the slightest idea who had shot me. I'd just been in the motel for the science fiction convention. I was a science fiction fan. That was when I began to get a grip on what he had, because I actually saw him rolling that explanation around in his little brain and I could see that it flew a little. Not much, but just enough to let me know that it was only highly likely but still not definite in their minds that I was a big doper shot up by other big dopers.

First he tried to sweeten the kitty with all the weird electronic boxes they'd found in my room. I blushed. That was good, that was the right thing, although what a blush looks like on the face of a near-corpse is something I never got to see myself.

"It's my hobby," I said.

"You got yourself an illegal hobby," he said. "Some of that stuff you can't get licenses for no matter who you are, so it don't matter if you do have licenses for the rest of it."

"Yeah, I know," I said, and blushed some more and tried to look repentant.

"It could be serious. It's not our beef, though. It's federal, those FCC boys, maybe the FBI, I don't know. I could overlook it if you'd tell me what really happened to you."

"I'm trying to tell you, but I don't know. I went to the convention and I brought all that stuff with me. I like to travel with it. It's fun to play with, drive around at night with some lady and broadcast to Mars or California all over the bands. I didn't think anybody'd ever catch me."

"Well, somebody did," he said sort of nastily. "It could be trouble. We're obligated to cooperate when federal statutes are broken, you know, even if we don't care one way or the other."

I was petrified. The last person who'd actually gone to jail on a broadcasting rap had been Tokyo Rose. And this would have been my first Dixie Kicker offense to boot. Truckers with linear amplifiers were waiting to go to trial on their eighteenth offense out there, with shittier lawyers than I planned to get for my first pop.

If this was the heaviest threat the cop could come up with, I just might be able to live through this.

"Well, I guess I should have expected I'd get busted for the radios one of these days. I'm really sorry." Sheepish.

"That don't wash," he said. "You're in to marijuana smuggling up to your ass, son, and don't try to kid me any other way. The radios are the easiest thing you got hanging over you right now."

"Marijuana? Look, okay, I smoke pot. Everybody smokes pot, a little. Teachers smoke pot. But I don't smuggle pot, man. That's too weird. I'd rather pay somebody twenty bucks for a bag."

"So you admit you had marijuana in your possession at the motel?" His voice sounded as if a gear had just clicked into place and a tape of a litany had come on.

*Sure. Where do I sign?* There was no fucking dope in that motel room.

"You mean you found marijuana in the motel room?" I asked. I was stupefied, sort of.

"I asked you if you admitted to possessing marijuana in the motel room."

Amazing. This fool had nothing, and he was just trying to bag a quota to justify his time and effort. Anything. Pot possession, Dixie Kickers, foul language and blasphemy, public urination, witchcraft, tampering with produce scales. Far out. So I decided to give the scumbag a hard time.

"Look, I don't like this. I don't think I should say anything without seeing a lawyer."

"Look, son, we know what you and your friends are up to. You're in a lot of trouble, and the only way you're going to get out of it even a little is to cooperate, and that's just the truth. Now don't be dumb and start with all this lawyer stuff, because in the long run it ain't going to get you anywhere."

*You're right, dad, but I'm going to try it anyway. What you think about that?*

Eventually the nurse came in and gave the cop the heave. She was a bent-looking young honey, the kind who never quite gets with anybody's program all the way. I had the feeling she threw him out not for any medical reasons, but because she'd checked me out and checked him out, and she liked me and didn't like him. I also had the feeling she liked me because she knew I was entirely no good and a turkey and a loser and a pathological liar who did nothing but conjure up bad times and weird troubles, and she went in for that sort of thing in a big way, as long as it could be kept within reasonable bounds and she didn't lose her job.

"You want me to get you a lawyer?" she asked, after we couldn't hear the cop's wooden shoes down the hall anymore.

"Can I ask a silly question? Is this a prison ward?"

"Nope," she said.

"I didn't think so. How am I?"

"What do you mean?"

"Well, I mean, how am I doing? What's wrong with me? How long do I have to have these fucking tubes—excuse me, pardon my French—how long do I have to have these tubes in my arm?"

"You're okay. You're a mess, but you're going to make it. I think you lost some of your intestines, but they still work more or less like they used to, or they will when they heal. It's going to be a week or so before you can handle solids. I hope you like broth. Well, what about the lawyer? I can make a phone call for you if you want."

"I don't think I need one."

"It sounded like you did."

"It sure did, didn't it? But I think he's just jiving me, just trying to shake me up. Well, anyway, I won't bore you with that—could you make a phone call for me to somebody else, though? Or could you get me a phone?"

"I can't get you a phone because you're a public admission and they don't know yet if you're going to pay, so they don't want a phone on your bill, too. I'm sorry about that, but who do you want me to call?"

I gave her Becker's number in Key West and apologized that it was long distance. She said that was okay.

"There's a problem, though," I said.

"What?"

"Well, maybe somebody'll be there, but maybe it won't be my friend Dave. That could be a problem. Listen, this is all getting too complicated and you don't need to get involved. Just forget it."

"You've been a bad boy, haven't you?"

"Must have been. I got shot for it."

"I'll ask him a question and if he can answer it, I'll give him your message. If he can't, I'll hang up. How's that?"

I stared at her. This was certainly turning out to be one of those full-of-surprises days.

"You used to work for the CIA?" I asked.

"No. Haven't you ever sent money by Western Union? They let you ask a test question so the person on the other end can prove he's the right person."

"That's very fancy. Okay, I'm game if you are. If the guy says he's Dave . . . Jesus . . . okay, ask him the name of the army lawyer who went to school with his brother. His name was Hart. That's a good one. If he knows that, tell him where I am, that I'd like to see him, that I'm going to live, that I'm eating broth, whatever. You can tell him anything you want, anything he wants to know. He's a buddy. Could I ask you something else?"

"What? I got to go in a second."

"There's a tube up my, uh . . ."

"It's a catheter. You're okay down there, if that's what you want to know."

"Very much so, thank you. What's your name?"

"Denise."

"I love it. Are you married?"

"No. I was. Get some sleep."

I didn't see Denise the next day, but the cop came back in the afternoon. This time he had the really damning evidence. He'd found out about my bad discharge and that I didn't have a job in Key West. At this rate, he was bound to have an air-tight case against me in five or six years, first-degree getting shot or bleeding on the floor of a public accommodation. A couple of times I almost felt like confessing to something in his jurisdiction out of pity. Instead I just kept playing hayseed and telling him about my passion for science fiction and funny radios and threatening to cry or faint or call for a lawyer. He couldn't make much ground against it. The business about my bad-conduct discharge meant he'd been scraping the bottom of the barrel, because I didn't have a criminal record, and he would have found out about the discharge by running my name through the FBI files. If he'd had anything better on me, he would have flung it at me first.

"You're running out of time, son," he said. "If you want to make your deal now, things won't be too bad for you."

"No, that's all right. If it comes to that, I'll take my chances pleading innocent. As soon as you tell me what the charge is."

"There's no hurry about that. You're not going anywhere far. We got plenty of time to put your deals together."

I was thinking *Use it wisely* and wondering whether to say it out loud when another doctor came into the ward, looked around, saw me and the detective, and came over.

"You'll have to leave now," he said to the cop.

"Okay," he said grudgingly. "You think about what's happening, you understand?" he said to me. "You could be running out of time."

As soon as he'd left, the doctor, a nice-looking young fellow in a shirt and tie who was carrying a black clipboard and had a couple of pens in his pocket, sat down and looked at me.

"You really look like shit," he said.

"Hi, Beck. Took you long enough. Did Denise give you my message?"

"Nope. Didn't get any messages. Who's Denise?"

"Never mind. How'd you find me?"

"I'm getting good at finding people in hospitals."

"That's a really impressive bedside manner you have there," I said. "I particularly like your badge."

He grinned. "Yeah. I punched a hole in my driver's license and bought one of those pocket clips for it. Real nifty, huh?"

"What's in the clipboard?"

"A legal pad. I bought it downstairs. How are you?"

"Okay, they tell me. You should have seen me yesterday. I looked like a bathroom fixture. They just started giving me broth yesterday and letting me stagger to the can for myself."

"What's your major maladjustment?"

"Lost some of my bowel or something. Saw God a couple of times and apparently I've had extreme unction administered so I can die any time I want and it'll be okay. So what's happening with you?"

"I think someone's trying to kill us," he whispered conspiratorially.

"That's real profound, Becker. I'm glad you came all this way to tell me that. It sheds a lot of light on some experiences I've had lately."

"Well, in a nutshell, R.J. killed Lee and Michael's taken the rap for all the banking bullshit. I gave him the boat and he's headed for sunny climes, if that's okay with you. Do you know who shot you?"

"No. I can describe him, though."

"You don't have to. It was a cop named Roche, I'm pretty sure. R.J. must have sicced him on you. I'm sorry, man. That's all I can say."

"Well, look, you did your part. You warned me and I should have been more careful. What about the toot?"

"We're still sitting on it, by some miracle. What's the earliest you think we can check you out of here?"

"I don't know. It could be iffy if I try to leave too soon."

"Well, I don't like you here. If I can find you, so can R.J. What happened with the cops?"

"Oh, he comes in now and then and accuses me of having a bad-conduct discharge and threatens to call my parents or give me a bad mark for citizenship on my next report card. It's pretty pathetic. You wouldn't believe it. If they go all-out, I may have to defend myself about those loony radios they caught me with."

"Look, didn't you have one of those guns with you? One of the automatics from you-know-where?" He was talking very softly and he looked concerned and confused.

"Sure."

"You mean they haven't busted you for that? They haven't said anything about Benning?"

"Nope. The guy who shot me took it. I saw him pick it up just before I lost it. Ain't that a stitch, Becker?"

"Jesus. What a loony tune."

"I know. Next to still being alive, it's the best thing that's happened to me all week."

"Fuck, I been hanging outside of the prison ward waiting for you. I thought I was wasting my time to check the other wards. I was sure they'd have you nailed. This is insane."

"What happened to Lee?"

"They drowned him in the swimming pool."

"Laura and R.J.?"

"Yeah, she was in on it. She's with him. I think you're supposed to try to punch me out for saying that about the woman you love."

"I'll let it slide. Somehow I just don't have the energy to get outraged. It wasn't a very elevating relationship to begin with, except that you needed an elevator to get to her place."

"Still, I'm sorry. It's all pretty seedy."

"What are we going to do?"

"Sell the dope, uncle, and get rich. I'd like you to come north with me if you can, as soon as you can."

"What about R.J.?"

"What do you mean? Are you hot for revenge or something?"

"I don't know. Right now I'm not hot for anything except staying alive. But he's been doing some pretty serious things. I don't think he's going to throw in the towel now. Is he still running around loose?"

"Very loose. I don't have the slightest idea where he is."

Then an old bag of a nurse came in and started staring at Becker, who started staring back. She looked confused, off her feed.

"Are you a doctor?" she asked.

"No," he said politely.

"I thought you were a doctor," she said angrily.

"I never said I was a doctor."

"You have to leave. Visiting hours are over."

"Sorry. I didn't know."

"I'll bet," she said, and started tapping her toe.

"There's a nurse here named Denise," I whispered. "You can talk to her about when I can get out of here."

"Okay. Be good." He wasn't wearing his driver's license on his pocket anymore, but I hadn't seen him take it off. He cracked me up.

The next morning they moved me to a semi-private in another ward, with a television and a phone and a guy in the other bed who owned a couple of parking lots on the Beach and tried to teach me how to play gin better. He told me he had a strangulated hernia.

# 26

## RICHARD

**B**ecker had told me that Annie should be home any day now, but she still hadn't shown up by the time I decided I could chance checking out of Jackson. Becker somehow had made an old Country Squire station wagon materialize and had jammed the back with an old mattress for the trip from Miami to the Keys. Even though he drove slowly enough and we went down by night, the day heat never broke and it was uncomfortable beyond belief bouncing around in the back. We'd had less and less to say to one another during the last days I was in the hospital, which I guess meant that we each had more and more to think about. He broke the trip and pulled over about three times to give me a breather. He'd pull down the tailgate and sit on it while we waited for a breeze to come up, but we didn't talk. When I tried to get him to slide me by a pizza joint, he made me snarf down a Thermos of broth he'd brought along instead.

We got home in the middle of the night. First he parked the wagon a couple of blocks away and left me in the back with the .45 while he strolled over to the house with Roach's monster gun to check it out. Then he drove the wagon the rest of the way home and helped me limp into the living room and set me up on the couch. I'd made it and it didn't seem that we'd done any real

**241**

damage by pushing my discharge from the hospital, but the trip down wasted me and I must have fallen asleep in seconds.

The sun was streaming through the curtains when I woke up. Becker had his back to the wall facing the hallway to the front door and I couldn't tell at first whether he was awake or asleep. The revolver was in his hand but resting on the rug.

"Morning," he muttered.

"Morning," I wheezed back.

For the next couple of days and nights, whenever I awoke he was in the same position. Only when I was awake and somewhat propped up on pillows, under which I kept the .45, would he stir and make me some more broth, which we'd started to augment with some toast and finally a poached egg now and then. A perpetual pot of Cuban coffee brewed for him in the kitchen, and I imagined he was dipping into the toot to help him stay awake as well. It wasn't doing shit for his demeanor, but I wasn't inclined to argue with him that he ought to get some sleep. Despite himself, he was getting a little sleep somehow, and as the days went by I guessed he was putting a little more faith in the new locks on the front door and the downstairs windows and the old refrigerator that blocked the back door, enough faith to suppose that to get through them, someone was going to have to make a shitload of noise that had to wake one or both of us. At night he didn't play blackout or try in any other ways to conceal that somebody was in residence. If anything, he was playing it just the opposite. He was so wired to the max that I guessed he wouldn't have minded some kind of play against the house that might settle things, however they ended up being settled. Only a couple of years later, after I'd left the island, did he tell me his real worry had been that R.J. might try to burn the house down in the night. I was glad he hadn't seen fit to share that particular scenario with me at the time.

On the third night the phone rang around ten or eleven and I grabbed it first. It was the first time anyone had called, but Becker had already invented the drill. Answer, but don't talk until the person on the other end identified himself; no information given away free until we knew who it was.

It was Annie, shouting "Hello?" into the phone.

"Hi, toots," I said.

"Richard? Jesus, why didn't you say anything? Hey, I just got in on the bus. I'm at Searstown. Can you come and pick me up?"

"Well, I'm sort of laid up —wait a second." I looked at Becker.

"I'm not leaving here. And she shouldn't come here anyway."

"She lives here, Becker."

"She could die here. Give me the phone."

Naturally it developed into an argument immediately from what I could hear on our end. He gave her a real shit-eating tone but no details and ordered her to scare up a friend's place to stay and not to come over until daylight tomorrow. Obviously this didn't sit well with her. Although I couldn't make out many of her words as they leaked out of the earpiece, I recognized the tone: *Drop dead, Becker, give me a break, Becker.* She hung up on him.

He gave me a disgusted look. "She's taking a cab over. Fuck it." He picked up the revolver and headed for the front door. I heard the locks start to click and the chains drop.

When the cab pulled up a few minutes later, the door opened and closed again. I heard Annie start to bitch and then stop.

"What the fuck is that?"

"It's a gun," Becker sighed. "It's yours now. Richard's in the living room. He'll teach you the drill. I'm going to bed." I heard him climb the steps and shut his bedroom door behind him. Then it opened again.

"Lock the fucking door!" he yelled downstairs. The door slammed shut upstairs again.

She was pretty wide-eyed by the time she got to the living room. She was wearing cutoffs and some kind of silk flowered top that tied above her waist. When she saw me, her eyes opened even wider.

"Jesus. What the fuck is going on here?"

So I told her. When I got to the part about Lee, she started to cry, and though I felt a little imbecilic, I took her hand and held it and it seemed to help a little. Lee had never been her idea of Prince Charming and it used to annoy her that half the time when he was down here on his own he'd try to jump her, but she'd gotten more than used to him, and he used to spend money on her like crazy when he could get her to go out with him. Once he'd taken her to the Marker 88—her first time at a ritzy French restaurant—

and he'd pulled out all the stops. I didn't know if he'd ever drugged and wined her up enough to tumble, and I didn't want to know. Ordinarily he would have been the wrong sex for her and on the hot island nights when he might have been the right sex, he would have been entirely the wrong type. But he was the original manic Good Time Charlie who held firmly to the theory that if you start squiring any honey at five in the evening and drop three or four hundred bucks on her in food, booze and drugs until three in the morning, the lady will eventually get flexible. Of course if they had tumbled in that financially crippling accidental manner once or twice, that wouldn't have anything to do with why she was crying now. She liked him; even when he was annoying the piss out of her, he tickled her, and she'd spent as much time hanging out in the Grove with him and Michael as he'd spent down here with us.

I had the Kleenex box next to me and I helped her clean up her act to get to the other parts about R.J. and Laura and about Michael having to head for the open seas.

"Jesus," she whispered when I didn't have any more to say that mattered. "I can't believe it. I tried to call a couple of times but there was never anybody home. I would have stayed, Richard. I just thought you guys were doing a number with R.J. That's what Becker told me."

"Well, no, he didn't exactly say that, I don't think, but he didn't mind you thinking it. He knew you wanted to split for a while and that you'd been planning it. Of course he didn't exactly think it would turn into the St. Valentine's Day massacre, either. I don't know if he would have said anything different to you if he'd thought it was going to get this fucked up. By the way, he hasn't had any sleep to speak of in about a week."

"He looked pretty crazied out at the door. What are we going to do?" She was still sniffling a little and was red and puffy around the nose and eyes.

"Oh, I'm sure Becker's got a plan. Man's always got a plan."

She played with the revolver a little. "I've shot these things before, but never one that weighed as much as a brick. I guess he wants me to take over some of the guard duty."

"Well, actually, he didn't want you here at all. He told you that."

"What about you?"

"I'm not crazy about it either, Annie. I got to be here. I can't move around too well yet. Becker—well, I don't really know what's going on in his funny little brain, but that's no different from always. In his way, he thinks he's got to be here, too, and I'm not arguing. Under the circumstances, I don't mind a nurse who can shoot straight. But you can still get out of here, Annie. You know, it could get a lot heavier than just R.J. Everything's been really sloppy and this could become Cop City any day now. Any hour now. Who knows what they got that'll bring them down here?"

"They don't have anything on me," she said. "I been out of town."

"No, but when it all comes tumbling down, it sort of contaminates, you know. Cops aren't real discriminating. You're clean, but you might not stay clean."

"I live here," she said.

"That's one way of looking at it. The other way is that it was a nice place to crash and pay rent for a couple of years and then things got weird and you got sensible and decided to move across town. For Christ's sake, Annie—you've been muling coke for R.J. for a couple of years, ever since he brought you down here from Atlanta. You could have already bought it, honey. You could be doing twenty years for some of that crap already, and you would have been lucky if it had been an American bust. You could have landed in a fucking Colombian jail forever. If you wanted to consider yourself lucky, you could get out of here now. You're not part of it."

"I live here," she said again. "You're all messed up and Becker needs somebody else to pull guard. I'm staying, at least until you can walk around. Even if this is all crazy, I'm not going to leave you like this. If I'd known what you were going to pull, I would have wanted to be in it. Becker never gave me the chance."

"He didn't mean it like that."

"No, he just decided everything for everybody like he always does. Maybe all this shit wouldn't have gone down if I had been here. I guess he never thought of that."

"It would have happened. There's stuff you don't know about R.J. Stuff that I knew and Michael knew. R.J. was just waiting for a chance like this. That's another reason to pull out, Annie. He's not going to stop. Right now maybe he doesn't consider you part of it. But he's not going to stop, and you could be out of it when he makes his next move."

"But you still got the toot. Maybe you could deal with him."

"That's not the problem," I said. "And Becker won't even think about it. I'm sort of scared—well, fuck, I'm scared to death about how Becker's going to play his end. He's got this thing about R.J. walking all over him; he's not going to let it happen anymore. There might be ways out of this, but Becker's not up for them."

"I don't care. I'm staying, at least until you're on your feet. That's it."

We looked at each other for a few minutes and exchanged something, I don't know what—sadness, quarts and gallons of sadness, mainly. She was so much fucking younger than Becker and me and since we'd all started palling around at R.J.'s little house in Atlanta back in the army days, I'd checked her out pretty much as a kid sister. I'd never been quite sure how she'd checked me out, something a little different. Sometimes she'd come out of the shower and walk past me in the living room and shake it a little when she'd been jaded to the max but was too lazy or stoned to go out and scare up something more in her usual routine, a waitress at one of the pier restaurants or a group grope from the Bull or the Monster. Oh, she was tough to look at in any state, but I'd never wanted to mix it up with a housemate—the deal we had going without that bullshit was too mellow. And I knew myself pretty well—one quick bop wouldn't have been enough for me, and I had Laura on my mind besides. It hadn't seemed to piss Annie off that I hadn't reached for it when she'd shaken it in my face—maybe she was a little smarter than I usually gave her credit for. But I'd never expected anything like this to turn up—Annie and Becker and me playing the homesteader's last stand, waiting for the Indian attack and everybody saving one last round so we wouldn't be taken alive.

"Well, what the fuck," I said. "How'd you like a little toot?"

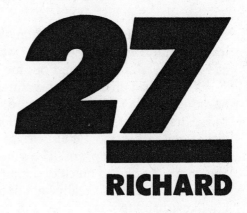

## RICHARD

**N**ow that Annie could give us some relief with the guard
duty, Becker started taking night trips around the island, to Luck's apartment down on Duval and then home by way
of R.J.'s. He refused to let Luck come to the house—enough is
enough, he said—but he counted on Luck to tip him if R.J. got in
touch with him. All he was able to gather about R.J.'s house was
that Lisa was there, because sometimes he'd been able to see down
the side of the house to the patio by the canal. Lisa was sometimes
out there, either sleeping in one of the deck chairs or getting a
moontan and reading her arcana. He still couldn't figure if R.J. was
there or not. When he realized how tempted he was to stroll to the
patio and talk to Lisa, he stopped short—it wouldn't have been
beyond R.J. to bait a trap with Lisa, to tell her the night was lovely
out by the canal and to enjoy herself while he poised himself in the
kitchen window.

After the first night, Annie gave up the monster revolver for
her Ruger .22 target pistol. Once she'd signed aboard for the
duration, Becker had forbidden her to leave the house, so she
couldn't go anywhere up the Keys and practice with the .357.
She figured she'd be able to do more damage with a pistol she was
familiar with and knew how to shoot. I traded in my .45 for a .22,

but for a different reason—with my stomach, the first shot I tried in any position with a .45 or a .357 would probably tear my stitches and sore muscles to shit and put me out of the game.

They'd had an argument, naturally, when Becker told Annie he didn't want her to leave the house alone. "You can't have it both ways," he said. "If you're with us, then R.J. might find that out and make you a target, too. Or else maybe he won't realize you're back, and if he tries anything, you'll be a nice big extra surprise for him." She didn't put up too much of a fight, though, and I kept out of it altogether. You didn't really fight or argue with Becker these days, not like usual. He was frazzled and near-wild and would fly off the handle if we crossed him or challenged him.

One night Becker was sacked out upstairs and Annie and I talked about it. "For a guy who freaks out every time somebody breaks one of his fucking rules, his schemes so far haven't been doing too well," she said, and gently patted my stomach.

"None of this is Becker's fault—well, none of it except the original get-rich-quick scheme. His plans were good, pretty slick. They made sense. I bought them, and I'm no dummy. They were simple for the most part, with a few very nice twists to them. I think he's so freaked out now because all his planning led to all this crap—it just all got out of his control. Also, he's the only one in the team who hasn't been shot or snuffed yet."

"So?"

"Well, he feels doubly shitty about that. Everybody else suffers from his schemes, that sort of shit. I don't have a lot of energy these days, but I'd put up a fight if I thought he was doing something lame. Right now he's in a corner, just trying to protect what we have left, the toot, what we got left of the cash, the house. Us. It may not make a lot of sense, but until I'm on my feet, it's all we can do."

It took a few days, but I was getting off the couch a little bit and for a couple of hours each day we'd all go into the back yard to catch the rays. A rotten and crumbling wooden fence shielded us pretty well from the street, and Becker just didn't think it was R.J.'s style to do anything in broad daylight with neighbors and people strolling by. It was making me feel a lot better not to be cooped up in the living room the whole time with no air other than the AC because of the locked windows. Annie or Becker would go out first to check things out and make a nest for me in the old lawn chair, and then they'd bring me out. I was walking on my own, but they still wanted it that way in case I stumbled. Then we'd set up and each of us would nonchalantly slide a loaded weapon under a pillow or a towel.

One afternoon I was outside talking with Annie and Becker was inside getting wrapped up in some more doom and gloom when somebody out on the sidewalk tried to work the gate in the fence and kept rattling it. The gate had never had a lock before, and people who were used to dropping over (strange and not-so-strange that none of them was sliding by these days) came in that way and went straight for the kitchen door. Now, of course, a big lock and chain guarded the gate on our side. Annie and I stopped talking and watched the gate.

"Annie? Becker? Anybody there?"

It was Lisa. Annie looked at me and I nodded for her to unlock the gate.

"You alone?" I asked.

"Yeah," she said. "It's just me. Can I come in?" She sounded spacier, more confused than usual, if that was possible. Annie had the lock off and was sliding the chain through.

Lisa came in and Annie closed the gate behind her. Looking at me and then at the chain sort of goofy, Lisa asked, "Is something wrong?"

"Been some rip-offs in the neighborhood," I said.

She walked over to my chair and sat down next to it on the grass.

"I missed you guys," she said. "I heard you were out of town. God, Richard, you look so thin. Have you been sick or something?"

"No big deal. I wiped out on Becker's motorcycle, got busted up a little. It's okay now. I'm getting over it. How've you been?"

"I don't know. I've had a lot of time to myself. I've been reading a lot. I found some books about Mu and Lemuria. They're real interesting. You'd like them, Annie. Have you read anything about that?"

"No, not much, I don't think," I said. "R.J. been around lately?"

"Not a lot. He says he's been hunting for mushrooms up north, but he hasn't brought me back any. He stops home sometimes—"

Her words degenerated into burbling and sniffling, but it was funny—she kept trying to talk to us and look at us as if she didn't realize tears were streaming down her face and her nose was running and as if she didn't realize her words weren't coming out right or making any sense.

"What's wrong, Lisa?" Annie asked. She stooped down next to her and put her arms around her, and Lisa kept crying and gurgling and making her awful little-girl noises. Out of the corner of my eye I could see Becker standing on the porch watching us and listening, but he didn't try to come out.

I could make out "—been so lonely—" but not much more, just bits and pieces, and she was shaking in Annie's arms. "Nobody's been around. R.J. comes home and then he leaves again and he hardly talks to me. He only stops to yell at me when he says I did something wrong in the house—"

Embarrassed, I just looked up at the sky while Annie tried to calm her down. I thought Lisa was on something, probably dust or much too much toot, but she got into that stuff a lot and it didn't usually do this to her. Annie was whispering to her, I think so Becker wouldn't overhear. "Did R.J. beat you up, Lisa? Did he hurt you?"

"No . . . he pushed me up against the stove and I got burnt a little, but he didn't hit me really." Then she really began to shake and bawl. "He got mad at me. He asked me if I was coming over here like he'd told me not to, and I asked him why I shouldn't come over here, and he pushed me and started yelling at me. He said Becker—he said Becker was trying to fuck him over, Becker and Michael and you, Richard. He told me not to come over here anymore. That's why I haven't called or anything. I been afraid to. . . ."

"What's wrong? What's wrong?" she wailed. "He won't tell me anything. He won't tell me what's wrong."

Becker was standing over us all now, holding a glass of lemonade.

"Lisa, you have to go now. You have to go home now," he said.

She looked up at him. She was in his shadow. "Tell me what's wrong," she sobbed. "Tell me what's going on. Nobody will tell me anything."

"You just have to go now," Becker repeated. He didn't sound angry. In fact it was the first time since we'd come back from Miami that he really sounded in control of himself.

"There's something awful happening and I can't see my friends. And even when I come over here nobody wants to tell me anything."

"There's nothing awful happening," Becker said calmly. "Just hard times. It has nothing to do with you, Lisa. We love you. It's just hard times. Now you have to go home. You shouldn't be here. This isn't the right time."

Annie helped her to her feet and walked her to the gate. She talked to her there for a few minutes out of our earshot but Becker didn't mind. All Annie was trying to do was to straighten Lisa out enough so she could get home. Then she looked over Annie's shoulder at us and started talking about bad drug deals, bad drug deals. "That's what it is. I know it," she said. "You shouldn't do them. There's always trouble. Nobody ever understands, nobody ever listens to me, and now I can't even talk to you."

Finally Annie had her calmed down enough to leave. Although Lisa had her bike parked outside the gate, she couldn't climb on it. She just walked it down the street and out of sight, still making those terrible noises.

"Great," Becker said, as he huffed back inside.

"Heavy stuff," I said.

"Oh, God, everything's so shitty. She doesn't know what's going on. I'm scared for her, Richard."

"I don't think she's in any trouble. Just getting knocked around a little, but she seems to be used to that. She's not any kind of threat to R.J., just his pet, sort of."

"God, she looked awful. Now she doesn't have anybody."

"Christ, Annie, she never has had anybody, not like normal people have somebody. Nobody ever really gets through to her."

"It's still sad. It's not right."

That night I heard Becker and Annie talking in the kitchen. They weren't trying to keep anything from me, but they thought I was trying to sleep and were keeping it quiet.

"I think we're going to be moving out in a day or two," Becker said. "Richard's just about mended, enough to travel. We got things to do, toot to sell. We still have the contacts up north and if we don't spark 'em soon, they're going to be stale. Everybody'll have put their money back in the bank or spent it on somebody else's shit."

"I'm going with you," Annie said.

"I don't know. Look, you've done good. Maybe because you were here we made it through the last couple of weeks. Maybe there were just too many of us for R.J. to want to fuck with. But this might be a good time for you to keep your distance."

"Not again, Becker." She seemed to have her willingness to fight with Becker again, and he seemed to be willing to make it an argument of sorts, something two-sided rather than dictatorial. "I told you I was with you. I'm staying."

"You don't owe us anything. Look, you're in for a piece of the action, a nice piece, even if you stay here, and that might be the best thing you can do. What's coming up isn't going to be simple."

"No," she said. "I never had a family worth shit, just that drunken colonel and his drunken Virginia society bitch. R.J. sure as hell wasn't family to me, but you guys are. And it's not just something I was born in. I picked you guys to hang out with. Don't try to shut me out again, Becker. It's not fair. You don't pull this shit on Richard. You deal square with him. Deal square with me."

There was a lot of quiet. I heard coffee being poured into a mug.

"It's going to be heavy," Becker said. "But if you want to stay in, okay."

# Part Four

## THE LIFE

# 28

## RICHARD

The Masked Man left me, his faithful Indian companion, behind to do some last-minute scouting around the island while he went on ahead with the Sweetheart of the Rodeo, a.k.a. Ruby the Dyke, to reconnoiter things in Miami.

I put the cat out, locked up the joint, paid the electric bill and did some general visible decoy work during the daylight hours. What a man and what a plan. One by one, like the musicians in the Handel piece who get up and leave the stage while the music's still going on, we were supposed to fade out of the island and head for Whereabouts Unknown to anyone but us: Now you see us, now you don't.

It made sense. We were suffering and R.J. had all the advantages mainly because he knew where we were and we didn't know where his ass was parked. We couldn't scare up anything solid on R.J. while I was lying around on the living room couch, so lacking that advantage, Becker decided to neutralize R.J.'s edge by making us as invisible as the old fart himself, and staying that way until it was R.J.'s turn to surface, to stick his cowboy hat up on a stick above the rock and see where the posse was.

Becker had gone up to Searstown and brought back four cheapo-cheapo electric timers the afternoon before he and Annie left for Miami, and I rigged them around the house, upstairs and downstairs, so that after I left (looking as much as possible as if I were just taking a little stroll down to the 7-Eleven for a Slurpee, be back in a couple of minutes), lights would go on and off in the house in a goofy enough way to fool your famous casual observer for a day or so. The stereo with the FM tuner on was hooked up to the rig so that anyone listening would get a little hit of disco now and then, maybe also the Mass for Shut-ins on Sunday mornings. Keep 'em guessing.

Of course it was only going to work for just so long, if at all. It would probably fend off the casual rip-off artist for quite a spell. For a final touch I was supposed to get Luck to slide by late each night and make the mail and the newspapers vanish. Becker figured that all his tricks and gimmicks wouldn't fool R.J. and his minions forever, but they'd be just effective enough to generate some uncertainty—maybe one of R.J.'s boys might get worried enough to try a forced entry one night. "He'll get in," Becker figured, "and he'll know for sure nobody's home. So he'll know where we're not, and to find that out I figure he'll be shitting bricks every time the window he's prying makes a noise. He can have that job."

I found Luck down at the Dog Beach getting his abbreviated sort of tropical tan.

"Greets," he said when I sat down. "You're looking pretty chipper these days."

"It's the sea air," I said. "Real dandy for recuperating."

"How's things with you guys?"

"Okay. Better than they have been. Like to hit you up for a favor if I can."

"Your credit's pretty good. What do you need?"

"Maybe slide by the house after dark for the next few nights, maybe for a week, and pick up our mail. So it doesn't pile up in the box, you know."

"I can dig it," he said.

"And maybe do it with a little *cuidado,* you know. You never know who might be hanging around these days."

"I'll oil the wheels on the skateboard."

"That's the ticket."

"Funny thing happened. I don't know if Becker knows or not. You might want to pass it on."

"What?"

"The cops are a man short, unexpectedly. Roach just up and left town a couple of weeks ago. He jerked out on a wife and two kids, as a matter of fact. She thought he might be dead or something, went down to the cop station and started raising hell, wanted an investigation. Anyway, he'd told another cop he had some kind of emergency and had to split, but that guy went on a three-day weekend and forgot to pass on the word, so they was tearing up the island—well, in a sort of mild kind of way; Roach wasn't all that much of a popular item to begin with—looking for his ass. They even got the scuba divers to check a couple of canals, I heard. Then the other cop came back on duty and set everybody straight, but nobody knows what the emergency was or where it was or where Roach is. I hear his wife's pretty ticked off. She may have to go back to bar dancing if the stretch marks don't show too bad. Hard times in the trailer court."

"That sounds like Becker's kind of story. Mine, too, could be."

"Yeah, I hear you and the officer knew each other."

"It wasn't very satisfying. We didn't have much to say to one another. But I appreciate the story just the same. I'll definitely pass it on."

That was my last errand on the island, so from there I just strolled north past the big public beaches and the fishing piers all the way up to the airport. Walking to an airport seemed so unexpected somehow that I felt pretty safe leaving town that way, and I timed the walk to be at the airport for the last Air Sometimes flight to Miami. Paid cash, gave a funky name, left no oil slick.

Becker was waiting on the bike down at the far end of the arrivals drive and when he saw me stroll out, he kicked the thing over and pulled it up in front of me. I put the extra helmet on and climbed on the back. We cruised over the highways and down to the boulevards toward Coral Gables and the Miracle Mile. Becker found a side street parking lot, locked the bike up and we strolled around the corner to a cafeteria-deli. We went through the line, me for a sandwich and some soup, Becker for his usual evening eight-course extravaganza. We took our trays upstairs to a corner table.

**257**

Becker looked at his watch. "Annie knows we're here," he said. "She should be here pretty soon."

"What's she doing?"

"Buying some kind of wreck of a car with the precious little we got left of our ready cash. While we're merrily sitting on a ton of coke, I predict that within a couple of days we're all going to be eating cat food. I hope you like cat food."

"I'm sure you'll find a way to make it appetizing. When are we heading north to make the rounds?"

"Not right away," he said. "Let's wait 'til Annie gets here to talk about it."

"No. Let's you and me talk about it now. Why aren't we going north?"

"We are. We got to. I can't snort all that coke by myself, and I still intend to become a moderately wealthy joe from this little jaunt. But we got some stuff to do first."

"Like what?"

"Like don't be an asshole. You know what we got to do."

"Yeah, that's what I figured was cooking in your seedy little mind."

"You sound like you're surprised or something," he said. "You know we have to do this. I'm not crazy about it. It doesn't happen to be my usual line of work, Richard. But that crazy sucker's not going to stop until we're all dead or lying around on heart-lung machines somewhere. I don't happen to be alone in this estimation. Michael was the first guy to point out R.J.'s grand plan to me, and I'm sure Lee would have backed him up on it if he could have surfaced for air. For one thing, there's that business with the *Coriolis*. By the way, you could have told me about that. It might have helped if I'd known."

"Yeah, well . . . it's not the kind of story you feel like passing around, and it was really Michael's—it was up to Michael to decide who should know and who shouldn't. Look, I'm not arguing that point with you. I agree. I think R.J.'s definitely trying to get us out of the dope-dealing business and I think he's trying to kill us."

"But what?"

"But I want out. I agree that's what has to be done if we're going to stay in business. You're completely right. Somebody's got to kill R.J. before he kills us. That's why I want to get out of the dope-dealing business now. You can do what you think has to be done. But I want to get out of the business, out of Florida, out of everything. I've had enough. It's what R.J. wanted, I guess, and he can have it as far as I'm concerned. I'm pussying out."

"Jesus Christ, you've come a fuck of a long way to get out now. Do you have any idea how much money we're going to have even if we make lousy deals up north? We don't have to pay any goddam money back to those banks. That wasn't my idea, but that's the way it worked out and there's nothing we can do about it now, and it means we're going to be rich as shit, Uncle. We just got a little bit more to go."

"No. *You're* going to be rich as shit and *you* got a little bit more to go. And R.J.'s going to be dead. I'm not complaining about that. I'm not getting ethical on you. No son of a bitch on this earth so richly deserves it, and when I read about it in the papers, I promise I'll stand up and cheer. But that's all I'm going to do about it is read about it. I'm not going to make it happen. I'm just not."

"He shot you, you know. He hired that geek to go find you and kill you."

"Hey, don't try whipping me into a lather about that, okay? I've already transcended that stage. That's the whole point, Becker. They tried to kill me and they shot me and I almost died, man, but I didn't. So now I'm back on my feet again, and all I want to do is cut my losses and throw in my chips and end the game and consider myself lucky. Very, very lucky. I want to get out of here and go back up north and do some stuff for a couple of years where nobody wants to kill me. The pay may not be as humongous, but it's a little more regular and you don't have to go through quite as many changes to collect it. I'm sorry, Becker, but that's the way it is. You can be the man of iron all you want, but you weren't the guy who had to float around for a couple of days and talk to God and listen to the angels make music."

His eyes were getting a little narrow and mean.

"I'm not any man of iron," he said, or sort of hissed. "I'm just doing what I have to do. I didn't ask R.J. to start bumping off my friends. That wasn't my idea. If he'd left it to me, there would have been peace and love and sweetness and light and Woodstock down on the island, but he wanted it the other way."

"Still no arguments with me. You're just doing what you got to do. But I'm not going to do it with you. Listen, Becker, there's something else. I mean, it *is* murder, you know, and there's laws against that sort of thing. Laws that never end, by the way, no statute of limitations. Okay, so you're going to make a neat, clean murder. Bravo for you. But sometimes even cops get inspired or lucky, and your luck hasn't been anything to rave about lately. Well, I'll be frank with you, Becker. I want to pull out now before I got to spend the rest of my days worrying about a murder rap. You do what you got to do, and if anybody ever comes knocking on my door to ask me what I know about it, I don't know shit. I don't know you, I don't know R.J., I don't know Luther Burbank, I don't know shit. But I don't want to be pulled into it. I got a chance to sleaze out of it now, and for once I am going to do what Ann Landers would recommend, as lame as that sounds. You weren't the only guy doing a lot of thinking down on the island, Becker. I'm just sorry that I had to come up with some different ideas from you, but I did, and I got to follow through on 'em."

He had to think the next tack through for a few seconds. I was proving a difficult customer. I wasn't responding to the standard sales techniques.

"There are implications," he said.

"What?"

"Implications, Richard. If you don't want to go through with it, that implies that you think I shouldn't. That implies that if we part company now, you're a smart man and I'm a fool."

"Becker, we had to part company sometime. Five years from now, fifty years from now. Nobody stays kissing cousins forever, pal. Believe it or not, I don't care what you do. I got no advice on this thing for you whatsoever. I don't think what you're doing is right or wrong or smart or stupid. But there's a hit associated with it. Ten, twenty years in some shit-sucking Florida penitentiary, and I just couldn't handle that, Becker. Maybe the hit'll never come due. Maybe nobody'll ever come knocking on your door to haul your ass away. But where I'm concerned, I couldn't handle the hit and I couldn't even handle worrying about the hit. The only thing

I'm making a big stand for is my sorry ass. Not yours, not R.J.'s. I'm only pleading for my one and only sorry ass. So I'm not going to do it with you. I'm just not."

I was dead serious, and it was finally beginning to dawn on him. Probably it was the first time I'd ever completely stone-walled him, put up something he couldn't get around or over or under. He looked pretty shit-faced. I didn't feel particularly good about it. I knew it was the end of us. He wouldn't be able to see things my way or feel them my way, and that meant I was going to have to leave and he was going to have to go on with his plans and his schemes, and once we started traveling down roads that were so fucking strangely different, we could never get back together again. Maybe we could meet again and pal around again, but we weren't ever going to be able to have anything tight again. That would be all gone the minute I stood up from the deli table.

"You're still going to have some money coming. A lot of it. Would you stick around and help us unload the toot? We still need you."

"No. If you're going to do what you're planning to do, I can't stick around, and I don't want any money from it afterwards. I got to hop off right here, and hop off clean. Don't you understand, Becker? If I don't hop off completely right now, the chance'll be gone. I'll still be part of it. So I'm giving you my share. You and Annie. And I don't begrudge it to you. I hope you score through the roof, I really do. But I got to jump off here and now, completely. You paid my hospital bills and you took care of me. We're square, more or less, give or take twenty bucks one way or the other. If you want to go on with the life, you get to take home the bennies and I don't."

"What are you going to do?"

"I don't know. You know I've always wanted to go back to school. I figure maybe I can suck up to the VA and try to upgrade my discharge. If not, I should still be able to swing something."

"You leaving now? You got money to travel?"

"Yeah, enough to get back up to Connecticut, see my folks, stay with them for a while until a semester starts somewhere where I can talk my way in."

"Well, good luck. I guess that's all I can say."

"Same to you, Becker. I really do mean that. Good luck thinking out what you got to do and good luck pulling it off, whatever it is."

"Can I pay for the dinner?" he asked.

"Sure," I said. "You can do that. You can do that anytime."

# BECKER

I was still upstairs at the table sucking on my fourth cup of coffee when Annie showed up. I wasn't feeling very talkative, but she started right off by popping the question; she wanted to know where Richard was.

"Come and gone," I said. She'd brought a piece of pie and some coffee up with her.

"What do you mean, gone? Where?"

"Out of town."

"What for?"

"I think they used to say to do his own thing. To seek his fortune."

"He split?"

"That's it in a nutshell. Very astute."

"I don't understand," she said. "Why didn't he tell me he was going? Why did he leave?"

I dangled my fork across the table and took a little corner off her pie, which was a pretty good restaurant rendition of Key lime. I was sorry I hadn't picked some up when I went through the line.

"Well, darlin', maybe this is where you and I part company, too. He left because he figured out what the next part of the big picture is. Do you know what the next part of the big picture is?"

"Becker, stop giving me all your bullshit. Get to the point."

"Okay. Before we go up north to unload all that toot and become rich beyond our idiot fantasies, it is my intention to make somebody dead. To make R.J. dead, to be explicit. Were you aware of that?"

She stopped picking at the pie and put her fork down. She was juggling several thoughts around inside her melon and trying to decide which one to toss out of her mouth next. She didn't usually do that; it hit me that she lived her whole life getting along fine with just addition and subtraction, and now I'd forced her to take a square root.

"I didn't know that," she said.

"Any suspicions? Come on, just the slightest hint?"

She was starting to get sullen. My fault, because I was starting to get nasty. I was trying to start a fight, I guess.

"Look, Becker. I know what R.J.'s been doing. I know we've all been running around with guns for the last couple of weeks. I mean, I'm not an idiot. Okay, so what I figured was we just defend ourselves. We kill him or anybody else who tries to do it to us. You can do that. You have to do that. But now you're saying that we go out of our way to kill him, and that's different."

"Bullshit. What you just said—we kill anybody who tries to kill us—that's just what R.J.'s been trying to do for the better part of a month, with pretty good goddam results and more to come on the late show, you bet your fucking ass. More to come. What I'm trying to say is that we may not get a chance, we probably, we almost certainly will not get the chance to be that nice, to wait for him to make another big move. He's not a complete idiot, either. He knows, he has *got* to know that we've targeted in on him as the chief villain of the piece, and that means he knows he's dealing with cornered, dangerous animals. He ain't going to give us a chance to defend ourselves, Annie. No way. And now that you've come in with us, you're on his shit list just like me and Richard and Michael and Lee. He'll kill you sleeping if he gets the chance, or blow you and some honey away through the head with one shot while you're balling one night. He'll fire-bomb your fucking house while you're on the can or put a dynamite bomb in your car and get you on the way to the 7-Eleven. Or he'll hire some complete, anonymous stranger to do it for him while he hides out in British Columbia for the summer. That's how Richard got his, from a complete stranger. We cannot afford to be so fucking ethical about this. We got to kill that man and stop him and we got to do it now."

"I don't see why we don't just get the toot and get the hell out of town right now. He doesn't know where we are. He can't get to us. We can sell it and take our time coming back. Maybe things'll settle down on the island after a couple of months. We don't even have to come back to Key West."

"No," I said. "We have to come back."

"Why?"

"Because that is where I happen to live this year. Maybe I'll want to live somewhere else next year, but right now I live in Key West. And I will move when I feel like moving, and not before." Through most of that I was clenching my teeth and hissing. I felt as if a couple of veins were about to pop.

"Look, cool out, Becker. What if I don't happen to feel that way? What if Key West, Philadelphia, Frisco are all the same to me right about now, especially with a shitload of toot and money? Can you handle that, Becker?"

"I can handle it. You can think that way. That's what I'm trying to find out right now. 'Cause I got to know now. But I got news for you. You got problems with your way. You're going to have problems with me. I am going to kill that cocksucker at the earliest possible convenience, starting now. I could use your help in that project, I sure as shit could. But I am going to do it with you or without you. And if I have to do it without you, that coke is all mine. And if I fuck up and die, that coke can stay in its nice little hiding place until it biodegrades into sludge and they come to find out what's stinking up the joint. The animal shelter can have that fucking toot for all I care. But if you want a cut of it, and your cut has just jumped to a third, by the way, thirty-three cents to the dollar, you're going to have to truck along with me on this next little part. If you don't come with me and you find me dying on the sidewalk later, I swear to whatever God we both believe in that I won't tell you where that coke is or how to get it."

"Becker, you're just cutting out everybody right and left so that you can have everything your own way and nobody can complain or they're out. I don't like the way you've been rigging everything up to now and I don't like the way you're rigging everything now."

"I didn't expect you to like it. You can like it as much as Richard liked it, and you can go fuck yourself."

"Well, maybe you've gone completely insane, and if I do help you, if I do what you want now, maybe you'll still cut me out afterwards. Maybe you won't like my color underwear or something, and maybe you'll just kill me because I broke another of your fucking stacked-deck rules."

"Well, that's a very good reason for you to get up and get out of here right now, sweetie. I sure as hell wouldn't stay around if I thought that was a reasonable possibility. Keep the car with my compliments, as a token of our enduring friendship."

"Becker, don't you see what's happening? We're already about to kill each other, or at least jump on each other and try to tear each other's throats out. Why is that, if R.J.'s the enemy? I'm trying to ask you to see it my way just for once, Becker. See it somebody else's way just for once. Let's take the toot and get out of here. Don't you see how if we do that, we've won? Maybe not everything. Okay, R.J. fucked us over real, real bad, but if we take the toot and sell it and just turn our backs on him, we've won as much as there is to win."

"I'm sorry," I said. "I know what you're saying. It makes a lot of sense. But I just can't see it that way. I mean, I'm sick with what I got to do, and I can't get well unless I do it. I don't know how else to explain it to you."

"Yeah. You're on a Clint Eastwood trip. There's a lot of that going around. But you could die from that trip, Becker, or go to jail forever, and so could I. Well, I'm entitled to pussy out, Beck, because I *am* a pussy."

"You can leave," I mumbled. "But then you're not getting paid."

She sighed long, a lot of air passing out over the table between us, and looked down at the ashtray on the Formica top, cold forms that clinked together whenever the table swayed.

"Okay, how much toot is there?" she asked.

I rattled off some weights and conservative sales figures that we could expect up north even if there was competing toot on the market, but I had contacts in a lot of cities and we could keep cruising and keep sitting on the stuff until we found the right places and the right times. Holidays coming up would make even the budget-minded freaks loosen up and want to buy a gram, and the dealers would need to buy more in advance for them. I didn't mind telling the truth now that it came down to how much toot we had. The truth was pretty persuasive.

"Jesus," she said. She looked like she was trying to work up a short sweat. "And I get a third?"

"Yeah. I didn't force Richard out of the profits. He just wanted out cold, his choice. That means we each get a third. Can you live with that?"

*Clickity-click. Divided by three now, not four. Three doesn't go into that, but it goes into that so many times. Five times three is fifteen, sixteen take away fifteen is one, bring down the zero . . .*

"Yeah, I guess so," she said. It was a sad answer and it made me feel dirty that I'd somehow forced her into it. Not forced, but led her along, used English on her like a pinball, fending her off with this bumper, easing her into that solenoid, keeping her just this side of the tilt button until we got the score up to the part where she got to divide the big number by three and put in the zeroes. Not much sadness ever passed between Annie and me. It was always either good times or tooth-and-nail down-right claw fights. But this was just sadness, sadness in her mouth, sadness hanging over the table, sadness being fried in the bright overhead fluorescent fixtures of the deli. God, there was so much fucking sadness all over the place.

"What do I have to do?" she asked.

"I don't know yet," I said. "We don't know where he is. We're just going to have to hole up somewhere and start trying to sniff him out. I don't know how long that's going to take."

"I think I know where he is," she sighed again. I could barely hear her.

"How? Where?"

"I didn't want to tell you. I really thought we could just pick up the toot and leave town. Well, I don't know if R.J.'s there, but when I was coming back from the car lot, I swung by Laura's apartment. I know her car, and it was in that open garage under the building. So I waited for a while, and she came out and I followed her."

"I don't believe this . . . ."

"It was hard to follow because it was getting dark, but that also made it harder for her to see my car. I got a tan VW, like you said, and it just wouldn't mean anything to her. It was a neighborhood off the Palmetto, way out, little ticky-tacky stucco houses. I didn't turn down the last street after she did, just stopped at the corner, but I think I saw the driveway she turned into. It won't be hard to find it again, and her car's probably still there. Oh, Christ, Becker, do we really have to do this? This is crazy."

"You're sure you can find it again? In the dark again?"

"Yeah. I even wrote down the street number, the name of the intersection."

"Anything else?"

"No. I couldn't see any other cars I knew or if any lights were on in the house. I told you, I didn't really get a look at the house. It's on the left side of the street down from where I stopped."

"One-story, two-story houses?"

"I think two stories mostly. Little houses, but two stories. Little front lawns, little yards. It looked like base housing for sergeants or lieutenants."

"A lot of traffic on the street?"

"No. Just a side street. That neighborhood, it's like twenty streets by twenty streets of the same kind of houses, a big development, but an old one. He's probably renting the house, it looks like there's a lot of rentals there, if that's where he is."

"That's got to be where he is. Jesus fuck, I don't believe it. Okay, darling. We do it tonight."

"There?"

"Yeah. Where the fuck else?"

"I don't know, Becker. Now that you know where he is, can't you just wait for him to go somewhere else, follow him? It's right in the middle of a million other houses."

"We do it there if he's there."

"What about her?"

I didn't say anything. I just looked at her.

"Oh, no, Becker. This is getting out of control."

"It's up to her. If she's not there, that's fine. If she is, it's not fine."

"We could wait until she leaves and he's there alone."

"No," I said. "We're going there, doing it and getting the fuck out of there. We're not waiting around down the block for the weather to get nice so somebody can call the cops about a strange car."

She had a million other objections, and that was how I had to outline what I knew of the plan to her, knocking down her objections one by one, explaining the way it was going to be, the way it had to be. We cleared out of the deli and walked to the car which was parked on the Mile. It was a tan bug, probably the most common car on earth now. If somebody remembered seeing it, that would be like telling the cops they saw a coconut palm or a stop sign. Inside, it smelled of old car, but it was pretty clean. A knob was missing off the radio, but you could still tune it and it still played. Annie started it up.

No place is as dead as downtown Coral Gables after dark, nobody walking on the streets, no stores open late, usually not even cops. We got to the parking lot and I bent down next to the bike and took the screwdriver out of the tool kit. One of the few cars in the lot was a Fairlane with Cuban trim that had been thoughtfully parked with its ass in, against a building wall, with just enough room for me to crawl behind it. The bolts that held the plate on were rusty, but they finally gave. I shoved the plate under my shirt and started the bike and got the fuck out of there, heading for 27th Avenue. The driver wouldn't notice his plate was gone when he came back to the car, and with any luck, nobody else would that night either, so we could use the plate and ditch it before it was even reported. I supposed they made the plates in the penitentiary at Raiford.

Annie followed me up 27th for a couple of miles until I turned off into Opa-Locka and found a side street where the bike didn't look too out of place. I parked it and got in the VW with Annie. I had her drive me to a convenience store, and while she waited outside I roamed through the little hardware section until I found some steel clips like the kind on clipboards. The spring action on them was powerful, and I figured they'd do to hold the new plate on over the old one for at least a couple of miles of slow driving. We pulled over a few blocks north of the convenience store and I rigged the plate.

*Because fancy wasn't going to get it. Fancy scheming and waiting around and staking the place out and tapping their phone wasn't going to do anything but give us opportunities to screw up and give plenty of people plenty of chances to see us and notice things about us. If it was going to work at all, we were just going to have to go there and go in and do it and get out. And it was going to have to be now, that night, because even old Becker didn't have infinite reserves of nerve. And so we were going to have to do it now while old Becker had a snoot full, while old Becker was crazed enough for both of us. The next night or the night after that, I was going to have less and less of the seething and the boiling fear and craze and finally she was going to be able to talk me out of it and it was going to seem much more reasonable her way, just to grab the toot and get the fuck out of town and leave him be, him and the bitch. We go, we go now, we do it now, we do it tonight.*

*I had the light backpack from the bike and when she said we were a couple of blocks from the house I had her pull over and I opened the pack and brought out the .22s. I loaded the cylinders from a box of long rifle cartridges I'd bought in Islamorada on the way up. They won't recoil, I said. If you can't do it, just use yours to cover them if it comes to that . . . .*

*I can do what I have to, she said, and she was close to biting my head off. Okay, I said.*

*One pass by the house, I said. One pass, not too slow, and she turned down the street. Are you sure this is it? I asked her. Yes, yes, dammit, this is the street, shut up. Look on the left, about three-quarters of the way down. There, there's her car.*

*Well, which house is it? I asked.*

*It's got to be one of those two, the green one or the pink one. . . .*

*There, I said, the driveway goes with the pink one. It's the pink one. Keep driving, don't slow down.*

*There were lights on upstairs, but the green house next door to the left had lights burning on the first floor like people were still up. I told Annie to start driving out of the neighborhood, go anywhere, just so we were on fairly busy streets and looked like we were going somewhere.*

*You mean you just want me to fucking drive around nowhere for a fucking hour? Goddam it . . .*

*Yeah, I said, just drive around, please. I think it's the best thing ιo do. You got to go to the can?*

*No, she said, I don't got to go to the can.*

*We'd slid by the house around 10:45, and now I wanted to give it until midnight so that asshole next door would stop watching The Twilight Zone and go to bed. I didn't want to do it during real weird hours like two or three. I just wanted to slide up around midnight like some slightly jaunty Bohemian pals paying a slightly risqué late-night social call, park, go in, shake hands all around, have a beer or two, trade a couple of stories and then goodnight all and out the front door and gone, at least as far as any insomniac neighbor who chanced to look out the window could see. The later the hour, the stranger the visit would seem, the more likely to get ten neighborhood outdoor monster guard dogs freaked out and howling and the more likely to make somebody debate a call to the authorities just for a reassuring drive-by.*

*The time finally piled up enough for us to head for the neighborhood again. If something was wrong on this pass, I was going to scrub it for the night because even a tan VW can look suspicious on a third pass. I told her where I wanted to park, a place I'd scoped out. The light that had been on in the pink house was upstairs left, so if we parked farther up the street on the right, about a house-and-a-half back, the car and most of our walk down the sidewalk to the driveway would be in a blind spot to that upstairs room. So we wouldn't have to skulk around behind trees and bushes if neighbors were watching, we could just walk like respectable people or semi-respectable people right up to the side door, which wasn't strange in a neighborhood like that; a lot of those houses used the driveway door more than the front door and some of them even locked off the front door entirely. I'd put electric tape over the plastic spring buttons in both car doors that turned on the dome light so when we got out, the dome light would stay out.*

*I could see what I wanted in time to make the decision to tell
her to park. The late-show guy in the green house must have gone
to bed and there were still no downstairs lights on in the pink
house. She pulled over and parked it just where I wanted. It seemed
a light was still on in the same upstairs room but it was dimmer, like
it was a table lamp instead of the overhead. That was okay with me.
I handed Annie her gun and told her to stick it in her waist. There
was no round in the chambers and the safeties were on both guns
for the walk. We could chamber and click the safeties off when we
figured out how to get inside.*

*I started to reach for my door handle and she put her hand on
my arm.*

*Hold it, she said.*

*What?*

*I want to know what you're going to do if R.J.'s not there but
it's just her. I don't see anything that looks like one of his cars.*

*I can't handle that now, I said. Just get out of the car.*

*I got to know. I'm going along with you about R.J., but I got
to know what we do if it's just her.*

*We play it by ear, I said.*

*That don't cut it, she said.*

*I'm getting out of the car now, I said. You stay in it or you
come with me, but if you stay here, you just fucking better be here
when I come out. I am not going to stay in this car and debate
what-ifs with you all night.*

*I opened the door and got out of the car and started to the
sidewalk. I heard the other door open behind me.*

*Don't slam the door, I whispered. She didn't.*

*It was maybe forty steps to the driveway, Annie single file
behind me, both of us staying to the house side of the sidewalk and
then up the driveway. We were in dark almost all the way, the street
lamps being few and far between. I heard a metal dog collar rattling
somewhere in one of the back yards, but nothing was barking or
even panting hard.*

*The kitchen door was up a stoop with two steps and it had a
metal screen door that had rust and squeak all over it. I opened it
probably the way the bomb squad meets a new anti-Castro infernal
machine, even though the last thing I wanted was to spend a half*

minute or a minute playing footsie with somebody's back door at that hour, but that was just the way it was going to have to be. I got it open enough to try the door handle without making any noise.

The kitchen door was unlocked.

I took out my gun and nodded to Annie to take hers out. I opened the screen door a little wider and then started on the kitchen door. I didn't believe what was going on in my bladder and my stomach. No sense checking Annie's condition out. However she was, that was the way she was going to have to go through with it.

Finally we were both inside the kitchen. I had the screen door propped open enough with the retainer ring on the suction spring so we could just slip out without fucking with it again. I'd brought a rag with me and used it on the doors. We stood with our backs against the sink and listened and listened and listened and couldn't hear a fucking thing except our body and throat and head noises. So finally it was time to move again. There was carpeting on the dining room floor and then on the living room floor. It stopped in the hallway by the front door and the stairs, which were wood parquet and old, probably full of squeaks, like the bannister. I stopped at the edge of the carpet and slid off my shoes and so did Annie. Then I walked to the stairs and pointed at the bannister and gave her a sign not to use it going up the stairs. The socks did a lot on the first couple of stairs to muffle the sound, but not enough for me. I could hear my feet making noises that sounded like a fight in the roller derby, so I told myself I was the only one who could hear them.

But I was hearing noises upstairs now, off to the left of the top of the stairs, from the lighted room, and they weren't alarm noises. It was voices talking and mess-around noises, not heavy fucking, but just the mess-around in the sack late at night, and that was good, because the noises—and they seemed to come from behind a closed door—would muffle ours a little, certainly the ones I'd made so far, and when the voices stopped suddenly, that would be the sign that there was trouble. They didn't stop, not suddenly, just every once in a while like lulls in the conversation, and when that happened, Annie and I froze on the stairs until the talking and the grab-ass started again. It was R.J. and the twat, that much I could squeeze out of what I could hear.

We got up to the top of the stairs, outside the open bathroom door. The voices were coming from behind a closed wood-paneled door with a little streamer of light leaking out from under. It touched the tips of my socks.

I wanted a rhythm, I needed a certain rhythm for the next part. I wanted to touch the doorknob, turn it quickly, open the door and get in there like Loretta Young and be facing them almost instantly and gracefully, but not faster than that, not too fast. I knew there was a way I could get in there and of course frighten them but not freak them out, a rhythm that would match the rhythm of a friend strolling in, someone they knew well, someone they almost expected, whom they would see and their minds would think, oh, it's just Becker. They would think that first, and then later, even an instant later, it wouldn't matter what they thought, what occurred to them after that. I turned my head and looked at Annie and had no sign to give her, no advice, no guidance. There was nothing to say anymore, nothing to fight about anymore.

Wipe the doorknob afterward, Becker, and that's the only thing you will have touched, I thought. Wipe this doorknob afterward.

I touched and turned the doorknob and swung the door open; it opened into the bedroom. The light inside wasn't enough to bother my eyes even after what had seemed like hours in the downstairs darkness, and the door swung silently. I was inside and facing the bed immediately, as if I had known in advance where it would be. It was a huge waterbed surrounded by a simple light wooden frame, and I could see it start to shake as both of them turned abruptly and sat up however they could to look at me. I already had the pistol aimed arm's length at them, with the aiming point directly between them.

Jesus. Jesus, Becker, you scared the shit out of me, he said. It didn't sound like fear. It sounded like annoyance, like the sound of someone surprised in the bathtub by his wife coming back from the grocery store. I felt Annie come into the room and walk behind me to the window and draw the curtains all the way closed.

Laura was sitting up in bed now. The bedclothes had already

been over her from the waist down and she didn't bother to rear-range them to cover her tits; she didn't try to cover her tits with her hands. I couldn't tell what was on her face—maybe annoyance, too, although hers would be real and R.J.'s would be bullshit an-noyance, a pose. She wouldn't be posing. Even if she knew for certain now what was going to happen, she would still feel annoy-ance more than anything.

What do you want? she asked.

Be quiet, I said.

Get out of here, she said.

Hey, hey, cool it, R.J. said to her. He wanted to play the scene, not her. I don't know why he bothered. But I was glad he shut her up. She worried me more than he did. All he was likely to do was make a grab for some gun and do it quietly, but she could scream her fucking lungs out and would, too, not from fear, not from fear at all. Just her calling card, to die but in dying to wake up the entire county and know the lights would be coming on and the sirens would be wailing and we would be just as fucked as she was about to be.

I nodded to Annie to walk behind me again and cover the twat from the right side of the bed where she was. The instant she had moved behind my back I started toward R.J.'s side of the bed.

Hey, Becker, look, man, if something's diggin' at you, man, we can work it out. I know we can work it out, but I don't even know—

I stooped beside the bed and in the same motion came up with a pillow in my free hand. He wasn't expecting it all to go this fast, he thought there would be time to talk, to think, but there wasn't. I jammed the pillow in his mouth and the muzzle of the gun right in behind it so it was buried a few inches into the pillow and then I fired and an explosion of feathers came back at me and a smell and a sound, not the crack of an open .22 but a Blat, something hollow and resonant but which seemed to be contained all within the room.

Yes. The twat started to scream then, and I was sorry because I'd been wrong. It was certain fear and panic and not calculated revenge and she lunged not at Annie but for the door. I got a good handful of her long hair before she was even off the bed and when

*I yanked it back hard it stopped her scream. I was on top of R.J.
now with my knee jammed on top of the bed frame, and he was
moving and thrashing, but uncontrolled, and none of his moves
were directed at me or at anything with any design. The noises he
was making under the pillow were noises not like puking or gasping, but throat noises, noises of choking in thick viscous liquid. I
yanked her head back toward me and her whole body came flying
after it, and before she could get her breath again, I had dropped
my gun to grab the pillow that was on R.J.'s face and I smashed it
into hers.*

*Annie stood there looking at her. Her gun was up and ready
but nothing was happening.*

*Now, I said, now, now, do it, do it.*

*She held the gun up more.*

*Jam it in the pillow, dammit, I said, jam it in the pillow.*

*She took her eyes off the pillow and looked at me as if she
hadn't understood what I'd said, but then it hit her and she did what
I said and an instant later she fired and fired again, five or six times
one right after the other so that I was afraid she'd jerk and hit my
hand and I pulled my hand away and sat back up off the bed. In the
dim bedroom light it seemed I was in a snowstorm of furious smoke
and feathers and cloth shreds.*

*Annie had stopped and was standing back from the bed.*

*Go downstairs, I said. Be quiet and go downstairs and put your
shoes on and listen for sounds. Don't touch anything, anything. Do
you understand? Don't touch anything.*

*Yes, she said, and she wasn't in a daze. She understood.*

*She was out of the room. The pillow that had been over Laura
had fallen off her now and some of the shots had ripped through
the sheets and ripped up the vinyl. Some had struck her in the face
but others had gone past her head, and now her arm, the arm closest
to me, was falling through the tear in the waterbed and already I
could see a pool of water seeping out of the bed and drifting up
to her shoulder. It was diluting the blood from her face, the blood
coming from her nose and mouth, diluting it in swirls snaking
around in the water and falling below into the waterbed.*

*I picked up the other pillow and braced up the back of R.J.'s
neck with it. I had my gun back now and I fired once into the base*

of his neck. It was strange, but this was the first one that frightened me, that alarmed me, that I wasn't prepared for. Then I went around the bed and did the same to her, for her. That shot frightened me, too.

On the way out I wiped both doorknobs, the inside and outside. I'd used the rag on the back doors so there was nothing else to wipe. I stopped Annie just as we got to the back door.

Walk the way I do, I said. Walk regular. Just walk the way I do to the car. Let me drive, I said. Give me the keys to the car now.

She reached into her pocket and gave me the keys. They were still on a ratty cardboard and string arrangement from the used-car lot. No lights had popped on in the houses on either side and none had come on that I could see across the street or anywhere down the block.

Your shoes, she said.

Oh, Jesus. Oh, God. Go to the car, I said.

I turned around and went back up the driveway and back into the house. I crossed the living room and had trouble getting the shoes on because I was starting to get into a panic because I had fucked up with something, and even though it was small and seemed correctable, something had gone wrong, something had gone wrong, but finally I had them on my feet, even the right shoes on the right feet, and I was out of the house and down the stoop again and down the walk and in the car. I put the keys in the ignition and started the engine. I didn't mean not to turn the headlights on, but I forgot, and we were most of the way down the block when I remembered them. Just as well, maybe better. I turned them on as we turned the corner.

# 30

## BECKER

**W**e collected the duffel bag and made a scuttling run deep into the 'Glades down Tamiami Trail. Where it all ended up —well, I wouldn't be able to find any of it again even if I wanted to. The license plate, the .22s, the last M-16, Roach's magnum, all gone forever unless the alligators find them and decide to arm themselves. While Annie drove into the swamps, I filed the serial numbers off the .22s just for paranoia's sake so that even if they were found, they couldn't be traced to a store or a sale. But nobody was going to find them. I got eaten alive by the mosquitoes just to make sure of that. If I'd still had the *Kelpie,* I would have been tempted to make the scuttling run on that, but the swamps would do just as well, maybe better. Florida's just filled with interesting geographical features that are plenty useful for young people engaged in monkey business.

Just before we headed north from Miami, I bought the papers, but nothing had shown up. I wished it had. A day of news reports would have given me a pretty good feel for what the cops knew or guessed or suspected and what they didn't. It would have told me whether I should start worrying or whether the cops just had their heads up their asses. We stayed in a motel in Coral Gables the last day we were in Miami and checked out the TV news the night

**279**

before we left as well; nothing on the 11 P.M. report. As we drove north, we'd be able to buy the Miami papers and keep in touch that way, but we were going to miss the TV news; when our bad boogie finally did come to light, it wouldn't make TV anywhere north of Fort Lauderdale. Not grisly enough, just your normal, once-a-week Miami drug rub-out, no big deal.

We'd done our best, but we'd only be hot stuff for a couple of days before some other geeks in Lauderdale or the Grove or Key West went to it and carved each other up to grab the headlines from us. You couldn't pull this kind of shit in Des Moines and get away with it for long, but in south Florida you had to take a number and stand in line before the cops could get around to chasing your ass down and catching you, what with all the competition. Of course if you were dufus unlucky, there *were* arrests and convictions now and then. All I asked was that they make one little mistake and set some kind of bail on me, however outrageous. I'd decided long ago what to do if that happened.

But it took us until Chattanooga for anyone to tumble to the news. Interstate 95 could be a bad road to take north if the heat was out for you, too easy to patrol and watch for plates, so I mapped us through Georgia and the Great Smokies and up the Blue Ridge Parkway instead. Those roads were better matched for the VW anyway. I found a day-old *Herald* in Chattanooga that had the story. We'd made the front page again.

From what I read and what I could guess, the discovery was a pretty pathetic business. R.J.'s habits had a lot to do with that. Probably quite a few people had come calling on him the next couple of days looking to buy this and that, but they weren't the sort of folks to bother finding a distant pay phone and dropping an anonymous tip to the cops about what they'd seen or smelled. One of them probably left the kitchen door wide open, and then the neighbor children started slipping in to seek their junior house-breaking fortunes. One of them finally had to explain to his mom where he got the dandy new tape recorder or whatever, and then things went public.

So things were starting well for us. By the time the cops got around to getting scientific, our little in-and-out had been fairly obscured by the comings and goings of perhaps dozens of anonymous people of all shapes and sizes. But the cops were right about one little detail they told the papers. They ventured that the whole business looked drug-related to them; it was nice to know Sherlock Holmes wasn't dead.

The cops didn't say anything about any neighbor witnesses. Of course there might have been one or two. But by the time anyone who'd noticed us figured out what we'd been up to, we'd have something going for us. The witness had seen two people who he now knew had snuffed two other people in their bed; would folks like that hesitate to repeat a job like that on a nosy witness? If the odds against any sharp-eyed witnesses were small to begin with, the odds against willing witnesses had to be even smaller.

It was Lisa I really worried about. There was just no way to call the shots with her, no way to anticipate what she'd say when the cops finally got around to cruising down to Key West to ask her about her late sugar daddy, assuming they were even sharp enough to realize he'd been keeping more than one residence. But if they were, how would that bubblehead act? What would she say and what would she keep to herself?

Possibilities abounded for our side here. Lisa was an old-fashioned type who latched up with her stud forever, even if it didn't last forever and even if the stud didn't recognize the arrangement. R.J. had always been able to do what he wanted as long as he didn't fling it in her face. His long vacations and business trips had always been largely a matter of getting his rocks off out of her sight, and she'd been satisfied with that arrangement, as long as when he came home they pretended like they were one-on-one. But now she'd had it flung in her face on the front page of the *Herald,* and that wasn't going to sit well with her at all.

She just might consider what she undoubtedly knew we'd done and then consider what she knew R.J. had done and decide that they canceled each other out, especially since he'd done it with Laura, whom she hated. Oh, Lisa probably figured that I only imagined I was doing something vile for greed and revenge; actually, I was simply part of the grand cosmic scheme by which innocent and self-sacrificing and long-suffering folks like Lisa were dispensed their ultimate smidgen of karma and justice; I was just an unwitting pawn in the wheel of karma to set her wrongs right. It was screwy, but there was a good chance she'd think of it that way by the time the cops came to call.

Beyond that, she was also vulnerable to the more concrete logic of knowing what we were capable of, especially since we'd whipped it out on her own notorious R.J., the original heavy-duty *macher,* juggernaut and Oilcan Harry whom no one had ever previously dared fuck with and hoped to survive the experience. What we'd done to him and to the lady who happened to be there at the time we could do to her; I just hoped she'd be straight enough to consider it that way for a moment.

That left Annie, who knew everything, in shorthand, in detail, warts and the little hairs coming out of the warts and all.

But for that matter, when she thought along the same lines, that just left me.

So what that boiled down to was the same crummy situation Michael had been in with R.J. after the last voyage of the *Coriolis.* Both of them had hopped off that tub knowing that each of them could kill the other from that moment on just by picking up the phone and dialing 911. No time limit, no home free.

No, there was a home free, and it sucked. If it boiled down to only two people on earth who knew, and both of them were part of it, equal partners, then it was plea bargain and state's evidence time. The prosecutor wouldn't get the leisurely opportunity of separating the good partner from the bad partner. The prosecutor would have nothing if neither partner ever decided to spill. But if either partner sometime down the line decided to spill, then the first one to the State Attorney's office with the sordid tale would be the one who got immunity, and the slow fucker would be the dead fucker, even if he missed the boat by ten minutes. Oh, there'd be a hit to pay, some nominal felony that would come out of the wash with most of it gone as probation for cooperation, but anybody could probably stand that—a couple of years on the farm, maybe even sent out of state as part of the deal because you were worried about what happens to informers inside. It beat the shit out of a big cloud of hydrocyanic acid up your snoot with witnesses watching you through the little window with the rubber gaskets. That's what the partner who called up second would get.

Well, there wasn't much to worry about there. Michael's

death-lock arrangement with R.J. had certainly stood the test of time. They'd lived in peace and harmony for two or three whole years before R.J.'d decided to rub Michael out just for good measure, along with anybody else who might have picked up a little loose talk, half the listings in the Key West phone book if necessary. No sweat.

We were just going to have to trust one another, Annie and me. Sucky as it sounded. We were just going to have to grow old and gray and not freak out three or four times a week that our old pal might get cold feet and reach for the Princess phone and its accompanying fast relief and perked-up ear.

I could live with that. I thought so, anyway, as we drove the bug through the Smokies and beyond, six inches from each other for ten or twelve hours a day, without a whole hell of a lot to say to each other for most of that time. But I wondered what corresponding bumfuck suck fest thoughts were rolling around in her head about me and my ultimate trustworthiness and exemplary character.

It wasn't a subject I felt like bringing up, and it must not have been a favorite with her either, because I didn't even catch the most veiled reference to it, even in those moments when we did have something to say, when we made the effort to shout something across the front seat in the face of the highway wind noise or when we talked in the evenings in our motel rooms. These were not cordial evenings. They were certainly not intimate, she being able without question to cite the privilege of her well-established persuasion to sleep alone. The only reason I argued it was that we were just about bone dry for bucks. At first we always ended up in rooms with two beds, and what we paid depended on how many of them we opted to mess up, ten or fifteen bucks more if we used both beds. In happier times on a trip like that, we would've probably shared the same sack, with or without a little mess-around, and if without, I wouldn't have minded sleeping all night (or staying awake) hoisted on the arc of my erection next to her. But now she wanted one bed to a customer, and she also started off by insisting that she always be that customer; if I wanted to save bucks, I could avail myself of one of her blankets and the spacious floor or one of the keeno leatherette torture chairs. I let that bullshit slide the first two nights, but then I fought her on it. First I fought her down to *her* sleeping on the chair and me getting the bed every other night, but the trip and recent events must have taken more out of her than I thought. By the fourth night we were sharing one bed. It was still a pretty joyless arrangement, two consenting adults consenting to keep the fuck away from each other. I've had better holidays before and since.

Things started to loosen up when we swung back to the coast and started hitting familiar towns. As low-key as we tried to make the sales and the dealing, we were Santa Claus and Mrs. Claus wherever we went and general cause for jubilation and rejoicing. There were parties, and the parties provided us with some new faces and some much needed one-nighters and tension relievers. Those in turn provided us with some breathing space away from each other, so that in the mornings after or the afternoons after when we showed up at our appointed rendezvous, we just naturally found ourselves getting more civil toward one another. A couple of towns later and we were doing our parts in an act that seemed pretty much like being buddies again.

A lot of amusing shit was happening in these atmospheres of instant conviviality that sprang up whenever word got around that the new coke truck was in town, with competitive prices, honest weights and primo, primo quality, discounts for quantity and slightly better discounts for buyers who didn't keep us standing in strange parking lots for three hours in the middle of the night or didn't at the last moment ask to bring a close friend but a stranger to us. Actually, there wasn't a whole fuck of a lot of that kind of bullshit. Although we had a lot of shit to get rid of on our rounds, my contacts were holding up pretty well. Each one of them was good for two substantial hits, first when we breezed into their town more or less without warning for those who could scare up the necessary cash within a day, and then maybe a week later after working some other towns, for the people who hadn't been prepared but who'd been told that Christmas just might come twice a year that year if they were very, very good and very easy to deal with on the return. So we ended up moving the vast majority of the toot under the best possible circumstances, only to people we knew in fairly mellow surroundings—although even the very best of circumstances always generates tons of paranoia. But when I breezed into town, I'd lay down my rules, take it or leave it, and most people who said they were willing to get with my program stuck to it to a degree that I could live with in exchange for big stacks of cash. The automatic stayed with me all the time, but it moved farther and farther back in my mind and to more and more inaccessible places on my body.

After the tally from the first few cities, we traded the bug in for a used Volvo sports job with overdrive, the first overdrive car I'd ever played with. I was so high on life by that time that when Annie would nod out on the interstates and wasn't paying attention, I'd gun the sucker to see what she could do, which was plenty. Life was authentically grand.

And that was about it. I don't want to make it sound too simple or too sweet, because it never is, not selling one Quaalude to your best friend, not selling a stick of oregano to a junior high kid, and certainly not pushing all the toot we were supplying to the northeast power grid. But I'd done these trips before, and this time relative lubrication was definitely everywhere. The prices we asked for we got, and they were mounting up to something unbelievable: the berserko fortune I'd been having wet dreams about since Richard and I had started scheming about the venture. Only better. Better and worse. Better because there wasn't anyone to repay the venture capital to anymore. And worse, for the same reason. But in pure numbers, far, far better, nearly an acid fantasy better, magnificent even when you divided it by three, magnificent again for being tax free. My only worry now was that it seemed to be coming in so easily and quickly that I feared (assuming I lived and stayed out of jail) I might make it go out just as easily. Champagne, new bikes, imported virgins who glowed in the dark and could whistle Mozart during a hum job, chocolate-covered hummingbirds' eggs, an operation to give me a third eye in the back of my head . . . Well, I had no choice. I'd have to risk it, take a chance, hope for the best. I reminded myself that I'd had worse worries recently.

We were gone on our rounds for six weeks, not all the time spent attending to business. In New York I took Annie to see her first Broadway show and then took her out for a midnight supper at a scandalously overpriced French tourist trap that, despite all the signs to the contrary, slung us some superb food and served us, and particularly the *mademoiselle,* as though the Russian missiles were on the way and we were the last customers they'd ever have. Later that morning we were both ghastly ill in our hotel room and even got in a fight when both of us needed to use the can at the same time.

By then I didn't really give a flying fuck anymore whether we were home free or living the last seconds of a doomed fool's paradise. I was ready to go back to Florida and fart in the face of whatever was waiting.

Which was nothing. The spectacular yawn that was lying in wait for us from the northern border to our front door in Key West was something less than devastating. During the next few days as I made the rounds around town, to sunset, to the grocery store, to Searstown, I was besieged by people who hadn't the slightest idea that I'd ever been away, mobbed by hordes who'd nearly forgotten my name, set upon by shoving and pushing rabble who didn't seem to know that there'd been any troubles I might even have heard about. Luck had been dutifully collecting our mail, which now overflowed a couple of shoeboxes with Radio Shack fliers, *Sports Illustrated* pleas for subscriptions, handy hints from the power company about conserving energy courtesy of Reddy Kilowatt. No five orange pips in a plain brown wrapper, no dancing men ciphers, no black hands, not even a summons for jury duty.

Of course Luck knew what had happened. He just didn't bring the subject up. I asked him if there was anything he wanted in return for picking up the mail. He hinted a few snorts wouldn't be considered an insult, and he'd been thinking that he might hit me up to help him design a new custom skateboard with a built-in radio and a little strobe light on the front for night street crossing. I told him to show up at the house and we'd get on it right away.

A postcard from a fellow in Mexico who seemed to know me read, *Wish you were here* and all that jazz. It was pretty recent and the tenor of it seemed mellow, nothing critical seemed to be crying out for attention. In my head I started mapping out plans to fly down there so I could deliver his third, as well as the boat papers if he wanted to keep the boat, assuming the *Kelpie* still floated and wasn't a permanent addition to some Caribbean reef. I felt bad about the way I'd pooh-poohed the difficulties he'd have on his maiden solo voyage. If I'd told the truth I would have told him it was tantamount to suicide, and I suppose I should have given a little more credence to the Bermuda Triangle, but I'd just had to get the boy out of town for his own sake.

Annie didn't have a whole fuck of a lot of trouble readjusting to island life. Within a couple of days there issued from her bedroom at various hours an assortment of rutting noises from herself and an assortment of new ladies, with a few new gents thrown in just for some occasional convex pleasure with the concave. When we passed in the hallways, things were pretty straight and livable between us, sometimes even jovial. She kept hitting me up to let her put on her New York dress again and take her to the nearest wildly expensive French restaurant where the lady's menu had no prices, and after we finally got around to it one night, we ended up back at the house and I got to help her remove the fancy New York dress and squeeze the mangos for the rest of the evening, an episode I laid largely at the doorstep of another sixty-five-dollar bottle of blue velvet wine. I think that was the last time we got into that situation, but not because I didn't enjoy it.

One evening when she was ripping the downtown area apart and I'd passed and decided to stay home, the front door opened— I'd locked it for the first week or so after we got back and then one by one the new locks fell into disuse, and then finally the door stayed unlocked most of the time—and I could see someone, a woman whose silhouette in the dark I seemed to recognize, come in and come toward me down the hall to the living room where I was reading. It was Lisa. She stopped just outside the entrance to the living room, still mostly in the dark of the hallway.

"Hi," I said.

"Hello, Becker," she said, quietly, nervously, uncertainly.

"Come on in," I said.

"My eyes hurt. I've been having headaches. Can you turn the lights down?"

I clicked off the overhead, and she came into the room. Although she didn't look dirty or exactly unkempt, her clothes and her hair gave me the impression that she was still going through the motions of female vanity but getting them all hopelessly mixed up.

It was definitely a waif look, and a look far more lost than I'd ever seen on her. It was a little spooky. She knelt down beside me on the couch.

"I'm all alone in the house," she said.

"Do you have money? Money for the bills? The mortgage or the rent?"

"What?" She was still blinking even in the dim table lamp light, and the question hadn't seemed to register or to make sense.

"Can you pay the bills? Has anybody shut anything off, the phone or the electricity?"

"Oh. No. I have money. Do you want some?"

"No. You keep it."

"I saw Annie on the street today," she said. "But she didn't see me. I should have said something. I had this headache. I went home and went to sleep. That's how I knew you were home. I'm all alone in the house, Becker."

"Are you frightened?"

"No. I'm lonely. And my eyes hurt. I thought I was pregnant. I missed my period for a couple of weeks, but I got it yesterday. I didn't have any Tampax. I had to run down to the store and buy some."

"Oh. Is everything okay now?"

"I guess so. R.J.'s dead. Did you know that, Becker?"

"Yes. I'm sorry."

"The police came and told me. They came to the house. There was some other woman who was dead, too. You knew her, didn't you? Laura? She was a friend of Lee's."

"Yes. Yeah, I knew her."

"Lee's dead, too, Becker. I thought R.J. was going to come back. He was gone so long. He's been gone longer before, but he didn't tell me he was going to be gone that long this time. Can I move in here, Becker? I can pay, I can help pay the rent. I don't want to live in the house anymore, Becker. I can cook. I don't think you ever tasted my cooking. You used to come over to the house, but I don't think I ever made you dinner."

"What did the police talk to you about?" I asked.

"Well, they wanted to know a lot about R.J. It's funny—if anybody had asked me before if I knew a lot about R.J., sure, I would have said sure. I mean, I live with him and he lives with me, so, sure, I know a lot about him. But when somebody did ask me, when the police asked me"—she started to giggle a little and I didn't know quite what, if anything, it meant—"I really didn't seem to know much about him at all. I wasn't lying. I just really couldn't tell them much of anything, except things they already seemed to know or things they didn't seem to be interested in. Oh, please, Becker. I won't be any trouble in your house. I really won't. I can keep things clean if you want. You know I'm quiet. I know you like quiet sometimes. I remember that."

"I don't know. I guess I'd have to ask Annie first, but if it's okay with her, I guess it's okay with me. I guess. You don't look so hot, Lisa. Why don't I put you to bed? In Richard's room, if that's okay."

I led her upstairs. I didn't think she was on anything particularly, nothing more than usual, anyway, but she was impassive and had a lot of trouble undressing herself from the start. I helped her, pretty clinically, and got her into bed. I sat next to her on the bed in the dark.

"Becker, I've always liked you. I've always really liked you."

"Yeah, I know, Lisa. I've always liked you, too. We make a pretty good pair of friends."

"I've always wondered what it would be like to live here with you and Annie. I think I love Annie more than any friend I have in the world. I don't know why she helps me out so much, but I know I always come to her when I'm in trouble. Can you get in the bed with me, Becker?"

"No, darling. Not tonight, I don't think. You're not feeling too good. Are you hungry?"

"I don't know."

"When's the last time you had something to eat?"

"I think I had some peanut butter. There was some peanut butter in the cupboard. I don't like peanut butter, but they got mad at me at the store when I went there to buy groceries last time. I know you like the way I look, Becker. I saw you once, looking at me on your boat. Do you like the way I look?"

"Yes. You're a very beautiful lady. That's no secret. But I

think you better go to sleep now. We'll talk about this stuff tomorrow when you've gotten some sleep."

"I don't think I can sleep, Becker. You could get in the bed with me."

"When's the last time you slept?"

"I guess I've slept. I wake up sometimes in the kitchen or out by the canal, so I guess I've been asleep, but not much lately. I don't like going to bed alone anymore."

I called the doctor and he told me what I guessed he was going to tell me, that I should take her up to the emergency room or call an ambulance if she didn't want to go. She didn't mind, she said, as long as I was going with her. She knew she wasn't feeling well.

Annie and I went back to the hospital a couple of times over the next few days to see her and to talk to the doctor. It didn't seem to be as serious as I'd thought it was when I'd brought her in, but she was going to have to do some time there, at least to clean her system out so they could figure out how bad off she was when she was straight, and to get some weight back on her, which the doctor said was the most immediate problem; she had been about a day away from losing a couple of organs from malnutrition when we'd taken her in, or something like that. They asked us to stop coming when she started to go into withdrawal problems, which weren't helped much by hepatitis. Oddly enough, it wasn't the kind you get from spiking up, although she'd been doing her share of that. Annie and I had to go down to the clinic for gamma globulin shots on our way out. Mine was a roaring bitch and Annie didn't seem to like hers very much either.

Annie said we were going to have to go over to R.J.'s house and take care of it, close it up and clean it up while Lisa was in the hospital and make sure everything was paid up and in order. I didn't want to, and some unpleasant words passed, but she finally put the screws to me and I agreed to go. Even knowing why I was there and that it was aboveboard and necessary and the Lord's work didn't make it very pleasant. I was roaming around R.J.'s life, seeing little details of it that I'd never seen before and never had wanted to see before, nothing terrible or shocking, just personal things like boxer underwear with a Valentine on it and a stack of hardcore stroke books, the intimate details of a person who didn't exist anymore, Christmas tree ornaments with no tree to put them on. I tended to business, checking the window locks and cleaning out the refrigerator before shutting it off, while Annie did the dishes, but even tending strictly to business didn't make the job any less spooky. Palmetto bugs were all over the kitchen because Lisa hadn't been keeping anything clean for a long time, and I'd have to come back in a couple of days to see if our cleanup had helped the bug situation.

I didn't find much cash around the house, but I checked drawers and boxes for any important papers and bank accounts and bank books, which we put in a manila envelope and saved for Lisa. If we were lucky, the hospital wouldn't give us any trouble about letting her sign some checks to keep paying her bills. While she was in the hospital, I didn't want to ask her to make decisions such as giving up the house because they might not be the decisions she'd want to make when she straightened out. The bank books indicated that she wasn't in a bad way and that she could keep the house going for whatever number of months it took her to get back on her feet. The bank accounts seemed to be household money, though, and we found no trace of where R.J. had stashed the money from his deals. Where that was only he knew. Or if Lisa knew something about it, maybe she'd chase some of it when she got out. Taking care of Lisa and her house put a nice fat pall on things between Annie and me for a week, and the conversation dropped down to a chill.

During the next couple of months I spent a lot of time by myself or palling around with Luck. Sometimes I'd drive up the Keys to check out boats for sale, but I never quite got around to commissioning a marine survey or putting any money down. For one thing, there was a half a chance the *Kelpie* was still afloat and that Michael might want to give it back to me or make a deal on it when I got down to see him. A solo cruise back through the Caribbean would be nice, and I even felt jealous that Michael the landlubber had taken an extensive one before I had. But the main reason I stayed shy of doing something about another boat was that I just didn't seem to have much high-test gas in me for anything, and on top of that I found that I was pretty raw and taut in my dealings with Annie and most people around the island, ready to pop off and stalk out and get pissed off at pretty much anything, even though on the surface there shouldn't have been much cause for it. I was, after all, in Fat City and for all appearances Home Free. Anyway, nasty, disgruntled, testy people have a right to reach Fat City just as well as pleasant, laid-back types.

When the time seemed right, I flew down to Mexico City, doing my famous tourist impersonation with camera in case any eager beaver feds suspected what I was really up to, and after a couple of days in Mexico City, started my disappearing act into the countryside via local buses and eventually made my way to Michael's Gulf coast town. By the time I got there, I was pretty satisfied nobody was interested in my comings and goings, but I spent the first couple of days checking out the local tourist attractions without trying to get in touch with Michael, and when I finally felt 99 and 44/100 percent pure, I started hanging around on the patio of a tourist gringo bar off the plaza each afternoon. I was drinking a cold bottle of local beer when the man himself strode up to the table and asked if I minded if he join me. Not at all, says I, be delighted for a little gringo company.

"God, it's good to see you," he said.

"You're looking tan and fit," I said.

"Yeah, well, the climate's great if you like the climate. Personally, I think it sucks the hairy wazoo."

"How you been?"

"Miserable, man. Really miserable. That's the truth. I mean, I appreciate not being in jail, that's for sure. But I ain't too happy down here. Jesus, you didn't tell me they still ain't invented gay people down here. These people have just barely heard of heterosexuals."

"Yeah. Well, I figured you'd catch on to that. There's a lot of homo stuff in jail, I hear."

"Right, but I never went in for being held down by eight dudes with pieces of lead pipe and broken glass. People just imagined I'd dig it, but it's really not my thing."

"What about the gringo tourists?" I asked.

"Well, they're usually about as happy to see me as I am to see them. By the time they drive down here, they're so sick of their dream Mexican vacations that they see somebody who looks like an American and they're buying me drinks and keeping me up all night talking English. But they're here and gone, you know, catch you later. I've even cruised a couple of them. It happens. Guys from Akron who always thought they were straight arrow, but down here and lonely and so far away from everybody who's keepin' tabs on them—you know, anything for a thrill, even bopping a fag South of the Border. I get a little trade, it keeps me going. But I miss you, sweets. You're the man for me."

"Yeah, well, here I am, and that's all you get, a hearty hand-shake and a Hi-Yo Silver. Where you living?"

"I got a couple of rooms in a sort of rooming house a couple of blocks from here with a little refrigerator and a hotplate. I been running out of money. I was even thinking about trying to get some kind of work, but you were right about how they jerk you around if you're a gringo trying to work down here. I been hearing stories."

"You can cancel the alert. I brought you a little bit of change. You ended up with a third of the take, you, me and Annie."

"Oh, Christ. What happened to Richard?"

"Nothing, really. He healed up, but then he just didn't want to play anymore. He'd had enough. I didn't blame him. I offered him his share, but he just wanted to leave town. I think he's gone back to school. We haven't heard from him since."

"How's R.J.?"

"He died."

"Whoa."

"That's what I read in the papers, anyway."

"Yeah, well, I don't get the papers down here. Sometimes real late at night if I twiddle with the dial I can get some American radio stations on the AM, but I haven't picked up Miami yet. I get weird shit, Pittsburgh, Texas, some guy who plays redneck truck driver music to truckers all night out west somewhere."

"You learning any Spanish?"

"Oh, sure, man. I got six, seven phrases nailed down solid so almost everybody understands 'em. I ain't like you, man. The world ain't my oyster. You think every place is Disneyland. Well, it ain't. This sure as hell ain't, anyway. I just want to get out of here and get a hamburger."

"I don't know what to tell you."

"Yeah," he sighed. "I know. Listen, do you know anything about what's happening with me up there? Did you see that lawyer?"

"They still remember you, I'm sorry to say. Not so much Lee's murder—simple murder is easily forgotten and forgiven—but you done buggered their banks, or they think you did, anyway. You know, when it comes right down to it, I don't know what they can prove. Probably there'll be a time when you can breeze into town, turn yourself in and tell them to prove whatever it is they think they got against you. All it boils down to is that you were Lee's roommate, but you didn't snuff him and you never actually signed anything or picked up any of the money. They could have a hard time nailing you on anything."

"Got any idea when this magic time might come?"

"Well, here's the hard part. What Lee did with the money and the banks shook everybody up so bad—I guess nobody got caught at it before—that some congressmen came down from D.C. and held hearings in Miami, and they sort of made a big blowup of your picture—that high school picture, that's still the only one they got—and threw darts at it for a couple of days. It was a cheap shot. I mean, you weren't there to tell 'em any different. And the papers sort of dug it, fugitive bank-fucking queer. You're a media celeb, sort of."

"Oh, gross. Well, get in touch with that lawyer, okay? See what the real story is, 'cause I'm dying down here, man, I really am. I got to move out of this town, anyway. Did you know they got an American consul here? Anyway, he ran into me in the hotel bar a couple of weeks ago and he likes me. He thinks I'm real interesting. It's scaring the living shit out of me, man. I don't know what his trip is, but I don't like it."

"Well, you got the money to move now. I hear there's some gay folk in Guadalajara or farther west, a lot of gay gringo tourists in the Pacific Coast resorts. By the way, do you still happen to have the boat?"

"No. I made it here all right, no thanks to you. I got caught in a storm, man, and I thought I was going to die. After about eight hours of that shit, I was so sick I wanted to die. But I sold it a couple of months ago, man. I'm sorry, but times were getting hard and I was scared of being down here without bucks. They'll throw your ass in jail down here just for being poor, and they'll shoot you for being poor and queer."

"Hey, it was yours to do with as you liked. Good deal?"

"Shitty deal, man. That Mexican had me by the short hairs 'cause I didn't have any papers and stuff. Every time I'd argue with him, he'd say something like he wondered how much dope was run on this boat and if the authorities anywhere were looking for it. Or if they were looking for me. I just had to take what he wanted to give."

"Well, as long as it got you down here and kept you going, that's what I gave it to you for. And both of our church-mouse days are pretty much over for a while anyway."

"Thank God for that. You got the coke up north?"

"You betchum. Just in time for final exams at all our finer institutions of higher learning. We did real well."

I hung around the town for a couple of more days and settled up with him, and when I did, I imagine I left him the richest homosexual drug-running American fugitive in all Mexico. That didn't make him feel much better. Well, better, but not much better. To tell the truth, it wouldn't have done much for me in his shoes, either.

I promised to see the Miami lawyer to sniff things out. What I hadn't told him was that it might not be a scot-free situation. He might have to agree to come back and cop to some prearranged cheapo felony and do some time at some federal game farm. It was going to boil down to this, the way I read it: They might not have him nailed for Lee's murder, but he was the best asshole they had, the only asshole they had, and if he wanted them to find someone else, he'd have to talk to them and cooperate and give them some good ideas. That would be R.J., of course. Ordinarily, R.J. would have made the perfect fall guy, being dead and defenseless and all, but it was because he was dead that I didn't like it. If Michael pointed the finger at R.J. and Laura, that would just reopen the whole business of who killed them, and so far that had been dying down very nicely on its own. Well, when you got right down to it, even though I wanted Michael to spend a bit more time in outer space, it was out of my hands. One of these nights he'd be tuning in his radio and he'd hear somebody play his favorite rock 'n' roll song from his high school days, or maybe a nice Judy Garland tune—"Somewhere Over the Rainbow" would probably do the trick nicely—and he'd start to sob into his pillow and he'd jump up and pack his bags and head for the nearest airport and he wouldn't give a shit who knew about it. I just hoped that when he did it that way, he got a chance to have a couple of good hamburgers before they put the cuffs on him.

## BECKER

**T**he trip must have been good for my head, because when I got back to the island, people stopped behaving as if I were about to bite them in the leg, and I even started to go to some parties. Then Annie talked me into helping her throw one at the house, and I didn't even put up a fight. It seemed like a swell idea. I cranked up the stereo the day before the party and made a whole shitload of tapes, nice tunes off my records so we wouldn't have to depend on the Miami FM stations and the chancy radio propagation conditions and all that half-assed disco they were still playing anyway. We were out of our own coke stash by that time and I had to go out like a common citizen and pay for it; that was sort of a mild bring-down, but it had its amusing aspects.

After a while the party didn't seem to require my presence; everybody seemed to be doing just fine without me around to tell them who to try to finger or feel up in a corner, and I drifted out into the back yard to do up some toot and mellow out by myself. I liked the feel of the house with all the people in it, the ones that I knew and liked and even the strangers who seemed to be nice enough folks having a nice enough time and glad to be there. Every once in a while somebody strange would whisper to the person who brought him and that person would point to me or to Annie, and

then the stranger would come up to me and say, *"Nice* party, man,"
and I'd tell him I was glad he was having a nice time, drop by any
time, and then he'd drift off to try to nail some honey. A couple
of honeys came up to me with the same rap, one of them with a
whispy little voice and a tight frame that made me think of the
future, but she'd come with somebody and they looked pretty thick
at the moment, so I just made notes. For companionship, Luck and
I sat around and shot the shit and he started needling me about
when the fuck I was going to get on the stick and build him his new
skateboard already, and I said I'd start soon, tomorrow, *mañana,*
whenever, just as soon as anybody ever got around to anything on
the island. "Key West time, man. I'll do it on Key West time."

But I felt like a little space and I drifted out to the yard and
hauled out one of the lawn chairs and plopped back on it and
looked up at the sky. It was half-and-half, huge, rolling cloud forma-
tions that were just for show but didn't threaten anything, with big
holes in them to let the stars shine through perfectly, a patch of sky
at a time.

It was the segment of the sky that belonged to me, the one I
could see from my yard, which belonged to me. Outside my house,
and from my house I could hear my stereo and my music and my
friends talking and playing grab-ass and eating my potato chips and
making cigarette burns on my furniture.

It wasn't really that much, not that much for anybody to ask
for. You wouldn't have thought so, anyway. But it hit me that it
sure had been a bitch to get it and an even bigger bitch to keep it.
It hit me that I was a smart boy, and there must have been easier
ways for me to have gotten something pretty much like it. Maybe
I would have had to fill out a few more forms (and then it hit me
that I'd been fixing things like crazy so I hadn't had to fill out
anybody's forms probably since the day I'd been discharged from
the army) and suck a little more ass—was that so fucking bad? Did
people have to get blown away just so I wouldn't have to suck ass
and wear neckties?

But I couldn't get anywhere with those hits. For the first time
in a long fucking time, they didn't seem to be self-propelled, they
didn't seem to be self-starters. They popped up in my head, hung
around for a couple of seconds, and then they moved on, like the

big puff clouds I was watching that were rolling from west to east because they had to hustle to put on the same show later that night over the Bahamas.

I guess that's when I thought about going up to see Richard, to see how he was making out.